Major Washington

MICHAEL
KILIAN

Major
Washington

ST. MARTIN'S PRESS
☙ NEW YORK

Design by Bryanna Millis

Library of Congress Cataloging-in-Publication Data

Kilian, Michael.
    Major Washington : a novel / Michael Kilian.—1st ed.
        p.   cm.
    ISBN 0-312-18131-0
    1. Washington, George, 1732–1799—Fiction.   2. United States—
History—Colonial period, ca. 1600–1775—Fiction.   3. United
States—History—French and Indian War, 1755-1763—Fiction.
4. Presidents—United States—Fiction.   I. Title.
PS3561.I368M35   1998
813'.54—dc21   97-36509
                                                                                      CIP

First Edition: February 1998

10   9   8   7   6   5   4   3   2   1

For my son Colin,
and mountain days

Author's Note

This is a novel—a fictionalized account of three key years in George Washington's life as a fortuneless young man ambitious for glory, social position, and wealth, however he might wrest them from his time and circumstance, yet a very singular young man, one who came naturally to the fore in the public service of his greater community, no matter the risk or sacrifice involved.

But, though this is in considerable part fiction, it has been the author's hope and intention to make this as authentic and accurate an account of Washington in this period as has been rendered—to have this book serve as a form of time travel for the reader to become acquainted with Washington as a living, breathing man and not simply a noble figure of history and sculpture, especially as concerns a period in his life when his remarkable character was forged and honed.

The story centers on three bold treks he made into and beyond the Appalachian Mountains—in 1753, 1754, and 1755—on the last one as a principal aide-de-camp to British General Edward Braddock in a monumental defeat that proved as consequential to the eighteenth century as Pearl Harbor did to the twentieth.

Rather than have this seem dry history, in which Washington and the others would speak only by means of letters and journals, I wanted to present these singular people as the real men and women they were, behaving as on best authority it appears they actually did, including their conduct in places and circumstances where historians may not always be willing to go.

There is considerable focus in this work on two lingering if little-known controversies in Washington's life.

The first is his ambush and apparent murder of an ostensibly peaceful French party led by Ensign de Jumonville at the glen that now bears the slain Jumonville's name—an act for which Washington was misled into signing a confession that was used to help bring on the French and Indian (or Seven Years') War.

Second is the controversy over Washington's deep and abiding passion for the wife of his best friend, neighbor, and chief benefactor—Sally (Sarah Cary) Fairfax, wife of George William Fairfax—and what is perceived by some, including this author, as their probable affair.

I also explore Washington's attitudes on slavery, from his magnanimous wish to have his slaves eventually emancipated to his acceptance of

Author's Note

"skinning" (whipping to draw blood) as a measure of discipline to be employed, even with female slaves. (Docents and guides of the Mount Vernon Ladies' Association now regularly and readily discuss this latter aspect with visitors to the Washington home.)

This book is an undertaking of more than three years' duration. I have walked upon and examined virtually all the ground on which it took place, including that at Jumonville Glen; Fort Necessity; the site of Fort Pitt; Braddock's Field; Braddock's grave; the length of Braddock's Road; Lord Fairfax's domains in the Shenandoah Valley; Cresap's Fort and trading post; Fort Bedford; Fort Cumberland; Fort Frederick, Frederick, Maryland; Alexandria; Mount Vernon; the site of Belvoir, Fredericksburg; Williamsburg; Yorktown; Annapolis; Valley Forge; Philadelphia; London; Paris; the Cayman Islands; other Caribbean locales; and numerous woodland trails through country traversed by Washington on all three adventures in Virginia, West Virginia, Maryland, and Pennsylvania.

In preparing this novel, I have read more than sixty books (a select bibliography follows).

Wherever possible, I have relied upon primary sources, including Washington's journals, official reports, and letters; Gist's journal and letters; official and unofficial eyewitness accounts to events at Jumonville Glen, Fort Necessity, and Braddock's Field; Sally Fairfax's (few) letters; Benjamin Franklin's *Autobiography* and other books, letters, pamphlets, and monographs; and archival material from the Mount Vernon Ladies' Association, especially as concerns Washington's treatment of his slaves, and the Pennsylvania Historical Association, among others.

My physical descriptions of characters are based on contemporary portraits and accounts. For Sally Fairfax, I relied on two drawings and several historical descriptions. Portraits of Washington, Franklin, the other Fairfaxes, and the principal military figures in this story of course abound.

Wherever possible and appropriate, I have tried to have the characters speak in their own actual words, as suggested by letters or official accounts.

Michael Kilian
McLean, Virginia

Acknowledgments

For their assistance, support, guidance, and inspiration, I would like to thank my friends, author Cleveland Amory; writer David Elliott; actress Roma Downey; former Director of the National Museum of American History and National Park Service, Roger Kennedy; Congressman (and Washington scholar) Henry Hyde; biographer Kristie Miller; White House Historian William Seale; Maria Downs of the White House Historical Association; historian John S. D. Eisenhower; art historian Elizabeth Wilson; and Dale McFeatters of the Scripps Howard News Service.

I am also grateful to Vernon Edenfield of Kenmore Plantation and Gardens and Washington's Boyhood Home at Fredericksburg, Va.; William Kelso, archeologist for the Jamestown project; the staff and volunteers at Mount Vernon; and the staff and volunteers at the Fort Pitt Museum, Pittsburgh.

I owe much to my longtime friend and editor Tom Dunne, and friend and agent Dominick Abel.

And I am grateful to my wife, Pamela, and sons Eric and Colin as only they can know.

Major Washington

Part One

George Washington a murderer?

I was there at his side that most consequential morning in 1754—great heavens, now twenty-four years ago—as I was so often in that dangerous and calamitous time. The two of us were then quite newly come to manhood and the soldier's art, I the more newly than he. For all our adventures in the wilderness, neither of us had killed a man before that day, white or Indian, though I had often thought and talked upon the prospect, liking it not. What happened at what is now called Jumonville Glen that morning perhaps came as surprise to us both.

I was standing as close as breath to Washington at the top of that well-forested little cliff as the early sun pierced the gloom and lighted the stage below for slaughter. Lighted it eerily, for it had rained heavily throughout the preceding night and the glen was filled with mist. I don't suppose those poor Frenchmen bundled and huddled beneath us had any notion at all of our presence—save for those few whom the fates had cursed with wakefulness.

Crouched behind the wet shrubs, we could not have been visible to any of those below. But standing, one must have looked a spectral fiend, most particularly towering George. One poor French wretch's hand went madly for his musket upon that sighting, as would have my own, but never reached it. At the sudden movement, gunfire from all 'round the rim slashed downward into the glen's foggy depth.

I saw the rising bodies fall—saw three or four who never again stirred from the spot where they'd been sleeping. I remember clearly Ensign Jumonville lying afterward wounded and helpless but in soldierly calm as our friend the Indian Tanacharison, whom we also called Half King, came and knelt to work war club on skull and scalping knife upon trophy hair. I had reached the rocky floor of the glen by then and was hurrying toward the wounded man. Coming close, I heard Tanacharison say, "You are not dead yet, my father."

But then he was, and there, I suppose, is where the war began. Soon all the world was rattling with cannon and musket fire. It was Horace Walpole who wrote: "The volley fired by a young Virginian in the backwoods of America set the world on fire."

I did not discharge my own pistol that bloody morning, happy I am to state, though I've loosed ball and shot enough on subsequent violent occasions. My forbearance that morning has been a solace on troubled nights years after, when those long-ago shouts and screams disturb my slumber—and that of my wife, for I sometimes rise and walk about the bedchamber, which vexes her sorely.

All told, ten of those mischievous if officially innocent Frenchmen perished in that rocky entrapment where Jumonville had made his camp. It need not have happened. I do know that.

But George Washington an assassin?

That old dog of a question hounds me still, two decades and more after the awful fact, even as that once-esteemed and now-outlawed Virginia gentleman skulks in the wintry wastes outside this city like some cur kicked away from the hearth. At last report, he was huddled with his ragged band of insurrectionists in hilltop hovels near Valley Forge, while I sit a fat spaniel here in Philadelphia in all the comfort of Tory plenty.

Pray forgive my overindulgence in canine metaphor. I have a fondness for the beasts, as I do for metaphor, though in all my years at sea, I kept only a cat in quarters.

Never a wench, mind. Do you know that the only women to have ever graced a ship's cabin of mine have been my wife and, of course, of great moment to this accounting, Mrs. Sally Fairfax, now residing permanently in Britain, far from the still-glowing embers of Mr. Washington's passion, as must be her intent.

Forgive me also my discursiveness. My sharp-tongued wife has observed that if I sailed a ship in the manner I bring forth words, I should never have completed any voyage but coursed instead 'round and 'round my every harbor. She finds my discourse so elliptical she calls me "Fielding without the sauce." Her own sauce, I fear, has soured from what was once the flirtatious stuff of coquetry to something far more astringent, though I do still love her madly. But, as she would now remind, this is to digress.

This question of Washington's criminality abides in a wide assortment of memories and minds—not to speak of mouths. It was asked of me not a fortnight ago by General Howe, no less, His Lordship raising the question at my own table, idly, as though the matter were supper chat or London gossip. Good God, base or noble, Washington's deed unleashed the forces that settled the affairs of an entire continent. All history begins in the grub, does it not? What are the grand designs of ministers and kings compared to the well-placed mischief of a few men with guns?

I cannot convincingly demur in this matter when the question is asked. My past friendship with Mr. Washington—as some King's regulars now sneeringly refer to the American commander, countenancing no military address for Damned Rebels—is well known, as familiar a fact in this city as the extent of my fortune and the beauty of my wife and daughters. Quite considerable, that, in all regards, incidentally; despite my wife's years, which are near in number to my own, and I am almost as old as Washington.

Certainly I would not deny the smallest aspect of that long-ago comradeship, however much it has lapsed in recent years and now complicates my life. Politics and the current troubles aside, I still much admire General Washington. I've known none greater in the tumultuous chronicles of this country, if country it ever should prove to be.

What I said to General Howe was this: "General Braddock did not believe it assassination, sir, nor did Governor Dinwiddie. The confession was obtained through guile. Washington was and is a soldier, sir, and it was a soldierly encounter."

A more honest answer on my part would have been that I do not yet know within my soul of souls what Washington should be called in this regard. If the real truth of it must be plucked from my own moral sense, I've not found it there, despite much searching.

What I can say in certain fact is that Washington was surely the most ambitious man I ever met, his eye ever on the most glorious part of any deed or action, and it was ambition that took him to that glen, not simply the counsel of Half King or the orders of Crown and Governor Dinwiddie.

I can say a great deal more about Washington, most of it good. He was and is among the very bravest I have known, never shrinking from mortal hazard or the most wretched trial and discomfort, though he never could abide the lice and bedding beasties of frontier ordinaries, and shares with me and Dr. Benjamin Franklin small tolerance for uncleanliness.

Some have thought Washington dull, though no lady has ever spoken thus. Unless angered, or embarked on the passionate poesy of *amour*—he showed me several of his letters to Mrs. Fairfax, and blushing works they were—he was a man otherwise clumsy with words, and is so today. He had paltry education, and was no reader. But he was thoughtful—his mind a great wrestler, ever in struggle. He was a man who honestly tried to do what was right, whatever the cost—many thousands paying the price sometimes, now as then.

He was in no infamous way mean or cruel, merely strict, if damned strict. He ordered numberless hangings and shootings of deserters in that conflict with the French, as in this with the British Crown, and he freely set the lash the prescribed hundred or more strokes to the backs of drunken soldiery. But in every instance, to my mind, his severity was owing to the desperation of the military situation. Given his difficulty with tactics, desperation was a frequent companion, though he was ever the man for it.

I've seen him act most mercifully, mind, sparing the life of at least one villain—an Indian at that—who in the most treacherous fashion had sought his.

It's a fair criticism to call him aloof—except with the ladies—and no real democrat. Though he has evidenced no unseemly care for noble title, he is ever mindful of rank and social class, and will frostily assure you of his own should you give evidence of harboring any doubt. But I have found him a singularly fair man in all the dealings of which I had acquaintance, and often kind. No one ever had a more useful friend.

If not gifted in the wisest military exercise of that power, he was a man born to command. His estimable physical presence embodied authority. In rage, he quivered with it. His bearing under fire was extraordinary, showing no more care for bullets than mosquitoes. It inspired us all, sometimes to great foolishness. We would have braved cannon and facefuls of canister for the man, as some did. It was small wonder no hesitation followed his order to wake those unsuspecting French with musketry. Small wonder indeed that those ragged wretches of the Continental Army now so willingly suffer the cold with him on that hilltop at Valley Forge.

Two

At this point, I daresay I owe you an introduction. My name is Thomas Morley. For most of my life I've been addressed as Captain Morley, though I'm now more concerned with the owning of ships than the sailing of them.

I was born in Bermuda, the second son of a middlingly prosperous factor for London-based merchants in Hamilton Town. My pa never married the fetching tavern wench who was my mother, but she lived with him as wife, when he was not off on his travels, which were frequent. She bore him seven children, five of whom died early on, leaving me and my older brother Richard as survivors. My mother herself died in giving birth to the last of her babies, a daughter who lived but two days longer.

In quick time, my father took up with a quite handsome mulatto woman, who subsequently bore him three children, all daughters. The two who survived to adulthood were eventually taken into servitude, and I was in later years ultimately to expend considerable energies and sums tracking down these dark half-sisters and securing their freedom. One has since been successful as a courtesan of New Orleans and the other is married to a good man in Boston. They both correspond, usually when in need of money. I am considered a fair and generous man—both qualities I found conspicuous and admirable in Washington. I seldom ignore their implorations.

My brother and I came in for scant charity from our dusky stepmother. When my father died—depending on accounts, either lost at sea or killed in a dockside brawl in Barbados—she claimed lawful marriage and bribed a local justice to declare the union so. Richard and I were disinherited in the process, prompting my resolute brother first to a drinking binge and then to bold and vengeful action. Binding and gagging our stepmother one night when she had invited him to her bed, he took possession of our father's money box, and with it and me in tow, secured passage on a ship bound for Charleston. From there we made our way north, finding eventual haven in Annapolis in Maryland colony. Using our "inheritance" to make partial payment on a small, much-weathered but still-seaworthy sloop, which Richard named the *Hannah* after our own mother, my brother and I went into the coastal trade and prospered. Richard, as senior partner and master of the vessel, prospered particularly. Eventually, he generously repaid that "inheritence" we wrested from our get-penny stepmother. Merchants everywhere came to esteem Richard for his honesty, though not many gave him reason to return the compliment. If he could keep rein on his lusty drinking, which was at times prodigious, much was expected of him.

He was nineteen when we arrived in America, and I five years younger. In Bermuda, I had sometimes been called "Leech" for the tenacity with which I had kept my brother's close company. In more woodsy America, this became "Tick," for I displayed the same dependency, serving as Richard's mate on the *Hannah* and hurrying along at his heels or side wherever he went, when he'd have me. Washington was later pleased to call me "Tick" as well—for much the same reason. Once we became friends, I was much in his presence—oft to my discomfort when Sally Fairfax was about.

Fortune smiled so kindly and so swiftly on my brother that he was in short time able to go into partnership with an Annapolis ship's chandler on the purchase of a three-masted merchantman, which he sailed as master on voyages to the West Indies, leaving me with the *Hannah* to continue our coastal trade, principally in the waters of Chesapeake Bay and the Delaware River.

It was as great an honor as it was a terrifying responsibility to command a twenty-five-ton sailing vessel and ten-man crew at my few years. But I was saddened to be separated from Richard and missed him. I suppose it only natural that I would turn to Mr. Washington as a substitute, especially after Richard, despondent over a lady's death and driven by unnamed demons, turned still more increasingly to spirits. For Washington's part, I think he came to find me a tolerable companion. Death had recently taken his own older half-brother Lawrence, and he suffered the sibling lack as much as I.

There is little more to say about myself. By the time I met Washington, I had attained the height of six feet, but no great breadth or strength. Our father, figuring on our apprenticeship in the merchant trade, had had us both schooled in reading, writing, and ciphering, and I developed a strong fondness for books as boon companions at sea. Whenever possible, Richard took crated books aboard as cargo so I might have them for the borrowing. I was also amiably disposed toward sketching from a very early age, and had some skill at it, but Richard disapproved. Art was a proficiency of little practicality, he said—certainly in the American colonies.

I had sailed small boats in Bermuda's Great Sound from the age of six, and came early to a mariner's skills, if not full confidence. I already had a fair authority with the pistol and could train a deck gun with usually successful result. I inherited the better part of our parents' good looks, but this attribute was tempered for much of my youth by an acute shyness and awkwardness with women, until Dr. Franklin's wise tutelage took hold. If quick of mind, as my brother always boasted of me, I am careful how I speak it. My wife does not always give me the chance, at all events.

I came to manhood with one eccentricity I have maintained unto this day—a fondness for bathing. Growing up on Bermuda, I was constantly swimming, fishing, capsizing, or for some other reason immersed in that island's clear, warm waters, and developed an affection for having my skin thus refreshed and consequently free of its otherwise natural covering of sweat and dirt. I am told by physicians that this penchant of mine is dangerously unhealthy, but I persist in it nevertheless—bathing once a week even in winter. I had one of those new shower baths installed at our Philadelphia house, but my wife is disinclined to use it. As she wrote to her sister, "I still find the experience of being wet all over inside a house most disagreeable, and one I hope not to repeat again."

I fear I am rambling overmuch in this account, as my wife would again remind. Allow me to return to a warm day in the late spring of 1753—an election day of some sort, with all the public places crowded and boisterous—when I was preparing to weigh anchor from the half-moon harbor of Alexandria, Virginia, with the sloop's hold loaded full with wheat and whiskey bound for Philadelphia.

It was to be my third voyage as temporary master of the *Hannah*, the previous two having been completed without any great misadventure and at some profit. I was by then all of eighteen years. Washington, a little-propertied but fully fledged member of the Northern Neck Virginia aristocracy, was twenty-one, residing at his recently deceased half-brother's house on Hunting Creek, a then relatively modest dwelling place called Mount Vernon, after Admiral Vernon, under whom his brother Lawrence had served in the military expedition against the Spanish at Cartegena.

Washington was "little propertied" by the standards of the Tidewater gentry, but not by those of ordinary folk. He had in fact inherited his father's small farm on the Rappahannock, by Fredericksburg, as well as some fifteen slaves, and had recently acquired the patent to some fourteen hundred acres in the wilderness lands beyond the Blue Ridge in the valley of the Shenandoah, though it was then a territory too untamed and dangerous to be of much more than speculative value.

In no respect was he satisfied. Despite these holdings, his income then was nearly all gained through his employment as a surveyor for the Fairfaxes, and acreage to his mind was best measured in the thousands. He had grand neighbors and grand friends. He dreamed grandly.

These particulars I was to learn later. At the moment of our meeting, I knew nothing at all about the man, not even his name, though I was enormously struck by the impressive figure he presented.

Alexandria was a new town then—planned, mapped, laid out, and auctioned as plots and parcels in 1749, just four years before this first encounter. At the south end of its waterfront was the dock of a shipbuilder's. At the north, there was a long wharf belonging to the Crown's tobacco warehouse. Between them ran a long, curving bay of the Patowmack River, exposed as muck at low tide and too shallow even at high tide to allow shoreside mooring. Ships large and small were compelled to anchor in the river channel and load and unload cargo by means of rowing boats or barges.

I'd planned to sail that morning on the change of tide. The Patowmack current there ran a good three knots, and the tidal draw southward could add two knots to that. The breeze that day was light, but favoring, tending westerly. Our hold was full, the deck cramped with lashed crates and barrels. All was ready to get underway. But the damned river pilot they'd given me was as drunk as a German, having taken early of the election-day bumbo and God knows how much tavern grog. My brother Richard would have departed at all events, hauling the sotted fellow as temporary cargo to his drop-off point and navigating the channel himself. Richard was the ablest seaman I ever knew, drunk or sober.

But I was mere eighteen, fearing the result of every order I gave. The sloop was partly mine, but by far the larger share was Richard's. He retained a seventy-five-percent interest in our little company, according me the remaining part, which was generous in a time when the older brother was often heir to all. The *Hannah* was registered in his name.

The river below Alexandria was relatively free of the rocks that bedeviled captains seeking landings upriver, but the shoals to the south were wide and many and the channel between them tortuously meandering. I dared not risk it. I got the listing, mumbling, rum-soaked fellow into our small boat again and had two crewmen row us back ashore, pulling to the landing at the foot of Water Street. Sending the pilot back to his alehouse, charitably promising to report him merely as ill, I set briskly off for the harbormaster's and a new pilot. But hardly had I put foot on the wooden walk when there stepped in front of me the tall figure of Washington, who stayed me with raised hand.

"By your leave, sir," said he, "are you Captain Morley of the sloop *Hannah*, there at anchor?"

His height exceeded six feet by a good two inches, perhaps three, making him tower over the ordinary man, and he weighed some two hundred pounds or more, by common measure. This stature was increased by the most military of bearings, his posture compensating for narrow shoulders and almost womanly wide hips. He had legs like trees and his hands and feet were large, as was his leonine head. His cheekbones were broad and his arctic blue-gray eyes wide set. Washington had a strong jaw and fine mouth, the latter usually grimly set as he was disinclined to smile for fear of exposing his teeth, which were in no way handsome and not much healthy.

His face was marked with the smallpox with which he'd become afflicted on his sole voyage to the West Indies not long before—his only travel ever outside the colonies, though as a youth, he'd longed for a career at sea and had been intent on an education in England, both prizes his pesky mother had denied him.

But the marks of the pox were a common disfigurement, and his were small and rather disguised by the burnishment of the sun, to which he was quite sensitive and exceedingly exposed as a surveyor and incipient planter. Though always distinguished in dress—after marrying the rich Widow Custis years later, he took to the aristocratic custom of having his fine suits and linen shirts laundered in England—he was not a man much for wigs, and wore his reddish-brown hair tied simply in careful queue.

He was wearing an unembroidered but well-cut suit of blue cloth that morning we met, buff-colored hose, and brass buttons on his coat and waistcoat, and brass buckles on his shoes. He had no lace at throat or sleeve, but wore a simple neckstock. He was a gentleman of the country, and the day was warm.

His manner, as you might deduce from those first few words he addressed to me, was somewhat cold. As I would learn, it was his way with all strangers, and with all inferiors, even of long acquaintance. He would later reveal his share of jolly moments, but this was not one of them.

"I am Captain Morley, sir," I said, standing as straight as I could. I recall being embarrassed by my appearance. Only a cocked hat distinguished me from my rough-clad seamen. I was not the certified master of this small sloop, and not yet entitled to the "Captain." I accepted the honor, however.

"And you sail for Philadelphia, as they say?"

I nodded.

"I am Major Washington, district adjutant of the Virginia militia. I would beg the favor of a lady's passage downriver to Belvoir plantation. There's a voting today and the roads are not safe."

There was no lady then in sight. I hoped she was not waiting at any great distance. In this apprehension, I must have frowned.

"It would mean much to me," he said.

"I would be agreeable to it," I said, "if some haste would not be inconvenient."

He studied me, his gaze steady, not unfriendly, but unsettling. He seemed much older than his relatively few years, an impression contributed to by the stiff formality of his language. I feared I might have struck him as impudent.

"You are well-spoken," he said.

"Thank you. I am fond of books."

" 'Let your discourse with men of business be short and comprehensive,' " he said.

"Sir?"

"A rule of civility, Captain."

"You find me uncivil, sir?"

"No. The contrary. I am impressed, and so observe: 'Superfluous compliments and all affectation of ceremony are to be avoided, yet where due, they are not to be neglected.' Another rule of civility, applicable to my observation of your speech."

"I thank you. As I say, the books."

"The reading habit serves you well, sir. I have another favor to ask. It's most important. And King's business, of some urgency. A parcel for Philadelphia. Another for Williamsburg."

"I'm Philadelphia-bound, but Williamsburg is forty miles up the York River. A beat against the wind as it holds today."

"The wind could change a dozen times before you reach the James, don't you think?"

True enough. Who was this young militia officer claiming the Crown's importance? And why choosing me? And why was I so obediently listening?

"There are other ships, Major," I said. "The harbor's full."

"No ship for Philadelphia. Not for a week or more."

"These parcels are of value?"

"Yes. Come with me, Captain, if you would."

"I mean to sail on this tide, sir."

His glance took in the river. "There's sufficient time. Please, I'd be most grateful."

Then, as in so many times that followed, I found it most difficult indeed to refuse George Washington's bidding. He had this compelling effect upon most men, save his scheming rivals, and sometimes even them.

"Very well, Major. King's business."

Tramping along with great purpose, he led me to a public house up the hill on King Street. The way was crowded with the usual swarm of sailors, carters, navvies, boobies, brawlers, idlers, horses, pigs, dogs, and chickens— their numbers swelled by the visitation of country folk attendant upon the election. The farmers absent their wives, of course. Only bawds and wenches and a few market women were visible in the throng, plying their trades with great vigor on what was of custom a profitable occasion.

Awaiting us were a young man named George Mercer and a lady named Mrs. Sally Fairfax—the latter, I would learn, was wife of Washington's friend and principal patron George William Fairfax, nephew of the almighty if eccentric Lord Fairfax. They sat not in the common room of the tavern, but in a private supping chamber. Even so, I was shocked to find so highborn a lady in such a place on such a day. The curse-laden chatter from the common hall was painfully loud, the scent of ale and rum and piss in the house most powerful.

There was but one large, round table in the private room, and they its sole occupants. Oyster shells, nuts, sweetmeats, the remains of a cheese and round loaf of bread, and a sugar cone were set before them—gentlefolk's fare. Mercer was drinking wine and she tea, then as now a costly refreshment. After making introductions—she looked up at me in the most wary way—Washington thrust me into a vacant chair and seated himself beside me, asking my pleasure.

"There is an excellent ragoo today," he said, "if you're in mind of bouffage."

"My hunger," I said, "is for the tide."

"I understand, Captain," he said. "But you'll attend at least to your thirst."

My nerves had thirst enough at this point. Ship and cargo beckoned worrisomely, but here was an important gentleman not to be displeased. "A whiskey," I said.

It was brought with dispatch. In the brief interval, my eye fell in quick blench upon the lady's bosom. This, at least, seemed to please her some, but she quickly looked away.

Mrs. Fairfax was without cloak and wore a simple straw hat instead of bonnet. Its ribbon was the same pale yellow as her dress, which was broadly full in skirt but bore little evidence of much petticoat beneath. In the fashion of the time, the bodice was tight but deeply and widely cut, lacking a modesty cloth and thus exposing an amplitude of girlish bosom, an enameled brooch pinned like a sentry at the cleave between her freckled breasts.

She had freckled cheeks as well. She was broad of brow and long of face and nose, and sharp if dainty of chin, but her features were arranged in agreeable symmetry, and it was in sum a very pretty face. Her hair was dark, with coppery glints when the sun shone upon it, and she had large, deep-set, mischievous brown eyes. Hers was the sort of beauty that diminished in solemnity, such as at that somber meal, but when she was merry, which was often, freely bestowing her sweet smile, there was none more radiant.

I have no doubt that Washington's love for her sprang forth the instant they were introduced upon George William Fairfax's fetching her home as bride from Williamsburg, where her family—the esteemed Cary clan—was among the most prominent in the capital.

A shadow passed over Washington's gaze as he took note of the reckless direction of my own. He paused to take from his waistcoat a small box of cloves—a remedy I learned later he carried against unfortunate breath—and pop one of the small bulbs into his mouth. Then he leaned close.

"What I ask of you is a mission of great necessity," he said. "This colony—and Pennsylvania—are at peril. Damned worrisome peril. And you must carry news of it. Governor Dinwiddie at Williamsburg must learn of it. And Mr. Benjamin Franklin of Philadelphia. Are you of that city?"

"No. Of Annapolis."

He frowned. "Maryland is at peril, too, in her western reaches, but chooses not to know it."

"I am little in Maryland, sir. My land's my deck."

The whiskey did not diminish my restlessness, but emboldened me to steal another glimpse of aristocratic bosom. You must understand the magic of this lady for me. I was then becoming quite fascinated, if frustrated, by women and relished their company with great excitement, though I knew not what to do with it. So much at sea and at my brother's beck, I was seldom in it.

At that age and station of my life, I'd spoken few words to any gentlewoman. She was every inch that—and a Fairfax! It was all the same as royalty to me. Yet I caught myself imagining the brown buds of her breasts, the softness of her furry flag, the silkiness of her bum. But for those freckles and a fashionable mole, her flesh was flawless.

Washington became abrupt—enough, I think, to be in violation of his rules of civility. He rose, seized up two leather pouches from the baggage by the wall and thrust them onto my lap.

"They are sealed, sir," he said, and so they were, by leaden fastenings.

"The letters they contain are sealed as well, and you will see to it they remain so until they reach the governor and Mr. Franklin."

I drank the last of the whiskey. "I've not yet agreed to this, sir," I said.

"I beg you, Captain. Serve your Sovereign. And safely deliver this lady." His eyes sought hers, but were rebuffed. There was some dark trouble between these two—spoken in wordless ways. I had the feeling he had entangled her in more than inconvenience.

Flustered, boyish now, he turned back to me, reproachfully. "As you observed, sir, the tide is running."

He called for the bill and paid it from what struck me as a less-than-weighty purse. The money prompted another thought. He called for quill and paper.

"I am a gentleman justice of this county," he said, "and can authorize compensation for your troubles. Will fifteen shillings suffice?"

"It's a fair sum," I said as he scribbled, having no idea. A gentleman justice at his age? The aristocracy, of course, won such titles simply through birth.

"Present this to the governor. He will see to it."

"George," said Mrs. Fairfax sharply. "We tarry overlong."

They were the first words she had spoken. She had a clear and charming voice, quite musical, if in that moment somewhat leaden. Mercer smiled and rose. He had not spoken either, having responded to Washington's introduction of me with a cursory nod.

The Major got to his feet as well, his eyes seeking Mistress Fairfax's pleasure. She stood with ladylike grace, revealing herself to be uncommonly tall for a woman, and brushed the crumbs from her gown as if they were a great nuisance.

Their horses were fetched, only two, Washington's a fine light gray of suitable size to bear his weight. The lady rode; the two men walking to either side of her to protect her from the rabble. I followed meekly behind. The crowd was too thick to permit me to walk beside them.

I would be taking her home. How had she got from that downriver place to this? 'Twas a mystery, with no answer the mere likes of me was privileged to.

At the landing, a plank was brought to spare the lady's dainty foot from the muck. She took a seat at the aft of my small boat, spreading her skirts and leaving no room aside her—not that I would have made so bold as to join her.

I hesitated. "Major, I have no pilot for the river."

"The lady knows the river, sir."

"The regulations are specific." I had no wish to present my brother an admiralty-court summons and a painful fine.

"I am a gentleman justice of this county, as I said. I'll attend to any irregularity."

I recall her last look at him as we shoved off—all dark and earnest. His own gaze was long and lingering. He and Mercer stood on the landing until we had drawn aside the *Hannah*, then mounted their horses and trotted off.

She held fast to my arm in ascending the ladder. On deck, releasing me, her hand brushed mine. I fear I flushed at the touch. The deckhands, surprised to find this guest among them, watched with some wonder and stifled mirth.

"I have quarters below," I said. "They're rude, but you'll find comfort."

"Not in this heat," she said. "I'll stay on deck. You'll need my guidance for your steering."

"I've sailed the river before, ma'am."

"How many times?"

"Well, the truth of it is once."

"The channel bears right below the town. It shifts to the opposite shore at the narrows."

"Yes, ma'am. I know." I straightened my hat and went to the helm.

There were seats aplenty for her on the numerous boxes, but she went to the starboard rail and stood, removing her hat.

The crew raised anchor and hauled on full sail without their usual lusty curses and ditties. A few had been to the bumbo punch while ashore for the cargo loading, and I wondered how long their good behavior would last. They worshipped my brother almost as much as I did, but viewed me mostly as a figure of fun and kept their own counsel as to what was prudent behavior.

To my regret, Mrs. Fairfax refrained from coming aft to join me, keeping instead to the rail, her eyes on the passing westward shore. I was surprised when, after sailing through the narrows below the town and coming nigh the wide mouth of a tidal creek opening on our right, she spoke to me as though in command.

"If it please you, Captain, I would have you steer to starboard."

It didn't please me. The tide was low. The inlet, though broad, was shallow.

"That's not the course, my lady."

She approached me, a different mood upon her face, and smiled. She had fine teeth. "I know that, sir. I would like to go ashore."

There were woods rising to a small hill on the north bank of the inlet. Alexandria Town was well masked by it. No other vessel, no small boat, was in view.

"Here?"

"To that wooded place. I'll not be long."

We had slop jars and chamber pots aplenty. "Madame, there are accommodations below."

Her smile became a laugh. "You err, sir. That is not my need."

This whimsy unnerved me. I knew not what to do or say.

"Mrs. Fairfax . . ."

"You've been paid for my passage, or will be. Let this be part of it."

I still hesitated—too long. The dark look returned.

"You are in Virginia waters, Captain. Will you not honor the name of Fairfax?"

It was then that I noticed the horses, halted by what I presumed to be a ford at the creek that flowed into this inlet. There were two riders, at too far a distance to recognize except by their clothing. One, as Mercer had, wore purple. The other, taller man wore blue. They seemed to be looking toward us. The taller man dismounted.

Our home at Annapolis lay just thirty miles overland beyond the river's eastern shore. Would that I could be there.

"As you please, ma'am."

I swung the heavy tiller myself, calling out the shift of sail. The *Hannah* turned into the shallows, slowing, then gaining speed again as the mainsail and jib were drawn close-hauled.

Too late I realized my mistake. I should have left the sails trimmed wide as they were, to brake against the breeze. Close-hauled, we glided well past my intended anchorage. The deck creaked and groaned as the *Hannah*'s keel mushed into the bottom. We listed gently to port.

I kept myself from swearing, though not easily. "You may take your leisure, ma'am. We'll be here until the rising tide. If the wind should shift to the south, you may not make Belvoir till after the sun is set."

"Thank you, Captain. Your kindness will not be forgotten."

I did not accompany her ashore in the small boat oared by a crewman, deciding whatever mystery those woods contained should be her private one. As the rower pulled away to return to the *Hannah*, I looked to the horsemen again. The tallest had now vanished. The other, in purple, was upon his feet, standing idly.

The stout Riggins, promoted to chief mate when my brother's absence put me in command, came to my side and gave a wink.

"I hope you've foundered us for good reason, Tick," he said.

"A militia officer in Alexandria provided the reason."

"And what is that?"

"Not your worry, Bob."

He watched the lady move toward the trees. "No strumpet, that."

"No, indeed. And neither is she your worry."

" 'Twill be your brother's."

"He need not know."

Riggins grinned. I decided to buy some friendship, as downpayment on discretion.

"Fetch me a cup of grog and the book from my chest," I said. "And draw a dram each for you and the lads. We'll be here a considerable while waiting on this tide."

"You're a generous soul, Tick. Or is it 'Captain' I heard?"

I endured his laugh. I'm sure their drams were refreshed more than once, but I countenanced it. They'd be sober enough by the time we hazarded the sea.

Mrs. Fairfax had scurried with some certain haste into the woods, as though she knew the path. The heat was increasing. With the yellow of her dress having vanished into the greenery, I stripped to shirt and breeches and hopped onto a barrel for a seat, resting bare feet on the rail as I settled into my wait, and book.

I sipped slowly, and read, as perhaps half an hour passed. Riggins refreshed my cup and also brought my pipe, having lit his own. We smoked.

"She could come to harm in that woods."

"She knows her mind. And this country. Be patient."

The remaining horseman had moved somewhat nearer the creek. He watered the animals, but was otherwise idle—waiting, as were we.

That's all you should really know of this, but I'll tell you a measure more. Riggins took no undue note of the stopped traveler, and had no ken of whatever ravary might be adance in those trees. I quickly sent him below to check the hour on the ship's clock, as I'd failed to turn the hourglass. When he reemerged, I told him I'd bring back the lady myself, and set about doing so, though she'd not yet reappeared from the woods.

I rowed until stopped by the mud a few yards from the firmer shore, then sat in the boat, my back to the trees, slapping at flies and dripping sweat. Here, the tall trees stilled the breeze.

I did not turn until she called my name, and that was a good while later. She stood at the edge of the marsh, hat in hand. The tide had fallen considerably by then and there was no hauling the boat farther. I'd have to tote this pretty burden to it. I slid my bare feet into the ooze and sloshed toward her.

"There's no clean footing, ma'am."

"Indeed, not. Then you must carry me."

She was flushed, but no more than I. As I lifted her, with the firm feel of her legs and back against my arms, my face warmed so I fear it must have turned the color of the King's uniform. Her skin was damp beneath the cloth, her throat and greade glistening with perspiration. The hem of her skirt was smudged with dirt, and there was some of it on her elbow. Bits of leaf and tiny twig clung to the fabric. Her curls were matted, and she snatched a leaf from her hair. I set her gently in the aft seat, then went to the bow and shoved hard to float the boat clear.

"It's a hot day, ma'am," I said after clambering aboard and putting oars to lock.

"There's a bliss to it." Her eyes were very merry.

"My cabin's yours for the rest of our little voyage," I said. "Perhaps you will want to refresh yourself."

Her flush deepened. "If you could have basin and water and cloth brought. I am in need of them." She studied me, much as Washington had. "What is your Christian name, Captain Morley?"

I pulled hard on the oars. "I'm not captain yet, ma'am. Not truly. The name is Thomas. I'm also called Tick."

"Will you be returning to this river?"

"My brother—he's the right master of this sloop—will be the judge of that. But Alexandria has become a prosperous port. I expect we'll find some cargo for it."

"Then tell me, Thomas—Tick—when you visit us again, or speak of us in neighboring parts, will you be a friend to Major Washington?"

"I've only just met him."

She leaned forward, her breasts bulging, and touched my knee.

"Be a friend to the Major," she said. "And be a friend to me."

She sat back, waiting.

"I will, ma'am."

That's all of this adventure I'll relate. I leave the rest to your surmise. Mind, ladies of the country oft take to woods and meadow for the health of it, seeking berries or flowers. Pity she found none.

She pressed a coin into my hand upon taking her leave at Belvoir landing. Something troubled me as she flitted down the dock toward the house, and I realized of a sudden that her dress was missing its brooch. I started to call out that loss to her, but wisdom caught my tongue. I still have that coin she gave me. My wife thinks it a souvenir of Mr. Washington's first war. I suppose it is.

———

We were still far upriver from the Chesapeake when evening fell. Leaving Riggins to keep a course midway between the riverbanks on the rising tide, I went below to my cabin. She had left it much tidier than she'd found it. I sat down upon my fresh-made bunk, spreading my hands over the coverlet as though she might have left some residue of touch behind. I closed my eyes in reverie, till a sense of foolishness chased my wanton thoughts. She was much older than I. A mature woman. My guess was twenty-three, which proved dead-on. Her affections belonged not only to a husband but, with the woods as witness, to another man. She and both of them were of a rank far superior to what I thought I might ever achieve. She'd graced me with her charm and friendship only in purchase of my discretion, or so it seemed. She doubtless thought me a silly, posturing boy. I should wisely expect her to treat me coldly on our next meeting, if there was to be that.

Nevertheless, I was smitten, and would do her duty as she bade, and serve Washington. But what errand had he set me on? King's business, but what?

The pouches were in the cabin corner, as I had stowed them. I went over and lifted the lightest of the two to my lantern's glow. The leaden seal was firm, holding the thong that bound the pouch taut and tight. I could barely poke two fingers into the small opening beneath the leather fold.

Tilting the pouch to slide its contents to my touch, I felt the folded paper of a letter, and something soft and furry. What, some wilderness cap as gift?

Putting down the first, I hefted the far more weighty second pouch, that bound for the governor. That seal had been clumsily applied, or weakened in carry. The thong was loose. Pulling it gently until less than an inch of it remained held by the lead clasp, I turned back the pouch's cover and found I could slip my hand inside with ease.

My fingers discovered another letter, which I left within, lest I tear or wrinkle it in pulling it to eye. Probing farther, I touched another furry thing, this one much silkier than the first. I pulled it out, merely curious at first, then shaken. I'd never seen a human scalp before, but this met every description I had read, complete to stains of red on the underside of the delicate, terrible leather. The hair was yellow and long, fine and fair, that of a child—or, more likely, woman. I shuddered, and shoved it back.

The weight of the tote came from a more benign but equally curious object, an oblong lead plate bearing a French inscription. I was already master then of some words of that tongue, and made out. *"Année 1749, cela sous le règne de Louis XV, Roi de la France."* Good grief, the French king.

I returned the plate to its place, in my haste pulling free the thong. Swearing, I tried several times to thread it back into place, but the opening would not admit it, not without damage to the seal.

What now? What punishment would a Royal governor select for such offense? The stocks? A flogging? A hanging on the Williamsburg commons?

I'd put my mind to some excuse. Setting the pouch beside its mate, I stood. I was still unshod, mind, and when I moved my bare foot, it was to sudden pain. I looked beneath and fetched up my lady's brooch, happily undamaged.

Here was a souvenir I dared not keep. But how return?

Three

Williamsburg sat in the very middle of a long peninsula bounded by the York and James rivers, but at some distance from each, a somewhat awkward situation for the capital of a colony so dependent on maritime commerce. Creeks led to the town from each river, but none was very deep. I had to leave the *Hannah* at anchor, row to the shore, and then hike three miles to the town, lugging Major Washington's leather parcel for the governor.

I'd not been in Williamsburg before, but had heard much of it. This was a very large place for Virginia, a town of at least one thousand inhabitants, and boasted a theater among other diversions, though gaming was frowned upon and horse racing within its boundaries banned by governor's decree to discourage wagering by the colony's poorer folk.

This was a military town as well, with more than a hundred muskets, some cannon, and a small war's worth of powder in the arsenal. But all such was locked and guarded—a Royal concern for rebellion even then, though Virginia had not had one for more than sixty years.

Few were in the streets and lanes in that sultry heat, but a small crowd had gathered near the end of the common where some men and boys were hectoring with sticks and pebbles a most unfortunate African woman, who ran about in mad, shrieking circles with a sharply studded iron collar hanging bloody around her neck. I inquired of a bystander her offense.

"Runaway," I was told. "Too frequent fled, too often found."

"Is this torture necessary?" I asked.

"It is the law. She'll be out of her misery soon enough."

He gestured to a stout post that had been erected in the meadow grass, much scorched about the base. Women were piling straw and wood about it.

I was not then and certainly have never been since much tolerant of the slavery custom—"the peculiar institution," as Charlestonians refer to it. An Englishwoman found guilty of slaying her husband in dembulation would face no more than a quick noose. I turned away, much sickened.

In the way of more unpleasantness, I spied nearby two men drooped in the painful fastness of stocks, their heads hanging numbly, unmindful of the clamor of the slave woman's torment. In that heat, I wondered if either would live the day.

I passed on, unregarded, until I reached the governor's palace. Washington had given me a letter for Dinwiddie, but none of introduction for myself. I was treated rudely by sentries and servants until finally admitted to the large central hall and brought to a desk behind which sat a clerkish official who was able to comprehend my purpose.

I had feared reprisal for the one pouch's loosened seal, but the fellow paid it no mind, snapping off the lead with a knife and dumping the contents on the desk before him. His eyebrows lifted and his nostrils flared at the sight of the fair-haired scalp. He pushed it aside and turned more happily to the letter, the waxen seal of which he left untampered. Adjusting his spectacles, he squinted at the address.

"Major Washington, y'say. Why did he not come himself?"

"He said it was a matter of urgency, and better by my ship than his horse." I withheld any "sir."

The man sniffed. "Very well." He gestured dismissively at a chair against the opposite wall. "Seat yourself a while, for a while it will be."

He returned the scalp and letter to the pouch, which he sent upstairs with a servant. I waited, and waited more. The servant returned. Others came and went. Two finely dressed gentlemen entered the hall from outside, arguing volubly—their heated discourse continuing unabated as they climbed the staircase.

I waited still. When what I judged to have been the better part of an hour had passed, I approached the clerk again.

"May I go?" I asked. "My ship is waiting."

"There may be a reply," he said, scratching at some document with his pen.

"My vessel is bound for Philadelphia and I'm overdue. I'm not returning to Major Washington."

"The governor may wish you to. Sit down, sit down." His hand flicked at me as though at a fly.

Dinwiddie, of course, was in fact officially only the lieutenant governor of the colony. In the custom of the time, he acted as agent for the true holder of that title, who administered his American domain from England, if at all. But the bewigged Robert carried the King's writ, and his word and whim were law. I dared not trifle, even with his clerkish servant. Obediently, I sat.

If my first period of idle waiting was near an hour, the next was longer. No one descended from the upper floor, but the clerk finally summoned me forth, as though at whim.

"You may go," he said.

I looked to the stairs.

"If the governor had wished further service of you, I'd have heard his pleasure by now," the clerk said. "Be off."

Starting for the door, I recalled the note promising fifteen shillings. Richard would want something of recompense for this detour. I placed the paper atop the desk. The man frowned, peering at it more disdainfully than he had the scalp.

"Major Washington should have paid you and listed the item among his expenses."

"Yes, but he did not."

"Very well." He scribbled something at the bottom of the note. "Take this to the bursar."

"And where is he?"

"In Charlottesville, actually, but he'll return by Saturday."

That was four days hence. There was nothing left but to bid a pleasant farewell, which I refrained from doing. All I had to show my brother of this adventure was a note in the hand of a rustic militia officer named George Washington. Richard would find that of negligible value indeed.

All told, we lost a good three days in this perambulation. And, wouldn't you know, just as we passed the bar off Cape Charles and onto the open sea, a great dark storm began rising from the southern horizon. Squalls and thundery showers from the west and northwest were the customary inclemency here in summer weather. They could be nasty, but they swiftly passed. Coming from nor'east or southeast, a malevolent sky like this promised an enduring trial. From the look of it, it would be a hell of a blow. My crew commenced a lot of chunter, with me and Mrs. Fairfax the objects of their unhappy scorn.

The Virginia capes and the Maryland and Delaware banks provide no friendly waters for a ship of any size caught in a storm. The sandbars and shoals run far off the shore, and a mariner foundering on them when the weather's coming straight from Hell has small time left on Earth. I steered east by nor'east to seek a healthy depth, but the course prolonged our visit with the furious weather, which, in vexing perversion, was passing easterly from south to north, spreading its terrors widely to either side as it came. We were in it a good five hours or more, though none of us frantically busy and terrified hands bothered much to keep the time.

Good God, every damned minute seemed an hour in itself. I counted the remnants of my life in terms of each approaching mountain of wave and every increase in pitch of the wind screaming through the rigging. Where the sky was not black, it was as weirdly, brightly green as the heaving sea. Even if through some miracle we should survive, I thought, there'd be no sparing the sloop and her cargo from serious damage, visiting calamity upon my brother's heretofore prosperous fortunes—not to speak of my own.

But, praise be to Providence—and to my brave crew and stout little ship—I brought us through with far more injury to nerves and temper than to flesh or oak. It remains one of my proudest attainments, that passage, and I recount it still today—that is, as often as my wife will let, so impatient is she now with my retold adventuring. Certainly the feat was not accomplished without good Riggins' constant counsel. We reefed all canvas but the forward staysail in the worst of it, and lost only a shroud.

Many were my prayers when wind and seas were at their fiercest. I was in rage with myself for having allowed Major Washington and his Mrs. Fairfax to delay us to such devastating effect, but when we'd at last found gentler winds and finally rounded Cape Henlopen into the welcoming shelter of Delaware Bay, I forgave them, reminding myself of my fondness for this lady, and my noble promise—as it then seemed. I took our survival as a sign I should serve them both. They had both worked a magic on me.

We had moonlight for our quiet reach up the Delaware River and arrived at Philadelphia on a clear morning, marveling as always at the height and abundance of the church spires and the breadth of the city. Thanks to our small size, we were able to obtain dockside mooring without much wait. Of course, before the unloading could proceed, I had to pay my respects to the merchants for whom our cargo was bound and complete the commercial paperwork that would secure our payment for it. I also had to find customers for the whiskey I had bought on my brother's credit in Alexandria, so my stops included a few of the taverns. And there was as well cargo to obtain for our return voyage to Annapolis, where Richard had bidden me to await him. Sailors can look forward to a jolly time in port, a reward not granted their vessel's master.

Then as now, Philadelphia was the grandest town in America, surpassing in all its spendors and appointments Boston, Newport, Charleston, Baltimore, and upstart New York. My one good suit of clothes, all of a solemn black, was better fit for a rougher place, but at least it marked me as more than a deckhand or tradesman, though were I wearing common trousers with my somber coat, I'd be thought the one or the other.

Among the places I was to call upon was a large aristocratic house on Chestnut Street belonging to a rich merchant and grain trader named Nathaniel Smithson. I'd been told he kept his office in his dwelling place, an arrangement that provided me little convenience that morning, as he was absent. The maidservant who answered the door knew not where he had gone nor when he might return. I protested that I had ship's cargo waiting for him that I could not unload until he had attended to the proper papers, and demanded to know how long I would be required to wait. My triumph over that colossal tempest at sea had rather puffed me up, don't you know, and I was feeling very much the man, not the boy, quite the contrary of my station when last I'd visited this great port.

The wench gave me no useful answer and proceeded to close the door in my face, or tried to, as I quickly stuck my foot in it. This rash impertinence produced a few disagreeable exclamations, until the servant girl was shouted away from the door and her riled countenance replaced by that of an extraordinary pretty young lady of perhaps sixteen or seventeen years. She had fair hair somewhere between the color of brass and gold, enormous light-blue eyes, small nose, and large mouth—its corners turned down in decided disapproval.

"What is the meaning of this intrusion, sir?" she said, holding the door firmly against any further entry on my part, an act which bulged her young bosom forth enchantingly.

"I was told Mr. Smithson could be found at his office here."

"He has an office here, but does not receive visitors to it—except by invitation. Who are you?"

I explained my business, introducing myself, with some confidence and aplomb, as Captain Morley. She looked over my dusty, mildewed, unimpressively plain clothing, and gave a little laugh.

"You look more a reverend without his stock," she said. "Actually, you seem too young to be either thing."

She opened the door a few inches more, but still held it fast. I removed my foot but did not step back. She was the prettiest female I'd seen in all my young years, or ever expected to. The cut of her bodice drew my eye far more frankly than even Mistress Fairfax's had done—much, much too frankly. I'd visited perhaps too many taverns that morning. She blushed, but with no great degree of indignation.

"I'd admit you, sir, but there are only women here, and you are a stranger."

"I do very much need to see Mr. Smithson," I said. "You are his daughter? Perhaps I might wait."

Too bold, this. She retreated a few inches.

"I am his daughter, but you've no business with me. My father should return midday for his dinner. You may present yourself then."

"My lady—"

"*A* good-bye, *Captain.*" The door closed fast.

As you might surmise, I'd been instantly smitten. My "ardor" for Mrs. Fairfax drained away like wave water through a scupper. In its place in my heart there sloshed the nectars of a much likelier *amour.* This young lady, I felt quite sure, was unmarried.

It was nonsensical of me to expect a desirable result of any sort of amorous ambition with her as object at that point, but life is so damned short—no member of my family had lived beyond his or her forty-fourth year—and you took your chance when it flew to hand. This was such a pretty bird.

Also, as I confess, I was fairly drunk.

So my step was light and lively upon the dusty street as I departed. Everything about this day now seemed delightful. I would have gladly camped there on Smithson's front steps to make certain of keeping the appointment, but realized I should make use of the interval to inquire after this Mr. Benjamin Franklin and deliver Major Washington's mysterious parcel.

Franklin, I'd been told upon inquiry, was the proprietor of a substantial mercantile establishment and print shop on Market Street, and possessed besides a fine, tall house down a nearby lane running off that thoroughfare. It was to the house I was directed. There I was welcomed at the door by the gentleman himself—far more cheerily than I'd been greeted at Mr. Smithson's.

He was a tallish man but decidedly unimportant looking, and I wondered how Washington's "King's business" could have to do with this unremarkable and very unmilitary Philadelphian.

Franklin was wigless, his long brown hair worn loose almost to his shoulders. His forehead was high. Indeed, he was close to baldness and could have handsomely done with a wig. As it was, he augmented the thinning hair on top by reinforcement of a few strands combed up and over from one side. I was curious at such vanity on the part of a man in possession of no great handsomeness, but he had a charm to him—an amiable smile and something of a merry twinkle in his eyes, which also seemed to impart a considerable intelligence, this effect enhanced by his fragile spectacles.

His clothes were as modest as his countenance and colored the dullest of brown. His height was tempered by a soft and paunchy roundness. He had quite delicate hands, which were stained with ink and smudges of some other substance. I took him to be about fifty, an estimate that proved to be off the mark by only a year.

"Come in, come in, young man," he said after I explained my purpose and he had taken hold of the sealed pouch. "I know you not, sir, nor this Major Washington, but he evidently has had word of me. Come in and rest yourself. Would you have punch? My wife has prepared a milk punch. We are putting a supply to bottle."

"That sounds very agreeable, sir."

"Indeed, indeed. This way, please."

He ushered me into an abundantly windowed room that would have seemed commodious were it not so crammed with books and papers, piled high in great stacks upon almost every flat surface, and what looked to be medical or scientific instruments jumbled upon a long, broad table in the center of the chamber. Among them was a mysterious contraption of fashioned wood and metalwork and large glass globes. A candle was burning beneath one, and I feared I might be in the presence of something explosive.

He noted my apprehension, and accompanying curiosity, but provided no explanation. Having summoned the punch and snuffed out the candle, he pushed forth two chairs and plumped himself upon one.

"You have news?" he asked. "Any sort of news from Virginia?"

"Only what might be contained in that pouch, sir."

He snapped open the seal and pulled out the dark piece of hair and scalp, examining it as though it were an object of great scientific interest, then took to the letter, reading it studiously, with some blinking of his eyes.

The punch came quickly, brought by his wife, a small, plump, but handsome woman named Deborah, and it was an invigorating and delicious brew. I sipped as he read and reread the letter, waiting patiently until he set it down on the table beside him.

"An interesting man, this Major Washington of yours," Franklin said. "What can you tell me of him? What is his age?"

"Not much more than mine, sir. I'd say he is just past twenty, and I think not long in his militia commission."

"He has produced a decidedly cogent *militaire aperçu* of distressing affairs in the Ohio country. French on the move. Our Indians wavering in their loyalties. And he knows his politics—knows the politics of this province. Knows it well. Unusual for a Virginian. They have small concern for the other colonies, or the rest of this earth, for that matter."

I knew that to be true enough, but refrained from comment.

"Still, this is a curious letter," Franklin continued. "Indeed, I might pronounce it derivative."

"Derivative? Derived from what, sir?"

"Derived from another's letter. He quotes a frontier scout named Christopher Gist: 'a report from Gist . . . ' 'Gist observed . . . ' 'It is the opinion of Gist . . . ' et cetera." Franklin paused to give an impish smile. "One might adduce that there was an original dispatch sent to Williamsburg by Gist, which was intercepted by your young Washington at Alexandria and then forwarded by him, along with his own remarks, to the proper authorities—to His Excellency Robert Dinwiddie, and correspondence to my humble self as well—if you ken my meaning."

"Not exactly, sir."

"I think your Washington took hold of this message from Gist to attach his own name to it, to connect himself to its import—and great import it bears indeed. Am I to presume you have his confidence?"

"His confidence?"

"His trust. He trusted you to bring me this. Does he count upon your discretion?"

I thought upon the charming bits of leaf upon Mrs. Fairfax's hem. "I think so. Yes."

"Then henceforth I shall presume to count upon it as well. This is a grave matter. The Major's 'news' arrives preceded by others'. An Indian trader named William Trent has sent back alarms of Indian mischief on the frontier, and Governor Clinton of New York has just now dispatched letters to all the several colonies telling of French activity up there. Large armed parties, moving at will throughout the forests. Have you heard of the dreadful occurrence at Pickawillany last year?"

"Mr. Franklin, sir, I've not heard of Pickawillany."

"It is a small trading town on the Miami River, far in the west of the Ohio country. It was the seat of government, as it were, of the principal chief of the Miami Indian tribe. Unemakemi his name. A chief so loyal to the Crown he was given the name 'Old Britain.' Last June his town was set upon by Ottawas and Chippewas led by a half-breed French agent named Langlade. There was a horrid slaughter of the Miamis. Old Britain had his heart torn out and then was boiled and eaten. Of the seven English traders resident, two were killed outright and the rest taken north to Canada as captives. And three thousand pounds' worth of trade goods were burned. The Indians in that region were most impressed by this boldness—and our weakness. If these native peoples turn against us, Captain Morley, the French need hardly send a single fusilier against us. A gang of carpenters will suffice to seize the region."

I'd never been farther west than the fall lines of the Rappahannock and Patowmack rivers. "Which region do you mean, sir?"

"West of the Blue Mountains, west of the Alleghenies, in the vastness of the valley of the Beautiful River, as the French call the Ohio. It is an Indian territory, though that will change."

"Is that a scalp, sir?"

Franklin picked it up. "Yes, alas. According to your Major Washington—or more truthfully, to Mr. Gist—it is the hair of an unfortunate man late of the mountains beyond the Shenandoah. Murdered by Indians, Major

Washington reports, along with his wife and children. The devil's own work—and the French king's, I fear. Know you of the Ohio Company, Captain?"

"A military organization?"

He smiled, rather wryly. "Not yet, though that may be in the making. It is a company of investors—Virginia investors for the most. They are bent on acquiring vast properties in the Ohio country. Their goal is profit. Their intention is to open the territory to settlement. They boldly claim it for Virginia, though Pennsylvania is disposed to dispute that. They have patent from the King to some five hundred thousand acres, with two hundred thousand to be opened first. And there's the rub, Captain. The King's grant was issued in seventeen forty-seven—but to remain in force only seven years, unless the company has managed within that time to settle a hundred families in the country. That leaves them little more than one year, and I don't know that there are now more than a dozen English families in that entire territory." He shook the scalp. "This will not increase their numbers."

"A hundred would not seem so many. I read in some place that there are approaching one million British subjects in the American colonies."

"So there are, so there are. But all but a handful are confined to this side of the mountains. They won't go beyond them until assured it's safe. And if they don't go, the investors are out their shares—plus the sundry bribes applied where necessary in London to secure the King's grant, which was not initially forthcoming. There's your patriotism, sir, lying where most usually found—in profit, or in fear of the loss thereof. Governor Dinwiddie is among the shareholders, and so, I gather, is your young Washington. At least he has that interest. He writes on behalf of the company."

"What has this to do with the French, if the land is King George's to grant?"

Another, smaller smile curled Franklin's thin lips.

"Everything, Captain Morley, for the French assert the right to all the lands drained by that great river that runs from Canada to New Orleans—the Missippi, or some such—have you heard tell of it? And that of course would include all the land of the valley of their Beautiful River, as the Ohio indeed flows to the Missippi quite resolutely. They are building forts in there now, these damned French. Numerous forts—their ambition a chain of forts extending from Montreal to New Orleans. Leaden plates have been recovered that mark all the land west of the mountains as that of the French Louis. Washington says he has sent one of these leaden plates to Dinwiddie. Were you the bearer?"

I now felt more important. "I was. I also delivered letters, and one of those scalps. I fear, a lady's."

Franklin frowned, shaking his head sadly. "The mate of the owner of this hair, I'll wager. It's distressing, Most serious. Vexatious. Our population swells with every ship arriving from England, yet we must pen them up on this coastal plain, fearful of trespassing on what by right and logic are our westward domains. Short of war, I can think of no solution. But there is no war, nor prospect of one—not waged by our King. They are a poor and common people, these settlers. I hold small hope that our good King George is going to stir himself much over their miseries. There've been three bad fights with the French these past hundred years. The King will require mighty provocation to embark on a fourth. There are debts yet unpaid from our late dispute with the Spanish."

As you may by now have gathered, this Franklin suffered no poverty of words or reluctance to use them. I'd call him garrulous, but there was no waste to them. I learned something from every sentence.

I asked about Gist. He seemed more the player in this game than my new friend the Major.

"You are not acquainted with this remarkable gentleman?" asked Franklin. "He was in the merchant trade himself. In Baltimore. One of the wealthiest men in that town, with land aplenty. But he had more an eye for opportunities than the management of them. Far from frugal. Reckless. Sometimes daft. And a man who attracts bad luck. He had a warehouse burn down full of pelts belonging to the British Fur Company in London. Gist borrowed mightily to pay for that loss, but he never did repay, not fully. Borrowed from me, among others. I've yet to see tuppence of what he so blithefully pocketed. Trust Gist with your life, young man, but not your coin."

I noticed Franklin had a slight rash of eczema on his forehead. He rubbed at it.

"Gist took flight, I daresay wisely. Moved far beyond the reach of writ and civilization, first to North Carolina, then deep into the mountains and beyond. He has or had a house at Will's Creek, near the upper reaches of the Patowmack. He fled our civilization a goodly while ago, and he's used the time well. He now moves about that frightful territory with the ease you do over your ocean waters. As surveyor for the Ohio Company, he's scouted the great valley all the way out to this country called 'Caintuckee.' He knows that wilderness as the Indians do, knows all the ways of the Indian. He's all but become one himself. Has established a small settlement of his own not far from the forks of the Ohio. Our Sovereign has no braver or more knowledgeable guardian on that frontier, scoundrel that Gist is with ledger work and promissory notes." Franklin picked up the dark-haired scalp. "I'm sure 'twas Gist who procured this tragic artifact. And the woman's hair you brought to Dinwiddie. And he who recovered that leaden plate, now near to four years in the ground. I'm sure of it. But it matters not. I am pleased to be hearing from this Major Washington."

Franklin set down the scalp piece, then rose, clasping his hands over his round stomach as he began a stroll of the room.

"I can be of help to him, as he can be to our cause. I publish a newspaper well read in this province; I have a wide correspondence and not inconsiderable influence in political affairs, serving as a member of our Pennsylvania Assembly, among other worthy offices. I raised the funds that provided cannon and defense for Philadelphia during the late troubles with the Spanish. I also am postmaster general for these several colonies. Curious that Washington trusted this correspondence to you and not our general post. We provide a most reliable service, Captain Morley. You may count upon it."

"He was in haste, sir."

Franklin paused by a window and stood staring out it.

"Your Major wants to know whether Pennsylvania might share in a military response to these French provocations. I don't know if he asks this as agent for the Ohio Company, or for Dinwiddie, or simply himself, but it's an excellent question, though the answer is not excellent."

Franklin turned to face me.

"The answer, alas, is no. We have many Quakers here. They dominate the Assembly. Good, hardworking, dependable citizens, but a people who look upon the musket as an instrument of sin. When the Spanish threatened—yes here in Philadelphia!—we had to fund our little force through private contributions, for the Quakerish legislature would have none of it. Attempt to raise a militia troop from among these folk now through an Act of Assembly and all you'll raise is a righteous cry of refusal."

"But hasn't Pennsylvania settlers on the frontier?"

"Ever increasing, settlements as far west as the Blue Mountains, and beyond. We'll have no choice but to levy troops eventually. But not at the present moment. No, young sir. It's not possible. Yet Virginia cannot bear this burden alone. This is occasion for our colonies to unite. Not mere occasion, but grand chance!"

Franklin stuck his hands in his pockets and recommenced his stroll about the room.

"These colonies were created for different purposes—confoundingly, too many of them concerning the most quarrelsome aspects of religion. But the time for that is past. If we're to have any worthwhile future—in commerce, in politics, in expanding our domain—we must unite the colonies in some working confederation, wed them to some common purpose. The King, I'm told, is reluctant to have this happen. He is unhappy with the 'Democratick' that flourishes here, and is jealous of allowing the colonies much military power of their own. But, King be damned. We might yet prevail. I'd thought Dinwiddie reluctant, too, but now, perhaps not. Governor Sharpe of Maryland is strong for cooperation, as are New York and Massachusetts. We may have to instruct our noble Sovereign sharply."

He paused. "Does this not interest you?"

I'd been staring blankly, and had yawned. I'd read about some of these matters in newspapers, of course, but it had meant nothing to me, and less to Richard, whose mind and eye were always on the West Indies and their promise of wealth.

"It interests me, Mr. Franklin, but I do not see my place in it."

"You are Major Washington's courier. A messenger who knows the import of what he bears will carry it the faster. You've drained your cup. Would you like it refreshed?"

Before I could reply, he shouted for his Deborah.

"It is a fine punch, sir," I said.

"Fine? The finest! Would you like the recipe? It originates from Boston and is deserving of a fame widespread."

He went to a writing desk and quickly put quill to paper. He was still at this labor when the good Deborah returned with her pitcher. "The brew was worth some fame, and remains so now. So I'll spread its renown further by sharing his recipe with you." He handed me a printed card:

> *Take 6 quarts brandy, and the rinds of 44 lemons pared very thin; steep the rinds in the brandy 24 hours; then strain it off. Put to it 4 quarters of water, 4 large nutmegs grated, 2 quarts lemon juice, 2 pounds of refined sugar. When the sugar is dissolved, boil 3 quarts of milk and put to the rest hot as you take it off the fire, and stir it about. Let it stand two hours, then run it thro' a jelly-bag till it is clear; then bottle it off.*

I pocketed this formula and glanced again at the assemblage of globes and whatnot upon the central table.

"Is that for the making of punch?" I asked.

Franklin laughed. "No, sir. It is an apparatus of my device for measuring the weight of air."

"Air? But air weighs nothing!"

He seemed surprised by my pronouncement. "You struck me as a young man of some education."

"I read books, Mr. Franklin, as often as I can get hold of them."

"But nothing of the physical sciences, I fear. No matter. As a seafaring man, you should know the truth of what I say without benefit of a single written word. You have felt the breeze in your face, seen your sails bulge taut in weather?"

"Aye, sir, but that's the wind."

Franklin shook his head in mild exasperation. "That's the air, Captain Morley. The weight of air set in motion. We can observe and measure that air heated weighs less than does air at normal temperature or cold air. The volume is the same, but the weight less. Thus lighter, it must rise. Cooler air, thus denser, must sink. More to the point, the cooler air moves to displace the rising warmer air. In such manner, we are given wind."

I looked, I fear, somewhat stupefied, and not simply from the punch.

"Have you not noticed," he asked, "the cloying warmth that accompanies a tempest, and the coolness of the calm that follows?"

I nodded, but without great comprehension.

"A means contrived to measure the weight of air should tell us much about the coming weather, don't you think?" he asked. His eyes were quite twinkly again.

All I could do was bob my head some more. He took up Washington's letter.

"This requires a reply in detail," he said, "and some thought beforehand. Will you be returning to Major Washington soon?"

"I'm not sure when or if at all," I said. "I'm bound for Annapolis, to await my brother, who's also a sea captain. It's where we live. Our ships' home port." Franklin seemed disappointed. "But it's not a long road from there to Alexandria," I quickly added. "I could send your reply the distance that remains by your, er, excellent postal service."

"In this event, I'd rather you delivered it in person, and a letter to Dinwiddie as well. These gentlemen may well have wish to know my mind, and you should be there to explain it. Can you return here this evening?"

I shrugged. "We won't sail till the morrow. I've cargo to unload and load."

"And there're sailors' pleasures to be had in the meantime, yes? This is a town of abundant amusements."

I thought of Riggins and my lads, no doubt already well into their fun.

"I've other business," I said. "I must call on a merchant named Smithson. I was at his house earlier, but he was not."

"A mean fellow. All avarice—his rascally ways cloaked in pomposity. There are too many of his like in this city." Franklin's eyes brightened with a thought. "You've cargo for him?"

"Aye. Some barrels of grain."

"I advise you then to complete your transaction with him upon the wharf, with an honest witness at hand. He has a mind for greedy tricks. One is to demand delivery to his own storehouse. Once your barrels are settled with his and bear his mark, he'll demand a final count, and you'll find you'll come up short, with no means to prove the contrary."

"He's that much a thief?"

"Knavish as there be, sir. He'll measure his prospects of successful swindle by your youth. Be warned."

"I am, and I thank you. Are you acquainted with Mr. Smithson's daughter?"

Something more wicked than merry came into his eyes.

"He has three—had four, till a fever took his eldest last spring, poor girl. I think you must mean his Susannah, for she is nearest your age, and of a quite uncommon beauty. A handful for the fondle, that one. The tits of an angel. And exquisite of leg. I had occasion to glimpse these divine limbs one recent hot day as she alighted from her chaise. Sublimity, Captain Morley, sublimity. If I were younger, or she less bound by the proprieties and convention of this town, I . . . well, I gather she's won your fancy."

All my thought lay upon those angelic "tits." What had o'ercome me? "Wholly, sir."

He studied my drab clothing dubiously.

"Though I commend you on your circumspection and frugality, young sir," Franklin said, "you'll not fetch her eye much in such clothes. We've Quakers here more splendidly dressed than thee." His hand went to his chin. "There's no time for a tailor's work, but we can provide you with something finer. My establishment trades in cloth and clothes among its enterprises. There's a fine blue coat there with brass buttons, bartered for rum by a sea captain too long without ship. I think we might discover a suitable pair of britches as well. Something in white. You'd look a captain then. My partner, an honest man, is David Hall. I'll provide you with a note of introduction."

"You spoke of too much money in this city, Mr. Franklin," I said as he quickly scribbled out the note. "I fear I cannot share in the complaint."

He waved my concern aside. "Your promise of repayment will suffice with me, Captain Morley. I assume this will not be your last voyage to our port—as long as Miss Smithson here abides. Such clothes are a worthwhile investment, would you not say, if they lead to a more abundant knowledge of her charms and attributes?"

Franklin winked. I knew not what to make of this man, but I liked him.

"You will sup with me tonight then," he said. "Call upon me here at eight o'clock."

———

I returned to Smithson's shortly past three and found Mr. Smithson at home and in ill humor. Actually, he may well have been in what for him was good humor, but it promised little amity for me.

"Produce your manifest," he said curtly after allowing me into his office without pleasantry or greeting. His delightful daughter, alas, was nowhere in view.

I'd by then acquired the coat and breeches Franklin had suggested, plus a fine linen shirt, finding myself seriously in debt for the first time in my life. Two doubloons! The coat's fit was awkward—that rum-loving captain had been a narrower man in the shoulders than I—but if I stood mast-straight, it was not too binding. Unfortunately, I'd paused with Riggins at a dockside grog shop before coming back to Smithson's house, and rather than straight, I stood altogether wobbly. I would have been grateful for a chair, I daresay, but he provided none.

Smithson read my papers as though they were full of dark secrets and lies. "These seem in order, much to my amazement," he said finally. "I doubt I'll find the same true of my cargo. Have it brought to my storage house, and I'll take inventory there."

Aha! Mr. Franklin's prophesy was proving correct. I wasn't so tipsy not to be ready in reply to this rascality.

"I am sorry, sir, but the count must be done in the hold or on the dock. It's not my ship, but my brother's. Those are his instructions and I am faithful to them."

"Your brother be damned. I'll not do business on the docks like some common boobie."

"Then I'll find another customer for these commodities."

I felt bold enough in this dispute. Prices for grain and such in Philadelphia had risen handsomely.

"Damn you, sir! I have a contract! I'll have you sleeping with the rats in gaol! Not one more impertinence!"

"If impertinence it be, so be it!"

It was more grog and punch speaking than I, but I was pleased to hear the brave words come out of my mouth. I hoped my brother would be proud of me in this moment.

"Get out, you pirate! Get out of my house!"

Smithson snatched up a piece of wood from the stack upon his hearth and brandished it. I had hoped the man would back down. I couldn't fathom the reason for such a depth of foul temper, but wanted no more of it. I retreated. In truth, I fled.

My fear was that his beautiful daughter had been witness to some part of this, and so it proved. She called out to me from the front door as I was descending the outside stairs in clumsy haste.

"Captain Morley!"

I turned, stumbling a little. "Miss Smithson, I must apologize—"

"Your hat, sir." She came partway down the steps, extending the object, a ratty thing in contrast to my new finery. "You left your hat."

I bowed in accepting it, an error. The sound of my coat rending up the back was inescapable. She began to laugh. I could not well enjoy the moment, but tried to make something of it, smiling as though to share in the amusement. I also reached again to take the hat, but my balance was far from sure. I careened a little backward, gripping the hat. As though to right me, she tried to pull it back, but came tumbling forward against me. I raised my hands to steady her, but in faulty manner, my right hand coming firmly to her breast. Gads!

We froze in that position, not in any great happiness in it, but from the sudden terror that struck us both by reason of the hideous bellows coming from her father, who was standing in the doorway, looking murderous.

Washington had called me "well-spoken." Not then. A few idiocies burbled from my mouth and I took off running, wondering, should I reach my little ship, if the best end to this adventure would be found in setting sail immediately.

This time Smithson threw his damned stick, but it missed me.

———

I did not set sail, but slept off a few hours of the rum in my little cabin, while the sailmaking member of my crew attempted to repair my new coat. He'd been into grog as well, and his labors produced a poor result.

Arriving at Franklin's house at the evening hour requested, I was not this time welcomed into it. Instead, he bade me wait outside while he had a brief conversation with his wife. I heard the words, "a matter of great importance to the united colonies."

Rejoining me on the street, he set us off at a brisk pace. "We sup tonight at a private house," he said. "In a sense, it is a public house, but not one licensed by civil authority. A public house, if you will, of private arrangement. Its proprietess is a Mrs. Jennifer Calderwill. Are you familiar with her?"

"No sir."

"And you a sailor? How often do you visit our town?"

"This is my sixth voyage to it."

"And what do you do while in our town? What amusement?"

"A bit of ale or rum and the company of my good crew. In the larger part, though, I stay about my ship, and read."

"A moderate fellow. You're a friend to your mind and body, I'll grant that, but you must learn more of life, young man."

The house he took me to was large but dingy, set in a gloomy lane near the river and at some distance south of the city center. A few windows were bright with candles, but most were dark, with curtains drawn.

Mistress Calderwill was near Franklin's years. A large, bosomy and roughly pleasant woman, she admitted us to a small room with a round table just off the main hallway and stair. There was much boisterousness elsewhere in the house, but we were left alone, except for the serving wench who brought us our supper—a cold soup spicily flavored, roast beef, some cheese and bread. Franklin drank punch. I chose Madeira. My head was throbbing from my day's refreshment. I needed a calming potion.

Franklin took from his coat two letters, sealed and folded.

"I follow propriety and convention with these," he said, laying a finger on one of the seals. "But I'll tell you of the contents, lest either go astray or meet with misadventure. To Washington I write that Pennsylvania wants no war but that there are important gentlemen here who view his alarming news with profound seriousness, and wish him well in whatever counter Virginia may take against the French. I ask your Washington that he become my correspondent, and extend my hope of meeting him in person. I promise him I shall do whatever I can to assist him in Virginia's fortunes."

He sipped. He did not strike me as much of a tippler.

"To Dinwiddie," he continued, "a briefer letter. I tell him I've been apprised of the worrisome activities on his frontier and remind that Pennsylvania and New York are experiencing similar troubles. I inform him also that I shall in my newspaper encourage a meeting of the several governors to prepare themselves cooperatively to meet this emergency. I suggest that his wisdom and stature commend him to take the leading role in such a conference. As always, Captain, flattery advances politics. It's a useful grease."

I took the letters, folded them carefully, and placed them within a pocket. I refrained from telling him I had no intention of delivering either correspondence in person. I now had little hope of encountering Miss Smithson again, and wanted quit of Philadelphia. My ardor was for Annapolis. I wanted to rejoin my brother. I had tired of decisions and responsibilities. The honor of serving as courier in all this "King's business" and "united colonies" had lost its charm.

"How went your renewed acquaintance with the lady Smithson?" Franklin asked. "Was she suitably impressed with the improved dignity and fashion of your appearance?"

"I fear my impression was calamitous." I went on to relate my unhappy encounter with Miss Smithson's father, and my embarrassing one with her breast.

He laughed indulgently. "You may yet get a reply. She now knows your touch, and may have deemed it welcome." He grew more serious. "Fear not Smithson and his cheating, thieving wretch that he be. I can settle the matter of his cargo for you. I have the use of an ample warehouse. You can have Smithson's goods brought to that place and if you'll provide me with your papers, we'll have the count completed on that neutral ground. I shall give you a note of payment, and to obtain his goal, Smithson shall have to pay that sum to me. Have you arranged new cargo for your return voyage?"

"Perhaps more than my sloop will hold."

"We'll have it aboard in time for you to be well downriver by the next sunset."

"I owe you much, Mr. Franklin."

"Consider it simply the hospitality of our friendly city. And now, Captain Morley, I am happy to offer you more. Your sundry business today has denied you much chance for recreation. I am at Mrs. Calderwill's regularly, if circumspectly. I think you will find it a charming house." He winked.

"It was an excellent supper, sir."

Franklin gave a mock scowl. "It was not meat for the stomach I had in mind, Captain Morley. Deprived of Miss Smithson as you are, might you fancy another in her place?"

His meaning struck me with blushing result. "I . . ."

"Your hesitation confounds me, Captain." He paused thoughtfully. "Are you not in good health?"

"I am, but . . ."

"But what, then?"

"I am unused to such, er, arrangements."

"Are you acquainted with the Hellfire Association of London?"

"No sir."

"Best put, it's a society of accomplished rakes—all good patrons of the daughters of Venus. Its members—and I am one of them—mark themselves with necklaces of pearls, each pearl standing for a virgin seduced. As you might judge by my years, my strand is full. I fear, Captain, your own would be merely string. Am I correct?"

I gulped some wine. "It's true."

"And," he continued, "if some lady should find the favor of you, she might come away with the right to such an adornment herself?"

As though in great shame, I nodded.

"I daresay," said he, "you are the only sea captain ever to call on this port who could honestly admit to such a thing. We must attend to this at once, so you may sail tomorrow a better fellow to your crew. Yes?"

"What I'd like most right now, Mr. Franklin, if this sound not strange, is a bath. The voyage was longer than I'd hoped and the season is hot and sticky."

"A bath! Excellent. The one pleasurable thing will enhance the other. I'll inform Mistress Calderwill of our desires. She won't mind them, but the heating of the water will take a while."

"I'm in no hurry," I said, "I shall have more wine."

I drank with abandon, but still felt as fearful climbing those stairs as I had in apprehending that storm.

"Early to bed and early to rise," Franklin said in parting, with another wink.

———

The wench I was brought to was named Margaret. She was a small, even scrawny, lass with eyes set perhaps too closely together and a longish nose, but she was young, well favored in the torso, and on the whole, not uncomely. Unfortunately, she needed a bath with far, far more desperation than did I. More unfortunately, she thought me perverse indeed when I politely suggested she share the small, brimming tub with me to attend to that matter. If I insisted upon this eccentricity, she said, it would cost more. Much more. She had never heard of such a thing.

As Mr. Franklin had kindly assumed all the expense of the evening's diversion, I told her the cost was agreeable to me. With some grimacing, she removed her clothing—there wasn't much to remove, as she wore neither petticoat nor corset beneath her simple shift—and lowered herself into the tub and upon my lap. This cramped situation promised only discomfort for both of us, so I bade her stand, and did so myself. When I had scrubbed the both of us as clean as the *Hannah*'s deck—I daresay it was the first such experience she had had in years, if ever—she fled the soapy water and fetched some cloths with which to dry ourselves.

The scrubbing had put me in a mood for the next phase of our encounter, but I was unsure just how to commence it. She assumed this duty, with far more relish than she had the bath, leading me to the bed, laying me down upon my back, and then straddling me in practiced fashion. She was knowledgeable of considerable eccentricity herself, and at the rapturous end of it, I found myself remarkably well-schooled, and eager to continue my education.

But first, sleep. I was uncertain of Mr. Franklin's whereabouts during this interlude, though from time to time my ears were witness to numerous sounds, both joyous and exuberant, arriving from the adjoining room. If Mr. Franklin was the source of them, he'd not likely be adding another pearl to his collection. Not in this establishment, whose whereabouts I well noted in my memory. If Franklin's intent was to give me appetite for another visit to his pleasant city, this had been richly accomplished.

Though I liked this scrawny Margaret, and hoped I might pay my respects to her again, I of course felt no true *amour*. The object of that remained the fair Miss Smithson. What dreams I had were of her, and marvelous they were.

I promised myself I'd make a sketch of her. I promised myself much else besides.

Five

I left Mrs. Calderwill's at first light, and not finding Mr. Franklin about, set my course first downhill to the river and then north up the shore to the wharf. I had expected to find Riggins and my crew slumbering well in varying degrees of stupor, but lo, they were up and busily about, assisting with the loading of Smithson's share of cargo onto two wagons, which I discovered had been sent with some dispatch by Franklin. Early to rise, indeed.

With the wagons finally creaking up the street, my men were disposed to return to their hammocks, but I set them to labor in greater earnest, loading the cargo bound for Annapolis that had by then arrived on the dock. We were in the midst of this effort, the sun now rising swiftly above the Jersey shore opposite, when a woman appeared in our midst—the same maidservant who had closed Smithson's door upon my foot. She bade me accompany her back into the town, and swiftly.

"Mr. Smithson sent you?"

"Nay, sir. Miss Smithson. She said to make haste."

"Why? To where?"

"Just come."

Urging Riggins to continue the work without any slackening of effort, I followed the girl from the wharf. She led me off the main street, down a lane behind the garden of a large house, then up an alley that led to a churchyard. There, lurking only partially hidden behind a large tree, I discovered precisely what I'd hoped I'd find—the graceful figure of a young lady, this day dressed in pale blue and carrying a parasol, with which she masked her face.

As I approached, the parasol fell away.

"Good day to you, Miss Smithson." I said, realizing how unkempt I must appear after my night's adventures and morning's labors.

"It's not a good day for you, Captain Morley. You are a rude and impudent young man, sir, and I would not in any normal circumstance speak with you again. Yet I am impelled by conscience to do so now. My father treated you meanly and poorly—grievous unfairly, to my mind—and he intends to do so again. He has already gone this morning to a magistrate of his long acquaintance to obtain a writ of seizure for that cargo. He claims you intend to dishonor the contract. Once he has his paper in hand, he'll be down to your ship with this gang of louts he employs for such ill purpose. I urge you, sir, produce his goods in the place where he demands, or remove your vessel from this city. Do either, but don't tarry."

"I don't understand any of this," I said. "Your father may have his cargo. I simply asked to deliver it to him in an honest place of counting."

I stepped nearer, but with care, for she seemed most tentative about this rendezvous. She was no less lovely this bright morning than in memory.

"And right you were, for he's clever in his dealings. But that dispute is not what riles him so overmuch. It's your manner of ending it. And, I daresay, your unfortunate embrace of my—" she blushed "—which I shall presume was the most unintentional of accidents."

"It was, miss. I am not known for giving such offense."

"I should hope not. I will forgive you." Her eyes held mine, then glanced away. "You may kiss my hand."

Bold lass! Bold me. This was encouragement to friendship, to more than that. I could scarce understand my luck.

I performed the gesture in as courtly a manner as I could muster, recalling how it was done by an actor in a play I had once attended in Charleston. I cannot express the wondrous effect it had upon my senses, except to say that nothing had been done for me in Mrs. Calderwill's establishment, or imaginably could be done, that might produce the rapture that followed the touch of that fair flesh against my lips.

She withdrew her hand, but seemed unsure of what next to do or say.

"I would visit with you again," I said.

"You've more chance of visiting Cathay, or sailing on the seas of the moon, Captain Morley. I'll not take this risk again. Good-bye to you. Make haste."

I stayed where I stood until she, followed by her servant, had fully vanished from view—though not from my affection. Gads, no. Now I truly was in love! What an extraordinary voyage this was proving. The awkward, inexperienced youth who had been myself was now thrust upon such a brimming tide of life. Beautiful ladies, militia majors, governors, scalps, intrigue.

And knavery. Miss Smithson's warning, however much well intended, had come tardily. When I returned to the wharf, her father and his scruffy associates were in attendance upon my vessel. Smithson and a stout fellow who proved to be a bailiff were engaged in argument with Riggins, who had incomplete knowledge of the nature of the dispute but was emphasizing his side of things with the aid of a brandished belaying pin.

Smithson seemed to relish my appearance. "There you be, you bastard whelp. Thief! Scoundrel! Produce my cargo or you shall be placed under arrest this instant!"

" 'Tis so, sir," said the bailiff, nodding. "Aye, 'tis so."

"The cargo awaits you, Mr. Smithson, in a safe warehouse in this city."

"A warehouse of mine, sir? As I required?"

"No, sir. In another, belonging to a most trustworthy gentleman."

"Damn you then! Bailiff, arrest him!"

The portly court officer took a tentative step forward. The gang of louts were less hesitant. Two of the biggest moved menacingly toward Riggins.

"Which warehouse would that be, Captain?" the bailiff asked. He seemed ill at ease, as though his errand had now struck him as much different than what he had set out upon.

"Its proprietor, for these purposes at least," I said, "is a Mr. Benjamin Franklin."

They stopped, looking as dumb as if struck to stone by Heaven. The bailiff appeared at once both mystified and relieved.

"Franklin? Benjamin Franklin, of Market Street?"

"Aye, sir." I turned to Smithson. "Present your papers and the sum agreed upon to him and the transaction shall be concluded to what ought be your satisfaction, in strict accordance with manifest and contract. He gave me last night a promissary note in the amount of full payment for this shipment." I pulled it from my coat and waved it about with much flaunting. "You'll have to settle accounts with him before you touch a barrel."

Smithson commenced to hurl oaths at me like the worst of my sailors, throwing his hat down fiercely. His rowdies stared at him in confusion. The bailiff smiled.

"In that event, sir," he said, "I'll trouble you no further. But I'd advise you wait your departure until all is seen to."

I nodded to him, feeling most gleeful.

When they had gone, I felt the grip of Riggins's powerful hand upon my shoulder.

"You got yourself into and out of some bad trouble here, Tick. Your brother will be powerfully curious."

I searched for the line from remembered reading: " 'All's well that ends well,' Bob."

He gave a snort. "Do we 'wait our departure'?"

"We flee like rats," I said, "just as soon as we can get this load aboard and spread canvas."

"You're a bold one enough, without your Richard near. I wouldna thought it."

Six

It was a smooth sail down the Delaware and Maryland coasts. The head-winds rounding Virginia's Cape Charles proved troublesome, however, and our westward progress into the Chesapeake was slowed by endless tacking into them.

I still had not made my decision. Annapolis or Williamsburg? There was reason enough to hasten to Maryland, steering north and coursing homeward on a fast beam reach. I'd rejoin my brother with both purse and hold abulging, full of news and tales to tell of unscrupulous mercantiles undone and monstrous tempests bested, fair beauty found, and friendship made with a most consequential if eccentric gentleman of Philadelphia. I could scarce wait for the puzzlement to spread across Richard's face as I related Mr. Franklin's notions of foretelling the weather by measuring the weight of thin air!

And later, in brotherly confidence, perhaps enhanced with a dram or two, I'd make revelation of my vanished virginity.

But these damnable Virginians. They had the cleverest ways of imposing obligation. To honor my brother's wishes to the mark would be to shirk the duties asked of me by the Major—not to speak of the respected Mr. Franklin. I sensed then that my choice could have a profound effect on the furture course of my life. These were important men. To get caught up with them would thrust me into matters of which I'd till then had little ken.

What most turned my mind—and ship—to Williamsburg at last was the thought of that bloodied piece of fair yellow hair and the tragic woman who had worn it. If what Franklin said of French designs and Indian attacks was true, we all were obliged to this lady. More should be made from her sacrifice than this grotesque pelt. I tried to think of what she must have looked alive. Blue eyes, a large and merry mouth, perhaps. 'Twas Susannah's face I conjured, and that impelled me all the more.

One stop, I decided—at the capital, all accounts settled—and then off before the wind to home. Richard would allow that much, if not happily.

I had let the James River pass, but when we reached the mouth of the York, I called out a change in sail and course.

The helmsman gave a look to Riggins, who turned and offered me one even darker.

"Be ye lost, Captain?" he said, the last word bitten hard. "It's the Severn you'll be wanting, not the York."

"I know where I am, Bob," I said. "And it's the York I want. I've a brief stop to make at Williamsburg."

"Brief? It'll cost us a day. If your brother's back, he'll be counting every hour, Tick."

"He'll have no complaints. Not with all we've managed."

"So it's that, is it? You're full of yourself now, and it's turned your brains to shit. Begging your pardon, Captain."

Only the helmsman could hear us, but that was a man too many. I pulled myself up to the fullest possible height.

"You'll heed the call of course, please, Mr. Riggins."

"But Tick, damn all, why?"

"King's business."

———

Williamsburg seemed not to have stirred a blade of grass since I'd left it, though when I passed by the gaol and place of public punishment, I found change enough. Only one of the poor wretches in the stocks remained, and he was as near to death in that hellish heat as one could manage while still drawing breath, and I wasn't sure he was doing that. The large post nearby bore fresh scorch marks, and in the ashy dirt around it I saw bits and tatters of homespun cloth. As with the scalp I'd borne here, the paltry remnants of a human life.

This, apparently, was small concern to the occupants of the governor's palace. The clerk was at his desk in the foyer, dressed, as memory served, in the same dull clothes as before, scratching away with his quill as though he'd not risen from his chair since he'd last so curtly dismissed me.

"You've returned, Captain Morley."

"You've awesome powers of observation, sir." I set Franklin's letter on the desktop. "For His Excellency. From Mr. Benjamin Franklin of Philadelphia."

The clerk took it to hand diffidently, squinting at the name it bore, then set it aside and picked up a small bell, ringing it twice. A Negro servant, well dressed, approached from the far end of the corridor, then carried the letter away upstairs on a tray.

"I hope His Excellency will like that one better than the last you brought," said the clerk. "It fouled his humor for two days."

"I am sorry for it. A good-bye to you then."

"Where are you going?"

I thought upon that. "To find your bursar and attend to the recompense for my expenses. Major Washington's chit."

"Oh, yes. That matter. It has already been attended to—so many days ago that I'd near forgotten. In truth, I'd not expected you'd come back for it, but here you are. Sign this first, if you please."

He thrust forth a small scrap of paper—a receipt. There was writing on the back as well, with lines drawn through it. Paper was an expensive commodity. Nothing was wasted.

I took the quill he proffered and scrawled, "Thom. Morley."

"You neglect the 'Captain,' " said the clerk with a slight smile. "No matter. Here you are. Your recompense."

He plucked from a chest on the floor beside him three rope-like twists of tobacco—one only half the length of the other two. There was coin aplenty in Philadelphia—in New York, Boston, and Baltimore as well. In Virginia, this weed was currency, by the twist or hogshead. Fortunate were New Englanders that Boston did not declare the cod to be money.

"Thank you," I said with some honesty. In truth, I'd not expected even one shilling in the end.

"Now seat yourself, please, and wait His Excellency's pleasure."

———

It was a remarkably short wait this time. A secretary, or an aide, descended half the staircase, stood at the railing and gave full unpleasant voice to "Morley, Thomas Morley" with such bombastic sternness I felt as a man summoned to the gallows.

I leapt up and hurriedly followed him to the next floor, and to a large corner room with many windows, all open to the breeze, if any there was, instead of standing dark and shuttered against the heat and sunlight, as in the rooms below. Beyond the windows were the branches of a large, sheltering, shade-providing tree.

Dinwiddie lounged by the sill of one window in only shirt, breeches and hose, his coat and waistcoat removed and hung over a chair back, his throat lace pulled askew, his monstrous dark wig set on a stand, his own sparse hair flattened moistly with sweat against his head. His high-heeled shoes, with gleaming buckles, stood empty by his writing table. He was a short, pudgy man, ruddy of skin, with a face overfed and not handsome, and he was old—some sixty years. But he had sharp eyes, without evidence of malice but with plenty of canniness. He was a Scot, and said to favor Scots in his dealings. I wondered if he thought me one, for he was most pleasant.

"Sit yourself, Captain. I'd have you served a cooling drink if such existed in this infernal season. How perverse of Providence to provide us such a superfluity of ice when we least have need of it, and none at all when we are desperate for it."

My thirst was such I would have settled for water of any temperature, but the subject of refreshment quickly fled his mind. He plumped himself back down into his chair and lifted Franklin's letter to his eyes again, glancing through it in snatches.

"This is correspondence of the most interesting nature," he said. "Are you acquainted with its contents?"

"In part." Should I, a mere courier, be so acquainted? "Mr. Franklin shared the general sense of it with me—should the written form fall into misadventure."

"What interests me more is what it does not contain, which is any word at all of Pennsylvania's claims on the Ohio country. Did Mr. Franklin speak to you on this matter?"

"Only in passing. To the effect that claim to these lands, wherever they are, is in dispute, though disputed more by the French than any other party."

"Did he mention new settlements, a place on Chartiers Creek, established there by a scout named Christopher Gist, and a trader by name of Thomas Cresap?"

"He mentioned Mr. Gist, but nothing at all about a Thomas Cresap. And he said nothing of new settlements."

Dinwiddie rose and walked with waddling step back to his window, wiping brow with handkerchief. "Do you return to Philadelphia soon?"

I thought of Susannah Smithson, and blushing cheek, and more. "It is my fondest hope, sir."

He gazed out the window. "I have no written message for Mr. Franklin. But I would have you tell him this. I find myself in strong accord with him on most every matter, including his suggestion of a conference of the several governors, a matter to which I have already put my mind. Yet amity depends on Pennsylvania yielding to Virginia as concerns the proprietorship of these lands, lest in our own division they instead become French and thus we all are diminished. Make him understand that Virginia is already in the Ohio country—has won the race—and this must be recognized. Otherwise, every interest will perish. Tell him I welcome his wise acceptance of this truth, and his newspaper's promulgation of it. Inform him of this, and I shall be most grateful."

I promised I would do my best to play the parrot.

"That's all then, young sir," he said, mopping his head yet again. "I'll have my servant find you some refreshment."

"Thank you, Your Excellency."

I bowed and started for the door.

"No, wait!"

I halted, fearful I had managed to do something wrong after all.

"Major Washington," said the governor. "You brought me a pouch from him. He is here in Williamsburg now today and I'm certain would be pleased to speak with you."

"Where might he be, sir?" It was too hot for a search. I thought of my ship, and of Riggins' temper rising to match the heat of this afternoon.

"There is a tavern across the mall, east along the lane past the arsenal. You should find him there. He has been asking after you."

———

There were few in that public house, but Washington's corner of the taproom seemed crowded enough—though it contained only his imposing self and two large companions, one of them the George Mercer I had met before. They were seated at a round table, chairs pushed back, legs stretched out, coats removed, and tankards in hand. They'd been playing at cards, but the game seemed to have been forgotten in their general merriment. The Major appeared more the stripling youth now, and not at all the august bearer of sundry public titles. But maturation assumed itself quite quickly upon his seeing my approach.

"Captain Morley!" He stood, extending his huge hand for the shaking. "I'd hoped I might come upon you again. And here you are! Had you a safe journey?"

I might have shared with him some circumspect version of my adventures with storm, Smithson, and Smithson's daughter, but was a stranger to his two companions and felt constrained to describe my journey simply as "tolerable." Washington introduced the other fellow, a pleasant enough man, as Robert Stobo, and had me seat myself, summoning another tankard.

He seemed in extraordinary spirits. I knew not how much was from ale and how much from circumstance, but his liveliness was in marked contrast to the somber figure who had greeted me on the Alexandria waterfront a fortnight before.

"And do you bring news?" he asked. His two companions leaned close as well. News was a precious commodity.

"I bear you a letter from Mr. Benjamin Franklin," I said, producing it.

Serious now, Washington broke the seal and unfolded it, squinting in the poor light. They'd closed the shutters against the sunshine and heat.

"Hmmm," he said, refolding it.

"And I recovered this brooch. From a passenger. I thought perhaps you . . ."

I held it up. He took it quickly from my hand and brought it close to his gaze, turning in his chair to escape the shadow.

"A handsome piece of jewelwork," he said. "Its mistress should be well pleased by its return." He thrust it back into my hand.

"Yes, and so I thought—"

There was a loud scrape as his chair went back and he stood, a sudden tower. He excused himself to his two friends with the words "King's business," threw a heavy arm around my shoulders and propelled me up and toward the door, snatching up his coat behind him and pulling it on as we went out the door.

"It's hot for such garments," I said. I'd been about to remove my own coat.

" 'Put not off your clothes in the presence of others, nor go out of your chamber half dressed,' " said Washington. "A rule of civility."

The yard outside the tavern was even less peopled than the interior, but there was a stable hand loitering by the hitching post, amusing himself by pelting chickens with bits of stone. Washington took me up the lane and to the shade of a well-spread oak. He read Franklin's letter through thoroughly, alternately smiling and frowning, then put it carefully to pocket.

"Well done, Captain Morley," he said. "I am in your debt." He paused. "Did Mr. Franklin speak further of me than this?"

"Yes."

"And?"

"He appreciates your comprehension of matters politick and military," I said. "He seemed surprised at your few years, and that you are so, er, newly come to your responsibilities."

"I've been adjutant since February, Captain Morley. My major's commission dates from then. What else did he say?"

Four months drilling militia—if even that—hardly made one the Duke of Marlborough.

"He was curious as to your relationship with Christopher Gist," I said.

Washington's eyes fell to the ground. "I have not met the man, though he is well regarded. A frontier scout, don't you know. A dispatch of his came to hand from Winchester—came to me in my capacity as adjutant. I sent it on to the proper authority, with my own remarks appended. And I made summation of his report in my letter to Mr. Franklin. You say he found this curious?"

It was time to be more politick. "I would describe Mr. Franklin as being very interested in you, Major Washington. He perceives usefulness. A useful friendship."

"You think?"

"But he's adamant, as he's written to the governor, that nothing military can come to your assistance from his colony. The Quakers, sir."

Washington kicked at a pebble. I proffered the enamel brooch again. It bore the Fairfax coat of arms and had fine gold workings about the edge. It must have cost her husband dear.

"Your lady's," I said. "You will want to return it." I placed it in his hand. "Now I can be off."

"No, no." The brooch came back to me again swiftly. You'd have thought it had just been plucked from some boiling cauldron. "Captain— uh, your Christian name again? I've forgot it."

"Thomas, sir. Or Tom. Or Tick, as my brother calls me."

"Tick, then. And I am George. And Tick, I have a considerable favor to ask of you."

I'd been hoping for some reward, not further errand. "And what is that?"

"On your voyage to Alexandria, I should be gladdened indeed if you could return this handsome piece to Mistress Cary by yourself in person— and so, I'm certain, would she be grateful."

"Mistress Cary?"

He flushed. "Her name before she was given in marriage to my friend. Sarah Cary, daughter of Colonel Wilson Cary of Ceelys, a plantation on the James not far from here. Now she is a Fairfax. She'll be missing this. It's a favorite. I wonder she hadn't mentioned it, except . . ."

He flushed again.

I extended the brooch once more. "I shall not be sailing up the Patowmack. I'm not going to Alexandria, but Annapolis. I am much overdue and my brother will be displeased."

Washington had us walk a bit down the lane, then stopped by a wooden fence. Ahead of us, some children were having sport with a sick dog.

"Have you a worthy second-in-command?" he asked.

"Oh, yes. My Riggins is the best."

"Annapolis is not far. A voyage with little hazard. Trust your vessel to your mate and your brother's needs will be attended."

"But—"

"Tick, the lady must have her cherished property. Better it be brought by you, who properly found it after having provided her passage, than by a gentleman without wife who should of necessity have no knowledge of a missing jewel that day."

"Yes, but—"

"Then there's nothing else for it. It's a comfortable ride to Belvoir—no more than five days. We can talk of Mr. Franklin and the worrisome events in the Ohio country. You may use my manservant's horse. I'll send back later to fetch him. Once your mission's done, you can ferry across the Patowmack at Alexandria and find yourself in Annapolis in a day's good ride. A small diversion, sir."

"Perhaps, but—"

"I want you to talk to George William Fairfax and other gentlemen of the Northern Neck. It is well you know the mind of Virginia should you soon be in Mr. Franklin's company again. These are trying times. Serious times. We've had more reports of outrages on the frontier."

He paused, leaning closer, lowering his voice. He smelled of cloves.

"The governor is fretful," Washington said. "He is putting much in motion. He is writing to His Majesty himself to apprise him of our troubles. He asks approval of stern measures to be taken against these French encroachments."

He leaned closer still. His excited eyes were staring weirdly, as though completely through me at some prospect a thousand leagues distant. "He means to send a few bold men into the wilderness to deliver to the French an ultimatum to leave. Their trespass is not be countenanced."

Now Washington's eyes, for all their cold, blue-gray color, seemed afire.

"I have told the governor that I should be as happy as honored to deliver this message. He must hear from London before it can be done, but Morley—Tick—I do believe he will have me do it!"

Seven

So there it was—a dividing of the ways: one clearly leading not just to Alexandria, but ultimately into those forbidding mountains and the mysterious lands beyond, the other over water back into my life.

As you perceive, Major Washington's persuasive energies were difficult to withstand. Once he'd set his mind to some attainment, he'd move toward it as resolutely as a strong plow horse to the end of a furrow. Had Sally Fairfax not been so capricious as to marry Washington's best friend and patron before George had even made her acquaintance, I'm sure he'd have hounded her to the altar himself if it took all his days.

He could wheedle, beg, flatter, bluster, and otherwise importune to gain his will as cleverly as any lawyer. As I have mentioned, the aura of command he bore was singular—and no one who has passed a sociable evening with him could say he was without charm. But his principal quality was resolution. He would not give up.

Treating me as old companion and not the brief acquaintance I truly was, the Major stayed with me all the long, dusty journey back to my sloop's mooring, urging me to his will with such compellingness that by the time I reached Riggins, I could do no more than instruct the fellow to take the *Hannah* home without me, asking him to carry back to my brother a muttered excuse about being detained by "Virginia authorities."

Riggins' mocking look remains with me to this day. He had the *Hannah* sailing smartly downriver within minutes.

———

I don't know if I've yet related how unfamiliar I was with that noble beast the horse at that young age. I'd ridden one only very seldom, almost always in a town or to or from some dockage, and always at a walk.

Washington was regarded by some as a man of large and clumsy movements. But, as I have noted, he was even then an excellent dancer, and upon a horse, he was magnificent. No matter how fast he rode, or how rough the road or countryside, he sat his mount as though in the comfort of a fireside chair.

I, poor devil, jounced and tottered like a badly bound sack, over the evenmost ground.

The Major's gray was a fine steed, as muscular as it was proud-spirited. The servant's nag I'd acquired was a less ambitious creature, but with my untutored hands at its reins, it behaved disagreeably from the first.

There was a rhythm to such a long ride—walk, trot, canter; walk, trot, canter. In deference to my inexperience and the soreness that swiftly enveloped my backside, I think Washington spent more time at the walk on our journey than normally was his custom.

This was the longest journey overland I'd ever made—from Williamsburg north to Chiswell's Inn, then Doncastle's, and across the Pamunkey River at Claiborne's. We followed the south bank of the Mattapony for the longest piece of the ride, crossing it at Todd's Bridge, and then following the northern bank to Bowling Green. A morning's ride from there, we reached Fredericksburg and the fall line of the Rappahannock River. It was the town of Washington's childhood. We were greeted with many welcomes along the high street, and our midday stop at a tavern there was exceedingly jolly. The Major was a popular fellow among his people, and enjoyed himself in their midst.

But then came time to make the ferry crossing to the river's northern shore, and the Major turned as grim as though Hades itself lay on the opposite bank.

All that was there was the house of his father and the small Washington family holding called "Ferry Farm," then the abode of his mother, Mary. I've seen him since plunge into the rage of battle and streams of singing bullets with far more relish than he showed there for the prospect of reunion with his lone surviving parent.

As he confided as the ferry reached the muck of the northern shore, he'd failed to stop there the last time he'd passed through. He feared his mum had learned of this.

And so she had.

She stood in the doorway as we rode in—looking like some Gothic gargoyle come to life, a pinch-faced woman with large, blue-gray eyes the size of George's, staring starkly at us from beneath an enormous bonnet.

Her tongue stayed still as we dismounted, and remained in check as we passed through the door into the house. But when George moved on through the large central hall to a rear bedroom in pursuit of a washing-up, she cut between us, followed him into the chamber, closed fast the door, and then launched into a screeching tempest of complaint and self-pitying lamentation the like of which I've not heard since, except when compelled to witness aspects of the slave trade. I wondered if my place were not better found on the other side of the Rappahannock, though I'd no doubt her squall could be heard over there as well.

Instead, I seated myself in one of the leather-bottomed chairs set at different points about the hall—eleven of them, by my count—and prepared to wait out her tempest as I might one at sea. There were two large tables against the walls, suggesting this was where the family, such as remained here abiding, took its meals. The walls were recently painted, but bore no pictures or other adornment save a mirror. The Washingtons, I gathered, lived comfortably there at Ferry Farm, but were not rich.

Mary Washington emerged first from the rear bedchamber, passing by me without glance or comment, heading darkly for the kitchen as though to prepare a large pot of poison for the both of us. George stepped out only to beckon me forth, saying, "There's whiskey here. We'll be wanting it."

Later we escaped the house, glad for a walk along the bluff above the

river despite the hot afternoon sun. The Major told me of his early yearn-
ings to go to sea and how much he'd been struck by envy watching me
move about the *Hannah* when we were at anchor at Alexandria. His voyage
to Barbados two years before—an ultimately unsuccessful mission to restore his consumptive elder brother Lawrence's health—had been, for all
its tragic conclusion, a happy excitement.

At age fifteen, the Major had had serious hope of a career at sea, and
inquiries had been made of influential relatives in England as to whether
a midshipman's berth might be found for him. His brother Lawrence was
for it, and his mother had not closed her mind. But his Uncle Joseph, brother
to his mother and guardian of that family's fortunes, rejected the notion
contemptuously. George's mother's mind then closed with a snap.

George recalled a dismissive line in the uncle's letter on the subject: "I
think he had better be put apprentice to a tinker, for a common sailor before
the mast has by no means the common liberty of the Subject, for they will
press him from a ship where he has 50 shillings a month and make him
like a Negro, or rather, like a dog. And as for any considerable preferment
in the Navy, it is not to be expected, there are always too many grasping
for it here."

The youthful Washington had accepted the maternal "Nay" as philo-
sophically as could be expected, finding solace in the prospects shortly afterward offered him in the practice of surveying, and the possibility of
becoming a planter and landholder more prosperous than his father.

Oddly, the subject of seafaring returned to the Washington family table
that night at dinner, for which we were joined by George's younger brother
Samuel and his married sister Betty. The Major sought to warm the cold
silence generated by his mother's lingering displeasure with him, this by
encouraging me to seek from memory's store amusing anecdotes from my
shipboard adventures. No sooner had I seized upon a tale about pirates in
the Turtle Islands of the West Indies south of Jamaica—the pirates being
two bloody-minded women named Anne Bonney and Mary Reade—than
Mother Washington cut me short with a murderous look, followed by a
misremembered and unfactual retelling of the message in her brother's letter.

The meal was good—roast pork and beef, a stewed green of some sort
and sliced squash, corn bread, molasses, watered whiskey, and a fine bread
pudding—the latter an indication that for all her meanness, Mary Washington harbored some good thought of her son and his guest.

There was ample china, and if most of their glassware had fallen victim
to breakage, I counted at least two dozen silver spoons.

After supper, George suggested that he and I might revisit the town of
Fredericksburg and converse with the gentlemen of the town on matters of
Crown importance, but his mother would have none of that. We sat uncomfortably in the central hall after the tables had been pushed back
against the wall, talking in trivialities, then repaired to bed. George was in

no way deferential to his mother in insisting that our business the next day required an extremely early start.

The mattresses in this household were firm and stout, the linens in good repair and recently laundered. I was happy to slip into sleep, and there, in dreamy fantasy, rejoin my fair Susannah. I'd done a successful sketch of her—a frilly work all curls and eyes and lips and bosom—but had left it on the *Hannah*. I could only hope Riggins and the crew would treat it with respect.

————

The next day's ride began at the first peek of light, and the Major had us canter a long distance from his mother's house before relaxing finally into a walk. He did not talk much, but pressed us ever on, anxiety coming onto his face, which I noted was suffering greatly from the sun, as it had been burning down upon us with little intervention by cloud since we'd left Williamsburg. Relieved as he'd been to be away from the Rappahannock, he became increasingly apprehensive the closer we came to Hunting Creek and its confluence with the Patowmack.

We camped our last night in the open country. The Major insisted it was because he could tolerate no more the beasties with which the straw bedding of the wayside ordinaries were so infamously acrawl, but I thought this a feigned excuse. He'd chosen for us a deeply wooded glen out of view from the road and common traveler. We lit no fire. The next morning, we again were in the saddle before the sun was up, and Washington kept a wary eye on the meandering trail both fore and aft.

When we drew nigh the lane that led east off the main road to Belvoir, George William and Sally Fairfax's Patowmack plantation, the Major bade me dismount, taking the nag's reins.

" 'Tis best you arrive by yourself and on foot, with no notion of my whereabouts," he said. "They're hospitable people. You'll find their welcome extends to dinner, tea, and supper, and a night's good bed. You can be off to Alexandria and homeward on the Annapolis road the morrow."

I gestured at my blue coat and soiled white breeches. I still looked much the seafarer. "How do I explain to them a ship's captain arriving afoot—and from such a long way?"

"Tell them your hired horse went lame and you were taken up by a farmer's wagon. I shall come calling this afternoon or evening. I'll have you a fine mount for the morrow's travel, worry not."

I shouldered my traveler's satchel and started down the lane, but was stopped by his call.

"Have you the brooch?" he asked.

Searching my pocket, I smiled at its finding, holding it up.

"Take care not to lose it now, good friend," he said. "The loss of it vexed her sorely, and she blamed me." He paused, looking down, then up, his gaze resuming quite direct. "I would ask no man to utter falsehood, least of all for me. But there're careful ways of speaking the truth."

Waving, and with a sigh, I turned and put foot to path.

———

The proprietor of Belvoir, a civil gentleman but one in no doubt whatsoever of his social position, received me coolly. When I produced the missing brooch and a suitable explanation of its whereabouts this past fortnight, George William Fairfax mellowed a small measure. I might err in my perception, but it seemed to me this oblong fellow with dour, oblong face was quite amazed that a ship's captain was capable of any honesty, let alone traveling all this distance from any port to accomplish so chivalrous a deed.

He offered me a few shillings' reward, and if I'd step out back to the kitchens, some small refreshment before I continued on my way. Then up swept his wife, her charm as fully evident as her smile, and my welcome improved surpassingly. Upon taking the jewel and hearing me repeat my succinctly discreet story of its travels, she clutched the brooch to her much-displayed bosom, reuniting with her heirloom as though with the most beloved kin. Eyes rapturously aglow, she then reached and grasped my hand most warmly.

"Captain Morley, you are a true friend," she said. Her eyes fixed sharply upon mine. "I had worried so fretfully over this."

I mumbled something I hoped was suitable, wishing she'd release my hand, but instead, she pulled it back toward her with both of hers, almost within touch of that now so sweetly nestled brooch. I fear I turned as red as poor Washington's face had become on the sun-hot trail.

"You must stay to supper and pass the night with us," she said. "You can have no ken how deep my gratitude runs." She turned to her husband, who seemed still frozen in amazement. "We should send for the Washingtons to fill our table. I do believe they and the captain have mutual acquaintanceships." She turned back to me. "In Williamsburg?"

"Yes," I said, puffing up a bit. "Governor Dinwiddie, and I think we have a common friend in Philadelphia as well."

"Philadelphia!" she said, still all asparkle. "Our rustic Major Washington has friends in Philadelphia?"

"Yes. A Mr. Benjamin Franklin."

The names of governor and wealthy merchant statesman sufficed to ease George William Fairfax's worries that his present company might be too far beneath his social station to long endure. He seconded his wife's invitation. He seemed a husband made happy by his wife's pleasure. I liked that.

Major Washington arrived as the afternoon began to cool, in company with his brother Lawrence's widow, Anne—herself a Fairfax and close kin to George William.

The five of us supped at sunset, afterward walking the bluff to enjoy the river twilight, returning then for the pleasures of cards and, once two musicians were summoned, of the dance.

The ebullient Sally was much the mistress of that night. I knew only sailors' jigs and such, but she taught me a few steps of current fashion, her merry eyes beguiling in every glance.

Then she was off for a romp around the room with the Major, such lighthearted but noisy thumping as I'd ne'er been witness to—at the turns, his hand slipping 'round her waist most intimately.

But then she'd return to the side of her proper husband, all cozy, rosy coquetry as she clung to his arm, and, with upturned jaunty chin and elbow into ribs, seek mischievously to prod forth a smile from him.

I don't suppose I've known a man who could long resist this woman. How Washington could abide so much in her proximity and not be driven mad with frustration, I found most remarkable. After a year or so of this, I might well be disposed to kill myself, or her husband, or her—anything to end the torment. I was even happier now in my discovery of Philadelphia's Susannah. Without her blushing face to keep in mind, I might have succumbed to Mistress Fairfax's charms again with far more reckless ardor.

Belvoir was a large house, but not enough for Major Washington and me to avoid having to share a bedchamber. We left, with his sister-in-law and two African servants in tow, after an early breakfast. Washington, as promised, had brought along a spare horse for my conveyance. Before parting from his sister-in-law at Mount Vernon, he showed me about the hilltop establishment, which possessed one of the finest views of the Patowmack I've ever seen.

Unfortunately, I was made privy to one of its less happy aspects. Washington had added his inherited slave holdings to those of his late brother's plantation, and among the poor creatures there abiding was a young woman named Charlotte. While showing me about the grounds to the east of the main house, Washington was approached by the plantation's overseer. I think his name was Whiting.

"Charlotte, I guess, will be reported sick this week," the man said, and then proceeded to horrify me with a commonplace relating of that place and practice.

"I gave her a whipping on Saturday," he said, "and I find she don't intend to work, in order, I suppose, to be even with me. When I was cutting out the river hogs, she sent David, requesting I would give her a spare rib, as she longed for it. I thought it a piece of impudence in her, which she has a great share of.

"I did not send it, but on Saturday, I sent one to each of the women at the quarter. Of course she had one with the rest, but she, I fancy, watched me go home, and as soon as I got in the house, she brings the spare rib and throws it down at the door—affronted, I suppose, at my not sending it on

Thursday. Told me indeed she wanted none of my meat, and was, in short, very impudent.

"I took a hickory switch which I rode with and gave her a very good whipping. She certainly could deserve nothing else. On Monday morning, she was sent sewing work, but I believe she has not done anything yet under a pretense of her finger receiving a blow and was swelled. She threatens me very much with informing Lady Washington, and says she has not been whipped for fourteen years past, but I fully expect I shall have to give her some more of it before she will behave herself, for I am determined to lower her spirit or skin her back."

I watched Washington very closely. He stared at the ground a long moment, then nodded curtly and moved on. This was acceptance, whether concurrence or approval, I could not say. I do not believe he was happy with the necessity, but necessary was his apparent view of it.

We quickly afterward remounted, then pressed on the eight miles north to Alexandria.

Without mentioning the slaves, I spoke admiringly of his estate. He explained that his brother Lawrence had left it to the Widow Anne with the understanding that he, as brother, was always welcome at it and should keep a hand upon its management. Should Anne die, the place was to be given over to George. She was fond of the Major, and had told him that should she remarry into a suitable circumstance, she'd be just as pleased to have Mount Vernon his by lease or other arrangement. I was happy for him when that proved the case scarce a year later.

We reached Alexandria in time for the midday meal—enjoyed in the same public house to which he'd taken me on our initial acquaintance. We ate in leisure. There were boats enough to make the Patowmack crossing. I knew I'd not make Annapolis by nightfall and had reconciled to another night's shelter on the road, no matter what.

So I was in no haste, and suggested a walk about the town. The Major countered with another notion. There was a hill just to the west of us, rising as an upward sweep of a long ridge. If I'd ride to it with him, he'd present me a view as I'd never seen from any mast top.

I accepted the invitation. I'd become used enough now to the back of a horse to stay upon it without recourse to manic gymnastics, and saw no awesome challenge in the ascent of the hill, especially if there was a trail— as the Major promised. We trotted along King Street, following it west out of the town until it dwindled into a country track that meandered upward to the lip of the ridge. Thence, we bore off right onto a narrower trail that led up to this hilltop, which, like much of the surrounding slope, had been largely cleared of trees.

Dismounting, Washington reached into a saddlebag and pulled forth a spyglass, a handsome piece with highly polished lens and brasswork.

Climbing up onto an outcropping of rock, he handed me this instrument, but when I turned it east to look down upon Alexandria Town and its river anchorage, he shook his head and put a hand on my shoulder.

"No, Tick. Wrong way. All that's old to the eyes. I know every brick. I was apprentice surveyor when we laid out the plots and lots four years ago." He turned me the other direction. I shifted feet quickly, to avoid being toppled.

"Look there," he said, extending his arm to the west. "The air's of uncommon clarity. You should be able to see all the way to it."

"To what?"

"To the Blue Ridge—the first ridge of the Appalachian Mountains. There. You see?"

I put lens to eye and ran out the spyglass to its fullest travel, bringing into focus a hazy line of grayish-blue that rose above the distant greenery beneath the remarkably azure sky.

"Just over that ridge is the valley of the Shenandoah," Washington said, resting elbow on bent knee as he stared in the same direction. "It's broad and wide, and home now to increasing numbers of Irish and Germans. The great Lord Fairfax now lives there, too—friend to all but women, whose company confounds him sorely."

I kept looking, as though I could see this all.

"There's a small settlement called Winchester in that valley—the last town in the colony as you travel west. What you are looking at, Tick— from here to there—is all that most know as Virginia. Sea to mountains, nothing more. With a captain's glass, one can see it all."

I lowered the glass. He was staring at the westward horizon as if in no need of lens.

"Beyond that ridge and valley, Tick, are six more lines of mountains. And once across them, the land sweeps on and on, flat and sweet for, I know not, possibly thousands of miles. Past the Beautiful River, past this great river which flows south into New Spain and New Orleans. On and on, westward without limit. Imagine it, Tick. The land as the sea. Land as the sea."

I tried envisioning it, but my mind went blank.

"I've been into those mountains," he said, "on a surveying trip for Lord Fairfax. But never before beyond. Dinwiddie's word can send me there, past those mountains. I'm going to see all that, Tick. Before the winter's done, I'm going beyond those mountains. And the French be damned."

I waited, almost expecting an invitation. But none came. He was trans-fixed. I don't believe even Mistress Sally dancing naked on the rocks could have drawn his gaze from that distant vision—not at that moment. Perhaps it was the rare clarity of the sky.

Eight

My return to Annapolis commenced the unhappiest summer of my young life. I was greeted by the *Hannah* waiting at dockside, Richard's three-masted brig anchored a ways off in the Severn, and himself plunged into rage and despondency.

He was reeling drunk on rum when I walked into our small house off Duke of Gloucester Street near the waterfront market square, and it was well before midday. To find him thus on a morning, sprawled in a chair by the window, with his dark glower aimed at the front door like a cannon barrel, was unprecedented and truly disturbing.

"Five days with no word of you! Your ship sails home without a master, and where are you?"

He knew the answer surely. "Virginia."

"Virginia! Yes! So says faithful Riggins. But for what sensible reason? Your ship first and last, Thomas! Abandon that principle, and you're not fit to scrub scum from its deck!"

"But Riggins is most competent, and—"

There came then the most amazing procession of oaths and curses, including several I'd heard not before, despite my mariner's upbringing.

This was as unexpected as the morning rum. Richard, don't you know, fancied himself a gentleman—the gentility advancing with every pound and shilling he acquired. Here 'twas all undone, the grand fellow transformed into some foul dockyard lout. His shouting and curses rose to such vehemence that his pet monkey, a prize brought back from the north coast of South America, took to madly leaping about the house, shrieking its own shrill complaint. The cat of the house commenced flight at this, leaping beneath the skirts of our kitchen maid, a Negro woman whom Richard had fetched from Port-au-Prince on a previous voyage. She added her own fearsome imprecations to the bedlam, which unnerved me all the more, as her faith was the dreaded Voudon.

Fueled by his rum, Richard's anger flamed far longer than was good for him—or me—but at length he subsided and I seized the opportunity to attempt explanation. It developed that the good Riggins had told him very little—relating the digressions to Williamsburg, my commerce with Major Washington and Governor Dinwiddie, and the fierce storm we braved off the Virginia capes, but nothing of what had transpired in Philadelphia save that there had been some dispute over the count of barrels and sacks.

When I perhaps foolishly laid out the bare facts, at least of that, Richard lost all hold. He threw things—a chair, his pewter mug of rum, a hearth broom that struck the hysterical ape. Riggins had delivered my rolled-up sketch of Susannah to the house for safekeeping, and Richard threw that as well. And me he threw from the house.

I repaired to a grog shop at the waterfront—one now decidedly beneath Richard's social station—and was fortunate in finding Riggins there, taking his midday meal with some mates. We found a table to ourselves, where he sadly brought me up to date on circumstances.

Richard had got himself a new partner, the earlier having abruptly died, and had borrowed with the new fellow a substantial sum to purchase a new brig, the loan provided by a syndicate of wealthy Philadelphians—none other than the rascally Smithson their chief.

For all his wealthy trappings, my brother had reason to worry for money. The *Hannah's* voyage had been immensely profitable, but our three-master's had not. The casked rum had traveled well, but the raw molasses he'd loaded at Sainte Dominique had fallen prey to the heat and doldrums.

His new partner, Ambrose Butler, also a Philadelphian, had become taken with the notion that they'd prosper much more quickly in the slave trade, and it was to that end that he'd pushed the issue of the additional vessel.

Richard was no friend to either indentured servitude or slavery outright, but he hated poverty more. Fearing to sunder the partnership if he adhered to principle, he'd acquiesced—but this had only added to his inner torment. Not to speak of mine. I could think myself no more greatly cursed than to be anywhere on a vessel carrying such cargo.

Worse for Richard, he'd fallen in love—not with a local lady, but with one down in the far remove of Jamaica, where he'd sometimes idled. The woman was married, to some island planter. Of course, there were deadly fevers enough in the tropics to kindle hopes of a change in that situation. The lady had certainly kindled something.

Here was the point where I should have set my foot on some other path of life. There were ships enough needing experienced mates, if not masters. After that storm, I had no qualms of any sort. There was also, I supposed, some promise in Virginia, where I could count one good friend at the least.

But my choice was to stay and abide a while with my brother. I had not got Susannah Smithson in any fashion out of my mind. And family was family, whatever the state of sobriety.

If I was to extricate the name of Morley from this odious slave trade, I could not do it from some far remove. I would have to keep my hand in the game—though if at all possible, without coming near a slave ship.

"Have you counsel for me in this matter?" I asked Riggins on our second rum in that public house.

"I'm Irish—Celtic, Catholic Irish—with forebears as what felt goddamned Cromwell's boot and flail," Riggins said. "You need not ask my views on the servitude."

"But if Richard makes you master or mate of a slaver?"

"He and thee have been damn good to me, Tick, but I swear I'll seek another berth—if one I find that pays as well."

Riggins had a wife or two at harborsides.

I drank, a modest sip—my brother's state firmly in mind. "He has already asked that of me—in a firm way. It's not something he'll have forgotten in the soberness of morning."

"It's dangerous work, Tick—master, mate, or crew of a slaver."

"It's appalling and vile, but how so dangerous?"

"Why, because of escape." An odd gleam there was in his eye.

"But there are all those chains and leg irons and such."

"Nay, no matter. Happens all the time—disastrous loss always. Worth a lot, those Negro people. Consider 'em gold pieces with legs. They run off and you're out some treasure. Enough to put one off of being in the business."

"I do not ken your meaning."

"Well, you think upon it, Tom, and perhaps you shall. For myself, my wish is to be mate with you on the *Hannah*, or her master if you won't be. No good for the slave trade, that little ship."

We ordered rum three. I put what he'd said out of immediate mind— but not far from its reach.

———

As it turned out, I did sail a voyage with Richard, though not on a ship yet in slavery commerce. He had decided the time had come nigh for the *Hannah's* bottom to be scrubbed, and the sloop recaulked and refitted besides. Leaving Riggins and crew behind to attend to that, he ordered me aboard our three-master as second mate on its next voyage—to Jamaica, with rum in mind, and of course, *amour*.

Our first stop was at Port Tobacco in Maryland, where we loaded with the weed for which the town was named. Thence it was due south for the Windward Islands, encountering some bother with that great wide current of warm water that flows north along the American coast by Spanish Florida. Once free of that, we had a day's good sailing, then fell becalmed for more than a week. After sailcloth spread once again, though weakly, we finally dropped anchor at Kingston in Jamaica in mid July.

I advanced my mariner's education in all this, learning, as I had not occasion to do before in our little sloop, the names of the several sails to be found on a big square-rigger. If they be of use to you, I'll call them out here with pen as I might to a ship's company. From bowsprit aft by foremast, mainmast, and mizzenmast, they are: flying jib, jib, fore topmast staysail, fore staysail, foresail, fore topsail, fore topgallant, main staysail, main topmast staysail, main topgallant staysail, mainsail, main topsail, main topgallant, mizzen staysail, mizzen topmast staysail, mizzen topgallant staysail, mizzen sail, spanker, mizzen topsail, and mizzen topgallant.

Try your luck bellowing some of that at a deckhand high up the mainmast shrouds in a howling gale. Of course, gale we had not on that limp of a voyage. I for one would have welcomed it.

So, as it turned, would have Richard. On Jamaica dwelt his ladylove. En route, he kept much to his cabin in the daytime and took all the lonely night watches, brooding.

His slough of despond deepened upon arrival, with horrible cause. The lady of his heart was gravely ill—and of that damnable disfiguring small-pox. Her husband the planter, a man of vigorous temper, forbade Richard any visitation at sick bed—not even letters. Each Richard sent was returned, the last accompanied by a note from the husband that threatened, though it did not demand, an encounter of honor if Richard persisted.

It made me think of Major Washington and the risk he ran in so closely gathered a friendship with Mrs. Fairfax. What if he had to contend with a fellow like this Jamaican planter, and not his meek and dour boyhood friend?

For Richard's part, he shrank back from the possibility of challenge. Good thing. He passed each day in such diminishing sobriety, he surely would have perished from wavering aim in an encounter.

Nearly a fortnight we endured the heat, damp, and myriad winged beasties of this tropic place, all to no good purpose, as the woman's health did not rally. On the last of twelve days, Richard's lady died. He was inconsolable. He thrashed about, throwing things, shouting curses at the heavens, then wholly succumbed to the juice of the cane. I waited for a particularly deep stupor, then had him lugged back aboard the ship and ordered anchor weighed.

My brother passed nearly all of the return voyage in his cabin, and most of that lying near motionless on his bunk.

Awaiting us in Annapolis was a sprightly looking *Hannah*, eager for sea, and Richard's partner, Ambrose Butler, eager to commence the African commerce.

———

Both Richard and Butler took sail on the new slave brig to Afrique, having prudently—for the purpose of their scheme—signed aboard some stoutish manhandlers with experience in the management of human chattel. Sad I was to see the brig disappear into the southern haze of the Chesapeake, knowing the misery the holds would bear abrim upon returning.

But I was free of it. Richard wanted so very much for this first transaction to go well, and nothing to mar it. As I was so demonstrable against the trade, he decided at the last to leave me behind, lest I cause some row. As before, he gave me command of the *Hannah*—even had me certified as master. So I was truly "Captain" now.

The instructions given me offered generous latitude. I was to obtain whatever cargo the Chesapeake could provide, then sail to Charleston and a factor of Richard's long acquaintance, there to sell my freight and load the sloop with indigo, bringing that to whatever port I deemed the best market.

Well, there was little question as to that, was there? The sudden end of Richard's inamorata prompted a new resolve within my own heart as concerned the fair Susannah. We'd had but two brief meetings. What if some fever were to take her before there was a third? Her own sister had perished, had she not? At times in these colonies, there seemed more death than life.

Three letters were awaiting me in Annapolis, two from Alexandria. Of these, the most verbose—creaking with the weight of words—was from my new friend Washington, informing me of Great Events, gatherings of Burgesses, further dispatches from the frontier, a request sent by sail from governor's palace to King's for money to raise and arm Virginia militia companies, and dashing about in the midst of it all, our young Major, seeking his important place in the scheme of things. He also found space to thank me for my companionship and honorable and gentlemanly conduct, by which I presumed he meant my discretion concerning the brooch and how I'd come to have it.

Further reward for my diplomacy with the Fairfaxes was manifest in the other letter from those Patowmack shores—this one unsigned and badly spelt, but its author, brooch restored to freckled bosom, unmistakable. The sense of it was that happiness was to be had everywhere in her household, and that the lady considered herself in my debt far more deeply than the worth of that copper with which she'd paid for river passage.

Her sentiment fluttered my heart a bit, but the third letter that awaited me set it to thumping wildly. It was from Mr. Franklin. Chatty and discursive, it was full of news and amusing accountings, but the lines my eyes embraced most joyfully were those that told of a visit to his mercantile establishment by a young woman of the town and her maid, both unnamed but of my recent acquaintance. The lady had asked of Franklin that he relay to me her most sincere concerns for my health and safety, adding that if I had wish to maintain these same, I should take care to keep far from the vicinity of her city, as a powerful relation of hers had been plotting a powerfully disagreeable welcome should I return. She regretted this, for she had been amused and charmed by me in our last meeting, she said, and her fondest wish now was for another. She was much discomfited, she said, by the impossibility of it.

Father Smithson and his plots be damned. The implicit invitation was far more powerful than any consequence I thought I'd have to fear. But the voyage to Charleston was not to be avoided. It took bloody forever in this summer's weary air—the heat stirring it not, no matter Mr. Franklin's strange theories on weather and rising vapors.

I had liked Charleston in our time living there, but then it had been refuge, after flight from Bermuda and a stepmother's wrath. In remembering it, I'd quite forgot that here was a city state not merely with views on the "Peculiar Institution" of slavery most tolerant, but a place where the subjugation of the black man was nigh the dominant religion. In stopping by the customhouse, I was compelled to pass a slave auction and found it as pitiable as the smoky scene in Williamsburg—perhaps more pathetic. That poor wench was delivered from her miseries. These unfortunates were but beginning theirs.

It was fair September when at last we set course for Cape Henlopen and the happy land of Pennsylvania up the river beyond.

Nine

When Mr. Franklin had described the uncommonly well-formed bosom of Susannah Smithson as angelic, it was, as no one could doubt, a judgment arising merely from surmise. My own assessment of this particular of her many charms was just as superlative, but to my utter amazement, became one based—how shall I say?—on firsthand observation, of both a visual and, yes, bless it, tactile nature far more thoroughgoing than that first encounter on her steps.

Indeed, all my secret dreams came astonishingly true almost from the instant I rapped upon the Smithson portal. Yet you must wonder how could this possibly be when her awful father had levied every kind of fearsome threat upon me save homicide?

Prudence was a virtue that served me well—at least initially. Shortly after arriving in Philadelphia, I sold our cargo of indigo at the Delaware River dockside to the master of an England-bound ship with space in her hold and a generous market across the ocean. While both vessels' crews attended to the transfer of cargo, I hastened up Market Street to Mr. Franklin's establishment. He was absent, off in the country pursuing some scientific notion, but his partner David Hall had cheerier response to my further inquiry: Mr. Smithson was absent as well! And, at much agreeably farther remove. The terrible man had taken himself off to Baltimore the week before on what he'd advertised about as a fortnight's visit.

Armed with this happy news, I sped to the place now dearest to my heart and pounded on the door as though bearing urgent message. And so I was. I loved Susannah. I was sure of it. The flame had burned without pause or flicker ever since our parting and was now a veritable blaze.

The same maid answered my summons. Far friendlier, the wench, this time, but not more helpful. She left the door standing only slightly ajar, and after a moment, hers was replaced by another face. My heart leapt high, then fell far. It seemed Susannah's face, but it was not—too young, too plump, and not quite so pretty, yet remarkably resemblant.

Of course, one of the sisters.

"I am Captain Morley," I said. "I call upon Miss Susannah Smithson. In response to her letter."

Pretty lie. It was Franklin who'd writ me.

The girl's face lit all up with smiles and mischief. "I shall fetch her, sir," she said and vanished, leaving the door still no more advanced in welcome. I heard giggling.

I glanced behind me about the street, wondering if the father might have posted some of his louts about in wait of me. There were none, for how could he have known of my coming?

A slender hand reached from the door and, grasping my arm, yanked me within.

"Thomas! You cannot be here!"

I smiled, searching for an appropriate salutation, but she continued to haul me in the manner of a ship on tow. The corridor was empty, but I could hear women's voices near.

"Susannah . . ." I protested.

"Hush. You mustn't be seen!"

She opened a door to the side, revealing a narrow, dark staircase—a servants' passage, leading both up and down. Still gripping my hand, she hastened upward. I followed as best I could manage, slipping once and cracking my shin painfully.

At last we emerged into an attic room, with four or five cloth-covered straw pallets set about variously beneath dormer windows. None was occupied. Here would sleep the maids, the cook, the scullery wench, the drudge, I guessed, but not until their day's labors were done, which meant hours hence.

"None shall discover us up here," Susannah said. "For now." She stared at me happily, slightly out of breath.

"Your father . . ."

"He never sets foot up here. It would be an annoyance for him to have to do so."

"And he's away in Baltimore."

"Lucky for you."

"Lucky for me indeed."

"Oh Thomas, you cannot imagine. But you shall know."

In aggregate, I could not have hitherto been in her company more than an hour in all our meetings. But some blazes take not long to kindle. I stared back into those merry blue eyes. Her breath was still heated, but I thought no longer from her exertion. I kissed her hand. She pulled mine close to her bosom.

"Welcome, sir."

"I feel very welcome."

"Then feel it more."

Her lips came to mine with a sudden swiftness. My hand remained in hers, and thus was caught between us in this panting crush, my palm flush against a curve of soft, warm, moist, silken flesh.

My, but her breath was sweet. All of her was that, attic heat or no, even when her clothes, as though by invisible hand, swiftly began to come undone. My only previous experience in this endeavor, mind, had been with the skinny lass Franklin had arranged for my entertainment at Mrs. Calderwill's on my previous visit to Philadelphia, and that slattern had worn only a thin shift. Susannah's bounty was encumbered by a silk outer dress, hoop petticoat, stays, camisole, underpetticoat, shift, panniers, stockings, and garters. It made a fine pile of cloth indeed when I'd finally stripped her to her shining glory.

Another kiss, a snatch at bare, smooth, soft bottom, and then I stood back as she began tearing away my own garments, quite literally as concerned my proud captain's coat, which I had had let out a bit to accommodate better the width of my shoulders. Rent up the back again by her urgent pull, it became portmanteau for two one-armed men.

On she went, with such zeal I could not participate but only wait, fearing for the knee buttons of my breeches—though it was not for very long. The both of us now exuberantly naked, we fell to one of the pallets, rolling and kissing and hugging and then—well, no mere strumpet was ever anything like this. I was quite surprised and remarkably impressed by Susannah's abilities. I'd not heard any of the crew on the *Hannah* talk of some of these things. How could so young and well bred a girl have learned them?

Indeed, she was prodigious in her knowledge of what I had looked upon as deepest mystery. Her magic brought me new wonders and amazements with every twist and turning. I wished it to go on and on but, climbing astride me, she commenced this wanton, irresistible bouncing and swiveling and clenching. I could no more hold back than restrain a cannon's fire once match was lit.

I was spent, exhausted, but she pressed on with groans and cries and endearing exclamations, at last collapsing upon my chest and clutching me tightly. We rolled to and fro, almost off the pallet, then back again, at length parting to recline arm in arm, with the both of us facing upward, lying perfectly still except for our rapid breathing.

We each were bathed in sweat, and her smell had changed—though in no way soured. I took a long, deep breath, then turned to look with savoring proximity upon this beauty I felt I now possessed as fully mine. She had this marvelous upward tilt to her small nose. Her bright blue eyes were jewellike in their clarity and luminosity.

"Oh, Susannah."

"Ah, Captain Morley."

"I am in heaven."

She laughed. "You are in my father's attic."

"It's heaven enough for me."

She paused, listening, then squeezed my hand. "You do speak in lovely ways, sir. No rough seaman, thou."

"I love you."

She seemed to think upon this a moment, then sat up. Her back was so perfectly formed. I reached and stroked it, down spine to the softness and cleft below.

"Thomas, we are but recently met. I know you not well, nor you I."

"Not well? What is this then if not knowing, and not well?"

"You know exactly what this was. The common term for it is fucking."

"But you—we . . ."

"Dear boy, with my father gone, I thought . . . You have some charm to you, sir, and great handsomeness. I did not want to waste an opportunity, when so sure there would not be another."

"There had better be another." I slid a finger into that cleft. She jumped a little, pulling my hand away and settling it with both of hers in her moist and furry lap.

"Not soon. Not ever again, perhaps. My pa would kill you if he could. You were rash and impetuous to come, Thomas. I am greatly flattered, but powerfully fearful."

"I want to marry you, Susannah."

She jumped again, pushing my hand aside and moving farther from me on the pallet. I stared at her breasts. A runnel of sweat ran down the nearest. The bud was so pink.

"You are rash and impetuous and impudent. You have no claim to my hand, sir, nor are you in a position to ask it. You're not nineteen. In this colony, you cannot marry without your father's permission until aged twenty-one years. Have you that?"

"My father's long dead. Mother, too. I need no one's permission."

"You need mine, and greatly do you need my father's. There's no way you can have it."

"He and my brother are now connected in business."

" 'Twould help more, then, were you your brother. He is the monied and propertied, not you."

I'd just a moment before been imagining myself dropping anchor in some sleek three-master and hurrying ashore to a stately house with this beauty waiting at the gate in the swirling company of many gay and cheerful children.

"Life is not long, Susannah."

"That is why one must be wise about how one lives it, and with whom."

I sat up, cooler now. Ecstacy to euphoria to melancholy, in so small a matter of minutes.

Perhaps worse. How distant was Baltimore? How many days the overland ride?

"So that is that."

"Of course." She bit her lip, staring off toward the window.

"You'll remember, at least, that I love you?"

"Oh, I shall indeed. You are a sweet man, Thomas, and I bear you much affection. I shall not forget you. Not soon." She reached with her hand to stifle a yawn. If not so anxious, I suppose I would have felt sleepy myself.

Susannah rose. I ran my hand along her long, well-formed leg, but she moved away, to the window.

"The question now," she said, "is what's to be done with you. Surely I can't allow you to boldly saunter out the door, coat in twain and breeches awry, and all in the full light of day. We must wait for dark. Then away with you fast—and far."

"But that's hours yet." I stood as well.

"You'll stay here. The servants are well occupied for the day." She began to get dressed—skipping, I noted, the camisole and corset. "I'll fetch some food. There're sage scones and strawberry jam, I think—and some crab cakes waiting for dinner. And ale. No wine, I fear. I dare not meddle with my father's casks."

Barefoot, but otherwise with sufficient cloth in place, she eased open the door and slipped out to the stairs. I looked to my ruined coat, then pulled on my breeches against the possibility of a surprise entrance by one of the servants or sisters, but remained otherwise unclad. Reclining back upon the pallet, I loosed my mind to wallow in its reverie. Yet, another worrisome thought intruded. If I was to be delayed so long, I should get word to my ship and its fellows, but how? I could ask no one from this household to present such a message to the docks.

Susannah returned bearing a well-laden wooden tray, setting it on the floor next to me and seating herself cross-legged on the other side of it. We ate—I with much appetite, for it was easing well into the afternoon and I'd had no sustenance save that of *amour* since breakfast. The ale tasted odd with the sage scones, but I had great thirst. I drained the mug quickly, and felt quite heady.

I lay back, watching Susannah's dainty progress through her meal. She had splendid manners. Her food had flown to her mouth with even more delicacy than Sally Fairfax had managed.

"You are well-spoken, and you write a lovely letter," I said. "You are educated, and possess every grace."

She patted her lips with a cloth. "I am well-instructed. I have been to school. In England. Three years."

"What I mean to say, Susannah . . . you are in every way a lady, truly a lady, but . . ."

"But?" Her eyes widened as her brow shot up.

"But, so . . ." I paused—a polite cough. "I am surprised, er, curious." I gestured at the disarray of flung garments around us. "I am surprised at your your—impetuosity."

"What do you mean?" It came out a growl.

"What I mean to say is that you are most startlingly knowledgeable. I have learned so much from you in this brief, er, lesson. Yet I am at least a year your elder."

"This speaks more of you than of me."

"And for a lady, so impetuous, so generous—and with a man so recently met. I am confused."

She set her plate aside and leaned toward me, her breasts slipping forth from her loose garment and hanging deliciously at hand.

"You are, sir, a comely fellow. You have a handsome and endearing face, without blemish, and a fine, manly figure, for all you drape it in unseemly clothes. You move with great energy, but with gentleness. And you have courtesy. In sum, there looked to be pleasure in you, so I took it."

"Took it?"

" 'Twas the same with you. Confess it. What drew you to me but my face and form? You've no knowledge of my thoughts upon the philosophic."

Truth to tell, I hadn't considered that she might have any.

"As for my experience, sir, a gentleman would not inquire after it."

"I sincerely regret . . .

Kneeling, she leaned farther forward, grasped the unbuttoned turns of my knee breeches and yanked them free. Then she stood, stepping out of her skirts and letting them fall with a flutter.

"Do not regret," she said, kneeling again, this time athwart my legs. "Enjoy. As you say, life is not long."

———

We slept. When I woke again, she was still in slumber, a curl of golden hair lying across both her closed eyes. I found a chamber pot in a corner and discreetly made use of it, then finished the ale she'd left in her tankard and returned to her arms. She stirred, turning toward me, and we both found dreams again.

When wakened next, I thought at first it was to a dream, and a hellish one at that—a slamming sound, a muttering mob of men, candles, angry faces, shouts and oaths.

But 'twas real life. I saw a pistol raised and fired. There was a shattering report and the acrid smell of smoke and powder. Susannah was sitting up, screaming. Her father was there, thrusting her aside. And then my bare shoulder felt the sting of a lash.

Ten

There was straw bunched and scattered about the low-ceilinged dungeon to which I was taken, but I took what little rest I could manage on the bare earthen floor instead, with only my arm for pillow. The straw was so full of tiny wildlife it at times quivered and rattled with their movement, especially the burrowings of mice. The resident rats were bolder and ran hither and yon as they wished—at least once skittering over my very head—but their interruptions were not frequent.

I had other companions in that gaol besides wee beasties. The two men who shared my bricked-and-barred subterranean chamber were condemned murderers. One was a lad of I think my own age—apprenticed, I believe, to a tradesman—who had without explanation save that of some demonic impulse killed a younger boy in the same employ toward whom he had borne some affection. The other felon, a much older, stouter man, a leather tanner by occupation—and damned noisily remorseful—had caught his young wife in the midst of an ill-advised frolic and cut off her head with one of the implements of his calling.

A third inmate, confined by himself in space across the passageway—Ranting Edgar, we called him—had spent most of his life committing every imaginable sort of crime. He stationed himself at the bars nearest us, screaming and banging and carrying on in the most barbarian manner about all the crimes he intended to commit once he was free again.

No large chance of that. All three of these men had been sentenced to hanging—in the case of Ranting Edgar, I think some dismemberment was prescribed as well—and were waiting only the arrangements of a public occasion.

I was as good as hanged myself, or so it seemed. I had only one visitor—the ever helpful Mr. Franklin, who came as soon as conveniently possible upon hearing of my misadventure. He was as concerned about my dim future as was I, though he maintained some cheeriness.

He brought news almost as distressing as the prospect of the noose. Smithson had secured a writ ordering the impoundment of the *Hannah*, and my crew had departed the city for fear of sharing a fate like my own.

"Your first mate, a Mr. Riggins, leaves word that he's bound for Annapolis to seek your brother's intervention on your behalf," said Franklin. "In the meantime, your ship will be safe here—under the Crown's protection until you might be brought to trial. On the matter of your own person, however, you've less to hope for from the courts and the law. Friendships bought with money make strong bonds, and Smithson has acquired several friends at the bar. The charges he brings against you are numerous and severe—two of them capital offenses."

"Capital? What could they be?"

We were conversing in a deep recess of the dungeon, as far from Ranting

Edgar as practicable. Well acquainted with Franklin's importance in that city, the gaoler—an older fellow named Billy—stood watching us as best he could manage, making sure of my visitor's safety.

"One concerns the ravishment of a female person or persons—as you have good reason to expect. The other complaint is that you assaulted Mr. Smithson with deadly intent."

"That's monstrous. I told you what occurred. I was set upon by Smithson and a gang of his hired men. I awoke to them where I was sleeping. The son of a gun fired a pistol at me."

"He claims it was discharged by you, after you'd wrested it from his possession. His tale is that, warned by his daughters that you had broken into the house, he armed himself the better to deal with you and mounted the back stairs to apprehend you, finding you drunk on ale, lying naked in wait for his maids and serving wenches, and in possession of valuables, to wit: two of his finest pewter tankards. There was a struggle. You took his pistol from him and fired it with a desire to murder. Only the intervention of his, uh, associates spared his life. So states the preferment of charges."

"If I had discharged that weapon with a desire to murder, the gentleman would have a very large hole in his breast."

Franklin bent his head forward to peer at me over his spectacles and treat me to a slim smile. "That is hardly a wise choice of words for one to argue with from the dock," he said.

"But it's the truth! He fired at my head. Had I not awakened when I did and sat up with such a start, the ball would have found its mark sure enough."

"Truth, truth. But we are dealing with the law."

"And this nonsense about my waiting for his serving wenches. His Susannah was lying in my arms, as naked as I, and quite content!"

"Not by her father's reckoning. According to that, she was with her sister Penny, huddled downstairs in fright."

"Damned lies!"

"But taken as fact. And quite understandable, when their intent is to defend a woman's honor—a man's own daughter."

"The intent of those words is a noose around my neck!"

Franklin patted my shoulder and rose. "Fear not, young friend. We'll find a way to spare you yet."

———

Days passed. My three companions each went off to their somber fate—on separate grand occasions. I could not, of course, join in the public amusement of witness to their demise, but was richly informed in the details thereof by my keepers. Apparently, the strange young man who'd killed the boy went stoic and quiet, while the older man perished wailing for the beloved he had dispatched before him. Edgar went raging as usual—exhibiting a particular strength of opinion, as the law saw fit to commence the mortal ceremony with the carrying out of a lesser sentence involving the loss of both hands.

I wondered at the possible punishments available for the ravishment of serving wenches and theft of pewter tankards.

Yet more days passed, mysteriously without the addition of new companions—or the removal of myself to a place of judgment.

"Why am I left to molder?" I asked Mr. Franklin on his next visit. "The *Hannah* sits idle, without cargo or market. Our loss of profit could be considerable. Why am I not brought to trial?"

"Justice is taking her time," he said. "She awaits Smithson's pleasure."

"I thought his pleasure was a swift cessation of my respiration."

"He now reconsiders—or at least considers. He seeks the course that profits himself best."

"He's contrite, then? He suffers guilt for my predicament?"

"Not that selfish fellow. No, he's guided now by circumstances not of his contrivance. His daughter grieves for you. It's she who feels contrition for your present unhappiness, and it's she who's set herself to doing something about it." He produced from a pocket a letter, bound by ribbon, which he carefully undid. Then he handed it to my view, which I improved by moving closer to the pale light.

Addressed to me, it contained no confession of true fact as concerned the specific arrangements of our dalliance. It was indeed quite vague as concerned any meeting between us. It did, however, impart the sense that there were such meetings and that they were regular, of long standing, and most carnal. Susannah's words were powerfully sensual and intimate—even crude. This was a missive of extraordinary flagrancy—a worldly writing, the like of which I'd heard spoken of but never read, certainly not from a lady's hand. It was a communication one might expect from Franklin's friends in the Hellfire Association, written and read in the utmost secrecy.

"I cannot believe this," I said, staring at her signature, which was writ with the clearest, boldest hand. "Why would she write it?"

"She has wisdom, that lass. She wrote it with an eye to the court and its credulity. A simple protestation that you had not done the things her father claimed might be dismissed as a charitable mercy, perhaps borne of infatuation—the sweet lies of a young girl smitten. But these flaming words cannot be so easily dismissed. They attest to carnal knowledge of the most willing sort. Note that the clever girl has predated the letter for a time well preceding your return to Philadelphia."

"But what's the point of this? And how did it come to your hand? How could she . . ."

Franklin held the paper up as he might a magic wand, stilling my voice.

"This document would destroy the lady's honor and reputation beyond redemption and repair. She'd be damaged goods for any prospective suitor of this city. Whatever bountiful marriage alliance her father might contemplate would be for naught. She'd be as ruined and useless to him as spoilt milk to the dairyman. So she will be should this come to judicial eye or any other public view.

"Yet I think she had it brought to my hand, not to deliver it to that end, but to make it worrisome to her father. A mighty threat, is it not? And, in my possession, one beyond the reach of his paternal power."

I reached for it, but he pulled it away.

"No, young sir. You cannot keep this, warm thoughts though it might provide you. Smithson knows of it, and would have it from you easy, and then you'd see trial, judgment, and rope in quick succession."

I slumped back against the cool brick.

"I am vexed by that letter," I said. "It speaks too little of love and too much of 'fuck.' This is a maid of sixteen summers. I cannot imagine . . . I thought her coy and flirtatious, yes, but also virtuous and innocent."

"You mean virginal. And you know now your folly. She was educated in England. You cannot imagine the effect upon even the most noble young lady of the sexual experiences to be had there in these times, Captain Morley. I doubt any returns a virgin. And London thus quite spoils them all for the chaste, conservative life to be had in these colonies. I cannot comprehend how any maid with schooling there could be happy here. May our academies in these colonies prosper."

"She brought you that letter?" I asked.

"No. She sent it by means of a personal maid, one unblessed by the learning of reading."

I paused to vigorously scratch myself. This was not a happy abode for a man so fond of bathing.

"Her father—is he aware that the letter speaks truth? That she is so unchaste?"

"Doubtless painfully."

"What does he need to ponder, then?"

"He ponders whether I would do it—circulate this letter in the coffee houses, the public houses, as she has threatened him. Would I let it come to judicial eye? Destroy her marriage value? Turn her honor base?"

"But he thinks you might—to save a life. My life."

"Yes, I do believe he does. Hence this long passage of time as he weighs his course. He may be seeking some new advantage over us."

"Would you do that—ruin Susannah, for me?"

"No, young sir, I would not—friend that you have become to me. I could not do this to any lady, and I am fond of this one." Franklin returned the letter to his pocket. "But Smithson will not know that. Restrain your fears. While the threat holds, you still live. And I am hopeful we shall yet secure your deliverance. In the meantime, reflect on what you might learn from this."

"Learn? My prison has taught me that I do not like it."

" 'Experience keeps a dear school,' " said Franklin, " 'yet fools will learn in no other.' "

A roach crawled over my foot, pausing midway. I kicked it off.

On his next visit, Franklin brought me more to read—a letter to him from Major Washington. It was most verbose, if not well spelt, but contained news. The French had moved to the headwaters of the Ohio and were building forts between the forks of that river and Lake Erie. A fortification near or at the forks themselves, at the juncture of the Allegheny and Monongahela, was expected soon.

But there was encouraging news as well. Not all the native peoples were scurrying to the French. Among the Iroquois, the Half King, known also as Tanacharison, had gone to the wilderness town of Winchester as emissary of the Iroquois' Six Nations to meet with Colonel William Fairfax, father of Washington's friend George William Fairfax and father-in-law to Sally. The elder Fairfax went representing the colony as president of the governor's council. Such amity did flourish there with the Indians that Colonel Fairfax had become godfather to Tanacharison's son, giving him the name Dinwiddie.

The governor had been flattered and pleased by this, Washington said. He was now inclined to lean heavily on Colonel Fairfax's counsel in appointing a leader for an expedition to warn away the French—ultimately perhaps, to drive them away. Dinwiddie had asked the Lords of Trade in London for money to raise a force to build British forts on the Ohio. The enterprise needed only a bold man at its head to lead it forth into the wilderness, where glory and profit lay in abundance.

Exciting times these were for young militia officers of great ambition. Less so for fledging sea captains locked up and itching in dark dungeons.

The Major had inquired of Franklin after me, saying I had proved a capable fellow and boon companion. He raised a hope I did not yet share of seeing me again.

Two days later, Franklin returned with a small cask of rum—for warmth, as I found the nights now cold—and another letter, or rather, a copy of one he had written to another young man years before, a fellow sorely troubled.

"*Amour* had presented him with a predicament," Franklin said, "for he'd become much attracted to lovemaking and wished it in constant supply. There's counsel in this that I wrote him that may be of use to you— at such time as you might find yourself at liberty, as we so devoutly hope for."

I accepted the letter, several pages long, from his hand. The copy had been freshly inked on new paper. It bore the date June 25, 1745, but was addressed anonymously to "My dear Friend."

> *"I know of no Medicine to diminish the violent natural In-*
> *clinations you mention,"* it began, *"and if I did, I think I should*
> *not communicate it to you. Marriage is the proper Remedy. It*
> *is the most natural State of Man, and therefore the State in*
> *which you are most like to find solid Happiness. Your Reasons*
> *against entering into it at present, appear to me not well-*
> *founded."*

I'd been reading aloud. I lowered the letter and gasped in protest: "But I *would* enter into it! I love Susannah. This is hardly applicable."

Franklin frowned.

"Sir, there can be no such marriage. Is that not clear to you? Friend Smithson hovers between two fears—one, that should you be set free, you would immediately elope with his daughter or otherwise make off with her, and, two, that if he prosecutes you, she, or I, might reveal the contents of that scandalous letter. Nowhere in this will you find harbored an incli-nation to weddings. I offer this monograph of mine as helpful instruction. What's applicable in this dissertation, which I have entitled 'The Old Mis-tresses' Apologue,' is the rest of it—my advice on how you are to deal with those violent natural Inclinations with the beautiful Miss Smithson forever removed from your life. You will seek a new port for your vessel, and here I offer an experienced pilot's guidance."

He rose and shook my hand. "I wish you well, Thomas Morley. And a good night."

Another twinkly smile, and he turned and summoned the gaol keeper. In a moment, he was gone.

Moving slightly nearer the light, I took his letter up again and read, leaping past the thoughts on marriage to those on violent natural Inclina-tions, which commenced thus:

> *"But if you will not take this Counsel, and persist in think-*
> *ing a Commerce with the Sex inevitable, then I repeat my for-*
> *mer Advice, that in all your* Amours *you should* prefer old
> Women to young ones. *You call this a Paradox, & demand my*
> *Reasons. They are these:*
>
> "1. Because as they have more Knowledge of the World, and
>   their minds are better stor'd with Observation, their Con-
>   versation is more improving & more lastingly agreeable.
> "2. Because when Women cease to be handsome, they study to
>   be good. To maintain their Influence over Men, they supply
>   the Diminution of Beauty by an Augmentation of Utility.
>   They learn to do a 1000 Services small and great, and are
>   the most tender and useful of all Friends when you are sick.
>   Thus they continue amiable. And hence there is hardly such

a thing to be found as an old Woman who is not a good Woman.

"3. Because there is no hazard of Children, which irregularly produc'd may be attended with much Inconvenience.

"4. Because thro' more Experience, they are more prudent and discreet in conducting an Intrigue to prevent Suspicion. The Commerce with them is therefore safer with regard to your Reputation. And with regard to theirs, if the Affair should happen to be known, considerate People might be rather inclin'd to excuse an old Woman who would kindly take care of a young Man, form his Manners by her good Counsels, and prevent his ruining his Health and Fortune among mercenary Prostitutes.

"5. Because in every Animal that walks upright, the Deficiency of the Fluids that fill the Muscles appears first in the highest Part: The Face first grows lank and wrinkled; then the Neck; then the Breast and Arms; the lower Parts continuing to the last as plump as ever: So that covering all above with a Basket and regarding only what is below the Girdle, it is impossible of two Women to know an old from a young one. And as in the dark all Cats are grey, the Pleasure of corporal Enjoyment with an old Woman is at least equal, and frequently superior, every Knack being by Practice, capable of Improvement.

"6. Because the Sin is less. The debauching a Virgin may be her Ruin, and make her for Life unhappy.

"7. Because the Compunction is less. The having made a young Girl *miserable* may give you frequent bitter Reflections, none of which can attend the making an old Woman *happy*.

"8. thly & Lastly. They are *so grateful!!*"

Amused and charmed—and no little instructed—by this, I read it through again, then folded it to fit my ragged pocket. I knew no old Woman, as Franklin defined, save that practitioner of the Voudon who kept our Annapolis house. Unless by some stretch I might embrace Mistress Fairfax with this description, for she was now twenty and four years old.

———

That night I lay in my dirty straw, listening to Old Billy the night gaoler rummaging and clanking about. I thought of my last meeting with good Riggins, and in what bold, cavalier fashion we had discussed freeing whole shiploads of captive Negroes. Now, but for the lack of leg irons, I lay there as good as one myself. The principal difference was that the cold earthen floor did not heave and sway like a ship's planks belowdecks, and that those poor African passengers were seldom in receipt of gifts of rum casks.

Unable to sleep, I filled my drinking cup halfway with the liquor and huddled against the wall as I sipped it. I'd lost count of the days and nights I'd been kept in this place. Now here I was succumbed to my brother Richard's solace—strong spirits. Would I now beg for more from Franklin as my prison stay extended, till I was as puddled a mess of a man as my brother? Or would I do something resolute at last to free myself? I could not imagine Major Washington tolerating such a circumstance for long. He'd do something bold, without doubt.

Old Billy the gaoler was laughing again. I'd read him Franklin's dissertation and it had vastly amused him. Billy was as much a man for the lifted skirt as the dissertation's author. In fact, in one of our increasingly friendly and ribald conversations, Billy'd told me that he often crept down here from his quarters above at night when prisoners had had their wives to visit.

I gave him a cup of the rum and then bade him a good night as he finished his labors and returned upstairs. Then I sat staring at the opposite wall for the longest time. When I finally went to sleep, I think there must have been a smile upon my grimy lips.

———

It was a week before Franklin's next visit, or more. He brought no letters, but did provide another rum cask and issues of his newspaper. I begged him return again as soon as possible, bringing as large and as fine a bottle of brandy that he might possess or acquire, a fresh meat pie, and some sketching paper and lengths of charcoal.

"I shall repay you to the last penny," I said.

"No need of that," said Franklin. "Your deliverance from this predicament will be all the repayment I require. But bear in mind that these things cost dear and cannot be supplied regular."

"Well understood," I said. "I think I shall not be needing them again."

He was puzzled, but only briefly. Without inquiring further, he was off—and back in short time with all I'd requested.

"You spoke of repayment, Thomas Morley, and I of deliverance. If you should find yourself with opportunity to rejoin Major Washington in the service of our cause, and do so, then consider all acounts paid full."

———

I waited a day and a night more, eager for all circumstances to be just right. Mostly, I wished Old Billy in a mellow mood, no other prisoners about, and an hour when the town was quiet.

Fetching up the meat pie, I bade Billy take it upstairs to heat, for it had to be eaten soon and I wished we might share it. While he attended to that, I set about making a sketch of a woman. I'd scant practice with such subject, to be sure—artistically, at least—but certainly now I had a few memories to draw from. I gave the woman a bum most exquisite, then provided her and it with a most excited gentleman to balance the sketch.

I had feared Old Billy might just say to blazes with me and consume the pie all for himself upstairs—as good as a mile from my reach—but he was at heart a kindly soul and he did return, most astounded and pleasured by my drawing. I made him a gift of it.

Only a nibble of pie did I take, leaving him all the rest to eat, while I continued to draw. When I noted pie plate emptied but his belly full, I retrieved the brandy and bade him decant it. Again, I gave him the most generous share, continuing on with my naked ladies.

I took my time now, as I hadn't a lot of paper. He stared raptly, moving up close to the bars that made one entire wall of my part of the dungeon, and fetching a candle better to see my work. A violent man might have struck him right then and effected his end, but that was not my way. I let the brandy work its way as a gentler cudgel, and sure enough, Old Billy's eyes began to glaze, and eyelids droop and flutter. Soon he was asnore.

His keys were on a ring tied to his belt. There was a nervous moment as I pulled his body nearer to better grasp my object, but I had the knot undone with great celerity. Soon I was through the dungeon door, leaving him slumbering among a plenitude of illicit art. The poor man would have some explaining to do, but perhaps the good Mr. Franklin could intercede on his behalf, as he had on mine.

Eleven

You've an easy guess where I was headed. As Gist had turned to the wilderness for sanctuary from debtor's court and Royal writ, so might any man—at least one with George Washington a friend. Judging by his last communication, the Major was straining at the leash to bound across the mountains. My wisest course now seemed to be to join him in that journey to the far removes.

When free of the gaol, however, I wished first to stop at Mr. Franklin's house there in Philadelphia. I'd presumed from his most helpful visits he'd not mind my calling, especially as I was yet in extremis. My clothes were torn and ragged, and where not that, stiff with old sweat and dirt. They were also few—shirt, breeches, and linen small clothes not in the happiest state. It was October now, and the night air was chill. I had no shoes!

I waited in a hiding place—the same quiet churchyard where Mistress Smithson had bestowed upon me her first tendering of friendship—allowing any hue and cry over my absence from the prison to rise and pass. So satisfied, keeping to the shadows as much as possible, I followed back streets to the lane that led to Franklin's house—all without apparent detection. There were candles alight in windows both upstairs and on the street level, and smoke coming from two chimneys. My heart was made glad.

Prematurely so, alas. Reaching the door, I heard from within the most awful bellowing and caterwauling. I almost thought some foul play was at hand, but the imprecations were both familiar and domestic, most of them emanating from Mrs. Franklin. They continued without pause or diminishment, even when I knocked sharply on the door several times. I crept to the side of the house and lifted myself to peer within a high window, obtaining only a glimpse of Franklin and his Deborah in a room just beyond—he in agitated movement back and forth, she standing like some fortress—before the weakness of my grip compelled me to drop back to the ground.

I'd heard enough to ken that no guest this night was welcome. Their dispute sounded as though it turned on long-held grievance, but not, as I had supposed, some long-held wifely resentment of Franklin's patronage of Mistress Calderwill's amiable establishment. Both Franklins had what sounded just complaint: she of neglect, the superabundance of wifely chores, the lack of servants, and insufficient income to support his travels and sundry interests, plus their large household. He spoke ill of her coarse nature and common values, of her entangling him in grubby mercantilism, of her holding him back from any lasting fame or worthy accomplishment, that all he'd be remembered for would be his trade as printer and purveyor of salt fish and dry goods.

I had heard from my gaol keeper and others that Franklin held his wife in the most affectionate regard and that they had a brood of numerous children. I'd heard as well that one of Franklin's sons was of another mother but his Deborah had nobly agreed to the boy's adoption. I'd heard, too, that Franklin and Deborah, for all their years of habitude, had never legally wed.

A curious man indeed. I decided I'd not disturb him this night, or linger longer, lest some sighting of me in his precinct give voice to suspicions of his hand in my unexpected departure from behind municipal bars.

My bare feet suffering from the cold stones and hardened mud of the streets, I repaired to the Delaware River waterfront and the King's wharf, where after some careful, quiet search, I spied the *Hannah* tied fast among other small vessels and a man of the night watch idling at some distance along the quay.

There was no means of releasing the little sloop from its dockside bonds without attracting the watchman's attention, nor really any way to rig it and sail it by myself, even if I could manage to steer it free of surrounding craft. But, hopeful that not all its secrets had been discovered, I slipped aboard, broke open a shuttered hatch forward and crept into the sloop's well-remembered darkness. In the master's cabin, kept against all emergencies, including plunder, was a secret cache under a floorboard within the cupboard beneath the bunk. There, undiscovered, though much else in cabin and hold seemed missing, was a leather pouch containing slightly more than twenty English pounds in Spanish gold coin that I'd hidden toward some rainy day or maritime emergency. I'd not have to swim to Virginia, though my travel would have to be most circumspect.

My thoughts, of mixed flavors, were on Susannah as I left this city. She'd saved my life, I had no doubt. But what had moved her so? Love? Pity? Or some secret design? I had no expectation of a re-encounter, but knew not whether this should render me miserable or content. Either way, I knew she'd remain fixed in my memory.

––––

Twenty pounds in gold means little if one looks a beggar and must avoid all public view, though the latter concern eased once I had distanced myself from the city and was into the open country to the southwest. Judging that my pursuers would expect me to escape by sea or move along the coast, I chose instead an overland route that took me toward Lancaster, then south for Baltimore. I had a few small adventures, including a charming one with a widowed farmer's wife who graciously outfitted me in her late husband's ill-fitting best, seeking no other payment than my company, though I was more sparing with that than I judged she would have wished. There followed numerous progressions in slow country wagons, and some delay finding a ferry across the broad Susquehanna.

Baltimore was obtained without any notice of me taken by lawful authority. There I outfitted myself with much handsomer clothing and an aged but still ambulatory horse. Crossing the Patowmack above the fall line on the Frederick, Maryland, road, I reached Alexandria about noon of my eighth day of liberation, there to find Washington and seemingly every other gentleman of station well absent.

It was the "publick time" of the fall season. The House of Burgesses in Williamsburg was in session, and all the worthies of the colony gathered there for reasons official or social. The innkeeper at Alexandria's Gadsby's Tavern, known then by another name now beyond my recollection, said he was uncertain where, but Major Washington was most definitely gone on important Crown business.

But *all* his business was that, was it not?

I stopped at Mount Vernon, Washington's house at Hunting Creek, but only his sister-in-law and a visiting woman friend of hers were in residence, the former telling me the Major had ridden to Williamsburg, for how long a visit she knew not, except that he expected it to be brief, though his return would take some time, as he was volunteering himself in service to the King and governor.

She did not offer nor did I seek accommodation for the night, though I suppose it might have been provided, as she remembered me from before. I was anxious to rejoin Washington, but the prospect of another stay in his mother's house at Ferry Farm was most forbidding, should I find him there. So I hurried more hopefully to where I was sure there would be the best possible knowledge of his present and future whereabouts: the plantation Belvoir, not far along the southern road.

What luck. The mistress of the house was in and the master was not. George William Fairfax had ridden off to Williamsburg with his father, Colonel William Fairfax—the "important business" was stirring everyone of prominence and authority in Virginia. Wife Sally was to join him there in a few days, removing herself to the capital at a less harried pace by carriage, but here she was. Would I stay to sup with her? To take my night's rest at Belvoir? To accompany her the next morning on the road as far as Fredericksburg, where she, too, hoped to greet Mr. Washington, or farther, depending on where along the road the Major might be?

I am a most compliant person—especially when hungry and in need of a bath. And the lady one so lovely.

The requirements of chaste propriety that evening were addressed through an invitation dispatched by well-horsed servant to the same sister-in-law, Anne Washington, and her guest, a Mrs. Carter, to take supper at Belvoir. It was happily and readily accepted.

For all my licentious behavior heretofore chronicled, no thought of such possibility in this instance had crossed my mind and I was just as pleased to have such fit chaperones present. My Philadelphia torments had quite disengaged my mind from considerations of dalliance, for which at all events there was no real prospect with or without chaperones. As it was, I needed whatever wits I had about me just to keep up my manners, which had largely been learnt from books and proved clumsily performed in the actual practice.

These three ladies represented the highest quality to be had in the way of Virginia aristocracy. Sally Fairfax was a Cary, one of the noblest—as they styled such things—families in Williamsburg. Anne Washington was a Fairfax, about which clan you know aplenty. And Mrs. Carter, herself English-born and of proud lineage, had married a descendant of the tobacco empire's King Carter and bore one of the oldest names in the colony—not to speak of one of the greatest fortunes. All three were my elder, with Sally the closest in age to me at five years senior.

I knew not whether to play the humble recipient of roadside charity, the eager and artless boy, or the worldly sea captain who could discourse upon the exotic excitements of Caribbean isles and Carolina coast—not to speak of bustling Philadelphia. As it developed, I took turns at all three—the latter role drawn out from me by Mistress Sally, who kept full rein on flirtation, but otherwise let fly more than charm enough to keep the evening at full sail. Mrs. Carter, for her part, was tittery, whilst Anne Washington seemed somber, not unreasonably, given the recentness of her husband's passing.

Following dinner, coffee and chocolate were served in the upstairs central hall, and the ladies engaged me in a game of whist, with most of our play devoted to my instruction, as I had little experience with the diversion. There was scant talk of the French and Indian menace looming over the mountains. Rather, the women wanted to know in most particular all I could tell them about Philadelphia's new Dancing Assembly, in which the ladies and gentlemen attending were made partners by the drawing of lots, and remained so for an entire evening. The custom attendant upon this was for the gentleman and lady who had thus passed the dancing hours, strangers that they might be, to have tea together the following day. Susannah, lying naked in my arms, had gone on and on about it.

I hadn't opportunity to discuss my troubles with the law with Sally, whom I now viewed as good friend. The two other women stayed the night and all company retired early, as Sally meant to rise at dawn for her journey to Williamsburg, having yet many preparations to complete. I was accorded the same bedchamber usually given to Major Washington on his overnight visits. I took note that it was directly across the main upstairs hall from the master of Belvoir's bedroom. As fearless and foolish as the Major and Sally might be, neither was so bold or brazen, I was sure, to take advantage of that geography. But it occurred to me that Washington's mind must have been plagued by the most vexing thoughts as he lay in this bed alone—just a few paces and a thickness of wood distant from his dearest desire.

———

The morning commenced warm and bright, offering a good dry day for travel. Sally had a small entourage—a coachman, two armed manservants riding horseback at the rear, and a maid. The latter rode in the carriage with her, in the rearward-facing seat, so our conversation was of necessity circumscribed. The journey would be long—to Dumfries by the first night, Fredericksburg the next. From there, Mrs. Fairfax would have two days to Richmond, and then another two—with good weather—to Williamsburg.

I knew not where in all this we'd encounter the Major, who could be either in Fredericksburg or Williamsburg, or around the next bend.

Once on the road, I told Sally of all my troubles in Philadelphia. Did I tell you I knew the French language? Not so well then as now, but I had command enough to make myself understood in some complexity, and Sally had the knack as well. With that advantage and the artful use of elliptical English, I managed to recount my misadventures concerning Susannah Smithson and explain my present fugitive status without the black girl kenning much notion of it.

Sally seemed sympathetic to my plight, but was not immediately responsive. She put tooth to lip for a moment, then leaned out the coach window and called to the driver to stop. As we had begun the slow ascent of a long rise, our movement ceased at once.

She opened the door herself and alighted, bidding me to follow.

"I will walk to the top of the hill," she said to the coachman. "Await us there."

She bade them all move along. We followed at a distance well out of hearing, at an ambling pace. The road was a well-traveled one, the principal route from Alexandria to Fredericksburg, but the earth was lumpy and full of stones. She held my arm as we proceeded.

"You were treated unjustly by both daughter and father, I think," she said. "But it was your own reckless dash into the brush that caught you up in the snare. You seem to me a prudent young man, Thomas. Certainly I have had cause to rejoice in your discretion and good judgment. How could you do this?"

"*Amour* is a powerful master, Mrs. Fairfax."

"So is selfishness. Your leap at this lady was utterly without any due regard to her situation."

"Situation? Her father was away in Baltimore—or so I had understood."

"Her situation, sir, was and is that she is a lady and unmarried."

"Madam, it was precisely that *situation* I hoped to undo. I asked her to marry me, but she put me off."

Sally's grip tightened on my arm, in earnestness, and she turned to face me. "Comprehend me, sir. The heart does flutter many times in life, as yours has done, and mine."

My heart was fluttering just then.

"But marriage is until death, and a contract of the greatest consequence," she continued. "Whatever else you may know of me, know that I was born to be a Fairfax. A fate happily met and kept."

I sought her eyes. I wished to ask how happily, and how long kept. I think she sensed this. Turning her eyes from mine, she continued with her instruction—as though all I'd seen between her and the Major were just imagined fancy.

"This lady, Thomas—and know that I bear you much affection though we are so recently met—but Thomas, she was not born to be the wife of an Annapolis sloop captain, if you are even that."

I could have angered and blurted some nonsense. Instead, I caught my breath and said: "Her father is a mere merchant."

Ha! There a stab at Virginia prejudice. In that colony, ever aping the mother country, the aristocracy viewed itself as cultivated from the soil. To the landowners, mere merchants, traders, and sea captains are all of the same class as tinkers and innkeepers, if not worse.

"A very rich merchant, Thomas. And in Philadelphia, that counts for much—a high station. You could have had no hope of what you asked of her. You endangered her sorely, to be so careless of her situation. Hence the severity of your punishment."

"Penance of sin."

"Precisely." She urged us forth up the hill, her hand still upon my arm. "I would ask my family and my husband's to bring some influence on your behalf, as I know you otherwise blameless of these high crimes of which you stand accused. But I fear . . . 'twould not be wise to explain too well how I come to be in your obligation. Best this be asked for you as the Major's friend, and not mine.

"Still, I would help you, and will do for you what I can. But you, Captain Morley, steer you a course that leaves that proud lady over the horizon. Find you a port more suiting. A gentleman of your attractions need not look long." She paused, stood tiptoe to kiss me on the cheek—to reassure me, I supposed, of her friendship—then hurried us on again up the slope.

So there I was, armed with Franklin's advice to take an old mistress, and Mrs. Fairfax's to find one poor. Some sage would likely next suggest I find one lame and sickly as well, or ugly.

No matter. Sally was being kind to me, and I was grateful.

"I have a small present for you," I said, "in my traveling bag."

"You need your money, Thomas."

"That's small concern, my lady."

Along with the twenty pounds in Spanish coins, I had taken from the *Hannah* all else remaining in the master's cabin—that amounting to just three books that I had set there, having "borrowed" them from a small box of odd cargo.

The first was Marcus Porcius Cato's *De Agri Cultura*—this, mind, being Marcus Porcius Cato the Elder, he of the great and lasting prose, not Cato the Younger, the minor Roman poet. Then also I'd "borrowed" Samuel Richardson's light and sentimental novel *Pamela*, having much enjoyed his *Clarissa* and *Sir Charles Grandison*.

Lastly, I'd purloined—though borrowed with all good intention of putting back—Racine's play *Phèdre*. Mistress Fairfax seemed to speak more excellent French than I. This would be her gift.

But it was not to be bestowed in the gallant manner I was preparing for. I've said I'd hoped to encounter Major Washington on that road. Well, this was not the desired time or place, but here he came cantering over the crest of the hill where the coach awaited us, hesitating only briefly upon recognizing the ownership of the conveyance, and then resorting to full gallop upon sighting the owner herself where we stood a good way down the hill.

The Major was in a crowd of horses and men. On clattering mounts behind him were two black manservants, each clutching the lead to a trailing packhorse. To his side and slightly to the rear was a stout but tall white man, well mounted.

They all came to a stop before us in a great cloud of dust, which Sally, shielding her eyes with one hand, tried to wave away with the other. Washington seemed chagrined by her discomfort, but unsure what to do. Four expressions hurried quickly over his face—the change from heroic pose to embarrassment to sour suspicion at my presence to mannered gentlemanliness. He alighted with a thud and swept his tricorne from his head in a gallant gesture.

"Mrs. Fairfax, good day. My humblest apology for the dust."

It was still hanging in the air. Through it, I noted that the Major wore a wide leather belt with a huge flintlock pistol stuck into its fastness. He was in the uniform of a Virginia militia major: dark blue tricorne hat and coat, red breeches and waistcoat with gold trim and buttons, simple white stock, the silver gorget indicating his officer's rank hanging 'round his neck by a stout cord. There were muskets strapped to the back of one of the packhorses. This was a young man off to war. But there was none, was there?

"You are forgiven, Major," Sally said with a slight cough. "I'm sure that you were spurred forth by the pleasure to be had in my company."

Exactly so. Washington bowed deeply, thus averting his face and allowing time to search for some eloquence in reply.

He found none, muttering, "Always a pleasure, madam." But he resumed his stance with his face now blessed with the happiest, boyish, closed-mouth grin—which I'm sure gladdened Mrs. Fairfax more than could have any graceful arrangement of mere words.

The grin faded as his eyes caught mine. "And Captain Morley here? How strange. I wrote to this gentleman at Annapolis, yet received no reply—save later word from mariners who heard tell of him voyaging to the Caribbean. And that was months ago. Now here he stands."

"The captain's had some sorrowful times," said Sally. "As I'm sure he'll be obliged to relate when you have some leisure. He came to Virginia seeking you, sir, and has kindly honored me with his escort as far as Fredericksburg, where he hoped to find you."

"But now you shall have a proper escort, and all the way to Williamsburg."

"That's very gallant, George, but too generous. I know the urgency of your business. You must be about it. But I should be most grateful for your company as far as Dumfries. I do enjoy it. Then we can each of us go where we should."

"And Captain Morley?"

"As I say, he would be with you."

———

And so I was displaced. Washington's great, creaking weight slid onto the coach seat that had been mine and there he sat with her the whole long, slow, hilly way to the tavern north of the Rappahannock that bore the Dumfries name. I, relegated to the less charming company of the other men, rode glumly behind, inhaling more dust.

The stout white man in Washington's party was an Abraham Van Braam—Washington always spelt it all one name, "Vanbraam"—of Fredericksburg. The fellow was a teacher, of all things, instructing in foreign languages and fencing, and counting, in the latter regard, Washington as one of his pupils. Van Braam had considerable military education, having served some years in the Dutch Army. Some of this service had been in wars fought against the English Crown, as the Dutch were always fighting, but this apparently was no obstacle now to serving Washington in his mission.

The Dutchman was not verbose, and after introducing himself, rode along content with his own thoughts. As I was to later learn, he was no better a speaker of foreign tongues than English, save his native Dutch, and thus clumsy at translation, the task for which Washington had hired him. I tried speaking a few words of French with him, without much success. I wasn't sure whether the lack was in his part or mine.

I gave Mrs. Fairfax her book upon our leave-taking. She professed to be delighted with it, and there was again a kiss on the cheek. Her farewell to the Major also involved *un baiser sur la joue* as well, but one much sweeter and most reluctantly withdrawn from by both. It was also accompanied by the warmest embrace of body and arms permitted in such a public circumstance.

———

I had given Washington the Cato volume in the same instance, but he'd simply nodded his thanks, sticking the book into his saddlebags.

Later, with Mrs. Fairfax well behind us, and my rump and legs already quite sore with the pace the Major was setting, he finally slowed his horse to a walk and bade me come up alongside. He held the book before him, squinting at the cover.

"I am not well acquainted with the Latin, Captain Morley," he said.

"It's about farming, and the verities of a farmer's life," I said. "Only the title's in Latin. The text is an English translation, except for a Latin phrase here and there that eluded the translator's grasp."

"Farming?"

"In the Roman sense—farming as what you Virginians do on your plantations is farming."

"Hmmm." He dropped his reins to the pommel and began leafing through the pages.

"I've not read it myself, but I'm told 'tis highly regarded, as was the author. It's his only complete surviving text."

"And you would give this to me?"

"Yes. I could think of no volume more meet to your life's occupation."

It occurred to me he might consider a military book more appropriate for that description, but he continued looking through *De Agri*, then gently closed it and returned it to his saddlebag.

"I thank you, sir." He looked at me then indulgently, elder to boy. "Now what do you wish of me? After so long a disappearance."

"You are going into the mountains, into that wild country, on King's business?"

"I am."

"I wish to go with you."

He looked at me dubiously, and now with some displeasure. He had truly not been happy to find me with his Sally. I could deal two blows with but one swing here—explain my presence truly, and allay his dark suspicion as well.

"I've serious reason," I said. "I'm in love, but it's all gone bad."

"Love?" A deep frown now.

"With a young beauty of Philadelphia."

The frown vanished.

"She's a lady of wealth and charms almost as plentiful as your . . . Mrs. Fairfax's. This girl and I, I do confess she took me to her bedchamber, or one convenient. It's an old story, I suppose, though the first time happening to me. I was discovered by her father, a mean and powerful man. Failing to kill me, he had me jailed, and so I am fugitive from there—at liberty now only thanks to a friend you yourself have acquired through correspondence."

"Mr. Franklin?"

"Yes. My eventual fate is most uncertain, but I know it will be a better one in those woods and mountains than on coastal roads within reach of Philadelphia. If you'd allow, if I could perform some service for our Sovereign—assist you in some way—I would count it as the best fortune had by me in many weeks."

"How do you know of my mission for the King?"

"I don't in any exact sense. It's my surmise from your own words to me and what I've heard in public houses and from Mr. Franklin. It goes worse now on the frontier?"

"And worse yet to be." His horse began to quicken the pace of its walk. "The damned French are taking over everything. I'll tell you more in full, precise detail when it becomes convenient. For now, Tick, you should be warned this is an undertaking of the most extraordinary importance and deepest gravity. It's damned dangerous and full of hardship. The roughest imaginable country. Murderous Indians. The treacherous French. A vastness of uncharted territory. We might not come back."

A sailor says that to himself upon leaving every anchorage.

I glanced at one of the packhorses. It was bearing two large casks of wine.

"But if you're willing to brave these rigors and dangers and can keep up with us and will obey all commands necessarily given, then, hell yes, Thomas Morely, I'd be damned glad of your company. Vanbraam here's an old friend and a fine fellow, but not talkative. It's a damn long ride I've got here. You've no idea. When I wrote you in Annapolis, it was in prospect of having this mission, and inviting you to come with me on it."

"It's no matter now that I'm a fugitive from prison?"

"Not to me. Not to Virginia. I carry a commission from Governor Dinwiddie himself. It empowers me to engage whomever I will. I'll need more men than three, Tick, before this is done."

With that, he put heel to horse and was off at a mad gallop toward the next curve in the road. As always when with him, I struggled to keep up.

Twelve

Governor Dinwiddie had selected George for the mission into the Ohio without hesitation, but principally because he was strongly urged to do so by Sally's father-in-law, Colonel William Fairfax. Both father and son Fairfax were among the weighties assembled in Williamsburg in response to the frontier emergency. The House of Burgesses had just the day before gone into session. All this the Major related to me—in bits and pieces, and phrased most carefully—as we proceeded westward toward the mountains.

King George, exasperated by the French and vexed by reports of rampages by the savages, had commanded that funds be placed in Dinwiddie's hands for the protection of the colony and his subjects within, and for the establishment of a British military presence in the valley of the Ohio.

Military stores would follow, though not troops, as at this point His Majesty was willing to rely on colonial militia in all measures of defense. Dinwiddie was to send letters under the Royal Seal to inform his fellow governors of these actions and the need for them.

Of more moment, Dinwiddie was also sending under the King's Seal a stern message to the French to cease all construction of forts, destroy what structures had been built, and remove themselves from south of the Great Lakes and return to Canada. It was Washington who now carried that message in a leather pouch on his belt, to be delivered to the senior French officer commanding in the Ohio country, a general named Pierre Paul, *Sieur de Marin*.

Washington had another task on this mission as well, and it would compound the hazard. He was to be a spy.

"Those French will not heed us," the Major said. "I'm sure of it. They'll not budge. If they lay down their axes and hammers, it'll be to take up muskets. We must know how strong the French, how many their Indians, of what design their forts and how numerous, what war canoes, supply routes, artillery. I'm to bring back answers, maps, lists. A full report. We must keep sharp eye and remember well everything we see."

I looked to the guns on his packhorse. "The French won't take us for a war party? For spies?"

"Sir, I travel as an envoy of His Majesty the King. I carry diplomatic papers. They dare not impede or harm us."

I'd later mark those words well. "Will their Indians observe such niceties—respecting diplomatic parties?" I asked.

He paused, frowning. "I would have that hope."

———

We pressed on along the dusty road for all that day and into the night, passing by Belvoir and Mount Vernon without so much as "Hallo," not stopping for sleep until Alexandria.

I was desperate for it. My gaol stay had weakened me prodigiously, and as I've explained earlier, I had small talent for the horse. At the canter, I still rode gripping the saddle pommel.

The Alexandria inn where we stayed was not badly crowded, with so many now gone to the capital, and we were able to obtain a room with a bed for the three of us. Van Braam fell snoring almost at once. I wished to follow, but Washington was in a mood to talk. He wanted to know what it was like with Susannah that long afternoon up in the servants' quarters. I told him enough to satisfy manly curiosity.

There were two roads that led west from Alexandria into the mountains. We took the more southern and direct route, which crossed the first line of the Blue Ridge at Ashby's rather than Vestal's Gap, as surveyor Washington elaborately explained when we finally drew nigh that long rise. He had been this way before, most notably when, hardly more than a boy, he'd undertaken a long surveying journey in the company of Sally's husband George William Fairfax, whereby this land had been mapped and their friendship lastingly cemented.

This Piedmont was pleasant, rolling country, with many open meadows and farms between the sprawling forests—most of the trees still bearing the gold and crimson colors of the season, though the autumn was now well advanced. The mornings were damned chill, but the sun shone brightly most of the time and kept us warm on the road.

As we drew westward and higher in elevation, the big plantations vanished behind us, giving way to ever smaller farms. The people seemed poorer, dressed in rougher clothes, and sometimes barefoot despite the weather. My own secondhand Baltimore suit seemed quite the noble finery in comparison. We encountered no coaches, only wagons. And, except for the Major's two servants, I saw no Negroes.

Once through Ashby's Gap, we descended through long folds of hill and entered upon the flat expanse of the great Shenandoah Valley he had described, bordered on the distant horizon by another high, blue-gray ridge and cloven south of us by a sharp-edged mountain that rose from the fields like the prow of a great ship.

"This is the northern end of the Shenandoah," Washington said at a pausing, speaking as though he were proprietor. "The Great Valley of Virginia. I know of no man who's traveled its length, though I suppose the Indians have done so. Hundreds of miles it is to the other end, perhaps a thousand or more, terminating in southern mountains that the Indians say are perpetually on fire. Here in the north, though, there is much cultivation and settlement—Scots and Irish in good number, and many, many Germans. They have more commerce with Philadelphia and Baltimore than with the ports of Virginia. They keep no slaves. They are without much manners. But they're friendly enough, and I fear for them. Any war with the French would come to them quickly."

"How far from here to the French?" I asked.

With a quick little grin, Washington faced toward what I judged by the sun's position to be the northwest. "Several weeks' ride, Tick. You see that higher summit, that which sits forward of the others along that ridge?"

I nodded.

"We steer by that and pass beyond—over many, many mountains. Once down into the valley of the Ohio, we make for the Forks and from there strike north for the French forts. Gist writes of three now in place: Venango, Le Boeuf, and Presque Isle on the Lake Erie."

I envisioned a very cold place. It was now November. I looked again at that summit to the northwest. I do not know why, but I had been thinking we had traveled the better part of our way. Several weeks?

Ah well, 'twas better than gaol straw.

Or would it be? Susannah seemed very far away.

———

By ferry, we crossed a lovely river, that which gives its name to the Shenandoah Valley and flows into the Patowmack at what Washington described as a glorious confluence of rivers and mountains. We made no digression to see this wonder, but the Major did stray from our route in two regards.

First, once across it, we followed the Shenandoah River downstream for a half day's ride, coming at length to a sharp bend to the right. At this point, Washington took us left through woods and out upon a high-grass meadow. This time it was meet that he acted as though he owned it, for he did. This was his Bullskin Tract, which he had come by through inheritance and purchase through quit rents. I knew little of such things, but it struck me as rich ground indeed, its only lack that of proximity to seaports and the amenities of civilization.

Returning upriver, we parted again from the road—now a rude trail—in a southwesterly way, coming at length to our destination for that night, Greenway Court, the country seat of none other than the great Lord Thomas Fairfax, proprietor of all Northern Virginia.

In its way, his high-roofed house was as grand an English country manor as you'd expect to find on the western shores of the Atlantic, with stables and numerous outbuildings and an avenue of sugar trees leading to its front door. And this was the wilderness! No woman was to be seen, but there were two Indians lounging by the fence of His Lordship's paddock—the first I'd ever observed at firsthand.

Unfortunately, they withdrew at our approach, slipping into the shadows of the gathering dusk. I could not say what might have repelled them. They did not return during our overnight stay, but the absence of Indians was not a lack we would suffer long.

I'd expected Lord Fairfax to be as imposing as his residence and doubtless as grandly a snob as his nephew, if not more so, but he was nothing of the sort. There was a vagueness, a paleness, a lack of substance to young

George William Fairfax, reminding one of a painter's canvas only just begun. His Lordship bore a definite resemblance to his kinsman, but differed in being so fully etched and colored—a most completed work. His eyebrows were thick and dark, his blue eyes bright and burning, his lips and jowls emphasized with deep lines, his chin bold. He had not shaved that day, or for several preceding. He wore a wig, but it wasn't elaborate. His leather breeches and waistcoat could have been a farmer's.

Once he'd ascertained there were no women in our party, His Lordship bade us come inside with great welcome and treated us to a most convivial evening, with food and drink flowing in abundance, a huge fire ablaze at the central hearth, great romping dogs, and hearty laughter. At an opportune moment, when His Lordship and I were standing together by the fire, I asked about the Indians, for they fascinated me considerable. He explained they were his friends. Had they not been, they would not have ventured this far out of the mountains, he said. They found the white man far too numerous down here on the plain.

"Treat them as men when you meet them," Fairfax sternly advised, "for that is what they are. He who would exalt his own race over another in this country is a fool. Young Washington there. He's a good fellow. A brave one. I like him well. But he knows too little about these people, and misjudges them. I fear he condescends. In the mountains where you'll travel, in the lands beyond, these Indians are much your superior. It's a lesson that can be taught harshly."

"Will they take the King's side if there's war with the French?"

He took a big swallow of ale, then belched. "Some will. Many won't. Is Major Washington intending to engage Christopher Gist as guide?"

"I believe that's his plan."

"He'd be a great fool to advance one foot past Will's Creek and not do so. And you, young man—George says you're called Tick. You'd best be a tick in the hide of Mr. Gist. He'll see you through this with your scalp intact if you'll heed what he tells you." Fairfax leaned close. "Best you can, in the event of dispute, bend young George in the direction of Gist's counsel. You understand me?"

"Yes, m'lord."

"You promise?"

"Yes m'lord."

He thumped me on the back and called for more ale. How far I'd risen, gaol or no. Friend to Mr. Franklin, guest of Governor Dinwiddie, now I could claim the amity of the mightiest Fairfax. Brother Richard and beloved Susannah ought be be magnificently impressed—were there any chance of their ever again speaking with me.

Retiring for the night, we found ourselves sharing a bedchamber but accorded the luxury of individual beds. I asked Washington the source of His Lordship's aversion to the fair sex.

"When he was young and a mere baronet," said the Major, "he was left at the altar by an intended who at the last moment decided it wiser to marry a duke."

"And he's hated all women ever since? For this one rejection?"

"Perhaps he loved her. If you have many more experiences such as you've just enjoyed in Philadelphia, Tick, you might have reluctance for womanly company yourself."

Ha to that. I wondered if His Lordship's aversion extended even to the charming Sally, and how a man of his aristocratic breeding could prefer the company of savages to hers. A strange land, this part of America. It was to grow stranger still.

———

From Lord Fairfax's, it was a short day's ride to the town of Winchester, a place in almost its entirety of log buildings and possessing the first frontier blockhouse I had seen. There was a well-stocked stable and a sutler's, and the Major used a letter of credit issued by the governor's palace to reprovision and re-equip us, tendering the King's generosity to my own humble person as well. He had my tiring nag replaced with a fresh mount, and acquired what he called "Indian clothes" for me and himself—thick buckskin trousers, warm fringed shirts, and matching deerhide caps—such as half the men in this town were wearing.

Additionally, I received from him a heavy blanket, a rifle, powder and ball, and a hunting knife. With all aboard my horse, I felt almost a medieval knight.

Shortly after we departed Winchester, which in complaint at its rudeness the Major described as "a vile hole," it commenced to rain, a cold, driving inclemency that abated only to renew itself with greater force a few minutes later. The now leafless trees provided small protection. Our progress degenerated to a succession of shelterless miseries, each longer than the other, slowing to a painful trudge as the now rocky trail climbed higher into the mountains. At some points it disappeared altogether, compelling the Major to backtrack through the wet, whipping brush and brambles to rediscover it. One such errant wandering cost us a good eight miles.

"Fucking horrible country," Van Braam kept saying, with his thick accent. I wondered if he would last the journey.

We crossed the Cacapon—a simple stream no doubt in normal times, but with these relentless rains, much swollen—then followed it downstream to the rude, fortified trading post that was Enoch's Fort. From there, we crisscrossed our way up and over a high, well-forested ridge, descending to the Patowmack and following its course west to a point opposite Thomas Cresap's Fort.

I was astonished at how narrowly the Patowmack flowed at this elevation, and at how roughly—its rising waters battering against rocks and boulders most vehemently. The rain had stopped, though the skies remained gunmetal gray. Washington had us make camp while we waited for the water to fall, though the warmly inviting structure that was our night's destination lay not much more than a hundred yards across the roiling river.

Clad now in his leather "Indian clothes" against the diminishing temperature and increasing wind, the Major suggested a walk along the shore. There was no trail here, and it was hard going. We'd leap from hillock to hillock over swampy mush, clambering over numerous fallen trees and dodging bramble. Finally, Washington stopped and took a seat upon a thick fallen log, bidding me sit beside him. The view was straight downstream.

"You know how far we are from the sea, Tick?" he asked.

I shrugged, then said, "From the sea or the Chesapeake?"

"More than a hundred miles as a bird flies from here to Alexandria," he said. "Much more than that by road, and as you have seen, the greater length of it passable only by horses, not carriage or wagon, and some of it at times not passable at all." His gaze was fixed upon the cold, rushing water. "Think how swiftly we could run the trip if we could use the river."

"It looks all rapids. There are rapids just upstream from Alexandria."

"There are rapids intermittently, but there's slack water enough as well."

"Enough for what?"

"A canal, Tick. Think upon it. A canal to run along this riverbank and bypassing every fall and rapid all the way down to the Patowmack's tidal waters. You'd open this country, wide and fast, with such a canal. You'd have a great parade of settlers marching into the Ohio, as day follows day."

And if sailing ships could fly, you'd have them there the faster.

I rose and touched his shoulder. "I'm dreadful cold, sir. Let's return to the fire."

———

The river level fell sufficiently for a fording, which we made just at dark, and we were able to pass the night in the warmth of Thomas Cresap's establishment, our wet clothes drying dankly by the fire. After breakfast, encouraged by news from Cresap that Gist and several traders were in residence at Will's Creek, we set out for it.

Following Cresap's instruction, we took a trail that crossed the Patowmack twice again at easy fords—leaving Maryland for Virginia and then to Maryland once more—to avoid a deep place where the wide stream that's called Will's Creek flows into the river.

The settlement actually occupied both sides of the Patowmack, at either end of the last ford. On the Maryland side was the larger part of it, built around the Ohio Company storehouse and ordinary. On the Patowmack side in Virginia were a large building and two small ones, the whole of that known as the "new storehouse." The business of the settlement was Indian trade and equipage for traders, trappers, and settlers. I thought that if the French could be removed and the settlers invited into this vast valley of which they spoke, Will's Creek could become a town or city with some swiftness—though one too far from the sea to suit my pleasure.

We passed by the new storehouse, seeing only three or four white men and as many Indians, offering them a few words of greeting and splashing on across the river to the main settlement—then swinging left into the woods to approach its palisaded log wall from the west side.

I saw then the most amazing thing of this whole journey, at least that far. A lean and lithe young maiden with long, dark hair streaming back over her homespun dress came leaping and dashing through the woods as nimble as a deer. In hot pursuit of a half-grown horse, she chased the thing in zigs and zags from our right to left and, coming to a winding lane with bordering rail fence, leapt over it without breaking stride or putting hand to wood.

"If she does that again," I said, in odd impulse, "I'll marry her."

Washington watched as fascinated as I, then clapped me on the shoulder. The lass had harried the colt into a sudden doubling back. It went over the fence—and so once more did she!

"Well now, Tick. You've made a vow I'll see you keep."

Thirteen

Christopher Gist was by way of being the founder of the Will's Creek settlement, having built for the Ohio Company the trading post and small ordinary that was its principal structure and place of commerce on the Maryland side. Though he'd moved to his "new plantation" on the other side of the mountain ridges to the northwest, he kept a small cabin at Will's Creek among the several that had sprung up since—most of them inside the village's log stockade.

His dwelling was just at the eastern edge of the settlement, along the river but within the palisade. It was to that place that Washington brought our small party after receiving directions to it from a couple of coarse fellows who greeted us at the gate. Before we could dismount, we were greeted again by another but not quite so pretty woodland sprite who came running pell-mell out the door of the cabin and up to Washington's horse, exclaiming, "Welcome, sir. We been expecting you."

The Major removed his hat in a gallant sweep, despite the resuming rain, and even bowed a little in the saddle. Charming fellow, George, when there was a lady about.

As I say, the maid was not quite so comely as the marvelous fleet-footed horse chaser, but certainly a handsome lass, tall and slim, with long reddish hair and freckly pale skin. She introduced herself as Christopher Gist's daughter Anne, saying her father was briefly absent on a visit to a nearby Indian camp. She bade us enter her father's cabin. Nearly all her words were addressed to Washington. She smiled at him as the sun shines on the earth. I think he was a little discomfited by this female admiration, but not much.

We gathered inside around the cabin's rude table, all of us adrip and smelling of horse and wet. The girl had us sit and brought us some roast meat fresh from the spit, rough corn bread, and some even rougher corn whiskey. We fell to it with great appetite; to Washington's mind, too great. " 'Feed not with greediness,' " he admonished Van Braam, his former teacher. "It is, sir, a rule of civility."

Van Braam gave him a lizard's look and kept on. We were into seconds by the time the door swung open and Gist himself came into the room.

He damn near filled it. The man was equal to Washington's great height, and broader in the shoulders. Where the Major was a commanding figure, Gist positively loomed. In part, it was his wildness. His dark hair was long, and he had a full, gray-streaked beard. His large eyes were wary, much like a wild creature's. As he came through the door, they'd darted quickly over each one of us, making quick assessment. His nose was high and narrow, remindful of a hawk's beak. Washington had told me Gist was forty-eight years old, an old man by many a measure. Yet he stood as straight and strong as a tree. Even my good Riggins would have thought twice or thrice before rushing into a fight with this "old" man.

On his feet were strange, high-topped shoes of thick black leather that fastened at the sides with metal buttons. He wore as well thick woolen leg wrappings, a buckskin coat that reached to mid thigh, long leather gloves, a woolen scarf, and a large fur cap. He carried a buckskin pouch and powder horn on a beaded Indian belt around his waist, which also bore a pistol and a wide-bladed knife longer than a bayonet and held in a beaded, Indian-made sheath.

Washington rose, introduced himself, and handed Gist a letter from Dinwiddie. Pulling off his fur cap, Gist took it to the fireside to read, squinting.

"Seems agreeable to me," he said finally, glancing back at the Major. "The compensation is fair—not generous, but reasonable. Am I to pilot you to the Forks or the French forts? That's not said clearly."

"You're to conduct me to the French commander in the Ohio country, a General Marin, I believe, wherever he may be. If we tarry here long, there may be a French fort at the Forks by the time we reach it."

"We'll leave in the morning," Gist said. "They got no fort up yet. You want to add more men to your party?"

"Yes. If there are good men to be had."

We had seen clumps of woodsy fellows camped around the Ohio Company warehouse, the principal structure in the settlement.

"There's a couple good ones. Maybe more. You bought horses in Winchester? Arms and provisions?"

"Yes."

"Better you'd bought 'em here—from me. I charge a fair price."

"Next time, perhaps. Depending on our needs."

"I got more necessities available up at my plantation. It's on the Youghiogheny, just past the last mountain ridge we're to cross. We'll pass it on the way to the Forks. If you need more mounts or baggage animals, there they'll be."

"A reassurance, sir."

Gist handed back the letter. "Dinwiddie says you'll want Indians on this party—friends to the Crown. Half King's at Logstown now, or maybe at his hunting cabin at Little Beaver Creek. He's a sachem of the Iroquois. Sachem, chief—they both mean the same. Some hold a sachem some sort of holy man and a regular chief one who leads warriors, but it ain't so. Sachems and chiefs are all the same and some of them are women. Powerful man, Half King, in the political way. Good he's our friend."

"I am aware of him," Washington said. "He is a friend to the Fairfaxes. How far is Logstown?"

"Beyond the Forks. Downriver on the Ohio maybe fifty mile, but there the river flows northwest, so it's on the way more or less to the French forts. Little Beaver Creek's fifteen mile from that."

The Major frowned. "Any Indians nearer?"

"Plenty, but none so friendly or useful as Half King. We'll hold a council at Logstown and see which way they're all leanin'. Half King'll be a help in that, but you'll need some wampum belts and tobacco and trade goods for gifts."

"I bought some of that in Winchester."

"You'll need more than what you got on those pack animals out there. Don't worry. You can buy it from me."

Gist took a cup of whiskey from his daughter. Then, the vessel quickly drained, he led Washington outside for the procurement of the rest of our party. I followed, leaving Van Braam the linguist to his preference, which was sleep.

There weren't but a dozen or more permanent structures in Will's Creek then, aside from the Ohio Company warehouse. Five of the buildings were set near it at the confluence of the creek and the Patowmack, the rest situated wherever their builders fancied.

It was to Mr. Ennis's ordinary that I was inclined, but not before Washington concluded his business. Gist led us to the encampments by the warehouse and called forth a few prospective recruits. Those he summoned did not come to us with any great enthusiasm, nor did those ignored seem much despondent at being left at their fires.

As "servitors," as Washington described them, Gist proposed a Barnaby Currin and a John MacGuire, both woodsies in quite filthy garments. He also produced Indian traders Henry Steward and William Jenkins, and as overseer of the lot, another trader named William Davison, who, Gist said, spoke several Indian tongues with even more fluency than he.

Davison, who seemed to have some intelligence about him, was a lanky fellow as tall as myself. The rest were shorter and stouter men, but all looked hard, strong, and weathered mountain men, each in some fashion marked by this wilderness. None, I estimated, was under thirty. It was interesting to observe Washington, not yet turned twenty-two, eye them speculatively as he might some stock animals for sale. He bade them turn about, show their hands and teeth, and suffer interrogations as to their histories, before concluding the discussions by informing them of their rate of pay and giving them instructions for the morrow. Why they did not grumble at this, I know not. Perhaps it was the King's shilling. I for one would not treat any ship's crew so contemptuously, but then, I was no aristocrat.

None of these men came close to that appellation. Observing Currin go about his business, the Major blessed me with another of his rules of civility, whispered low: " 'Kill no vermin as fleas, lice, ticks, et cetera in the sight of others.' "

"I'll keep that firm in my mind, sir," I said. "The thought will distract from the itch."

My remark prompted a dark look, and yet more rules.

" 'Speak not injurious words, neither in jest nor in earnest. Scoff at none although they give occasion.' "

The hiring done, with Washington in essence accepting all the recruits Gist suggested, I edged away and started toward the Ennis place.

"Tick," the Major called. "Where do you go? Mr. Gist's establishment is this way."

"There's a public house of sorts. I'll see if there's news."

"Keep an eye to your purse, and to your throat. These are hard men in this country."

I looked back, smiling. "You've not passed much time about the docks, have you, Major? These here are gentler souls than I'm used to."

Ennis's was not a large establishment, more like two cabins cobbled together than a proper house or inn, though each section was of two rooms, and each had a loft besides. The main public room had a roaring fire going. A bald man lay sleeping to one side of the hearth. Two others were eating at the end of a long table. Otherwise, it was empty. Gist's daughter had directed me to this place, but there was no sign of what I sought.

It was Ennis himself who came eventually from the kitchen, a strong-looking man with a ruddy Irish face and eyes, and hair as coal-black as a Spaniard's. He was sociable in manner, but stank and was in need of a shave. I was becoming used to such, and had myself not bathed since Winchester, though I wished to. Taking the lone chair by the fire, I asked for a whiskey, then pulled from my coat pocket my last remaining book: Samuel Richardson's *Pamela*. I'd read it twice, but as I say, it was all I had left. I wondered if its rightful owner could have any ken how far from its proper place it had strayed.

I need not tell you. The whiskey. The heat of the fire. The fatigue of the trail. The words blurred. My eyes closed. The book slid from my hand.

I did not hear it fall. I awoke to a more sizable sound—that of a heavy log being tossed thudding onto the fire, and then another, followed by the snap and sizzle of sparks.

My eyes opened. There on the hearthstone before me was the prettiest foot Providence has ever designed to append to human leg—high-arched, narrow, with dainty toes. The heel was coarse and callused, however, and the pale skin smudged dark in numerous parts.

The lithe little foot moved, disappearing beneath a fold of thick home-spun skirt. My perhaps too steady gaze lifted, following the lines of a lissome female form of a configuration to match the perfection of the foot. The lass wore only stays above the waist, with a wide kerchief or modesty cloth around the shoulders and tucked into the top of the stays, in country custom, but loosely, exposing ample greade. The long, dark hair fell near halfway down her back in soft tangles of curls.

She turned and looked at me. The face, though smudged, bore close inspection even better than at a distance. What was such beauty doing in such a wretched, far-off place? There'd be some impairment, I guessed—horrid teeth, perhaps. But no. Her smile revealed teeth that, if faintly discolored, ran straight and fine and without gap.

"Your book, Major," she said, holding it in grubby hand still near her waist. "You dropped it almost in the fire."

"I'm merely captain."

"Captain?"

"And a sea captain at that," I said. "Captain Morley. The Major is George Washington. He's with the Gists. Christopher Gist. He has business with him."

I was prattling. She glanced over my clothes and youth, finding contradiction.

"The Major's the tall one, is he then?" she asked. "He with the blue-and-red coat?"

"Yes."

"I seen him just now with Anne Gist. We heard there was a militia major bound this way with an armed party. You're off to see the French, are you? Save us from the scalping?"

"Something like that. Has there been a lot of scalping?"

"A family up at Loyal Hannon. Near the Conemaugh River. Don't know their name. Don't know no other. That 'twas a few months ago. There's been nothing since. But folks're powerful fretful."

"You're Irish, or is it Scots I hear?"

"A bit o' both. I was born in Derry, my father's city. He's of the Roman faith. My mother, God rest her soul, was lowland Scot . . . and Presbyterian. We come over here when I was five. Stayed in Philadelphia for a time, then tried Carlisle on the Susquehanna and then Shippensburg. Then the valley of Virginia. Now here. 'Tis the richest we've yet been, though we're hankering for better."

"I saw you when we came through the woods."

"Did you now? I saw you, too. Thought you was the Major."

"You are an agile runner."

" 'Tis well to be that in such country." She looked down at the book in her hand. " 'Pamela.' " She read out the word rather slowly.

"You can read?"

"A bit. My father has the knack better. In Cromwell's time, y'know, they was burning all the books in Ireland, so you'd read just to be fighting back. My family's strong on that."

She opened the book, glanced over a few lines, then turned the page.

"You may have it," I said.

"May have what, sir?"

"The book."

She gave me a slightly mocking look, as if I were jesting with her. "The book? For me? You cannot mean it."

"But I do. I've read it twice and know it well. Please take it."

She sank kneeling at the hearth, holding the book more gingerly and peering at it closely.

"I've not ever owned a book before."

"Well, we shall proclaim this yours for all to see." I reached into my leather pouch where, among the jumble, I had a couple of reasonably sharp quills and a small corked pot of ink. "Now hand it up."

She did so, still treating the book with great reverence. I held it open to the first leaf, dipped the quill, wrote the word "For," and then paused.

"I would ask your name, miss."

" 'Tis Mercy."

"Mercy?"

"Aye, Mercy. We've had Faith, Hope, Charity, Prudence, and Chastity in my family. My mother's doing. I'm Mercy. The family's Ennis."

" 'For Mercy Ennis,' " I wrote. " 'Wishing her pleasure in the reading, Thom. Morley.' "

I set it down on the hearth to wait for the ink to dry. She peered very closely now at what I wrote.

" 'Thomas Morley.' Where be the 'captain,' Captain?"

Kneeling beside her, I scratched the word onto the page beneath the others, then added the date, "the 14th November, 1753." We'd been a fortnight on the trail.

Our shoulders were touching. I had the most prodigious inclination to take her in my arms. I had a yet more overwhelming urge to give her a bath—as soon as I had done so to myself.

"Thomas Morley," she read again. "Captain."

Her own name was repeated, but not by me. It came bellowing forth from the doorway to the kitchen, where stood her pa.

Damn all fathers.

Mercy snatched up the book and scampered past him, almost as fleetly as she'd taken that fence. He apparently put her to labor in the scullery, helping with the preparation for the night's meal. I ordered another whiskey from him, and drank it with some slowness, but to no good end. The father hung about, and maid Mercy did not reappear. I thought of lingering in this place to take my supper, but knew Gist was providing that for our party and that Washington would be wanting to speak to us all before retiring. The general on the eve of battle, and all that. We were across the Patowmack and into the true wilderness at last. Once through the mountains now ahead of us, we would be on land claimed by the French king.

I emptied the earthen mug, threw on my coat, and pushed open the oaken door into the cold, rain-wet night. It was so dark I barely made a course before me.

Fourteen

W ashington was good to his word. He roused us from our fireside slumbers before first light. I stumbled out for my morning pee into utter blackness, pelted in the face by stinging, freezing rain and nearly killing myself trying to keep purchase on ground that was slippery muck where it was not sheet ice.

Once returned inside, I followed the example of Gist and the others by putting on nearly every garment I now owned, including deerskin trousers and shirt. Like Washington, who had acquired a buckskin coat as long as Gist's, I pulled my greatcoat on over everything and cinched it tight.

"Breakfast now?" asked Van Braam, slow to waken and not yet fully dressed.

"On the trail," said Washington. "And we ride as long as there's light—every day until we are there."

We loaded our firearms indoors with fresh powder and shot, but did not prime them because of the wet. I wrapped a blanket around my musket and put the flintlock pistol in my belt. How men could fight in such weather was beyond all logic, but Washington nevertheless wished to prepare for the natives, as he called them. Arrows, to be sure, could fly to their mark wet or dry.

Our departure was delayed briefly by disagreement between the Major and Gist. Washington took the scout out of our earshot for most of it, but we heard enough. Gist wanted Washington to leave behind here his two Negro manservants, or better, to send them back to wait his return in Winchester. I thought it must be that Gist had some marked peculiar aversion to fellowship with the African race, but his explanation was sensible. The two were household servants, unused to the extreme rigors of the wilderness, and so might slow us. Gist expressed the fear as well that these dark men might provoke some odd reaction from the Indians. Unsaid, but I think a factor, was his disapproval of having such luxuries as servants in this egalitarian country, though I'm sure he'd been master of a few himself in the happier days of Baltimore.

My estimation of the Major improved. Their argument concluded with his accepting Gist's advice. Gist's most telling point, I later learned, was his informing the Major of escaped slaves who in the past had taken up with the Indians and become members of their tribes, encouraging them in dislike of white men. So the Major's manservants were left at Will's Creek. They seemed the happier for the decision, now that winter was apparently upon us.

When we'd all mounted except the two blacks, Gist still bade us wait. His daughter and some of the other women had prepared a warm meal for us to partake upon the trail, and they came forth with it from Gist's house and one near it. Gist and the Major were gifted at first, then the lesser men of the party received their food.

I was not included. I sat there ahorse, wondering at the neglect, when I heard my name called out from behind me.

There, running nimbly over the mud and ice, with a shawl over her head and shoulders and a bundle in her arms, was my dark-haired Scots-and-Irish beauty of such recent and inconclusive acquaintance.

"Captain Morley!" she cried again. "Wait."

Wait? I was certainly in no hurry to depart. Not while she was running toward me. As best I could in that footing, I turned my horse to face her. She skidded into it, holding her hand out for balance. Then, regaining that, she lifted the bundle to me.

"For your journey, sir," she said. "Some pemmican, and mountain corn bread. And a small corked jug of my father's best whiskey."

I seated the bundle on my pommel, but took hold of her hand before she could withdraw it and bent low to bring it to my lips, grubbiness and all. She'd no experience with this gallantry and seemed astonished by it. I let her fingers slip from mine, then tipped my hat and smiled.

"I thank you for your kindness, Miss Ennis."

For a fearful moment I thought she might correct me and call out her proper title as "Mrs."—perish, perish that thought. Instead, taking a step back, she nodded her head once and said, "I thank you for the pretty book."

She smiled, came forward again, reached as though to touch my leg, but instead, patted the flank of my horse. She looked up, her eyes earnest.

"Safe journey."

"Will you be here when we return?"

"I pray to God we all shall be."

"I, too."

"Farewell to you, then."

"Farewell."

It was the perfect moment to turn and gallop off through the trees in grand dramatic fashion, but not in this foul inclemency. I urged my mount up close behind Washington's, then stopped. The Major looked back 'round at all of us—every inch the general surveying his forces—and then spoke to Gist, who nodded, once. Washington put boot to his horse's flank and it began to amble forward.

I studied my bundle. Mercy had wrapped the eatments in the modesty cloth she'd worn the previous day. 'Twas of a checkered pattern, soft to the touch, though getting wet. I pulled the skirts of my greatcoat up over it.

I'd read of the feudal times, when knights would enter tournaments wearing some bit of cloth from a lady, given them with the admonition, "Think, gentle knights, upon the wool of your breasts, the nerve of your arms, the love you cherish in your hearts, and do valiantly, for ladies behold you."

The knights were to have said in response, "Love of ladies! Death of warriors! On, valiant knights, for you fight under fair eyes!"

In the heat of such contests, I'm sure there was more curse and scream and spit than such sweet poesy, but no matter. 'Twas a lovely thought for the trail. And for our return, if blessed with one we'd be.

I looked back to the settlement. All three women were shrouded, huddled figures, hurrying through the chilly downpour toward the Gist house. I kept watching in hope Mercy might look toward us, but she didn't.

The Major observed this. Turning in his saddle, he said, "If you hadn't been two feet from me all the night at Gist's, I'd be wondering now where you found your sleep, Captain Morley."

———

As our little group wound its way through the wet woodland, I asked Gist if the "Will" for whom the place was named was still in residence.

"I do not believe he still walks this earth," Gist said. "Was an Indian, you know. Damn friendly. And helpful to the traders and settlers who first came up to this reach of the Patowmack, inviting them to stay and live among his people. After a time, he moved on, away from them, but everything hereabouts bears his name. That stream is Will's Creek, the settlement is so named also, and that high hill just to the north is Will's Mountain. Wish the man was here with us. I think you'd find him a good fellow. A better friend to us even than Chief Half King of the Senecas."

———

In his journal, Washington said of the next six days merely: "The excessive Rains and vast Quantity of Snow that had fallen prevented our reaching Mr. Frazier's, an Indian Trader, at the Mouth of Turtle Creek, on Monongahela, till Thursday the 22nd."

"Excessive Quantity" was the mildest possible term for this onslaught of cold and wet. If Hell actually were to freeze over, I thought, this was what it would be like. By the end of that first day out of Will's Creek, there could not have been a dry patch of cloth or skin among us. Before it could turn to mush, I ate all the food Mercy Ennis had given me. The whiskey I sipped sparingly, and just for the warmth.

The weather would have made us wretched enough were we traveling over a flat plain. Crossing those mountain ridges in it struck me as a very special form of madness. The trail, such as there was one, curved and twisted steeply in its every upward and downward course. Its surface was mostly slippery rocks and stones, loosely mortared with sodden muck. The downhill lengths of it were the worst, in most places the path as deep in rushing water as an actual stream.

Ascending the ridges, we'd walk to spare our slipping and sliding mounts the shifting burden of our human weight. Descending, we'd do it to spare our lives. Despite all care, horses and men were regularly going down, arms, knees, and bony backsides cracking against rock or splashing in wet. I once slid a good hundred feet to the bottom of a ravine, and later we had to kill a pack animal when its foreleg broke against a boulder, afterward spreading out the load among the other beasts.

Among the evils of these mountains was the laurel bush. An evergreen that looked absurdly tropical in the midst of all this winter, its bright and shiny green hue masked a stubborn woody stem and branch that stayed a man's or horse's forward progress as though a trap crafted by some devilish hand. And these bushes, most much higher than a man, were everywhere on these slopes. I quickly grew to dislike them, though they were pretty.

At night, we made shelter in our tents and slept rolled in blanket and buckskin and huddled close together. All that week we had fires only twice, the rain and sleet and snow were so relentless.

Washington, I'll say, held himself a bold, heroic, unbothered figure as he rode along at the fore of our column—head high, back straight, one or the other arm cocked back with a hand at his hip—though he kept his coat collar upturned and buttoned tight against his cheeks. Only occasionally—when we were following the summit of a ridge line in the face of a fierce squall or when the constant company of coughs and sneezes proved too much—did he comport himself as visibly discomforted as the rest of us. Otherwise, he rode on as a living form of some monumental statue, keeping an eye to the horizon.

I will say his manly example kept the rest of us going, though for my part, I forewent the pose and survived by huddling my body in thickness of heavy cloth and deerskin and my mind in the warmest obtainable memory. Having eaten the food it carried, I'd wound Mercy Ennis's modesty cloth about my neck, as though a scarf. The knowledge that my flesh was thus touched by fabric that had lain pressed tight against her bosom was of no little cozy charm to me.

Oddly, though, the most warming thoughts I had were of Italy. At that young age, I'd never been there, of course. But we'd once had a passenger on a voyage from New York to Charleston who had been to Venice. In 1748 or 1749 it was. The gentleman had just returned from a year or more on the continent—Paris, Vienna, but mostly Italy, which he'd been unhappy to leave. He'd brought back a folio of drawings he'd purchased in the city of Venice, capital then of a nation that reached from the Alps to Greece. He had some Ricci landscapes, gardens and canals; two Giovanni Battista Tiepolo sketches of the martyred St. Agatha; and four pastels by a woman artist, Rosalba Carriera, three of them of beautiful young women and the last a portrait of an aged nun.

But even that weary visage seemed to glow, as though the paper had soaked up the Venetian sunlight as it might have water. I cannot describe the delicate loveliness of those works, which the passenger so proudly

spread out in his cabin in response to my curiosity. Loveliness and decadence, all in one.

The American colonies, mind, then had virtually no art, save for the
occasional grand official portrait in one of the governor's palaces or the
wretched primitive folk portraiture of the self-taught itinerants—no better
skilled at painting, really, than the tinkers and cobblers and other tradesmen whose lifestyle they emulated. As a rich man, I now of course have
the obligatory Ralph Earl hanging in my parlor. Like most such, it depicts
myself and the beauty who is my wife seated in classical repose by an ornate
marble-like railing with a harbor full of ships, presumably mine, standing
at anchor in the background. It's quite good, though Earl never could get a
sitter's eyes to match exactly right upon a face, or keep a subject's limbs
in proportionate length. Still, for the nonce, he is among our best.

I have a few works framed and hanging from my own hand, which
some—including my wife—hold equal with Earl's, if not better.

But compared to Carriera! To see such magnificence set upon a single
square of paper. And by a woman! That struck me as quite wonderful.

I longed to be in Italy. To look upon these faces. To look upon Carriera's. Our passenger told me she was a most noble-looking beauty, and still
alive then, though she could no longer see. He had looked upon a self-
portrait of the gifted lady, but had not met her.

The imagined Rosalba, the remembered faces of the pastel ladies, the
light as it must look shimmering on the waters of the Grand Canal at height
of day, these and well-recollected youthful bosoms were my companions
of mind and soul in that mountain ordeal. I talked seldom, so much was
my mind absorbed by these visions.

Gist and Washington led the way together when possible. The latter
comported himself as though as knowledgeable as the former, though Gist
not only lived in this country, but had undertaken the most extraordinary
exploration two years before, traveling virtually alone through the entire
Ohio Valley to the Caintuckee country.

The scout conducted himself deferentially, hired man to employer, but
it seemed the two liked each other, for all their initial gruffness. Riding as
close to them as I could, given my inexpert horsemanship, I was from time
to time privy to parts of their conversation. Gist had much to teach, and
Washington was an eager pupil.

One day the weather broke in our favor—the cold deepening but the
skies clearing and the wind dropping to near stillness. We had reached and
forded the still-unfrozen Youghiogheny and climbed and crossed the high
Laurel Ridge, descending later to a wide valley that ran southwest to north-
east, which Gist called Great Meadows. Perhaps midway across we came
upon a swath of marshy bottomland, fed by two creeks and lying between
two low but not insubstantial wooded hills. Riding to a spot along one of
the creeks and not a hundred yards from the foot of the nearest hill, Wash-

ington proclaimed it an excellent place to camp—ignoring the sodden ground.

This was perhaps a tolerable notion at the time, for we were cold and bone-weary and in a mood to camp where we might drop. But once we'd put our beasts of burden to forage, got fires somehow going, and bedding settled, Washington proceeded to walk about the place as though fascinated by it, looking here and there, gazing off south and north, studying the fast-running creek water—and then described it as an ideal situation for a new settlement, and fort!

Fort? I'm a sailor. I claim no soldier's mind. I could no more drill troops than make my sloop fly. But I'd read Hannibal, and Xenephon's *Anabasis*, and Caesar's chronicles. 'Twas the high ground that favored a fortification, not this bottom. The Major thought the running stream gave advantage, not the height above. I looked to Gist, who only shrugged.

I rode quite a lot with Gist now. I was interested in his best guess as to the dangers we faced and how well we might fare with the French. I wished to know about these Indians. And this one called Half King. How came he to be our friend?

"I don't think it's a natural thing," Gist said finally, picking at his teeth with a small knife as we sat upon a log after our cold and meager supper—ignoring Washington's admonition that this violated a rule of civility. "Friendship between the red man and white, I mean. Given their druthers, they'd not have us in their country, but here we be. And they've grown a need for muskets, ball and powder; steel tomahawks; and the white man's whiskey. The trade.

"The French charge dear in pelts for their goods, which are inferior to the English. So you find the English trader fair received. But the French treat the Indian with more respect than do the English, and the French bring no settlers with them. Soldiers and priests is all. The Indian understands priests. He's got his holy men, too.

"Now Half King—he's also called Tanacharison, and by some, Monakaduto, but he is pleased when I call him Half King, thinking it in kind to what we call King George. Half King's a Mingo, a branch of the Senecas that moved into the Ohio country. The Senecas are one of the Six Nations of the Iroquois. The domain of the Six Nations runs all through these mountains and north and east, besides up into Canada.

"Half King, he's had some bad times with the French. He claims they killed and boiled and ate his father during the Queen Anne's war, but who can say? They've been disrespectful to him, sure enough, and they denied him trade goods, and refused whiskey when he had a thirst for it. When that French Colonel Celeron started going 'round burying those leaden plates to mark his sovereign's claim in the Ohio, old Half King, he got the idea the French were fixing to cheat the Mingoes out of their part of the valley. The English got no settlers in the Ohio yet to speak of except me and a few other traders. Lord Fairfax, he's been good to Half King; Dinwiddie, too. Many gifts and wampum belts. He's sure enough our friend.

"He's called Half King because he ain't the only powerful chief among the Mingoes. He shares his power. Think of England with two kings, or three or four. Tanacharison's an important man. But what Dinwiddie can't ken is that Half King doesn't treat with us as a chief, as a big leader of his people. His job is more what I'd liken to an ambassador's. He gets along so fine with the English that the other Mingo chiefs look to him to do their dealing with us. He's the Mingoes' Sir William Johnson. You know Johnson, up in the Mohawk Valley?"

I allowed as to how I did not. I hadn't any exact sense of where the Mohawk Valley might be.

"In New York, runs west of the Hudson," Gist said.

Washington was seated nearby, but busy with his journal or one of the letters he was endlessly writing.

"There ain't a man better with the Indians in all the colonies than Johnson," said Gist. "George Groghan, Thomas Cresap, Andrew Montour, William Trent, me—we've learned their ways and do well with 'em—live neighborly and no trouble. But Johnson they treat like one of their great chiefs, like he's one of them. He's the white man most respected in the colonies by the Indians, which is why King George has made Johnson his chief Indian agent for all North America. If he were situated down here on Virginia lands instead of up in New York, we'd have much less trouble. Considerable less.

"Anyways, about old Half King, what Dinwiddie and Fairfax don't realize—especially Dinwiddie—is that Half King's got a wife with a whole hell of a lot more power than he has. Women are chiefs in the Senecas. Lot of other tribes, too. I remember when I was down with the Shawnees once on my mapping trip for the Ohio Company, I came upon a village where I found Hokolesqua—"Chief Cornstalk," the traders call him—the principal chief of the Shawnees. But the chief of the village where Hokolesqua was staying, she was the most amazing woman I ever met. Nonhelema's her name. Sister of Hokolesqua. But the traders called her Grenadier Squaw because she was so huge. This woman, Tick, she stands six and a half feet. Taller than me. Taller than the Major here. And handsome. A most handsome woman. I'd a had some of that were I not a married man, and all the trouble it'd stir.

"But Half King's wife, now. Alequippa is her name. I do believe she is Half King's squaw, for she orders him around so. She is a chief, too. A squaw chief, but a mighty chief. Alequippa Town in the Ohio country is named for her. But neither English nor French will hold council with her. They do not understand that there can be female chiefs, no matter how much we tell them that is so."

Gist had taken out a small clay pipe and now began the laborious work of filling it and lighting it from flint.

"This Alequippa," I said finally. "Is she handsome, too—like the tall one, Nonhelema?"

Gist took in a big mouthful of smoke, then grinned as it came back out. "Alequippa's tall, but sideways," he said. "She and Half King, they like their meat . . . and their rum."

I produced my own pipe, accepting some tobacco from the scout. We sat and smoked a while, happy in the heat of the big fire before us. Washington continued scratching away with his quill.

"I am called Annosanah," Gist said, out of nowhere.

"Annosanah?"

"By the Mingoes."

"What does it mean?"

"I don't know. It was the name of a man who lived among them, and they liked him. They gave it to me after I performed a church service for them."

"Christian? Or some Indian ritual?"

"No ritual, but Christian enough. It was on this same mapping trip. On Christmas Day that year, I was in Muskingum Town, on the Muskingum River between the Ohio and Lake Erie. There was mostly Wyandots there, 'Little Mingoes,' they call them. It being the Christ Child's birthday, I thought it well to read from the gospels, for I am Church of England. Montour was in the town and he helped to translate for the Indians. Now there's an interesting man, Montour. I should not mind his company when we're up with the French."

"But his name sounds French. Isn't he one of them?"

"He claims he's the grandson of one of the French governors. His father was French, sure enough. A trader. I don't know the tribe of his mother, but she was Indian—come into this country from Canada and lived with the Senecas. It was as a Seneca she married his father. Montour, he can't rightly figure out which he is, white man or Indian, so he goes about as both. He has this blue coat he got off a naval officer—much like the one you have on underneath your greatcoat. He wears breeches and woolen stockings, and he's got this tall grenadier's hat. But he wears all manner of Indian jewelry, and he paints his face red."

"Red?"

"As red as war wampum. He was wearing red when he translated my gospels that Christmas."

"It sounds fitting for the occasion. How were you and the gospels received?"

"Oh, they were much taken with my 'medicine.' I am told this may well have been the first Protestant church service west of the mountains—in the Ohio country, at the least."

"The Mingoes then are taking up with civilization?"

"All of the Indians are civilized, but in the ways of their own civilization. That can get real different. Very next day, in Muskingum, the day after Christmas, those Mingoes recaptured a woman captive who had tried to escape from them. They took her outside the village and made a circle around her, hitting her by turn till she could scarce stand. They then stuck her several times though the back with a small spear—finally to the heart, then scalped her and threw the scalp in the air and from one to the other. Then they cut off her head. I don't know what they did with that, as I could watch no more."

I gulped. Then reminded myself of what I had witnessed at Williamsburg in the summer.

"Not so different from us," I said. "This very year, in the Virginia capital, I saw a similar torture practiced upon a black slave woman who had escaped and been recaptured," I said. "She was beaten and burned at the stake."

"She was white, this woman the Mingoes killed?" said Washington, abruptly.

"No. I think a Delaware, or some such northern tribe," said Gist.

Washington nodded and returned to his writing.

"Tell me about the scalps," I said.

"Of which do you speak?"

"A fair-haired woman's and a dark-haired man's. You sent them on by way of Major Washington here—one for Dinwiddie and one for Benjamin Franklin of Philadelphia."

Another grin from Gist, much hidden by his thick beard. Washington had stopped writing.

"I sent them on to Winchester and Lord Fairfax, to express farther as he saw fit, though I had mentioned to him how it might be a wise thing for Philadelphia to learn of matters out this way. I told him of Mr. Franklin, who is well known to me. His Lordship must have made courier of Mr. Washington. How do you know of them?"

"The Major made courier of me and my sloop. Dinwiddie has the woman's hair. The man's is with Franklin. Who were these people?"

Gist shook his head. "No one I knew personal. Some settlers north and east of here, on the Juniata River. I got the scalps off an Indian, in exchange for rum."

"What Indian?"

"Half King."

"He, he killed them?"

"No. He and a few of his warriors had a fight with a band of Abenakis. They took them prisoners and got those scalps off of one of them."

"And the Abenakis?"

"I think some were put to death, but in no unusual way."

The usual way seemed horror enough.

"The Abenakis are allies of the French?" I asked.

" 'Pears so, judging by that English hair. Though it may have been just a war party out for fun, no matter who the victim."

"And there are other tribes . . . who like the French?"

Gist shrugged. "Now, the Iroquois' Six Nations, I think, thanks to Sir William Johnson, they stay friends with the English no matter what—even the Senacas. But there's some Mingoes in the Ohio country ain't so friendly as Half King and Alequippa. And if things were to go bad against us, the Delawares and Shawnees, and the Ottawas out to the west, they'd fight for the French sure as shit. Those Ottawas sure would. They got a chief named Pontiac scares me just to think of him. Wears a big curved stone through his nose. Hangs down like this, like a mustache."

"When you say 'things go bad,' what's your meaning?"

Gist's grin was very wide this time, showing the gaps in his teeth.

"I mean, if the French and English decide to have a war again," he said. "The Major here's going to tell them to leave the valley. War could be their answer."

I shared with Gist some of Mercy's gift of whiskey, then drained the remainder—the better to sleep on all he'd told me.

"We'll be at my plantation tomorrow," he said. "It's just over Chestnut Ridge, the last before the valley of the Ohio. I got some corn whiskey laid by you might favor as much as this, though I can't promise you as pretty a bringer."

That night there was a musket shot that had me bolt upright in an instant and rattled echoing all around the hillsides bordering these meadows. Happily, no other discharge followed. It proved to be this fellow Barnaby Currin, who'd been left to take the first night watch and had loaded and primed with fresh, dry powder. Thumb or finger had slipped in the cold. The fired ball struck no flesh, only frozen mud. We went back to sleep, relieved, but wary.

——

Chestnut Ridge was the last mountain spine of the Alleghenies. The ascent of its eastern slope was surprisingly gentle, as least compared to my expectations. The summit was fairly broad, almost a plateau, rolling in sweeps and falls. The sky was perfectly clear; from morning on, the sunlight was dancing bright and the wintry horizon sharply visible when the trees allowed.

Ahead, I noted the trees were beginning to thin. Gist, eyes eager, quickened his horse to a jauntier pace, then looked back to us.

"Come see what it's all about, Major. Come see why we're all here. You too, Tick."

The ground was too hard and slippery to run the horses any faster than at a trot. I managed that, keeping Gist and Washington in view as they more nimbly weaved among the trees ahead, then burst out upon a small, scrubby field that ended abruptly at what seemed a precipice, though it was just the brow of the ridge.

There was a rounded hill line to the right, another that descended from the left, forming a wide cleft at the center. Beyond, below, limitlessly before me, was the grandest view I'd ever seen or could possibly imagine. It went so far that the horizon was only a vagueness, though all else was outlined knife-sharp in the crystalline winter air: field and forest, meandering river and stream, the brown and white of tree-dotted snow cover—all spreading off into a hazy blue.

How far could I see? A hundred miles? A thousand? Land as wide as the sea, Washington had said. Here it was. Here was land a million people could not fill. Not ten million.

Gist was right. Now I understood.

I turned to the Major. There was the most uncharacteristic look on his face, a fierce zeal in his eyes. He seemed about to leap forth from his saddle into the air, to swoop down into the valley and with outstretched arms, claim it all.

Fifteen

Gist's plantation, a few rude log buildings more primitive even than those at Will's Creek, lay on the wooded, rolling plain just a few miles out from the foot of that last westerly ridge of the Appalachians. We reached it not much before the next storm hit, and a nasty one it was. I had begun to think these relentlessly recurring tempests were a natural part of the rugged mountain climate, but Gist assurred me this was not so, that he had never in all his days upon the frontier seen a winter like this—and it had scarce begun!

In residence at Gist's place were his wife, his eldest son, another daughter, two hired men, a Moravian Indian girl who'd left her tribe and been adopted by the Gists, and assorted cattle, goats, pigs, chickens, and noisy dogs. I didn't know how he'd gotten this menagerie over the mountains, or managed to keep the wolves and Indians from helping themselves to so much tempting meat, but it bode well for the future of this country that these folk seemed to be flourishing here.

Mrs. Gist I judged to be a foot shorter than he, and she was poorly dressed. They all were. I don't know whether this spoke of the exigencies of the frontier, or of poverty, or both. Gist had told me he'd been paid one hundred fifty pounds for that mapping exploration a year before, and I gathered he'd asked, though not received, a similarly hefty sum for this journey. He deserved it, I thought. All the people brave enough to abide this wild country deserved better than they'd gotten.

Gist had himself a jolly reunion with his clan, prompting the happiest expression I'd yet seen on his careworn and weather-beaten countenance. The rest of us, after a huge meal, just as happily went to sleep.

Washington had us up before dawn yet again. Revictualed and refreshed, we set out north in now lightly falling snow, fording the Youghiogheny again and proceeding through hilly and wooded country up to Turtle Creek. At the mouth of this watercourse, where it emptied into the Monongahela River just a few miles upstream from the Forks of the Ohio, we found Frazier's trading post, and John Frazier himself.

Trader, explorer, and renowned as well as a gunsmith, Frazier was friend to Gist and proprietor of the outermost English outpost on the frontier. He told us he'd had another to the north at Venango, but that had been forcibly expropriated by the French, though he had counted them friends.

At this abode we were accorded another hot meal, a warm, dry place to sleep, and interesting news in addition to that of the loss of his other house. According to friendly red men who had only a few days before passed by, three nations of Ohio Valley Indians had just declared loyalty to the French Louis and could be expected to raise the hatchet on behalf of the Fleur-de-Lis should there be war. The French had moved substantial garrisons into their new forts at Venango and Presque Isle. A large body of soldiers had been heading south toward us, or at least toward the Ohio River, but had turned back at the news that their commander in North America, Pierre Paul, *Sieur de Marin*, had died. When their leadership was better sorted out, they could be expected to return.

Washington chewed over all this most thoughtfully, commander as he was of a mere nine men and bound for this dangerous territory. He had hoped to meet with Marin and be done with his mission swiftly, returning ahead of the worst of this harsh winter. Now he must find the French successor, if there was one to be found south of the lakes.

A more heartening tiding was the report that the Chief Half King of the Senecas was indeed in the area, as was Shingas, "King" of the Delawares, and a number of other Indians still favorably disposed to the British, though many of their fellow tribesmen were not. These two friendly chiefs had heard of Washington's coming, Frazier said, and were awaiting him in agreeable disposition.

It was a short distance from Frazier's to the geographical point that thus far seemed to excite Washington most—the fabled Forks of the Ohio. Gist led us there, but not until the next day.

Our party had to stop at the Allegheny River at all events, as it was swollen from the rains and snows and thundering along with a great volume of water. We'd have to swim the animals across and somehow float the considerable baggage. Currin and another man were sent back to Frazier's to return with canoes to ferry our goods across.

The wait was long, a large part of the day. Washington and Gist took the opportunity to ride down to the sharp point of land at the actual Forks, where the gentle Monongahela and more powerful Allegheny formed the great Ohio. The Major dismounted and clambered to a small prominence giving a full view of the confluence, eyeing it all speculatively.

There was a high bluff with steep cliffs along the southern shore of the Monongahela just across from us, smaller rounded hills rising to the north on the other side of the Allegheny. The hills continued along either side of the Ohio.

"There's a falls maybe two hundred miles downstream, just past the Miami and Caintuckee Rivers," said Gist. "But it's not a bad portage. Between here and there, it's all slack water, like you see."

Looking directly downstream, I thrilled more than a little with the realization that the wide, majestic river formed at this place was coursing *away* from the sea and seaboard from which I'd come and to which all the American rivers I knew flowed. The Ohio's waters not only traversed that infinity of land I had seen from the ridge above Gist's plantation, they kept going, joining with the legendary Mississippi—as Gist instructed me to pronounce the name, correcting Mr. Franklin—and eventually reaching south across the continent to the fabled port of New Orleans and the great warm gulf beyond. Our little party was striding the earth like giants. It seemed we might go anywhere we chose, that following Gist and the Major a few more days or weeks I'd find myself in China.

Washington brought me back to a ruder reality.

"We must have a fort here," he said. "On this very spot. It is the key to all."

"I had in mind another place downstream, on the high ground of the south bank," Gist said.

"No," corrected twenty-one-year-old Washington. "Here."

Later, after considerable delay crossing the cold, swollen Allegheny, we paused downstream along the Ohio to examine, with spyglass, the site opposite us on the south bank of the river that Gist had earlier surveyed and proposed for a fort.

"No," said Washington. "It is too far from the water."

I am no soldier, but it struck me that Gist's site was far more defensible from attack from the water, but like him, I stayed silent and let the Major command.

Our next destination was Shanopin's Town, abode of Chief Shingas. It was an Indian village on the north bank of the Ohio, with less than half a hundred in population—the larger part of that women and children. Indian protocol required we bestow handsome gifts on the chief. But why? Had Gist not included the Delawares among the tribes he thought would fight with the French?

"This Delaware likes us well enough," Gist said. "He's almost neighbor to me."

"The object, Tick," pronounced Washington, "is to maintain this friendship, to remind Chief Shingas of the might and amity of the English Crown. More than soldiers, we're diplomats in this place. I am the King's ambassador."

I looked back at our filthy, bearded crew, trailing behind us in convoy. As envoys, we weren't precisely fancy ones.

Shingas was fancy in his fashion, which ran to feathers and animal bones stuck on or in various parts of his large body. Odd designs and violent colors were painted or tattooed on his chest, arms, and about the face. He greeted us in his lodge, which was kept steamy hot and smoky with a huge fire in the center, near which he regally sat, not rising at our entrance. He'd removed his outdoor clothing and wore only loincloth, deerskin leggings, and moccasins. Several elders and warriors sat nearby, eyeing us as curiously as I stared at them. All had their heads shaved, except for a topknot, a peculiarity I'd noted among the Indians back at Lord Fairfax's.

Perhaps foolishly, as we all stood there in mutual visual examination, I whispered to Gist, "Why do they shave their hair?"

He whispered back: "Nothing sacred about it, Tick. Helps 'em evade the knife or war club. Head like that don't leave much for an enemy to hold on to when he's after cutting your throat."

I reached and touched my own hair, which I wore long and tied at the back, like Washington's, in a queue, in the common custom. We white men would commence any combat at a disadvantage.

Combat did not seem in the offing with these nice folk. We all sat, and before proceeding to any kind of discourse, accepted Shingas's invitation to smoke—a large pipe being passed around for the common pleasure, the tobacco harsher and drier than what I'd been used to, but in no way noxious.

There followed speeches, with Gist and Davison translating and an Indian who knew some English assisting the great Shingas in the understanding. I recall well the pomp and grand gesture with which the Major intoned the words he'd briefly practiced with Gist:

"I bring you, Great Chief, the greeting of the King of England, your father. He wishes you well. He asks that you stay on the way of peace and friendship and not take up the wampum war belt the French now send through your country. He warns you that the French lie and mean to take your lands and end your trade with us. He says again to you what he said in his treaty with the Iroquois, that no English man or woman save those who would trade for pelts shall come beyond the mountains to dwell on your lands. The King of the English is your father and your friend."

Shingas listened to the words as though they were food he was chewing upon, then grunted something in reply. So it went, back and forth, with much flattery and flummery, until finally Davison looked to Gist, who made a quick clicking or snapping sound with his fingers, at which Currin and the man named Henry Steward hastened outside, returning with a bundle of gifts for the chief.

These included a hatchet with steel blade, ammunition and powder for several muskets, wampum belts of a peaceful white-and-red pattern, two warm blankets, a kettle, and a cask of rum. Shingas seemed contented by them, though not o'erjoyed.

I was hoping we'd now be free to leave, much as I enjoyed the heat, but Shingas summoned refreshment: a pasty sort of substance with meat in it, carried forth on plates of bark by women. The rum, however, was not shared. We drank of river water from wooden vessels.

I had, like the others, removed my outer garments, and was sitting there in my brass-buttoned blue sea captain's coat, which attracted Shingas's curiosity and apparent fancy. He began talking to me with great specificity, and I feared he wanted it added to his collection of gifts, but Davison and Gist assured me otherwise. Apparently, with the coat on, I in many ways resembled Montour, and Shingas wondered if we were related.

He bade me come forward to sit by him, which I reluctantly did, finding his breath indeed quite gamy. Gazing at me intently, he said something to a women behind him, who leapt to her feet and scampered out of the lodge. She returned with a small wooden bowl containing some red substance, which I feared was food, some woodland delicacy like mashed weasel gland.

Shingas put a strong hand on my shoulder and drew me nearer still. I could sense my companions, all fascinated and amused, looking on intently as I leaned forward as if to examine this substance in some olfactory way and pronounce it delightful.

Before I realized what was afoot, Shingas, holding me tightly, scooped up a large dollop of the red stuff and slapped it against my cheek. The same happened to the other cheek. He then began rubbing, as an artist at work. Too stunned and uncertain to pull away, somehow restraining myself from sputters, I crouched there until he had my whole face covered with the substance. He exclaimed something happily, then finally freed me.

"He says now you are Montour," said Gist.

———

We moved on toward Logstown, also writ as Loggstown, with Shingas and a dozen or so of his people in train. I marveled at the names of these Indian villages. Shawnee Town was explicable enough, but what of Logstown? Was it uniquely abundant in the logs that were everywhere in this country? No, it was not. Most of its trees had been cut and taken. North of it was a place called Murthering Town—also called Murdering Town. Was that accurately descriptive?

West of us, far downriver, was White Woman's Town, and this place Gist said was aptly named—after a white woman, Mary Harris, who lived there. She'd been taken captive in New England more than forty years before when she was a little girl barely ten, raised as Indian by her captives, and sold from tribe to tribe as she reached maturity. Gist said they ought to rename the place Old Woman's Town, because when last he'd talked to her, she'd looked quite aged—white-haired, wrinkled, bony—a veritable hag. Yet she'd professed a fondness for the Indian life, and declined any and all offers to remove her to the civilization that had been her birthright. There have been times since that I've had sympathy with her reason, but then it struck me as most curious.

At Logstown, near the junction of the Ohio and Beaver Creek, we were brought to the ranking chief present, not Half King but a certain Monacatoocha, also known as Scarroyaddy. He was presumed to be a Seneca, but I later learned he was an Oneida, serving also as envoy for the head chiefs of the Six Nations.

He stared at my still-red face with much serious contemplation, but otherwise seemed a pleasant chap, spending much time smoking with us. Italy now seemed at a great distance indeed. Will's Creek, by the Major's calculation, was some one hundred forty miles behind us. Mercy would be going about her evening's labors. I wondered if she had thoughts for me.

For no good reason, my mind leapt forth to Susannah Smithson, imagining how it might be to have her in this strange place with me. What a hilarious notion, that. Surely I looked as wild and wretched as my companions, and smelled as vile. Her dainty, well-shod foot had no place here. She'd shriek to be free of this wilderness.

On the following day, our twenty-sixth since leaving Mrs. Fairfax on the road to Williamsburg, Half King and his wife Alequippa arrived close on to three in the afternoon with a small entourage and many pelts, and were greeted with much homage and carryings-on from their Indian brothers, especially the Senecas.

Both man and wife, if that they were, possessed the same short stature and stout physique, complete to round bellies. Both were richly decorated with painted symbols, feathers, bone necklaces, and other jewelry—he more than she, though neither quite so much as Shingas. As I would discover, Half King was usually less embellished, but he had fancied himself up on account of having just paid a visit to a French officer to the north, as well as in anticipation of meeting Washington, whose closeness with the Fairfaxes intrigued him, as Half King considered himself Fairfax kin.

I'd scrubbed at the color upon my face with snow and dried grass till the skin was rubbed raw and nearly as red in its own right, but the stain on my cheeks clung stubbornly. Alequippa was curious about this rosy hue and came over like a sniffing dog to examine me, but Half King paid me little mind. Summoning Davison, the Major invited the chief to his tent. Living up to my nickname, I tagged along. No one objected when I entered and seated myself quietly to the side.

As he spoke something of the Mingo or Seneca tongue, I'd thought Gist would have joined us, too. But he instead sought the company of Alequippa, prompting me to recall his intimation that she was the true power in this clan. To Washington, of course, she was merely a woman—one neither white, nor pretty, nor well-born, and thus of little interest. His business would be with the husband.

Half King needed no questionning to talk. He was eager to tell Washington of his journey to the north. He spoke well and with some eloquence, both in English and in Indian words that required Davison's translation.

The Indian first informed that the lowland way to the Erie forts, normally the quickest, had been made impassable by the heavy precipitation of recent weeks, which had transformed the plains and meadows into bog and swamp and lake. Instead, we'd have to go by a route through Murdering Town and Venango.

Half King said he had made a speech to the French officer in command at the latter place, and recited some of it for us:

"Fathers," he said he had said, "this is our land, and not yours. Fathers, both you and the English are white, we live in a country between. Therefore the land belongs to neither one nor t'other. But the Great Being above allow'd it to be a place of residence for us, so Fathers, I desire you to withdraw, as I have done our brothers the English, for I will keep you at arm's length. I lay this down as a trial for both, to see which will have the greatest regard to it, and that side we will stand by, and make equal sharers with us. Our brothers the English have heard this, and I come now to tell it to you, for I am not afraid to discharge you off this land."

In listening with some earnestness to this, I realized the true nature of the Indians' position in this territorial rivalry between the European powers. Gifts, trade goods, the price of pelts, insults and courtesies, tribal geography, all these things played their role; but essentially, the natives would give their allegiance to the side they most believed would leave them and their lands undisturbed. As both French and English were lying—Washington was not talking of canals to ease the transport of rum and trade goods to the wilderness—the Indians would inevitably lose, no matter which flag they chose. As I think few of them were aware, their only hope of continued tenure in this country lay in preventing war, in balancing French against English in a fightless tension, in keeping each circumspect in fear of the other.

Yet here came Washington, marching right up to the French Army to demand they get out—or else.

Half King said the French commandant had replied to him most rudely, saying, "I am not afraid of flies, or mosquitoes, for Indians are such as those; I tell you, Chief Tanacharison, down that river I will go, and will build upon it according to my command. If the river is block'd up, I have forces sufficient to burst it open, and tread under my feet all that stand in opposition, together with their alliances, for my force is as the sand upon the seashore."

I guessed that Half King's report, like the French officer's threat, was in some part hyperbole, intended to impress. Neither the French commandant nor the Indian chief could have much to gain from provoking one another with words so full of contempt and threat and exaggeration. At all events, Half King had used his visit for a cleverer purpose—espionage!

He described to Washington the two forts the French had built above Venango—one on the shore of Lake Erie, another some fifteen miles inland and south on French Creek, the former much larger than the latter. He said they'd built a wide wagon road in between. He made a drawing and plan of them on paper the Major provided.

As to hostile activity on the part of pro-French Indians, Half King said that a white boy of undetermined age had been taken, off toward the Great Lakes, and had been observed at Cuscusca Town, but he knew of no murders or cabin burnings in the area, not even where the boy had been seized.

There followed a ritual of gift-giving, feasting of a sort, and—well into the night—much drinking, and I found Indians in full swill a fearsome sight, and sound. But before all had gone stone drunk, a council was held in the longhouse of the village, wherein Washington gave a speech, upon which he had much labored. I cannot recall it verbatim, but I have the Major's later account of it from his official report. He was in no way timid or halt in his delivery. I would have thought him addressing the House of

Burgesses on some great issue—perhaps with the fair Mrs. Fairfax in audience attending.

"Brothers!" he commenced, with Davison translating and Gist looking on raptly, "I have called you together in council, by order of your brother the governor of Virginia, to acquaint you that I am sent, with all possible dispatch, to visit and deliver a letter to the French commandant, of very great importance to your brothers the English, and I daresay to you, their friends and allies.

"I was desired, brothers, by your brother the governor, to call upon you, the sachems of the Nations, to inform you of it, and to ask your advice and assistance to proceed on the nearest and best road to the French. You see, brothers, I have got thus far on my journey.

"His Honour likewise desired me to apply to you for some of your young men, to conduct and provide provisions for us on our way, and be a safeguard against those French Indians who have taken up the hatchet against us. I have spoken this particularly to you, brothers, because His honour our governor treats you as good friends and allies, and holds you in great esteem. To confirm what I have said, I give you this string of wampum."

With that, he sat down. I was much impressed with all that Washington had learned, as I don't think he had ever spoken words to any Indian before this mission. The tribesmen present pondered his remarks with great seriousness, talked quietly among themselves, and then at length Half King rose to reply.

He said he would provide a guard of Mingoes, Shawnees, and Delawares for us, but they would take three days to collect, and besides, he, Half King, had to return to his hunting cabin to fetch his speech-making wampum in the event he would be called upon once again to address the French. Washington was furious at this delay, but kept restraint upon his temper.

Everyone then got drunk, the Major and all his party partaking as well, myself most definitely included. There were no French near. It had been a hard journey, and would be harder still.

By the evening of November twenty-eighth, the various invited Indians had come in and Half King returned. Scarroyaddy, the Oneida chief, brought more news, acquired from an Indian on his way south from Venango.

His report was not a little alarming. The French at the forts had summoned all the Delawares, Shawnees, and Senecas they could lay hand upon in the vicinity and warned them not to make friends with the English, as there would be another French expedition toward the Forks of the Ohio in the spring.

Our Indians versus their Indians, and all belonging to the same tribes.

We were delayed one more day by Shingas's wife taking sick and some of the Shawnee chiefs having brought the wrong wampum belts. Then another council was held by the Indians—we English excluded—at which there was a change of mind. It was decided that Washington should be accompanied only by Half King and two other chiefs, and additionally by a small party of hunters, not the large force that had gathered here at Logstown. The Indians now feared that if the great mass of them were to go up to the French with us, it might be taken as an overture to battle and bring on war.

On the morning of the thirtieth, we set out at last—at nine o'clock rather than the Major's customary pre-dawn departure, the Indians seeing no need for such early rising. The weather was quite awful, full of snow and very cold. It was seventy miles to Venango by the longer upland Indian-trail route Half King had urged upon us, and we did not reach this place until December fourth.

I had lost this powerful feeling of striding the earth in seven-league boots. Out here, beset by a whirling blizzard, trudging through an endlessness of cold and misery and hardship, hundreds of miles from home with great walls of mountains in between, I felt lost and forlorn—as upon a strange and distant sea. My only consolation was that, assaulted by wind and wet, the red hue bestowed upon my face by Chief Shingas was fading.

When we finally reached Venango, the snow was so thick we did not see the French fort until we were within musket range of its palisades. There were Indians camped about the outer wooden wall, and some warriors came running at us with much ferocious whooping.

Sixteen

I would deem no man's fear unwarrantable in that situation. The French within the fort could have cut us down in a single volley if we so much as took aim at these leaping, screeching Indians hurrying toward us through the snow, agile as weasels despite its depth.

Washington, at the head of our column, halted his horse and moved hand to pistol. Gist stopped, too, but to look at Washington. Half King was ignoring those dancing fiends as he might a flock of birds and proceeding on nonchalantly directly toward the gate of the fort. I noticed for the first time that it was open—hardly a sign of belligerence. Washington, his attention devoted to the Indians, had not observed this.

I slapped my reins on my horse's flank, hurrying him past the Major and into the lead of our column, moving quite purposefully now for that portal. Some of our greeters turned to make a ring around me, without relenting in their whooping and hollering, but refrained from hostile act, even when I directed my horse through their cavort. It gave me a heady feeling, that bit of bravado. I hoped Washington wasn't angry.

He was. Drawing his horse up to mine, he leaned close and said, "Do that again, Mr. Morley, and I'll have you sent back to Will's Creek—alone." Then, stern-faced, he trotted forward.

Upon entering Fort Venango, we discovered this was less a proper work of military engineering than a simple stockade erected in perimeter around some Indian huts and a large log house I took to be that from which trader Frazier earlier had been dispossessed. The French colors, with all those fleurs-de-lis, flapped in the chill bluster from a pole set just before the house, and sentries stood to either side of the doorway on a porch of wooden planks.

They wore white uniforms with blue collars and cuffs. I recognized these from seafaring as belonging to French marines. Most of the men about the place, though, seemed simply woodsmen, clad in leather leggings, Indian-style moccasins, and long leather capot, or jacket, with what looked to be stocking caps. Gist assured me that these men were soldiers in the French colonial *Compagnies Franches*—though a few might be fur-trapping *voyageurs* or the irregular *coureurs des bois*.

"They're good soldiers, Tick," Gist said. "All of them. Regard 'em with respect."

Well, of course I did. I'd presumed they'd regard us with some hostility, intruders that we were, but they showed none of that. For the most, they seemed curious, as though we'd taken them by surprise.

Not entirely. As we halted our animals before the house, the door swung open and three officers came out, also in white uniforms, but without the scarves, long gloves, and woolly caps the sentries wore. These gentlemen seemed to know who we were.

The ranking man, a debonair and quite swarthy fellow of average height but evident muscularity, stepped forward, removed his hat, and bowed.

"*Bonjour, voyageurs,*" he said. "*Je suis le Capitaine Philippe Joncaire, et je commande ici. Bienvenu à Venango.*"

Van Braam had come up but sat there stupidly on his horse, staring. Washington gave him a cold eye. I didn't want to trample on Van Braam's sensibilities, what there were of them, or intrude upon his jurisdiction, but the circumstance suggested I or some French speaker intervene.

"He says he is Captain Joncaire and he's in command here," I translated. "He welcomes us to Venango."

"You speak French, Tick?" The Major seemed genuinely astonished.

"A little."

He waved me forward. "Well, both you and Van Braam assist me, then."

"*Ce n'est pas necessaire,*" said Joncaire. "I speak English. Please descend from your horses and come inside. You must be very cold, non?"

We'd been colder than I hitherto could possibly have imagined—from the morning we'd left Will's Creek on. Trooping over the porch, we followed the French captain inside and were made joyous by the great heat of the fire. As several of us hastened forward to it, Washington hung back, drew himself up into his most soldierly posture, removed his hat, and bowed stiffly to Joncaire.

"Major Washington, sir," he said, not saying whether King's regular or mere militia officer. "You are the commandant here?"

"*Bien sur.* My responsibilities embrace all the valley of the Ohio. Here at Venango." He swept his arm about. "*Le tout ensemble.*"

I heard these words with much happiness. Now Washington could deliver his letter, procure a reply, and—if the French were in a mind for hospitality, as this officer seemed—we could be off back for our own country after a good night's rest. Joncaire and his comrades appeared civilized fellows, not the sort to shoot us, imprison us, or turn us over to their Indians.

Washington produced from some inner recess of his clothing his leather pouch, and from it a folded and sealed document.

"Sir, I have come to present to the commander of French forces this letter from His Excellency Robert Dinwiddie, governor of Virginia, who writes on behalf of His Majesty, King George. The letter will acquaint you with—"

Joncaire threw his arm around the Major, steering him toward the fire.

"*Tres bien, monsieur, mais* . . . if you wish to make a presentation to the true commander, then it should be to a general officer. I believe one can be found to the north at Fort Le Boeuf."

"I was told Marin was dead."

"*Ah, oui. Quelle tristesse. Mais,* the man of whom I speak is Legardeur de Saint Pierre. He is *un grand homme, monsieur le Majeur. Un chevalier*—a knight—of the Order of Saint Louis. It is to him you must bring this important letter. For me to accept this in his place, it would be an impertinence, *non*?"

Washington looked downcast. His mind and heart must have been as much on the English side of the mountains as were mine.

"But we are made glad to see you nonetheless, *Majeur*," Joncaire said. "We welcome your company and look forward to your news. If you would sup with us this night, I should be most honored."

Washington looked about the room, uncertain. "I have nine men with me—and a party of Indians."

Joncaire's smile seemed to widen at the prospect. "No matter, monsieur. All of you are welcome at our table. And I shall also provide refreshment and entertainment for your Indians."

———

We white men settled our belongings in the large, rude room that was to be our lodging place. Then, on the Major's instruction, we washed as best we could to improve our appearance for this woodland dinner party. Washington was not content with that for himself. Sending one of the "servitors" for his personal baggage, he changed into the full splendor of his militia officer's uniform. Once done with this preparation, the Major, full of concern, drew Gist, Davison, Van Braam, and myself away from the others.

"Let them enjoy themselves as they will," he said with a nod to our lesser-ranked companions. "But if our hosts serve much wine or brandy, drink sparingly, and speak with care." He glanced at Van Braam, and then to me. "And you two, when they speak in their own tongue, listen well."

"I've heard of that Joncaire," Gist said. "He's not so young as he looks. He was with Celeron when they buried those plates, and has translated for the French governor with chiefs of the Six Nations. Done sizable business in these parts. Knows his Indians."

"He's very dark."

"Reason for that. His father was a French officer, his mother a Seneca squaw. He could be kin to Half King."

"He's a French officer? A half-breed?"

Washington seemed incredulous. This unpleasant snobbery of his would never leave him, no matter that there was doubtless some provision against it in his damnable rules of civility.

"Yes, Major," said Gist, with just a hint of grin. "Who better to lead in this country?"

"Well, watch him."

As we filed into the dining chamber arranged for us, there were but four Frenchmen at table—Joncaire, the two subalterns who had greeted us with him, and a fourth fellow I took to be a ranking sergeant. They had commenced the evening's enjoyment without waiting for us—in fact, may well have been at table when we first rode up.

At all events, the wine was flowing. As was good humor. And the table was heavy with simple but satisfying eatments, including a variety of roasted meats and good bread.

"Sit, gentlemen, sit," boomed out Joncaire. "And, please, drink. As much as you wish."

Following Washington's lead, I took my refreshment sparingly, as did Gist, though Van Braam drank thirstily, and our other men deemed this evening their jolly just reward for so much cold misery.

I kept my seat on our common bench close to Washington, to assist in the conversation as translation was required, for Van Braam was dulling his senses and the drink was also making the French officers difficult to understand in either tongue.

As I feared, there was ample occasion here for the Major to bring forth yet more of his rules of civility, and so he did. " 'Being set at meat, scratch not, neither spit, cough, or blow your nose, except there's a necessity for it,' " he said with an eye to our more vulgar tablemates. " 'Feed not with greediness . . . cut your bread with a knife . . . take no salt or cut bread with your knife greasy . . . keep your fingers clean, and when foul, wipe them on a corner of your table napkin . . . drink not nor talk with your mouth full.' "

If hard to comprehend, especially when in violation of the last rule of civility remarked by the Major, the French tongues came quite loose. Joncaire well understood the exact nature of our mission, and said so. Without really giving offense, he laughed at it.

"Je sais, je sais, je sais," he said. "You British have two men to our one under arms and a multitude of settlers waiting beyond the mountains. You wish us gone. You want to claim the Ohio for your own. But you British move with such slowness, *Monsieur le Majeur.* Your king is unsure, reluctant. Your governors quarrel with one another. And now the winter is here and it is a bad one.

"We have one hundred fifty men in each of our three forts north of the river. Come in the spring and you will find three times that number in the garrisons, and more to arrive. You will find a French fort at the Forks of the Ohio. You will be too late. You cannot stop us from taking hold of this valley. And once in our full possession, there it stays. How not? Be happy on your side of the mountains, *mon ami.* They are a natural frontier, and it is to our mutual content to honor them as such.

"You English claim this whole continent, yes? But for the most absurd reasons—because you have seen a coastline from a ship, because you have so presumptuously declared that Virginia's western boundary is the Pacific Ocean, because you have made treaty with the Iroquois Nation, who claim hegemony over all the other eastern tribes, though they do not have it.

"We French have walked these mountains, these forests, these marshes. We have paddled these rivers and lakes in our canoes and *bateaux*, made portages, traveled the Beautiful River all the way to the Mississippi, and the Mississippi from its source to the sea. We have built forts, buried metal plates to proclaim for all time that this land belongs to our Most Christian Majesty, King Louis. We claim this land, *monsieur*, because we are here!"

With that, he slammed his hand down hard on the table, causing nearby spillage. Conversation utterly halted, then there was nervous laughter.

My admiration for Washington, which had waned, began to grow once more. He did not rise to the provocations embedded in Joncaire's boasting by countering with accurate claims of British might, or any other dangerous revelation. As he was careful not to educate the French captain, so too was he cautious not to anger him. The Major's words remained full of amity and courtesy. He asked Joncaire's wisdom on foraging in such fierce weather—on the conduct of Indians in battle, the barbaric practice of scalping, Indian politics. Here, once more, he was told that the Indian Queen Alequippa was a power with whom he ought reckon, but this did not seem to take root.

The French heaped so much wood on their fire we eventually became discomforted by the heat—and made woozy. My resolve to follow the Major's admonition on drink weakened as the wine came to hand with increasing frequency, poured by the generous sergeant. At length, I left the bench and took my ease on the floor. A moment later, I was lying on my side, and asleep.

I awoke to note the fire down to a glowing mass of red coals and log ends, and nearly all in the room asleep and snoring—but for one of the French officers, who was singing croakily. I ducked my head as Washington stepped over me, moving to the door. There was a chilly draft and then the door shut tight. I dozed for a few minutes, then waked again, to see Washington settling his considerable person down on the floor beside me to take his slumber.

"Our damned Indians," he muttered. "Are all drunk."

———

It rained cold, hard, and without relent throughout the next day. Realizing it was French design to get and keep our Indians drunk, and thus divide them from our party, Washington labored diligently to get them sober, with small success.

By late afternoon, the Major had given up, as Joncaire was by then offering the Indians presents in addition to refreshment. A paltry offering, to be sure—beads, cooking untensils, a little gunpowder, a more generous quantity of rum. Half King had prepared a speech to make to Joncaire, but forgot too much of it.

When we finally broke camp, we were joined by the Frenchman La Force, whom I had taken for a sergeant at our welcoming banquet but who now identified himself as commissary officer in charge of the French stores. He brought with him three soldiers who could just as easily have been wild mountain men by their appearance—though you must realize that by now, my own was not much better. Only the Major still bothered with grooming, and that confined mostly to shaving.

These French said they were there to guide us to Le Boeuf. Gist could have done that, but Washington thought La Force's presence might help prevent any inadvertent hostile act. As we mounted, it commenced to rain quite hard. Later, this became snow. Washington wrote in his journal: "Excessive Rains, Snows, and bad Travelling, through many Mires and Swamps."

Half King and our Indians, fewer in number now, trudged along in that stoic manner of theirs. Our French guides, frequently nipping at liquor, were cheerier companions, making much jolly sport of our raft-crossing of French Creek, where we had to switch to the north bank on the last leg of our journey.

Fort Le Boeuf, which we reached December twelfth, was similar in size to Venango, but a much more military-looking fortification. Washington decided to camp outside it and took only Gist, Van Braam, Davison, and me with him when he rode up to the gate.

We were greeted by a junior officer who, like those at Venango, seemed to be expecting us—the Indian Express being most swift in the French employ. The officer, an ensign, conducted us to a house within the palisade and into a cold room, where we were received by the officer in charge—the Knight of St. Louis, Legardeur de St. Pierre, who, we discovered, was a mere captain, not a general. He was as well a rather elderly man, though possessed of a far more military bearing than Joncaire. The Major presented him with Dinwiddie's letter and his own verbal summary. St. Pierre glanced at the letter, rather wearily, I thought, then bade us wait in an adjoining apartment. He'd sent for the commandant from Fort Presque Isle, up on Lake Erie, whose presence here St. Pierre deemed imperative before he gave a reply.

That officer, one Captain Riparti, arrived within an hour, and Washington went through his formal presentation again. The French asked us to indulge them with some time to consider it, which Washington of course granted, returning to where the rest of our party waited outside the fort to prepare our camp. As our hired men went about establishing it, Washington and Gist—with me tagging along—set off on a perambulation of the land about the place. Washington pretended this was an idle promenade, spent as he might pass the time on a suimmer's evening on Williamsburg's mall, but in fact, he was very observantly taking note of the fort's situation and armament, and asked us to do the same. Now we were all spies.

The post had been built at a fork in the creek and was nearly surrounded by water. It possessed eight six-pounder cannon, two to each of its four bastions, plus a four-pounder at the gate. Those of our men the Major detailed to bring water from the creek were asked to count any and all canoes they might observe pulled up along the banks. They reported fifty Indian-made canoes of birch bark and some 170 French-built of pine, all of large size. It was a most considerable fleet for this country and spoke of a large quantity of Indians and supplies in the vicinity.

We were kept waiting a very long time for the reply from this bemedaled old captain, with no explanation given for the delay. In the meanwhile, much snow fell and the weakness of our horses became increasingly apparent and worrisome. Washington decided to send them back in the care of Currin and two other men, ordering them to wait for us at Venango.

The fourteenth of December arrived with us still there and no French letter in hand. Washington was sure they were delaying in hope of persuading our Indians to abandon us and remain at Le Boeuf, where they might be seduced to the French cause, Helped by Gist and Davison, he did everything he could to keep the Indians faithful, but French gifts and more rum, and now also brandy, took their toll of his resolve.

On the evening of the fifteenth, St. Pierre finally gave the Major his sealed written reply to deliver to Dinwiddie. Half King, Scarroyaddy, and the others refused to leave with us, the former arguing he still had important things to say to the French and that one of the lesser chiefs accompanying him, named White Thunder, had been injured and was unable to walk.

Gist learned of a more compelling reason for the Indians' decision to linger: St. Pierre was offering actual firearms. We departed with Washington showing some bitterness, though Half King promised to try to meet us later at the Forks, or if nothing else, to see us on the other side of the mountains in the spring. I made a point of shaking the chief's hand, which he seemed to appreciate, as it took me some time to extricate mine from his grasp.

The French gave us one of their large canoes in which to descend the creek, a vessel commodious enough for all our remaining party and baggage, though it proved unwieldly and dangerous in the bumping, careening, swollen waters. No fewer than seven times did we crack against rock—with such unnerving thumps and bashes that I feared I would end my sea captain's days ironically drowning in waters five hundred miles from the ocean.

Even without the collisions, can you imagine paddling such a craft all day in near-freezing weather, with rain and snow whipping about, fingers and hands utterly numb, arms and back aching, and bones so frigid they seemed to rattle against each other with every shudder and shiver of our bodies? And having logs and boulders come at you with almost every turning of the bow? But we were all for home now, and for one to let up would slow us all.

The creek turned ever more capricious. For stretches it would be frozen so hard we'd have to haul the canoe along by hand. Then we'd be back in our fast-flowing currents and slackwater eddies. And then, at turns, the water would be so shallow we'd have to get out and slosh along beside the vessel.

At one such interval, we found serendipity in the form of an overturned and abandoned French canoe with a great hole in its bottom. Some of the cargo from this wreck was found caught beneath the ice along the bank—several kegs of wine and brandy. Washington allowed us to take two kegs of brandy and one of wine abroad, but forbore the rest because of the weight.

"We'll husband it for the hard portages," he said.

Gist did not think it would last long, and he was right.

———

Currin and his lads were at Venango when we arrived, finding them living happily on French food and grog. Our party's horses were now much the sorrier, so weak and feeble as to totter rather than walk, especially in the wind. Washington wanted away from the French and onto the road to Williamsburg as soon as possible. We held our own council and it was decided that Van Braam, Davison, and the others would take the animals and as much baggage as could be carried and proceed via the snow-choked trails as best they could to Will's Creek and thence to Virginia.

Making haste, Washington and Gist would go on foot, traveling lightly and swiftly over the most direct route to the same destination. Gist disagreed with this plan at first. As he told me later, "I was unwilling he should undertake such a travel, who had never been used to walking before this time. But as he insisted on it, what could I do?"

True to the name of Tick, I'd no intention of leaving the Major's side—at least not till we were returned to English civilization. I pressed my case to accompany them. He frowned over this, then relented. Gist knew little French and we'd a long way to go before there'd be no need of it.

All three of us strapped packs upon our backs and placed upon our feet some clumsy-looking but most useful French and Indian contrivances called snowshoes.

Then we were off. Within a mile, though I'd thought myself by now a hardened veteran of the frontier, I found myself wishing I'd stayed with the main body—so rapid was Gist's stride and pace, and he an old fellow of forty-eight!

We went eighteen miles in all that snow, slept wrapped in our shelter cloth, and were in Murdering Town the next day, passing through the place quickly. Our plan was to quit the trail here and strike out straight south for Shannopin's Town and the Forks, avoiding Logstown entirely. All went well enough for a three-or four-mile stretch, but then, as we were ascending a ridge, Gist, in the lead, suddenly raised his hand. I listened for whatever it was he heard, but could note only the wind. Then at once I saw what had stayed him. From behind some trees ahead and to the left, came several Indians.

Seventeen

"Are they friendly?" Washington asked, though none of the approaching Indians appeared that. The Major had changed back into his woodland clothes and looked as much trapper or trader as we.

"Were we French, I guess we'd find 'em so," said Gist. "I make them to be Mingoes, but not from that bunch of Half King's that's been so well disposed to us. Half King would be useful here. These warriors have been following us, I think. Maybe all the way from Le Boeuf."

"I want to keep moving," Washington said.

"They may want to talk a bit."

"If that's their desire, then they'll be disappointed. We've no time to waste."

We moved on, single file, Washington in the lead. The Indians had drawn themselves to one side of our path, forming a line by which we had to pass. I recalled Gist's telling me of an Indian sport in which prisoners brought into a village were made to run a gamut of old men, women, and children who beat them with stones and sticks. Three of these Indians had guns.

They made no move against us, but watched us hard. They much resembled Half King in their dress and adornment, but I found no solace in that.

Gist raised his hand in form of greeting, but Washington, stiff as a board, just walked by the warriors, I think without even a blink, striding on up the hill. I followed, but could not resist turning and looking into one of those stern painted faces, finding no encouragement to contentment in it. Gist trailed now just behind me, as rear guard, his long rifle cradled but loaded and primed. I had a knife in my belt, though not much notion of how to use it against an Indian warrior skilled in all the arts of mortal combat.

Once we were past them, I held my eyes forward. Should an arrow, tomahawk, or bullet next be speeding toward my back, I'd no wish to observe its approach.

None came. It took three forevers to reach the top of the rise. When we got there, I finally risked another glance behind. The Indians had utterly vanished!

I was breathing heavily from our swift exertion. So, to a noticeable degree, was the Major. He smiled broadly in reassurance, exposing his bad teeth. I think he was more relieved even than I, and I was ready to embrace whatever religion had got us through that encounter, if got through we had.

"If you want to rest, we hadn't better," said Gist.

Washington took a deep breath, then shook out his shoulder muscles. "I know that." He started down the ridge's following slope, slipping a little in the snow.

———

Near the last of daylight, we had the good fortune to come upon an abandoned Indian hut that had no door, and may never have had one. It was dry inside however. There were a few bones and snatches of hide and fur scattered about the earthen floor, but they'd been gone over by insects and were clean of meat. Gist figured they'd been there many months.

He set down his pack and slowly lowered himself to the floor. He showed no pain, only fatigue, but had he hurt twice as much as I did, I doubted he'd be visible about it.

"Now we can rest a while," he said.

He shifted his seat to face the open doorway, leaning back against the wall with his rifle at the ready. He pulled some jerky from his pack with frigid fingers.

"I fear we've made a mistake in striking out just the three of us like this," he said. "We were safer as a big party."

"We were also slower," Washington said. He'd taken out his writing materials and was scratching out a few lines in the last of the light.

"Fast's no good if you're not gettin' were you're goin', Major."

"What do you mean? Are we lost?"

I looked to the fading sunset, which seemed more to the south of us than west.

"No. I'm just worried by those Mingoes."

"We'll stand watches."

"I'll take first'n," said Gist. "You two eat and then get some sleep."

I took one bite of the hard dried beef, chewed without enthusiasm, then put it away, rolling into my blanket and closing my eyes.

———

No one awakened me for a turn at watch. Emerging from my cold slumber in the morning, I found Washington in Gist's place by the door and the scout at the rear of the hut, each snoring. It was growing light, past George's favored time of departure.

I held no fault with the Major. True, our young commander had breached his own discipline, slumbering on guard, and maybe put us all at risk of a scalping knife, but we still had our hair, as the traders liked to say, and I'd gotten a full night's uninterrupted rest. Had I stood watch in turn as the Major intended, I doubtless would now be snoring in his place.

It was a stiffly painful business getting to my feet. I shuffled outside in all my wrappings, finding the early sky now colored a dim gray, dreary and gloomy in the extreme. I went around to the rear of the hut to pee and washed my hands and face in snow. Then, yawning, I retraced my steps.

But not completely. There, on the other side of the clearing the hut faced, standing against a tree, was an Indian. I wasn't certain of him at first, then recognized him as one of those Mingoes from the previous day. Who else'd be haunting us?

I called to my companions, wakening Gist. He came quickly out to join me, bringing his rifle. The Indian, I saw, had a musket himself, held straight against his leg and shoulder with the stock resting in the snow.

Gist called to the visitor in the Seneca language, apparently urging him forward. Gist's tone was initially harsh, but it quickly softened when the Indian was standing before us and the two fell into conversation.

"He's offering to guide us to the Forks," said Gist. "I don't ken how he knows we're bound there, but he says we're upriver from where we want to be, that we should be making more directly for the south."

"Is he right?" It was Washington, who had now emerged from the hut as well.

"Possible so. There's no trail. All these swamps and marshes we've had to go 'round—that's been shifting us east. If we don't shift back, we could miss the Forks by a far piece, maybe end up in New York."

He laughed, to show he was joking, but the suggestion made Washington shudder. He was mad for Williamsburg, or was it Alexandria that had him yearning?

"Do you trust him?" he asked.

Gist grinned. "Trust ain't the right word. I got a knowledge of the Mingoes. I think he might be a help to us. Surely he's been to Shannopin's Town and knows its way. You'll remember that place is within a shout of the Forks."

The Indian never gave his name. After Gist told him he was accepted as our guide, he went back to his tree and waited as we completed our toilet, grabbed a few bites of breakfast, and re-prepared ourselves for the journey. When Washington reached down for his pack, however, the Indian bolted toward us as though in a charge.

He had no weapon raised, so I felt no real panic, but wondered what he was about. Theft? He grabbed up the Major's pack, all right, but then stood there, muttering a few Seneca words to Gist. Washington said nothing, but his eyes were full of offense.

"He wants to carry your pack, Major," said Gist.

Now Washington smiled. He had a manservant again.

The Indian struck out toward the south, moving at a much faster pace than we had been keeping. At the first marsh we came to, he took us to the right, and continued to alter course obliquely, steering south by southwest. I was reminded of how I'd set the helm of the *Hannah* in strong winds and currents to compensate for the drift.

But was he steering us to the Forks, or Logstown? Or where? It was difficult to tell our exact direction with the sky so overcast. None of us had been over this terrain before except the Indian—a man of Half King's nation, but of what politics? This would have to be a matter of trust, yet why not? There was only the one of him, and three of us. We couldn't be truly lost. Ahead of us was either the Allegheny or the Ohio.

Hmmm. Could we tell the one from the other? Across the former was the road home. Across the latter, the vast wilderness I'd not yet seen: White Woman's Town; Pickawillany, where the trader's heart had been cut from his body while he lived; Caintuckee, a mythic land.

We were falling behind our guide ever increasingly, though he lacked our snowshoes. The Indian would stop, wait impatiently for us to draw closer, then hurry off again. It was an agony to follow him. I'd long become used to the constancy of the numbness of my feet and fingers, and almost wished that condition now upon my leg muscles and those of back and shoulders, to end their aching. Washington looked as discomfited. Gist, old man that he was, kept swinging along.

Pausing only briefly to eat, we'd made eight or nine miles by midafternoon. In the journal he kept, Gist later wrote of our progress at this point: "The Major's feet grew very sore, and he very weary." There was no such entry in Washington's journal. I read them both, when I had leisure to do so months later. They didn't contradict each other so much as leave out in the one what was put into the other.

Now the Indian offered to carry the Major's gun, in addition to the pack and his own firearm. I wished Washington would agree to it, in the hope the added weight might slow our guide down. But George declined the offer. When it was made again, he declined it once more—with some vehemence.

"Watch him," muttered Washington as the Indian moved out once more. "He's too helpful."

I grunted something in reply. Watching the Indian would require keeping my head up instead of letting it hang down as I wished, content to follow the footsteps in the snow ahead of me. But I complied with the Major's request. He struck me as close to staggering himself, his weariness all the more noticeable for his feigning otherwise.

Our guide now provided me with something to watch, all right—perfidious treachery. He trotted ahead some fifteen paces, then of a sudden whirled about, lifted his musket to his shoulder and took aim at us—as best as I could judge, the ball meant for Washington.

Happily, the Indian was in too great haste. The weapon discharged before I could give warning, but the bullet sang through the air between the Major and myself, striking a tree just behind with a loud crack that echoed in the cold.

I dropped to one knee. Washington just stood there. Gist, his senses still lively, plunged forward.

"Onto the bastard!" he shouted, " 'Fore he reloads!"

I'd heard that a trained British regular could get off three rounds from a regulation-issue muzzle-loading musket in a minute. This Indian was not so practiced with his weapon. As he struggled with ball and powder, Gist came loping toward him, butt of his rifle swinging 'round.

He struck the Indian in the shoulder, spinning him. The devil's firearm fell, but he still stood, reaching for his knife.

I attained the spot myself now and leapt forward, sliding under his knife swing and hitting his legs. Unprepared for this, he went sprawling.

Gist was on him in a blink, knees to the man's chest and shoulders, his own long knife out of its sheath.

"No!"

It was Washington, trudging up to us. I'd regained my feet and was standing over the Mingo, my rifle—not primed, as the Indian could not know—aimed at his face.

"Wait!" commanded Washington.

Gist looked 'round, impatient, angry. "Damn all, Major, this one's a hostile! You can count on him to fire another ball at us first chance."

"He's helpless," Washington said.

The three of us stood around the man. Gist growled a few Indian words, apparently a command to stand up. The Indian did so. There was anxiety in his face, but not what I would call fear. I think his apprehension had more to do with his religion and notion of afterlife than what he had to expect from us. He'd concluded we were about to kill him; there was naught he could do about it.

Unnervingly, the man suddenly began chanting—a mournful, primal sound. Some form of prayer?

"Let me put it this way, Major," Gist said. "If it was you or me or Tick caught by three of them, we'd be havin' nose and ears cut off by now, and they'd be movin' down to a place more painful."

"Ours is a peaceable mission," Washington said. "We travel as diplomats. I want no bloodshed."

Gist pondered this. I could stand this chanting not much longer.

"Very well, Major." The knife went back into the sheath, but Gist snatched up the Indian's musket. "You want to take him prisoner? It'll slow us appreciable."

"No. Let him go back to his people."

Like a fish returned to a river, I thought, except this one might want to come back. I stepped to his rear and pulled off Washington's pack, then pulled his tomahawk from his belt and plucked his knife up from the snow, stepping back. His chanting missed not a note or beat. His head was tilted back, his eyes closed. He was waiting for the blow.

Gist leaned close and shouted something at the fellow in Seneca. His eyelids snapped open. As Gist stepped back again, the fellow gave us all quick, dark glances.

"Go!" said Gist in English. "Be off, you bastard!"

Still giving us wary looks, the Indian backed away till he was as many paces from us as he'd been when he'd fired that shot. Then abruptly, like a startled deer, he bolted for the trees. In a moment, he'd vanished.

Washington wearily sank to the ground beside his pack, rubbing his knees and calves. He looked about the place. "Should we camp here?"

Gist grinned sardonically. "Oh no, Major. You've just made it damned perilous to be about this place. We don't know where that Mingo's friends are, or how many. But they may be near, so we want to be elsewhere, far, and fast. I am sorry, sir, but we must keep going."

And so we did—all night. How we kept direction, I know not. Large breaks developed in the clouds, admitting some starlight, and the snow offered its own faint glowing guidance in the dark. How we kept on as long as we did, I cannot explain in any way. Something put aside Gist's age and Washington's fatigue and my own plaguey numbness, which had come to envelop legs and arms and, so it seemed at times, the skin of my face. Came dawn and we were still moving, still with hair, no Indians in pursuit.

The sun rose. At the next halting, Washington looked at the older man with great imploring seriousness. The other shook his head and resumed his trudge. Washington shifted his pack, then followed. So did I, without much feeling, but still moving.

Gist took us several times sloshing through streambeds, to lose the trail we made in the snow, and at one point was clever enough to make trail from a creek and double it back to the same watercourse upstream. There was much I could have learned in simple observation of this remarkable man, but it was all I could do now to keep focused on his back.

Finally, we made cold camp in a rocky glen, eating dried beef and huddling together beneath a stone overcropping, surviving this night, too.

Another day, another night—none of us dropping dead—we at last reached the Allegheny, by Gist's measure some four miles above Shannopin's Town. Most, if not all, of Shingas's people had come with the chief to the French forts. If any remained, Gist was not sure we'd be welcomed in the village anymore, and so chose to avoid it. Washington wanted no more of Indians, at all events. He was desperate for a camp and sleep, but he knew, as did we all, that it had to be on the other side of the river.

But how to obtain this goal? The Allegheny was bewilderingly higher, fuller, and swifter than when we'd left it, with shore ice extending out some fifty yards from either bank—and the open channel between, a raging, killing torrent, filled with jagged lumps and crags of broken ice cascading along like weapons of war. There was no swimming it. We'd arrive on the other side dead, frozen, and cut up bloody, if arrive at all.

"Must be an ice jam upriver breaking up," said Gist. "Could take hours. Maybe days."

"We'll build a raft," Washington said.

Gist looked to the lowering sun. "Not tonight."

We made another cold camp without firelight, but next morning, Gist allowed a fire to warm us and help burn through the logs we fetched for the raft at measured lengths. For all our weaponry, we had but one poor hatchet—that Indian's—and the carpentry proceeded slowly, and at times, painfully. During one of my turns with the tool, my hand, clumsy with cold, let it slip and I cut my leg, having to bind it tight to stanch the bleeding.

We worked all that short winter's day, producing a fearfully bad-crafted vessel of four long logs, two crosspieces fore and aft, and a third long log running diagonally from port forequarter to starboard aft, the whole of it bound with vine.

The sun was down and the sky was fading.

"We'd best launch now," said Gist. "But we'll need poles."

"Poles?" said Washington. "The water's deep."

He was so bearded now, and dirty, he looked a bear in his leather clothes. I thought of one of his rules of civility that he'd earlier badgered us with: " 'Wear not your Clothes, foul or dusty, but See they be Brush'd once every Day at least, and take Heed that you approach not to any Uncleanliness.' "

"Deep in some places," said Gist. "In others, not. No matter what, we'll need poles to keep clear of those blocks of ice."

We got the raft, which creaked alarmingly but held, out over the shore ice. Then, with a dash, almost flipping our handiwork, we shoved it into the water. Gist leaped onto its nearest log, setting a pole to hold the whole still for us. I jumped next, landing astraddle the cross log and hurting myself additionally. When Washington went for it, the raft had begun to spin away with the current, so his leap fell a little short and his leg went into the water. I flung forth my arm and, grasping it, he pulled himself full aboard, half soaked.

With amazing swiftness, we hurtled along downstream. The poles worked well enough in fending off the ice floes and in pushing us into the mainstream of the central channel. But not farther across! Downstream, I saw the arrow shape of a small, treed island, with rocks and rapids to the fore of it. We had to get across before we were swept onto that nasty promontory, or into the wild water.

Gist, mustering more strength than Washington or me, managed to use some larger floes as brace to push with pole against, moving us grudgingly closer to the farther shore, but all at once, a bulky block he'd set pole upon abruptly spun around and came crashing upon us at the aft, heaving our clumsy bow around and sending us sideways against a jumble of ice chunks jammed against some underwater obstacle. Caught in these, we were held just long enough for a monstrous barge-like hunk of ice that came up swiftly to strike us full across the stern and knock the logs asunder.

I clung on, as did Gist, but Washington went into the water. He'd been trying to free us by pushing down with his pole, but with the force of the collision, the water end of his staff slipped and out over the side he went, clinging to the pole and somehow, madly, balancing upon it. There we might have lost him, but he had the wisdom to let go and swing for the logs of the raft as we swept back into the current.

With the raft of but two logs now, Gist and I astride them and Washington holding fast to one, we plowed along the river and crashed unavoidably onto the rocks just forward of the island, surviving, but having our crude vessel now come completely apart and losing nearly all our weaponry in the process. There was nothing for us now but to swim the few feet to the island's shore, which, though we were much banged about, we somehow managed.

The night was advancing rapidly. Gist had more bad news for us. In the tumult of the ice-jammed river, he'd also lost his fire-starting flint. With our rifles gone into the water when the logs were torn apart, we had only one pistol. Attempts to spark tinder with that failed utterly in the stiff wind. Marooned on that rocky islet, we would have to pass the night without a fire.

Using our remaining shelter cloth and some brush, we arranged a lean-to against one of the boulders and crawled within this sanctuary. Gist had us get out of our shoes and leggings and wrappings and dry our feet and other soaked places as best we could. Then he proceeded to do something most strange, commencing to rub his bare feet with snow, over and over, urging us to do the same. "To cure the bite of the frost," he said.

The Major followed the example for a few minutes, then tired of it. I didn't bother at all. Gist was wise in all the ways of the wilderness, I knew, but this eccentricity was just too much in my state of pain and exhaustion. I reclothed myself as dryly and warmly as I could manage and tried to sleep, wondering if it might be for the last time. I was bone-tired, but sleep wouldn't come. The wind rose, the temperature fell. Washington and I crowded and huddled together, but the cold remained unbearable. I could feel him shivering against my back.

"George," I whispered. "How fare you?"

"I'm freezing, Tick. Every damned inch of me."

"What will we do in the morning?" I asked.

"If we survive until morning."

"If we do, we'll try another raft," said Gist from wherever he lay or sat. "If that fails, we'll swim."

"We'll never make it across in water that cold," Washington said.

"Maybe not," said Gist. "But we'll die for sure waiting here."

We fell silent. Washington began shivering again.

"George."

"What, Tick?"

"What if we do die?"

"Then we'll die. All men die. My brother died."

"What if we die tonight?"

"Shit, Tick," said Gist.

"What will they say of us?" I said. "Three more unfortunates, vanished in the wilderness. All they'll find of us is our bones."

"They'll find us before we're bones," said Gist. "Frazier's trading post can't be but a mile or two along the river. People pass this island. Traders. Indians. And we'll be froze, like winter meat."

"Why not call out to Frazier?"

"He couldn't hear us if he were just across the water here."

"Be still now, Tick," said Washington.

More silence. More wind. I had my hands dug in my armpits, but there was no warm place for my poor feet.

"I almost died in your service once before, Mr. Washington," I said.

"When in hell was that?"

"Last spring. When we first met. The delays at, uh, Belvoir and Williamsburg brought me a day late into the sea, and we were pounded by the worst storm I ever experienced. I don't know how we sailed out of it again."

I was angry at myself for this whining, but I was truly despondent. This seemed the end.

"Then I am grateful to you, Tick. Thrice grateful. You did me service then. You and Christopher subdued that murderous Indian. And were it not for you, I'd have drowned falling from the raft."

"Only to freeze to death here."

"Do our duty," Washington said.

"I'm wondering what they'll say of us," I said. "How we'll be remembered."

"That Indian back there'll remember us as fools," said Gist.

"I delivered the governor's letter to the French," Washington said. "They'll find the commandant's reply on my person. We completed our mission. We'll be remembered honorably."

"Is that all you want to be remembered for, George? Carrying letters?"

"Tick," said Gist, "your chatter is getting damnable pesky."

"I'm sorry," I said. "It's the cold. I can't abide it."

"You got no choice. Though I wish you'd attend to your feet. Y'want me to?"

"No, thank you."

"Think of a woman you love," said Washington. "That'll warm you."

"The woman I love got me put in gaol," I said. "I've no hope of another encounter, and damned little wish of it."

"We live through this," Washington said, "and all things'll be possible."

He had stopped his shuddering.

"You have a woman to think upon, George?"

"I do, and let those be our last words tonight."

Eighteen

We slept. We lived. I don't know to this day how we accomplished either, as I was sure sleep and death would be all the same. In my desperation, I had a sort of conversation with God, as I understood there to be a God, but I don't know if it amounted to a prayer. Perhaps one or both of my companions had managed this more properly.

It was Washington who this time woke first in the morning. He crept from between the two of us out into the frigid air.

"We are saved," I heard him say.

Gist and I crawled forth as well. We all three then stood there in awe at what nature had wrought, staring at the river as though at biblical revelation.

It was frozen over in great completeness, the ice so thick it looked as though it could support an army.

Our limbs felt as thick and hard and lifeless as the ice. They barely worked. Even Gist dropped our lone pistol while just trying to stick it in his belt. Finally, we had our equipage all together in our arms and clung to it tightly as best we could, staring at the broad highway of white before us.

"Perhaps it's a dream," I muttered.

"Real enough, Tick," said the Major from beneath his muffler, which, like ours, was wound about the lower half of his face.

"Cold's twice what it was yesterday," Gist said.

" 'Twill be colder still if we don't get moving."

So we did, our breath a fog about our heads, Washington once again leading. From that morning on, there was never again any "Major," "Mr. Gist," or "Captain" among us. We were simply and always, unless the formality of a situation required otherwise, Tick, Chris, and George.

———

Once across the river, it was true enough a short way thence to Frazier's trading post, where we found the proprietor in a welcoming mood and all the delights of our imaginings: a big roaring fire, food, whiskey—also blankets, guns, and horses for the purchase, though at a dear price, all signed for by Washington on the King's marker. Gist offered cheaper if we'd wait till we reached his plantation, but George—the Major—wanted no more walking.

Subtracting from our happiness was the discovery of a party of some twenty Indian warriors at Frazier's, identified by Gist as belonging to the Ottawa tribe, which marked them as French in their presumed inclination. They seemed content to regard Frazier's as a neutral place, however, and accepted us as no more than fellow travelers. Frazier allowed them a little liquor, and with some of that in their bellies, they commenced to relate their recent adventure—all Indians, I judged, were compulsive storytellers—translated by Frazier in vivid form.

They were indeed Ottawas, from the west of the Lake Erie country. They'd been bound south and east into Pennsylvania and Virginia as a war party looking for enemies among the tribes there. At the head of the Cunnaway, also called Kanhawa, River—some hundred miles or more west and south of where we were at Frazier's—they'd come upon a log habitation belonging to seven white settlers, all of whom lay about the place murdered and, but for a woman with fair hair, scalped. These victims had been stripped of their possessions and most of their clothes, and there was at least one child among them. Hogs were running wild and free, they said, feeding liberally on these remains.

The Indians insisted they were innocent of this atrocity, which they thought might have been the work of Shawnee or Delaware. Not wanting to be blamed for it themselves, and then hunted down by the English, they said they had called off their expedition and were returning north. Some of them had scalps on their belts, but the hair was black and they looked to be old and ratty.

Gist said he had been by that place of the massacre on his mapping expedition of the Ohio country two winters before, but there had been no cabin there then. He wouldn't have settled that far out himself, he declared, not with a family. He wondered who would have advised these poor folk it was well to do so.

"It's no fit end for an Englishman," said Washington.

"End it is," Gist said. "Too far and too late for any burying. They all be gone to the pigs by now."

————

I do not think that the Major's opinion of the native population of America had improved much by that instance, and certainly their females had not risen in his esteem. But he was far more apt now to heed the counsel of those with a knowledge of these aboriginal people, such as Mr. Gist had. Upon hearing that Queen Alequippa was lately in residence at an encampment three miles up the Youghiogheny from Frazier's, Washington, once we had our new horses, elected to stop by that place and pay his respects to her before continuing on to Gist's plantation.

He took her two presents acquired at Frazier's: a warm match coat and a cask of whiskey. We all knew which would make her the happiest, and so it proved, but we left before she'd too furiously gotten into her merriment. At all events, her fealties seemed intact. We still could claim a friend, and maybe now a more loyal one than before—though George was little pleased with her advice.

"I asked her what the English should do," he said, "and she said to stay away from this country."

On the way out into the wilderness, time had passed so slowly that every hour seemed a journey in itself. Returning now on a trail become familiar, it was all the same as turnpike to us. We arrived at Gist's plantation long before I expected. Washington reminded Gist his obligation to us would not terminate until we reached Will's Creek. Gist had no objection, asking only that we stay the night.

Washington, his fatigue still a great weight upon him, retired directly after Mrs. Gist's good supper. I attempted a repair of my person, most immediately attending to the poor condition of my feet, which, with wrappings and stockings removed, appeared most horrible. Mrs. Gist fetched a basin and I attempted a bathing of them, but bereft of dirt and grime, the flesh still was disfigured by cuts and the sores of blisters. Worse, the dirt on the two outer toes of my left foot refused to come off, nor was any feeling in them restored by my rubbing, though I used a coarse cloth of Mrs. Gist's loan and strong soap and hot water.

"I fear they 're dead," said Gist, undertaking an examination. "Or will be soon."

"My feet?"

"The toes. The two on what you sailors'd call your port side. It's the frost. It kills the flesh if too long exposed. I feared for my own of this affliction, but I been spared, except for here."

He extended the smallest finger of his left hand. It had the same blue-black color as my toes along its outer edge, at the center of which was a white patch, but the disfigurement was in much smaller and fainter degree.

"I'll lose that skin for sure," said Gist, "but it's not got into the meat. Your foot now, that's another matter. 'Tis serious, Tick."

"What's to be done?" asked Washington, who'd drawn near.

Gist sighed. "Chop 'em off."

"Chop?" I asked. "Off?"

"Only way. Otherwise, the death in them toes is goin' to keep comin' at you. I seen it happen. Seen many a man's leg go black and dead from a musket ball and kill him, all in a week. Maybe less."

Washington leaned close in his own examination, exhibiting some repugnance. "It appears not so dire to me," he said. "Can he not be bled?"

"Bleed him? For this?"

"And drain the evil humours."

Gist shook his head. "The evil humours will go with the toes if we chop 'em now. If not, 'twill look dire soon enough."

I'd seen an amputation once—aboard a Spanish ship in the West Indies. A seaman had taken shot in his upper leg in some fracas with pirates, and the ball had shattered the bone. The ship's surgeon had used a saw with a fiendish curved blade, having cut the flesh farther down and folded it back in flaps before taking to the muscle and bone. Once this was sawn through, he'd burned the bloody parts to cauterize them, then sewn up the one flap of skin over the other. They said it was a perfect job.

The man was dead the next morning, but the doctor said if he hadn't operated, it would have happened all the surer and quicker.

I wanted none of this for my poor foot. Perhaps these toes might yet heal. If chopped they must be, I desired no recuperation here. I knew a nicer place for that.

"I can make it to Will's Creek," I said.

"You sure, Tick?"

"I am, George. Honest. If we keep ahorse."

"It's possible," said Gist. "But he gambles."

———

It alternately rained and snowed—as Washington noted, in all our journey we had but one day in which it had not done either—but we surely were no more miserable than before; rather, we were encouraged by the nearness of our goal, each mountain ridge behind us one less ahead, and only four to cross before Will's Creek.

In truth, worried as I was by whatever was amiss in my foot, it didn't pain me. If anything, stuck in that stirrup, the ailment was comforted by the pressure against it. Certainly it got no better, but I felt no worse. As Washington kept saying, I would soon be in the hands of a reliable physician who could properly bleed me. To keep my mind from it, he brought forth a new subject to occupy us: the theatre.

I'd no idea of this before, but the Major was quite mad for theatrics, comedy, and the dramatic. He'd only two years before seen his first stage production—*The Tragedy of George Barnwell*, performed in Barbados—and since had attended every play produced in Williamsburg, each more than once. He was among a group encouraging the establishment of a theater in Alexandria.

"Why not a theater wherever a habitation?" he asked with some excitement. "Why not a play from every book? This Cato you gave me. There's drama in it, of a sort. We could devise such a work ourselves."

I'd seen theatricalities in Charleston and New York. We exchanged our memories of actors, scenes, and lines. Washington had never read Shakespeare, but recollected much of it from the Tidewater presentations he'd seen. I vowed to bring him volumes of the bard's work if occasion allowed—if, that is, I didn't die of dead feet.

What merry mood we kept was taken from us by the long reach of Governor Dinwiddie. Three days after leaving Gist's plantation, as we descended the fourth ridge of the Alleghenies with but one between us and Will's Creek and the north bend of the Patowmack, we encountered on the trail a group of eleven men and seventeen horses, bearing tools and supplies. They were an advance party sent from Williamsburg to prepare for construction of a fort at the Forks of the Ohio!

Much as Gist and I were at first pleased by the contact, Washington was little gladdened, and showed us that in his face. Dinwiddie had sent these men without waiting for the Major's report and intelligence. The governor obviously had been already sold by others on the idea of the Forks as a site for the fort. Washington would arrive to find his counsel on the matter irrelevant. Our entire mission and all it risked—including the possible loss of my toes—might indeed be viewed as nothing more significant than courier's work. These brave men were going forth to set the King's flag in the Ohio. Worse, they spoke of Captain Trent coming later with a larger workforce and a body of troops. They, not Washington, would put a fort at the Forks.

What role then was left for our brave Major? He intended to find out— damned soon. Parting with these men—after offering them instruction of what lay ahead, which they much appreciated—Washington pressed on with great vigor.

There was one more encounter, this with settlers. They were two families, some fifteen folk in all, including children, with two wagons, which would be having a hard time of it on so narrow a trail. Why they had set out in this season and inclemency, and at such a rancorous time in the affairs of great nations, I could not fathom. They ignored Gist's warning to turn back, but accepted the invitation to stop at his plantation. I hope they heeded the wisdom of his advice not to think of settling beyond the Allegheny River. Perhaps Frazier, if they got that far, would tell them of the hog's dinner out at the head of the Kanhawa.

———

We rode into the settlement at Will's Creek to no heroes' welcome, for it was once again raining in sheets and all inhabitants were under shelter. Proceeding to Gist's cabin, we made no sound but to slump from saddle into mud, but a horse whinnied and at that, the door flew open. Out ran the fair and freckled Anne, her widened eyes first upon her father, then brightly turned to George. This flustered him. He looked away, setting to his saddlebags.

"Your mother sends her greeting, Daughter," said Gist, "We're now in need of dinner, and much else."

"I am glad to see you well, Father. And you, Major." Now she glanced to me, with a quick, small smile. "I'll fetch Mercy."

I nodded to Anne, wiping brow and face free of rain, then started forward toward the warmly beckoning doorway. My foot had been numb, but I'd paid it no mind. Now, with this first step, it failed me, and down into the muck I pitched.

Nineteen

They laid me on Gist's own bed—a pallet in the rearmost of the two rooms of his cabin—and gave me whiskey until I was raving. Then they gave me more. I remember talking with Washington for a brief time, and half the population of Will's Creek apparently in the room.

I could not quite comprehend what the Major said and began falling into sleep, catching myself quickly. " 'Sleep not when others speak,' " I said.

"What's that, Tick?"

"One of your rules of civility, George, which I was about to violate."

"Sleep, Tick. You've served me well."

He vanished. Then it was Gist and some old woman. The work upon my poor, wretched foot was done after I'd passed from consciousness.

——————

I awoke to awful pain, but knew its cause, if reluctant to examine said cause closely. From this point forth, the hurt could serve as measure. If it decreased, I'd be getting better. If worse, then I'd be ailing, more than likely bound for dead.

I tilted my head forward. After so much liquor, there was pain in that as well. My left foot, happily, appeared still to be there, extended from beneath the blanket and over the edge of the mattress. It was swathed in a clean cloth bandage so thick in windings it seemed a round thing. I could not tell what shape might be beneath.

But there came to me at the same time a most pleasant sensation—a soft touch of cool flesh about my left hand. I turned and there were the gloriously beautiful dark eyes of Mercy Ennis, wet and shining in their concern as she sat on the floor beside me, pretty bare feet tucked beneath her. Both her hands were holding mine. How had I not noticed this at once?

"Miss Ennis. Good day to you." My words came out clumsily in my pain.

"It's night, sir. All gone to sleep but us. Anne Gist and I been takin' turns here. Lucky me at havin' this one—now at last you're wakeful."

With my free hand, I scratched at my now voluminous beard. Some luck, indeed, for this poor lady. I moved the maimed extremity just a little, and quickly wished I hadn't. I'd not be dancing this night.

"Mr. Gist did some cuttin' there, Captain, but he left near most your foot."

"Most?"

"He and the birthin' woman did it. You lost the two toes but that's all. He poured whiskey over the bloody parts, then burned 'em some to close the flesh. Don't know how you kept from wakin'. You were ghostly pale for the longest time. She put a poultice on the burns, the birthin' woman did, and it's all been cleanly bound. Mr. Gist says you'll fare better here than you would downriver. He don't think much of those doctors and all that bleedin'. He says the Indians know more about medicine than those doctors, except for fevers, though some got the knack of that. You bled plenty, anyway, Captain."

She seemed surprised by the length of her little speech. With a demure smile, she sat back, removing her hands. I took one back, gently, and kissed it. All my pains seemed soothed by that.

"Why do you do that?" Her eyes were still friendly, but curious.

"It's custom."

"With gentry, maybe. Not 'round here."

"You are gentry to me, my lady."

She blushed. I doubt she'd heard such words ever come her way before. "I read nearly all that book."

"Did you like it?"

"Yes, I did, best I could understand it. I think I need more education."

"Just keep reading. Books are where you'll find it."

"I would do that. But there's naught about this place to read. Only writin' in this house right now is the letter left you by Major Washington."

"Left me? The Major's gone?"

I was stunned. On that frozen island, we'd been as good as brothers. Would he not stay even long enough to determine I might live?

"He rode off yesterday, Captain, with the two black men he left behind here when you went up to the French forts. They were happy to be gone with him, though no one treated them as slaves up here."

"The Major can't have left yesterday. We only just arrived."

"You've been here two days, Captain."

"Two? What day is this? What number of the month?"

"It be Thursday, the ninth of January."

We'd left Frazier's on the first. We'd been two months gone entire. A new year now—1754.

She fetched Washington's letter from the mantelpiece, then knelt to watch me read it. He'd written:

> *Thomas, I count your infirmity our worst bad fortune, but am grateful that I leave you now alive and not worse afflicted. I would that proper medicine could be brought you, but Mr. Gist assures me he has seen men in this country healed of worse without a surgeon's attendance.*
>
> *I ride now for Belvoir, and with dispatch from that place to Williamsburg to make my report the soonest to His Honour. I hope it pleases you to join me when you can travel, though I know that cannot be soon. Gist goes north to help with the preparations for the fort at the Forks.*

*I shall without doubt be returning to the Ohio, but know
not when. I would have you with me when I do. You now know
this country as well as I, and that'd be useful should I bring a
large body of men. Seek me at Belvoir when you can. They will
know where I am to be found, if not there.*

    Safe journey,
    Your Obedient Servant,
    G. Washington.

I'd not be in Williamsburg soon, abed with a maimed and tortured foot.

"What for you?" Mercy said.

"For me?"

"What can I bring you now? Have you got pain? Y' want more whiskey?"

"Yes. But there's something I'd like more."

"What be that, Captain?" Her face looked flushed.

"A bath."

"A bath?"

"Yes. And a shave."

"Have you forgot? 'Tis the dead of night."

"No matter. I've dreamt of this for weeks."

She had no tub on the premises, but there was a large bucket nearby, and a kettle hung by the fire. The cistern barrel outside was doubtless overflowing with the still-falling rain, which I could hear drumming on the roof.

Mercy had hot, soapy water ready for me within a few minutes. She returned to my bedside. "Your foot. Can you move it?"

"I'll try."

A thought occurred. Was I in any way dressed? I lifted my blanket and saw a nightshirt, nothing more.

"My clothes . . ."

"We kept your deerskin coat and t'other, and the deer-hide leggin's. The rest of it—breeches, shirt, linen—'Twas all torn and sweated through and crawlin' with beasties. Anne Gist burned those things this mornin'."

"Can I buy more here?"

"All you need, though not much fancy." She dragged the brimming bucket over, then fetched her cake of soap—a thing of much value here.

"Thank you," I said. She did not budge. "Miss Ennis. A bath requires some nakedness, at least if one's to do a proper job of it. 'Put not off your clothes in the presence of others.' A rule of civility. Just ask the Major."

"Sounds nonsense to me in the present figuring. You intend to wet yourself all over?"

"Every inch I can manage."

"All right, then, you'll have my help."

"Miss Ennis . . ."

"Sure and you won't be the first naked man to greet these eyes. In the summer, the Indians here go about bare as beasts. White traders, too, nearly." She looked away, speaking softly. "Truth be told, Captain, your manly parts will come as no surprise. Anne and I have both been frequent witness to them, helping Mr. Gist remove your clothes and prepare you for his surgery. And since then, too."

Now I flushed. "I see."

"And I saw. 'Twas not a mortal sin. Now let's be at it, 'fore this water cools."

I tried moving my foot again, but with little more success. I could, however, sit up, and did so. I took a deep breath, then pulled the nightshirt from my body. I truly, desperately, wanted that bath.

But with the next movement of foot, I cried out. Mercy shoved the bucket up close to the pallet.

"I fear you can't get yourself near enough, Captain. I shall bring it to you."

"What do you mean?"

She plunged a large rag into the bucket, then soaped it furiously after pulling it forth.

"Lie back, sir. Truth, I don't know how you find this tolerable."

I hesitated. "What if someone should come in?" I'd had enough experience of that in Philadelphia, and Mercy's father had a much more violent look to him than any of Mr. Smithson's thugs.

"They'll have a hard time doing that," she said, "seein' as I've barred the door."

———

I'd like to tell you that Eros took flight that night to unimagined heights, that all the ills visited upon me by merchant Smithson were avenged or at least assuaged in the arms of this dark-eyed woodland sprite, that I found *amour* in joyous abundance enough to make the direst amputation worth the while.

But in truth, I found none. Almost none. She scrubbed me well, every inch over. She cut off my beard and shaved with great care what remained. She washed my hair and combed it, and fetched me a clean nightshirt. In all, this lady's kind offices rendered me a gentleman once again, as much as I had ever been one. I relished her every touch.

Yet it was all done as might be kitchen work. I could have been a pot, for all she seemed aroused—and for all I was. No *amour* at all. Only kindness.

"You are well-named, Mercy."

"Thank you, sir. You've been through a terrible lot, and we're grateful to you. First time anyone from down in the towns done anything for us folk up here."

She pulled the bucket away, then tweaked the candle out, leaving us in the rosy firelight.

"I would kiss you, Mercy Ennis."

"Would you, now? Well, I'm a weary girl after all this, so I'll not be pleasing you further. There's another room around behind the fireplace, as you may remember. I'll be sleeping there. If you're hurtin' more, call out to me."

"Are you spoken for, Mercy?"

"Spoken to, enough, but not yet for. Me father appreciates me dutiful labors, and would rather not be sharin' 'em yet with a husband. I'm content with that. For now."

"You're sixteen?"

"Seventeen in March, sir. Now good night."

She started out the chamber, then paused, filled a wooden mug with whiskey and returned, setting it on the floor beside me.

"May it ease the hurt, Captain." She knelt. Her eyes flickered with the firelight.

"Thomas."

"Thomas." A smile found its way to her lips, then her lips found their way to mine.

But not for long. Before I could scarce catch my belief, she was on her feet and moving away from the pallet.

"I'm a virtuous girl, Thomas," she said, "and I mean to stay that." She passed into the next room. "For now."

I discovered the next morning that Anne Gist was sleeping all the while in the adjoining chamber. Her father had gone to join his wife at their plantation back over the mountains, and thence to travel up to the Forks. Whether Gist's swift remove from Will's Creek spoke of his great confidence in his medical handiwork or a prudent remove from the scene of incipient tragedy, I could not say. Mercy and his daughter Anne continued to abide with me in the cabin, watching over me by turn, with nothing more interesting happening—though when Anne was at my side, she talked almost continuously of the Major.

Five days later, Van Braam, Davison, and the others came in—hungry and dirty but otherwise fit, and with all our baggage and most of the horses. River ice had held them up, but they'd had no trouble with French or Indian.

I was hopping and hobbling about by then, and joined them all at table for a dinner's reunion. Davison and his traders wanted to remain at Will's Creek to await the first spring weather, but Van Braam was bound for Fredericksburg and asked me to take company with him and help with the pack animals much as I could, they bearing weapons and equipment purchased with the King's penny. My fondness for Mercy did not abate, but it was frustrating in her company, with no advantage to it. The well-populated world downriver, that from which I'd fled in the fall, now beckoned. Events down there had advanced as they had up here.

I accepted Van Braam's invitation. I could ride, after a fashion. I wanted to see my brother again—and George Washington.

It was well I went with Van Braam. He'd forgotten the way even to Winchester.

Twenty

It was not easy and was in no way comfortable, but I did succeed in reaching my home.

Disconcertingly, I arrived in Annapolis following stops at Alexandria and Belvoir to discover that my brother Richard had moved our home to Philadelphia. And when I finally reached that city, I was prepared to abandon forever any continuing interest in horses, journeys, or lands beyond the mountains. A hearth and chair would content me all my days, I thought.

But my first stop was at Mr. Franklin's, and my progress through the city to his dwelling was circumspect and discreet indeed.

To my surprise, he said there was no need to offer me refuge from gaols and gaol keepers.

"There are no charges here pending against you at all, sir, and none shall be brought—at least not by the lady's lamentable father. All is amity between Smithsons and Morleys, as long as Africa continues to yield its swarthy treasure."

I rubbed my eyes. "They have commenced their slavery trade, then?"

"Yes, your brother and Ambrose Butler—and now with friend Smithson not simply as backer, but as full partner in the ships and human commerce. They contemplate considerable profit to be made in this traffic. Fears of war are driving up the price of imported human flesh and muscle."

"I would undo this vile association."

"As would I, Captain Morley, in your place. But that shall have to wait for you to meet with your brother. He resides here now—in quite grand manner. I shall give you his street and number later, but first, refreshment, and an explanation, please, for your decided limp."

I briefly summarized the to and fro of our journey to the French, and explained my injury. Franklin insisted upon examining it. He was quite intrigued with my report of Gist's medical abilities and philosophies, and the rapidity of my recovery, despite three weeks on horseback over a route that took me from Will's Creek to Annapolis to the Delaware with little pause for rest or recuperation.

"Cleanly done and cleany kept," Franklin said, studying the once-afflicted flesh through a magnifying glass. "No residual infection. A touch of redness here and there, but mostly gone to scar. Most impressive job of work. Most. And testament to the medicinal purities of whiskey, I daresay, when applied to the external. The internal application too often produces the reverse result."

"I applied it both ways," I said.

He let go of the foot, which I commenced to reclothe, pulling back on my stocking with a slight wince.

"Does it pain you still?" he asked.

"Yes, but less each day."

"And you've not been to a regular physician?"

"That was my intention when I reached Alexandria, but I felt so fit upon arriving, I decided not."

"Then you've not been bled?"

"No."

"Well, you're a lucky lad. Strange I've not come upon a single word of your misadventure."

"How would you, sir?"

The look he gave me was knowing, and amused. "In what state was Major Washington when last you saw him?"

"A state of haste. He was hard for Williamsburg—anxious to make his report to Dinwiddie. I've not encountered him since."

"He's not angry with you?"

"Nay. He left me a most felicitous letter."

"He did, eh? Well, upon arriving at Williamsburg, he made his official report to His Excellency—a journal of his travels, commencing the thirty-first day of October last, and concluding January sixteenth just. The work has been rushed to the printed page and I have already been sent a copy of the complete." He rose from his seat and went to his desk, riffling through some papers until he found what he sought.

"Here 'tis," he said, returning to his chair and handing me a slim sheaf of pages without binding, held together with a ribbon run through a hole punched in the upper left corner. "Printed by the establishment of William Hunter, Williamsburg. A most fascinating account, this, but curious, for I've found not a word in it attesting in any way to your presence in Major Washington's company."

"What?" I was stung. He might just as well have hit me in the face with a hundredweight of snow.

"Your name does not appear anywhere. There's Christopher Gist, naturally. A Jacob Van Braam, a Barnaby Currin, a Henry Steward, a trader Frazier, and divers others, but no Captain Thomas Morley—no Morley of any sort."

"I cannot believe this," I said. "I was with him every mile, every inch, save on his return journey from Will's Creek to Williamsburg."

I turned my eyes to the frontpiece of the manuscript, reading. "The Journal of Major George Washington, sent by the Hon. Robert Dinwiddie, Esq., His Majesty's Lieutenant-Governor and Commander-in-Chief of Virginia, to the Commandant of the French Forces on the Ohio, to which are added the Governor's Letter and a Translation of the French officer's Answer."

"Take the time, please, to read through it at leisure," Franklin said, "while I have my good Deborah bring us some of that fine milk punch. Then tell me what you think. Of the Major's account, that is. I know what you think of the punch."

The Major's journal ran twenty full pages, and I read every word. Following it was a copy of Dinwiddie's letter to the French: "The many and repeated Complaints I have received of these Acts of Hostility lay me under the Necessity of sending, in the Name of the King my Master, the Bearer hereof, George Washington, Esq., one of the Adjutants-General of the Forces of this Dominion, to complain to you of the Encroachments."

This was followed by a translation of St. Pierre's reply, which Washington had not shared with us. I read it now with fascination.

> Sir,
> As I have the Honour of commanding here in Chief, Mr. Washington delivered me the Letter which you writ to the Commandant of the French Troops.
>
> I should have been glad that you had given him Orders, or that he had been inclined to proceed to Canada, to see our General, to whom it better belongs than to me to set forth the Evidence and Reality of the Rights of the King, my Master, upon the Lands situated along the River Ohio, and to contest the Pretensions of the King of Great Britain thereto.
>
> I shall transmit your Letter to the Marquis Duquisne; his Answer will be a Law to me, and if he shall order me to communicate it to you, Sir, you may be assured I shall not fail to dispatch it to you forthwith.
>
> As to the Summons you send me to retire, I do not think myself obliged to obey it; whatever may be your Instructions, I am here by Virtue of the Orders of my General, and I intreat you, Sir, not to doubt one Moment but that I am determin'd to conform myself to them with all the Exactness and Resolution which can be expected from the best Officer.
>
> I don't know that in the Progress of this Campaign any Thing has passed which can be reputed an Act of Hostility, or that is contrary to the Treaties which subsist between the two Crowns, the Continuation whereof as much interests and is as pleasing to us as to the English. Had you been pleased, Sir, to have descended to particularize the Facts which occasioned your Complaint, I should have had the Honour of answering you in the fullest and, I am persuaded, most satisfactory Manner.
>
> I made it my particular Care to receive Mr. Washington, with a Distinction suitable to your Dignity, and his Quality and great Merit; I flatter myself he will do me this Justice before you, Sir, and that he will signify to you, as well as me, the profound Respect with which I am,
> Sir,
> Your most humble, and
> Most obedient Servant,
> Legardeur de St. Pierre."

Franklin's wife had brought our refreshment. He studied my expression as he poured two tumblers full.

"An interesting work?" he asked.

"These letters," I said, "are remarkably indirect. They say very little, in very strong terms. Where they have weight, it is couched softly. In sum, though, one can distill from the French that they wish us most unwell."

"The diplomatic art, Thomas. When nations wish another a swift flight to Hell, they clutter the message beyond all excusability. But the Major's journal, my young friend, is it correct? Accurate? This is in truth what occurred?"

"Yes. He mispelled 'Duquesne,' and has, I think, some Indian names confused. Shanoah for Shawnee. He describes the Indian Monacatoocha, whom we also call Scarroyaddy, as a Seneca, and as a lesser chief than Half King, our ally. I thought as much myself, but was later told by Gist that Scarroyaddy is an Oneida, sent by the Council of the Six Nations of the Iroquois. A sort of proconsul, over the Shawnee. I do not know much about any tribe, but Gist knows, as you told me in the beginning. All else Washington writes is as it was, as it happened. I have no complaint, except . . ."

"Except with what is not therein contained, yes? Your own name, not a single mention."

"That's a mystery, true enough, Mr. Franklin. But more vexing is the paltriness of Gist's appearance in this saga. Major Washington was our commander, no mistake. 'Twas his mission, and he performed admirably. I was often in awe of his courage and fortitude and resolve. But our leader was Gist. If we were a ship, he was helmsman and pilot. He took us across those mountains into that fierce land and brought us back alive. It was thanks to him we survived that weather, which was a constant horror. Gist deserves better credit, and reward. Were I the governor of Virginia, I'd not venture another man into the Ohio without Gist's counsel and direction."

Franklin frowned. "But you say that in all other respects, our Major conducted himself well?"

"I do—in all but his generosity with glory, if glory there is to be shared from this."

"Oh, yes. Abundantly. His journal will be widely reprinted. I have myself obtained license to print excerptations in my newspaper—you recall the *Pennsylvania Gazette?*—and also in a magazine I publish."

He held up a prototype page. The text came under a large-lettered heading: "Major George Washington in the Ohio; A Hero for Our Time."

"I should not be surprised were it widely read in the capitals of Europe," Franklin said. "But 'tis puzzling, your neglectful treatment in it. I'd thought him more virtuous."

En route home, I'd stopped the night at Belvoir—at Fairfax invitation, mind—to rest my horse and self and see to a change of clothes from my woodsy garb. I'd been greeted anxiously by Mistress Fairfax and treated to sufficient hospitality throughout my brief stay. My wound—as the fair Sally chose to call it; I, the warrior returned from battle, don't you know—was attended to as though I were a man of the house taken ill. Her ministrations provoked the old infatuation.

But when I'd inquired after the Major's health and whereabouts, and what Washington might have told her of our travels, and how their friendship prospered, Sally had become most agitated. Her husband, George William, himself preparing to return to Williamsburg, had fallen into a somber mood. After a small supper, with discourse strained and kept to the most inconsequential subject, they'd left me to take their sleep.

In the morning, taking my hand in farewell and bidding me a good journey to Annapolis, she had pressed me to think well of Washington, and to keep our friendship.

'Twas all confusion to me.

"Well, he's hero nonetheless," Franklin continued. "And hero is what we need. Matters with the French—and the English Crown—cannot stand as they are, Thomas. They must advance apace. Washington serves this purpose well."

"Why not Gist for a hero, or is he too low-born?"

Franklin rose again, refilled our glasses with the warming punch, then began to walk about.

"It's not that," he said. "They are not that considerable in society, the Washingtons, though their position in it improves steadily. I inquired, discreetly, of those who might be acquainted with the family's origins. There is always someone to be found acquainted with a fellow's origins.

"The first here was a John Washington, fled from England utterly impoverished—a seeker of whatever might be wrested from the American wilderness, which in his time, scarce sixty years ago, marched to the water's edge. He was reputed to be a murderer of Indians—not in warfare, but as they came to him in diplomatic suit seeking parley. His first wife, Washington's grandmother, she was a moral lady. But the next two females this John Washington took to the wedding bed . . ." Franklin slapped his leg. "Harlots, sir! They were sisters. This John Washington had got himself made a country justice of the peace and these sisters were brought before him, the first for keeping a bawdy house, the second for selling herself in prostitution.

"Lenient judgment was theirs, I daresay. He married first the one, and when she perished, the other. Had a jolly time of his later life, I'll wager. No, you'll find few dukes and earls in the Washington tree. They've done as well as they have among the Virginia aristocracy through sycophancy and clever marriages."

I wondered. Would the Major be so obsessively enamored of a Sally Fairfax if she'd been born as poor and common as my lovely new friend Mercy Ennis?

And what of Anne Gist?

"Find no snobbery in my comments, Thomas," Franklin continued. "My father was a dyer, and his father before him. All literate, and that a great credit, but common tradesmen. Common, common, common. But is that not the delight of these American colonies? Those who might beg or steal in the streets of London rise to great consequence in these generous climes. The common, common, common become postmasters-general and members of assemblies, militia majors and gentleman justices, and of course, sea captains."

"My father was a Bermuda factor, whose fortunes varied perversely," I contributed. "Our mother, before she took up house with my father, I think had been a tavern bawd. He favored those."

"And who not?" said Franklin. He laughed, let that subside, then returned to serious subject.

"We need him very much, our Major. He's bold, that's evident enough. He wants back into the Ohio and would wrest it from the French with his own bare hands, if asked, and if it increased his good repute. We have here the makings of a most willing hero. And he has Dinwiddie's faith, trust, and confidence."

"Not in the fullest," I said. "It was Washington's intent to survey the Forks and persuade the governor of the best site for a fort, then return to the Ohio to build it. On our way back, we encountered an advance party already sent out by His Honour, en route to build the fort without a care to Washington's recommendation on the place for it. As much as Dinwiddie has prized the Major's journal, he had little care for the Major's counsel on that fort."

"And why should he? What can a youth of the Major's military inexperience know of fortifications? He's impatient, the governor. He has investments to protect. Nay, I think he sees another value in our friend Washington, as do I. There's opportunity here not to be squandered."

"Opportunity? There's great danger." I told him of the seven dead settlers, left for the hogs.

"Danger and opportunity wear the same face now, Thomas. Let me show you."

Back he went to his desk. After more riffling, he brought me a rolled-up piece of heavy paper, almost parchment, seating himself as he might at a theater to watch my appreciation of it.

Unrolled, the paper bore a drawing, with some small lettering, heavily inked. It was of a serpent chopped into eight sections, the pieces bearing the initials: "N.E., N.Y., N.J., P., M., V., N.C., S.C." Below the drawing were the stirring words, "JOIN, or DIE."

"Join?" I asked. "These colonies are already the King's domain. What are they to join?"

The twinkly eyes again, as merry as when Franklin was discussing Susannah's bosom. "They join each other, as should the parts of the snake. I would have them form, sir, a Union—a Union of the several colonies, for their mutual defense and security, and for extending the British settlements in North America. I would have the King's ministers and lordships and commons understand that without such Union, the colonies will fail and die. I would have all these American colonies understand that."

He was off his chair again, waddling about, gesturing as though addressing a great assemblage, and not mere me.

"I would like to see enacted, sir, a change in our system of government! I'd have, in addition to each colony's governorship, an overall President-General, to be appointed and supported by the Crown. And I'd have a Grand Council, its members chosen by the elected representatives of each colony, by their general assemblies. Their number would be in proportion to the population represented, say, seven members of the Grand Council for Massachusetts Bay Colony. For Pennsylvania, six. For Virginia, seven, and so forth."

And so forth he went, declaring how this fantasized President-General would, in consultation with the Grand Council, be empowered to make treaties and declare war, raise armies, issue land grants, print money, commission officers. More to my astonishment, empowered also to levy duties and taxes!

"But what would the King say?" I asked. "He'd declare you'd created an independent nation."

The twinkle disappeared, replaced by a look quite dark, perhaps even fearful.

"It's not what he says, but what he'd do," said Franklin. "And that I know not." He whirled about, presenting his drawing again. "Matters not. This must be tried. This serpent is not a jest. The country cannot survive in pieces, little morsels wholly dependent on the Crown, each to rot and shrivel if it's the King's wish, be the king British or French.

"Damn all, Thomas. You've been out there! You've had a view of the greatness of this continent. How can there be any taking of it if we huddle here by the sea, begging our distant Sovereign for the means of our safety?"

I sipped my punch. His ideas did not favor comprehension.

"What will you do with that drawing? With your ideas for Union and Grand Councils?" I asked. In truth, I thought he must be in some part demented. I'd heard that a fact of minds as inventive as Franklin's.

"This drawing shall appear upon the pages of my *Pennsylvania Gazette*, but only when I think the time propitious. Also when I deem it warrantable, I will propose this Union formally to all here in authority— that there be a convening of commissioners from every colony to discuss, agree upon, and draw up the requisite documents and petition the Parliament for an Act. Our argument cannot be lightly dismissed. There is no other way for these colonies to defend themselves."

"What do you consider a 'propitious-time'?"

Franklin shrugged. "I cannot say. What I can say is that I look to Major Washington to provide it."

Now at long last I comprehended! No mystery remained as to Franklin's interest in this obscure militia major, or in his desire for friendship with such an ill-starred and troublesome youth as myself. We were instruments of his employ and policy. We were to forward the Union of colonies.

Gads. I wondered if there were treason in this.

Franklin sought his glass of punch and sipped long, swallowing as though of dry throat. "I shall have another letter for you to take back to Major Washington. You do return to Virginia?"

"I ride the King's horse. I shall have to return it by and by. But as you observed, Philadelphia is now my home—or at least my brother's. So I was told in Annapolis. I must make reunion."

"With brother, or with Miss Susannah?"

"With both is my wish. How is she?"

"Her health is excellent. The exact state of her affections I have no means to measure, but I think you remain in them. And I know she is still angry with her father for his mistreatment of you. You recall the letter whose content was so scandalous I had to destroy it? Upon learning I'd done that, she wrote another even more, er, vivid. I have it here. Its disposition this time I'll leave for you to decide."

Again to the desk. He clucked his tongue.

"I would caution you not to read this while you remain in the same city as the lady, lest you are driven by sudden mad passion to a consummation perhaps not devoutly to be wished—at the present—and more trouble ensue."

I glanced only at the letter's salutation, which was unmistakably in her well-schooled hand and spoke of passionate love, then folded it and placed it in my pocket as safe as I might some large sum of money.

"But for the meantime," said Franklin, draining his glass of punch, "I've something else for your amorous spirits, if you're interested. They've just this week arrived." He started from the room. "Come with me to my chamber of scientific instruments and exploration. It is a space upon which my Deborah seldom treads."

———

Franklin had, don't you know, "forbidden" books, French in edition, well and blushingly illustrated. One was something entitled *L'Histoire de dom B . . .*," which he described as a novel wrought in opposition to the confining principles of the Catholic religion. The other was *Therese Philosophe*, an account of an innocent's progress in the arts of sexual congress. Though the latter had no pretention to be other than a work of pornography, it was of the two the most chaste. Though disguised as literature, *L'Histoire* contained much riper stuff. I'd not before seen such plates.

"Well, sir," asked Franklin, "what think you?"

"They serve to inspire a call upon Miss Susannah sooner than later."

"But you should not."

"No."

"Let me gift you with something more salutary for your moral health." From a small stack of exact copies, he produced a little volume. I recognized the title. *Poor Richard's Almanac.*

" 'Tis my seventeen fifty-four 'improved' edition—a few things added since that of seventeen fifty-three. There's no profit in writing books, make certain of that. I've lost count of what I've published, and wealth from it still eludes me. But there's amusement to it, and a means of gaining fame."

I tucked the book underneath my arm. "Thank you, sir. I'm honored."

He clapped my shoulder. "Call upon me soon—certainly before you leave us once more."

I walked down the street leafing through Franklin's *Almanac*, having heard of it before but having read nothing of its sage contents.

The writing had some wit.

"Love your Neighbor, yet don't pull down your Hedge," said one aphorism. "The Horse thinks one thing, and he that saddles him another," I liked, too. And also, "Don't think so much of your own Cunning as to forget other Men's: A cunning Man is overmatch'd by a cunning Man and a Half."

I'd gone to Mr. Franklin's first because I knew him to be a friend. I advanced upon my brother's fine new house unsure of his affection.

He was at once both pleased and displeased to see me when I greeted him—and also perhaps halfway between sober and drunk. It was just past the midday dinner hour. I found it distressing to find him so well aslosh. There was more to disturb me. Our Annapolis housekeeper, the lady from Hispaniola who practiced Voudon, she was nowhere about. When I inquired after her, Richard replied matter-of-factly, as if I had asked the time, that he'd sold her.

Sold her? He had not *bought* her. He'd hired her—for miserable wages, to be sure, plus all the chickens she could decapitate—but she'd been a free woman.

Richard lived now in the manner of a wealthy man, this circumstance troubling me also, for it was largely the work of credit. His tall, handsome house was on the highest reach of Chestnut Street, somewhat far from the river but provided with an excellent view of it. The furnishings were equally handsome, exceeding in quantity and quality what was to be found in Washington's Ferry Farm at Fredericksburg. He even possessed a painting—a crude likeness of some unknown country cleric done on wooden board, doubtless by some itinerant, but an artwork nonetheless.

My brother now drank fruit brandies and Madeira instead of commoner stuff. I joined him in a pewter goblet of the latter as we went through what had become our ritual of reunion—cool reserve and stiff civility; a lapse into an angry, self-indulgent bout of sibling wrath, recrimination, and finally righteous self-pity; and then at last a climb back to forgiveness and sentimentality. As is the burden of the kin of drunkards, I found myself matching him goblet for goblet, dram for dram, keeping company all the way along the road to the oblivion that came with the nightfall—though, unlike him, I took time out to eat.

In the process of all that and during the more sober succeeding day, I learned all I needed of the Morley family circumstance. Its debt was enormous, running into several thousand pounds now, but backed sufficiently by assets, barring an adverse turn of fortune.

This was all too common in the slave trade. Success or ruin was a matter decided by the health and content of the cargo, and disease and punishment took a fearsome toll. When some great tempest or siege of seasickness was factored into the calculation, a trader could find his hold filled with the human equivalent of spoilt vegetables.

Richard and partner Butler had already managed two ships back and forth to Africa—losing seven souls of 204 in the hold of one and only three of 117 in the other. The profit had been generous.

Riggins had been given command of the *Hannah*, but I should not consider myself displaced, Richard said. He wished me to join him as first mate on a new vessel they hoped to put into service. I'd be as good as captain, he said, as he'd be little on the quarterdeck.

"Bound where?" I asked.

"You know damned well where," he said. "Africa. From there to Hispaniola, where the cargo of labor is exchanged for one of rum and molasses, to be taken thence to here and Boston—thence all around again. If the first voyage goes well, she'll be yours thereafter—with a master's share of the profits. And they'll be considerable, Tick. Good thing. You'll need them."

"And why is that?" I let the words drop like heavy stones.

"My new partner, Mr. Smithson, has forgiven you. He now contemplates the prospect of a possible marriage between his daughter Susannah and yourself—though surely you are not worthy of it."

I sat dumbfounded. I knew not what to make of this. Franklin had told me the unfortunate news of another Smithson daughter lost to fever during my absence in the Ohio. I pondered whether Smithson thought his progeny too abundantly perishable to wait for an alliance much longer. Or was it the threat of Susannah's reputation being ruined by these letters of her own hand? Marriage to me would at least put an end to that.

At all events, here was all I'd asked of life not long before—now given me as on a plate. All I need do was make myself the same as brother Richard and partners Butler and Smithson.

After Richard had drunk himself to slumber one night, I finally did set about reading that second salacious letter Susannah had given Franklin. It surpassed in arousal anything to be found in those forbidden books of French origin. There was much to commend such a marriage, if slavery could be put out of it.

I should add that like the pretty coin given me by Sally Fairfax so many years ago, I still have that letter, hidden away in a very secret place as a souvenir available only for the most discreet revisiting.

———

Of course I wished to see the fair Susannah soonest. But I proceeded warily, like a ship in fog and shoal water. My second day in my brother's house, I sent my brother's manservant with a formally worded letter to the Smithson house, announcing my return, offering apology for any discomfit I might have caused, and asking properly if I might call upon her.

For a week, I heard nothing. Then one afternoon, without advance warning, Susannah came herself—rattling up to the house in her father's handsomest coach, sending her maid to the door to summon me. I'd prepared for a day upon the town, thinking of calling upon Franklin to seek his counsel, so I was dressed for the public street—in fine new clothes of nautical style provided by Richard, I think as inducement to the African commerce.

The maid prodded me to enter the carriage, herself ascending to sit beside the coachman, as though by previously understood instruction. Within the coach, Susannah bade me sit opposite her on the rearward-facing seat.

She was dressed in green velvet—a matching cloak with cowl pulled partially over her pretty blonde head. She gave me a kiss, bearing more politeness than passion, then sat back with no smile—only a cool, studying look.

The coachman shook the reins, stirring the driving pair forward with a lurch.

"Good day to you, Captain Morley."

"And you, my lady." Such formality for two who'd once been clutching at each other's rumps so madly.

We bumped and rattled along, careening badly as the coachman turned us into another street and over one of the municipal drainage channels of Mr. Franklin's design.

"I am informed by Mr. Franklin you are in receipt of correspondence I forwarded you through him," she said.

I cleared my throat. "I am."

"And you have read it?"

"Uh, yes."

"It was device, sir. I trust you do not take it seriously. It's served its purpose, and now I'd have you destroy it."

"Of course." I'm sure I meant to.

At last a smile from her, but it dashed away. We clattered on, downhill now. Her attention lingered out the window at the passing house fronts and strolling folk. We were moving with some deliberate speed.

"Where are we going?" I asked.

"To the river. Then the road north. It doesn't matter."

"It's a brisk day, Susannah. Not warm."

"You find not warmth in ardor for me?"

"Your father would not be happy to see you here."

"Yes he would. Come sit you by me."

I swung around beside her. She took my hand in hers.

"I am terribly sorry that you were kept in that gaol, Thomas. I truly am. I was so angry with my father for your many miseries. That is why I wrote those two letters, and would write again. I cried for you. I fear such tears do not leave my eyes often. But for what it matters, he has forgiven you."

"I know. I do not forgive him."

She looked again to the window. The Delaware was in view, blue-gray in color, whitecaps whipping up offshore. On the distant Jersey bluff, the trees still leafless so early in the season, I could see houses. This country was filling up.

"I am aged seventeen now," she continued. "Do you find that old?"

"I do not."

"Then you are in error. My schooling was abroad. I am an educated woman, sir—not only in the way of scholarly subject, but deeply steeped in the ways of the world. There are farm women in Virginia who will go to their graves at four score years not knowing things I learned at twelve. It was that year my virginity passed from me, did you know? A schoolmaster at an English academy, a man without much scruple, took it, leaving unhappiness and 'experience' in its place. Is this a concern to you? Do you find me thus afflicted? Tarnished? A lesser prize?"

"No. How could I?"

"I am become woman long before my time. And now, at seventeen, I feel old."

"You shouldn't. You are perfection."

She waved her hand in dismissal, then dropped it. "Do you love me, sir?"

"Of course. How not?" My foot was hurting. I'd thrust it against the carriage frame during a lurch and I feared my resulting grimace was mistook.

Her blue eyes were very cold now, on me like a cat's.

"I have made my confession," she said. "Now you. Was I your first?"

Did I blush? "By all but one, Susannah. The honest truth."

"And since last we met—have you looked upon a woman's flesh?"

"Only the bare foot of a serving girl."

What an awful, condescending thing to say. I held Mercy Ennis in much higher regard than that.

"Would you, sir, have me as wife?"

I'd been awaiting that subject's emergence for the longest time, but it found me as unprepared as might a lightning bolt on a bright, clear day.

"I would."

"I know every part of your body, sir, but not an inch of your truthfulness."

"I would marry you. But would you me? I've no fortune. No prospects. My brother's given command of our sloop to the mate. The horse I rode here is King's property."

This raised no question.

"You've prospects enough if you concur in my father's bidding, and your drunkard brother's. Would you do that?"

"I would marry you, Susannah."

She leaned forward, took my face in both her hands and kissed my lips again. Her breath was as sweet as I'd remembered. I wondered how she managed that.

"I would marry you," she said, "as I would not your brother."

There was some riddle hidden in that, but I did not hunt it.

"I've not decided," she said.

"It's not a hasty matter."

"Before I do, I would lie with you, Thomas Morley."

"What? But where?"

"I'll come to your house this night. At midnight. Your brother should be well asnore by then."

"Susannah . . ."

"At midnight. Leave the rear door unlatched."

"As you wish."

"You do not wish? God, Thomas . . ."

"I do wish."

"Why didn't you write me? Where have you been these last months since you fled from gaol? In hiding? On some ship? Gone to the West Indies?" From languor to chiding.

"Franklin didn't tell you?"

"He wasn't certain. He said you'd got free of Philadelphia is all."

"I was in the Ohio country, in the wilderness west of the mountains."

"You jest."

"No, 'tis true. I was with a Major George Washington and a party of Virginia men. We went to a French fort near the Great Lakes to tell the French King George wants them out."

She was staring with some mockery at me.

"We have all now heard of this gallant Major Washington, Tom. Mr. Franklin has some small book he wrote of this. It's all the talk at dining parties."

" 'Twas a hard time, Susannah. The winter has been deadly."

"Thomas, no one speaks of you in this."

"I know." What further was there to say?

"You needn't make false boast to me."

"I'm not. I was in the Ohio. In the horrible winter. With Washington." Now she fell silent. It was worse than more spoken doubt.

"We will talk no more of this," she said finally and called to her coachman to stop his pair and find a turning.

When we were back to my brother's street, stopped before his house, I opened the door and started to descend. She caught my arm, hard.

"I will come to you tonight," she said.

"I will be here."

———

She did, and for four nights after, entering my bedchamber only after we had made certain Richard was in his evening's stupor. She stayed only an hour or so each time, taking great care in her departure, but these interludes were a different kind of bliss than I think she intended. She employed with me fully all her alarmingly advanced knowledge of the amorous arts, and increased my education thereon surpassingly. Yet I felt most content not in exploring some maddeningly inventive new route to pleasure, but in the simple joy of holding her warm, slender, naked body in my arms. Yes, I thought, I could be happy married to this lady. Very happy. Kissing her tiny ear or the blossom of her breast—thinking back upon my shallow, unfulfilled life before our first earnest encounter—I was o'erwhelmed by this fact.

One night—the last, as it developed—I sensed as much as heard something amiss in our cozy, rosy private paradise. Gently, so as not to startle Susannah, I lifted my head and turned slowly toward the door.

It was ajar. In the opening was the staring, haunted, bloated face of my brother—his widened eyes agleam in reflection. Susannah saw him, too.

She came not to our house again, at least in that time.

Twenty-one

Richard apologized the next morning, claiming his intrusion unintentional:

"I heard a sound, wondered if 'twas you. Mind was a fog. Didn't mean to linger there. Quite surprised to find a woman, a proper woman, in the house at such an hour. Meant no discourtesy. Couldn't collect my senses. I am most sorry, brother. You may depend upon it."

What occurred to me was that I could depend on little from him, save as a source of sorrow and disgust. And pity, though my quantities of that diminished as the other increased.

I was trapped in the house, however, and in our brotherhood, as long as I elected to remain in Philadelphia. But where else? I dreamed through the days. When these reveries were not of Susannah or Mercy Ennis, they were of Italy. I thought, as though it were a practicality, that I might somehow take ship as mate on a vessel Italia-bound—an idyllic voyage, a landing at Venice, and all my paradise realized.

It seemed impossibly distant, as did the wilderness I'd crossed with the Major—both places as unreachable as the fantasy lands of Jonathan Swift's *Travels to Several Remote Nations of the World.*

The strange and beautiful Mercy seemed so unreal to me now she might have been a character in the book—indeed, an inhabitant of such an improbable land.

Swift had once suggested in a satire that Irish children be raised as food for the wealthy. Mercy had once been an Irish child.

So in melancholy fashion, did my mind wander. I could bear few more such days.

I called upon Susannah twice and was told she was not receiving. I sent letters that were received, but not answered. Mr. Franklin had no advice for me. Neither, of course, did brother Richard, for all his counsels with her father.

There then proceeded a most curious development. We began to receive invitations. Addressed to both Richard and me, they were to suppers, levees, teas, and receptions, and came bearing such consequential names as Schuyler, Shippen, Hawkesworth, some of the most esteemed "gentlefolk" in the city.

My brother was so thrilled by this prospect of social advance that he disciplined himself to some sobriety, at least for the few hours required. It did not occur to him, as it quickly did to me, that we were but feathers or chips in a mischievous parlor game. What drew my mind to this conclusion was that at each gathering there was always present Susannah—sometimes her father, but always her.

But to what purpose? Not reconciliation. She was not overly cordial. The politesse of coquetry is what came our way, especially mine: "How fare thee, Captain Morley?" "So good to see you well, Captain Morley." "You should partake of Philadelphia society more, Captain Morley." "Captain Morley, when do you sail? And is it for Afrique?"

The most casual words, and always come to me in company. I tried to maneuver her aside, if not to a private place, but she was very clever at avoiding that. Why this teasing? A punishment for that embarrassing incident in my bedroom? What of the punishment I'd already suffered in gaol at the hands of her father? Was it simply her perverse nature to vex a man so? In the many novels I'd read, it was a commonplace for the English lady of society to conduct herself in this peevish manner. To maintain a mystery about herself. To keep predatory men at disadvantage.

In part, at least, I thought Susannah might have been deliberately offering me a taste of the trivial life I'd find in permanent troth to her, a test of my willingness and forbearance to suffer it. If so, I can't say I was much willing or forbearing. These parties, except when they provided the occasional discourse with a finely read person of quick and healthy mind, grew wearisome, the more so in repetition.

These glittery folk were much the same as my brother—washed up ragged and impoverished on the American shore, taking root and flourishing in trade, devoting their subsequent lives and fortunes to comporting themselves as American reproductions of British aristocracy, whose customs they sought in every way to ape, if seldom successfully.

One night, following an indifferent theatrical performance of Congreve's *The Way of the World*, made all the worse by the audience's constant coughing and spitting, there was a late supper at the great house of the Chandlers'. There I found not only Susannah and her father, but my friend Mr. Franklin, who paid Smithson's old enmity only the most twinkly regard.

Susannah made Franklin all the more twinkly, with shameless flirtation, ignoring me all the while. We guests were gathered in a large parlor lit with an extravagance of candles—two foursomes seated at card-playing, and the rest of us idling and milling about, some at the sideboard, others, most chiefly my brother, by the punch bowl.

Susannah was engaged in whist at one of the tables. Seeing me pass from one side of her to the other, she spoke out loudly to a tablemate:

"This handsome young gentleman is Captain Morley, a man of extraordinary modesty. Did you know he was with Major George Washington on that remarkable march into the Indian country?"

I halted, face gone crimson. I should have kept going, but it was too late.

"They rode right up to the French forts and tweaked those cavaliers by the nose—telling 'em to be off our Crown lands. 'Twas most intrepid and heroic. Yet Captain Morley here did not allow a single word of his part to appear in Mr. Washington's journal. Know you anyone so self-effacing?"

But for Susannah's words, there was an uncomfortable silence in the room. The guests looked for the intended amusement in this, but they'd not yet found it.

I stared at her, my eyes as cannons, but she was not looking my way.

"It's true, yes," said Susannah. "You may ask him. He told me so. He was there. But not a word. What do you think of that?"

There were some titters.

"Yet how could he possibly persuade Major Washington to keep him out of the public recounting, when scamps and rogues and baggage men were honored with their names included?"

More titters. Now she turned to me.

"How was that, sir?"

"Miss Smithson . . ."

" 'Miss Smithson?' This is sufficient reply? Were you so long in what you declare as wilderness that you've lost your wit? Seaman that you are, have you no more elegant response? If I be wooed by heroes, sir, I like 'em better spoken."

Every eye in the room was upon me, all curious as to the cause and possible extent of this humiliation. I turned away, trying to mask my fury and helplessness, seeking an exit. There was no course for me here but retreat, and fast.

Not three steps taken, I was stayed by Mr. Franklin's now so familiar voice, which boomed throughout the room.

"Captain Morley is quite so to be commended," Franklin said, moving from the fireplace nearer to the center of the room. "He was indeed in the field with Washington, as I have cause to know well, as he went at my suggestion and urging. And I must add that he suffered a grievous wound to the foot, from which I am pleased to see him well recovered. As I requested, he has made me a full report, though careful to keep it out of public chutter. I remind you we are in danger of another war, perchance far worse than any yet suffered. In such times, secrets are worth many cannon. So I say, commend this young man for his modesty and sense."

A smattering of applause commenced, not lasting long. No matter, by then I was on my way downstairs en route to the entrance hall and exit to the street. Franklin's voice stopped me once more as he came pattering down the stairs after me.

"Thomas, wait!" I turned and he drew near, his voice then dropping low. "Miss Smithson plays with you. I know not why, but I think there's a message in it. She wants you away from here."

"She'll get her wish." I put hand to latch.

"You go?"

"With great enthusiasm."

"But when?"

"Now!" I was in a rage.

" 'Tis best, of course. You've lingered here weeks now—if no closer to the deck of that slaver, nor an inch farther away. And no closer to marriage with this lady."

"Not close at all!"

"I would wish you across those mountains again, Thomas. And soon. There's much afoot. The spring is nigh and men will be on the march. I await the latest correspondence for my newspaper. I want your reports to add to it. I want you there with Washington. His goad, his spur."

"If he cared—"

"For every action, there are many reasons. Don't cling to one until you know them all. Give the Major some chance to explain himself."

"I've no idea where to find him, even I wished to."

"You know well where to ask. The horse you keep in your brother's stable is the King's. I know you as a man of obligation, Thomas. Bring it back. Put it to the use intended."

I stared at the polished wooden floor. There was loud laughter now coming from up the stairs.

"I want no more of this place," I said. "That's for certain."

"Time enough in life for more of this place. I'll look after your interests here—and as best I can, your unfortunate brother. Susannah will keep her own counsel, but—"

I started quickly out the door, as though propelled by the mere mention of her name.

"How soon will you ride, sir?" Franklin called after me.

"This night," I said.

"And where?"

"I've not decided."

"Have you money enough? Clothes? Weapons? Food for the trail?"

"I have what I need."

"And your foot does not pain you?"

"Tonight the pain is welcome."

He dug into his pocket, producing a folded paper. "This will appear in my *Gazette* within the fortnight. I was hoping for it to be a surprise, but your Susannah calls my hand."

I nodded thanks. 'Twas too dark to read it, so into my own pocket it went. "You are a good man, Mr. Franklin."

"And you an intrepid one, Captain. Farewell. My greetings to the Major."

I ignored my brother's coach and pair and set into the chilly night on foot, limping some and slowing, but making my way.

A sound behind me, scurrying footsteps. It could not again be plump old Franklin, and certainly not Richard, who no longer moved so nimbly. I turned, fearing footpad or cutthroat, only to see the most astonishing thing.

Fair Susannah, rushed outdoors without her cloak, face still flushed, eyes urgent, running for me. Without a word, she threw her arms around me, held me fast, drew back, kissed me hard upon the lips, then turned and dashed into the shadows—an apparition.

Whatever else, it was a good-bye kiss. That was understood well enough without words.

I was almost to the Susquehanna by next nightfall.

What Franklin had given me was a printing of the article he intended to publish concerning Washington's trip to the French forts. It had been amended.

MAJOR GEORGE WASHINGTON, A HERO FOR OUR TIMES

How in the Company of the great Frontier Scout, Christopher Gist, and an Intrepid young Sea Captain, Thom. Morley, Now of Our City, and with them only Several Mountain Men and Red Indians, he Crossed the Western Mountains into the Valley of the Ohio, to Convey Upon the Commandant of the French Forces there Our Ultimatum.

They stand, United in Defense!

Herewith the Major's Journal of his Adventure, in excerptation, appended with the accounts of Christopher Gist and Thom. Morley. . . .

So. In Pennsylvania at least, I was now famous.

And still kissed, if knowing not why.

Twenty-two

Trotting the King's chestnut mare down the drive to Belvoir from the Alexandria road, I found Sally Fairfax standing before the house in welcome, as though expecting me. She was all smile and bright, shining eyes, looking as happy as the color of her yellow spring gown. But when I dismounted, she took me in the most urgent embrace, scarce waiting for me to beat the dust from coat and breeches, and I sensed a melancholy and disquiet beneath the outer cheer.

"I'm so pleased it's you," she said. "I was upstairs and when I saw you from the window, I feared at first it was Colonel Washington come back."

Feared? Colonel?

"I am most happy to see you again, Mrs. Fairfax."

"Your are too formal, Thomas, for so good a friend to me. Come."

A black servant took my horse's reins and led the mount off. Taking my hand, Sally conducted me similarly, not to stable but to house. There were African people seemingly all about it, though few of them were doing much of anything. If not at labor, why there at all? Every vestige of the "Peculiar Institution" now vexed me, though I'd certainly not call this lady to account for it. 'Twas not her fault being born to Virginia.

"Why 'feared'?" I asked. "And how a colonel?"

"I wanted nothing to be wrong," she said. "He rode from here this morning so happy. When I saw a rider in a blue coat, I feared something amiss."

She turned to face me, her prettiness of face enhanced by her animation.

"Thomas, George is off to the Ohio again! And this time he leads an army! They've promoted him Lieutenant Colonel!"

"Is there war?"

Sally shrank back. "Oh, no. We've had no such news. George marches to prevent war. The governor has mustered the militia to keep hold of the country 'round the Forks of the Ohio, while the fort is completed. Once that is done, the French cannot dare advance."

"George told you this?"

"No, my husband. 'Tis the view of the Burgesses. At Dinwiddie's urging, they've finally voted funds for the defense of the frontier. Ten thousand pounds. The French are as good as stopped."

"What did George say?"

She flushed a little. "Only that he would do his duty, and do me honor. The soldiers have been mustering at Alexandria all this past fortnight, making camp on the Falls Church Road. It took all this while to raise the funds. And the troops. The recruiting did not go so well as at first expected. I don't think George got quite the army he desired."

Riding through Alexandria, I'd noted no unusual stir. "So then, how large this *army*?"

"At least a hundred. I don't know. But many. And George commands. You should have been here. I've not seen so proud a figure in all my life."

I shook my head. Left out of the published journal. Left out of this. An army of a hundred? What we'd seen at the French forts had indicated they'd be raising a force of more than a thousand.

"Well, I wish them all good fortune. Where they go, they'll have need of it."

"The Colonel would have you with him."

"Would he? He's not told me."

We were mounting the steps. I glanced back toward the road, I know not at what. Perhaps just to avoid her look, which was very marked.

"He asked after you when he returned from Williamsburg," she said. "He had great concern for your wound, and was pleased to learn you'd ridden here in health. He sent a letter to you in Annapolis."

"My brother and I have moved our lodgings to Philadelphia. I've just come from there."

"Philadelphia? This he knew not. And now you've missed him, by scant hours."

I squinted at the sun. "By more than half a day, I'd guess."

"Where are you bound?"

"Not sure." Not true. I'd come to find Washington and I still hoped to, if only to be quit of my duty to deliver Franklin's latest letter.

"George would have you with him."

I did not speak.

"Have you a quarrel with him?"

There was no way to broach the subject of the journal without seeming a petulant child.

"None that he has told me of," I said finally.

"For now," she said, "I'd have you join me in refreshment. My husband's in Alexandria. But he would welcome you as well."

"I'm grateful to you, madam."

"And I you, Thomas."

Now I could not avoid her gaze. "I'll ride to him, Sally. I have a letter for him from Mr. Franklin. I was thinking just now I might leave it with you, but I suppose it is best he have it before he crosses the mountains."

"He will be most pleased to see you. I think he would like to have more friends with him than he has."

"It could be days before I find him."

"I think not. They travel with wagons and beef on the hoof. All very slow."

We ate lightly—a cheese and some pie, and tea. Our talk turned small. I was idling overlong. Off they were into the mountains again, and here was I.

"I gave you my word, madam," I said. "Now I must keep it."

She sighed. "Another farewell. My third this day."

The Fairfax groom had walked, brushed, and watered the mare. It looked a new mount, but was not eager for the road.

My foot hurt going into the stirrup, the pain lessening as I eased into the saddle. The road beckoned—but there was still something between us yet unsaid.

"Mrs. Fairfax, from the very first, you and Mr. Washington have made me privy to affairs that are not rightly my concern."

"What do you mean, Thomas?" She glanced back at the house.

"You asked me to be a friend to you two, and so I have been—gladly. But as your friend, I worry. Before I go to join him, could you tell me, lady, what did he do to make you so distressed when last I was here?"

"Distressed? You misapprehend."

"At my first mention of his name that day, your face darkened like a sea sky with a storm blowing up. Your husband's countenance, too. You seem content to hear the name Washington now, but then . . . If there's something amiss, if I can be of help, Sally. I sense you are not so content as you would appear."

She looked away again, this time toward the river. Then down to her neatly shod feet. Her eyes came back up sadly.

"It's his letters," she said softly.

"Ma'am?"

"He writes letters."

"He does that. He writes letters the way other men swat flies."

"Those he sends to me are far too ardent, Thomas. And too frequent, and too numerous in my collection. My husband, who is George's great good friend, better friend to him than I to you or you to me—my husband has read them, some of them, enough of them." She sighed deeply now. "Words of love, Thomas. Profusely strewn. My husband was grievously discomfited. He has recovered from this state, but . . ."

"Would you have me speak with the Major?"

"I've tried to tell him myself, in various ways, but he never understands. I can have no more letters. Not of any kind."

"That is much to ask of a man who rides where he does."

"I know, Thomas. But it must be done. My marriage . . ." She whirled about, then back to me again. "Please wait. I am going to say it to him as he cannot avoid it. I shall put the words onto paper. I'll not take long."

I took a deep breath. I was no meddler. But I wished to be a friend. "My lady, your words will mean nothing, will forbid nothing, unless you say that you do not love him."

Her eyes widened and fixed on mine. Then they fell, demure. "Of course I love him," she said. "He is a good friend. I love you as well, Thomas, though I know you less."

"Madam, I mean *love*."

She wiped at her eyes. "Yes. I shall do it. This cannot go on. Please wait. I shall not take long."

I sat patiently in the saddle. The moment became minutes, then more minutes. A ship was moving down the river. I watched its passage, ignoring the stares of the servants standing idle in the yard.

Finally, my lady, breathless and perspiring, came bounding out from the house again. Reaching my side, she handed up a folded paper, hastily sealed.

"For the Colonel," she said.

"To his hand directly," I said, placing it carefully in my pocket next to Franklin's letter.

"And impress it upon him. No reply."

I bowed there in the saddle, then set off down the dusty drive. She stood watching. When I looked back the second time, she was gone.

———

I had progressed not two miles upriver on the Alexandria road when I heard a rider pounding up hard behind me. It was a black youth, on a very good horse, and he came on unswervingly bound for me.

"Cap'n, sir," he said, reigning up amidst much dust. "Mistress Sally send this letter. She say it go for the other. You ken? She want you burn that other. You bring this'un instead."

I took what he handed over, paper folded and sealed just like the first.

"That's all she said?" I asked.

"Yes, sir. That all."

"Then I thank you." I placed it in my pocket, then moved on.

———

Armies signify themselves with dust and clank-and-clatter long before you can discern the sight of a single soldier. I caught up with Washington's that same day, in march on a rolling plain not five miles from where Sally said they had mustered. What I saw first was the rear of cows, then a few drovers, sutlers, tradesmen, and the usual camp women, then the militia column proper.

He had perhaps one hundred fifty or sixty in the way of soldiers, some of them close to boys. The muster list, I later noted, showed "two companies on foot, commanded by Captain Peter Hog, Lieutenant Jacob Van Braam, five subalterns, two sergeants, six corporals, one drummer, one hundred and twenty soldiers, one surgeon, one Swedish gentleman who was a volunteer, two wagons guarded by one lieutenant, sergeant, corporal, and twenty-five soldiers."

And now a sea captain.

His paltry two wagons carried provisions and tools for lumbering. There was no artillery save two small swivel guns, borne on packhorses. Few of the troops were in formal uniform, and some lacked shoes, but all in all, it was a fairly grand procession to be led by a man whose last and only other command had been a handful of woodsies, Indians, and youthful adventurers.

The Colonel appeared quite gratified to see me as I came riding up to him through his cattle and wagons, though he took pains to behave with the correctness of an officer of his new exalted rank, albeit one just now past his twenty-second birthday. He shook my hand, inquired after my late "wound," and abruptly offered me employment with his regiment as civilian aide-de-camp and scout, on strength of my knowledge gained on our expedition to the Forks—much the same suggestion he had made the last time we had spoken.

I couldn't feign reluctance, for I felt none, and accepted on the spot, though the resentment over the lapse in his journal commenced from that moment to burn hotly again. I decided to leave that bad thing between us till later. He seemed glad of Franklin's letter when I gave it to him.

As for the others I bore, there should have course been but one, but there were still two. It was perhaps no inadvertence that I'd carried them a while together. When I pulled them from my pocket later while resting my horse, I could not quite tell the one from the other. I could, of course, if I broke the seals and read the contents.

This I could not make myself do. I thought over it hard. I needed only break the seal of one and read it, sure that the other would be of the opposite sentiment. I could claim the breakage accidental—reasonable enough on a hard ride. But I found myself incapable of this deceit, and do you know, I could not imagine Washington resorting to it either.

My surmise, of course, was that the first she'd writ was the sterner—that she'd bit the bullet and cut loose from him, telling him to leave off—telling him, as I had urged, that she could not return the love that poured forth from him like a welling spring.

God only knew what this cannon shot might provoke. For all his officerly mien, George Washington was a man of deep and fiery emotion. He might rage like a madman and tear violently into the wilderness with his little army—or desert them, ruining his career, to return to her side, the beseeching swain.

Her second letter, then, must perforce be antidote to the first. And how dilute so strong a stuff? Only a profession of love, rashly, hastily, and intemperately proclaimed, a proclamation more powerful than her earlier denial because it was born of truth.

That was my surmise, and thus my quandary. If no meddler, there I sat with awesome power over Washington's prospective misery or happiness. I had in my pocket, I realized, the means to determine the future course of his life—at least for the immediate.

It was not a choice I could make deliberate and still remain his friend. I reached into my pocket, slipped fingers over one edge of paper and pulled it forth, entirely a matter of chance.

"This is sent also to you, George," I said. "From a lady."

He brightened as a rising sun, placing it within his coat, next to his breast, to be read later.

"I thank you, Tick. Once again."

The business of the journal still rankled. I wondered how I would rid myself of this resentment. 'Twould have to wait. He was preoccupied.

"I command only temporarily here," he said, resuming his part in the march with me riding beside him. "This is but the vanguard of what will deploy in the field as the 'Virginia Regiment,' six companies, each of fifty men at arms—and all under the overall command of Colonel Joshua Fry, late a professor of mathematics at the College of William and Mary in Williamsburg. I know him. A good man, though I'm not certain how good a man for the rough country."

He glanced back at the column, making certain not to be overheard. "These are not the soldiery I'd have wished. The generality of those who are enlisted are loose, idle persons, many of them quite destitute of house or home. Some came to me lacking shoes, stockings, shirts, coats, or even a waistcoat to their backs. We've provided clothing as we could. As encouragement to their enlistment, Dinwiddie has opened another two hundred thousand acres for free settlement—to the east of the Ohio River in those lands near Gist's plantation. But these poor fellows are all that offer got us."

"Van Braam is now lieutenant, and commands a company?" I asked.

"He has been a soldier in Flanders, Tick. 'Tis more than you or I can boast. My friend George Mercer is now captain and commands a company that will be joining us. Stobo, too. And a Scots soldier and doctor named Adam Stephen. Good men, all."

He smiled at me now in brotherly fashion, but, in his custom, without exposing his teeth.

"You will be addressed as 'Captain,' Tick, but your status must be the same as the Swedish gentleman who accompanies us as civilian. Dinwiddie and the Burgesses are the keepers of the militia commissions, and like me, they knew not that you would be here." He paused. "You found Mrs. Fairfax well?"

"I'm sure as well as she was this morning when you left her."

I could see that his mind was on the still-unread letter I'd brought him. I made an excuse and fell back farther in the column.

I rode along with Van Braam for a while, but liking that conversation not much, took up with Captain Hog and found him more than agreeable, earnestly curious about what lay ahead. A tall private I recognized as a misplaced sailor like myself offered salute. His name was John Shaw and he was Irish-born, but had taken berth in the coastal Virginia merchant service after Royal Navy duty as boy aboard HMS *Expedition*.

I'd last seen the fellow in the crew of a schooner moored in the river at Lewes, the old Dutch port in Delaware, when we'd shared a talk and a dram. I now dismounted to walk along with him a while, learning his home had most recently been in Hampton, Virginia, but that he hoped to acquire sufficient land in the Ohio out of this military adventure to set up housekeeping there, and bid farewell to livelihood from the sea. He was full of gossip of the maritime trade. It was now well known among the captains of the Chesapeake and Delaware that my brother had gone slaver.

It was not until we'd camped at the last of day and taken supper that I again had a chance to talk to Washington in private and at length. He invited me to his tent, which was commodious and well-furnished, with cot, two chairs, and small writing table, a bright lantern hanging above. We were attended by the same two Negro servants who had accompanied him initially on the last journey. This time I paid closer attention to them.

The younger, I think not yet sixteen years old, was a stable hand named Peter Hardiman, introduced as most excellent with horses. The older, near Washington's age and dressed in fine clothes, was a house servant and cook named Hercules.

"It's a remarkable difference from when last you and I dined in a tent," I said. "I recall hard jerky and melted snow. And talk of death."

"I'd like not to recall that at all. How is that frozen foot?" He studied my riding boot, as though that might reveal deformity.

"Well thawed, but peculiar-looking; a bit birdlike, I fear," I said. "Still, it gets me about."

"We must find a tent for you. As my friend and aide, it won't do to have you sleeping among the enlisted ranks."

"The sky's clear. I'll sleep in the open."

"If that's your wish."

Hercules set down a small wine cask on the table between us, then withdrew.

"Those two going with you all the way this time?" I asked.

"Yes. Excellent boys. And loyal. I think I worried overmuch about their being tempted to trade civilization for the Indian life. Hercules has learned the French art of cooking. I hope such can be practiced upon bear meat."

"I should tell you my prime reason for leaving Philadelphia was to escape my brother's business. He has gone into the slave trade—West Africa to the Caribbean. I want none of it."

Washington frowned. "It oft troubles me, I'll admit. To have a good man like Hercules as friend, yet in bondage. But what's to be done? He was born into it. Peter Hardiman also. My late brother Lawrence acquired only one man born free in Africa. A Sambo, by name. Fearsome brute. Tattooed face as marked as an Indian's. Gold earrings worth as much as he is. Now there's a one I'd not tempt with freedom. Could support himself well. A surpassing carpenter. Most of the buildings at Mount Vernon are by his hand."

"Yet you do not pay him."

"He is fed and sheltered."

"So is your horse." I thought of the young woman Charlotte and her skinned back.

"Don't harry me with this, Thomas. I cannot change the custom. The man at all events belongs to my sister-in-law. Let's talk no more of slavery. I had thought it was fear of gaol, not detestation for the Negro trade, that brought you to us."

"That's all withdrawn—the gaol and criminal charges. I am forgiven and held innocent. The lady and I may marry."

Washington came forward in his chair. "Excellent news! A young lady of both beauty and property. You're doubly blessed."

"Not blessed but cursed. The father has joined my brother in partnership. Wherever I turn, there I am a slaver."

Washington stood. "For whatever reason you come to us, Thomas, you are here welcome." He pulled forth a rolled map and unfurled it. "We go as we did before—by Winchester, then Will's Creek, and then I think make base at Great Meadows."

"That boggy place?"

" 'Tis spring. The ground will have dried. It's excellent pasture for the cattle and there are woods all about for meat to be hunted. But I don't mean to linger there long. If at all possible, I will be at the Forks a week hence. I intend to welcome Colonel Fry as officer in command of the King's fort there."

"All the more glory to you, then."

"I serve my King and colony, just as you."

"Better than I, I'd say. Mr. Franklin had a copy of your published journal, which he is reprinting."

"I'd not asked for any publishing. That quite took me by surprise. A disagreeable development, I can say to you. I am poorly learned in language, and the journal exposes that for all to see."

I took a gulp of wine. The moment had come.

"I searched and searched for my own name," I said. "But there was not a letter of it. Mr. Franklin made the same discovery."

Washington remained silent, staring at his map. Insects were buzzing against the lantern.

"I thought perhaps you'd left it out to save the expense of printing it, but you included all else, including the names of those rough men who did naught but paddle and carry."

"Tick, you had escaped from gaol and were a fugitive from the municipal writ of Philadelphia. I would not put to paper where you were. What friend would do that?"

That was one view of it. Another could be that including the name of a fugitive awaiting trial for assaulting a lady in the party described in the journal might diminish greatly the luster and honor of the feat in the wilderness.

I took another tack.

"What of Gist? He brought us there and back. Yet his share of glory was no more than Currin's, Davison's, and Van Braam's. You paid him handsomely enough for his risk and labors. Why not as much in words as in coin?"

"Damn it, Tick! Why do you hector me? Gist owes debts up and down the colonies. As I would not draw a map to you, sir, neither would I to him. I would not make much of his participation, lest his debtors think he's been made rich by it."

"I have never known you to lie before." God, I'd said it. I'd thought it. But did I believe it?

"Damn you, sir!" His faced was deepening in red. "Were we elsewhere, I would call you out!"

All my anger erupted from its inner well. I had a pistol in my belt. I jerked it forth, crying, "Where better?"—then slammed it down on Washington's writing table, knocking it over.

That was matchstick to his cannon's breech. His arm came swinging around by the side. I dodged as best I could, swinging my own fist. His blow struck my shoulder as mine hit his chin, but his was the stronger. I went flying against his cot. In a trice, he was on me, lifting me by the arms with his great strength and hurling me from the tent.

Several men stood there, having gathered at the sound of a quarrel—Captain Stobo among them.

"Arrest this man, sir," said Washington, his voice grim and low. "Take him from me."

I spent the night in the open as I wished—but tied to a wagon wheel.

In the morning, I was freed from my bonds and set upon my horse, the reins kept in the hands of a sergeant. After a few minutes, Washington, mounted on a large gray, trotted up.

"Ride with me." It was a command, not an invitation.

The sergeant handed me the reins. I took them, then followed Washington out of the camp.

We rode up a long rise to a tree, stopping beneath it.

"King's manual prescribes the lash for what you've done," he pronounced tersely.

"I am not a soldier in your ranks. Civilian scout I am, by your own word."

"What happened last night sets a damned awful example for the men. How can I punish brawlers now?"

"I don't care if you punish them at all."

We looked at each other. We could hear all the camp stirring behind us, down along the road.

"I will apologize to you, sir," Washington said. "I am thus bound by a rule of civility. Your name had a proper place in my journal. What I would have you know, Tick, was that it was not in my mind to belittle you in any way."

"No?"

"No. Not you or Gist. I meant that journal as a private correspondence, for Dinwiddie's contemplation solely—such as I've carried on with him all the time I have had a commission in the militia. I'd no idea he'd wish my report published. If I exalted myself at your expense with it—and it was only by omission, sir—it was to one end only. I wanted this command, Tick. I felt I must do everything in my power to commend myself for it."

I stared at him. I felt tired, emptied, and vaguely cold.

"There," he said. "It's all I have to say. I'll order no punishment. You may go, as I'm sure's your pleasure."

I breathed in, tightening my grip on the reins, but moving not. He'd spoken honestly. I was obliged to do the same.

"I've no other place to go, George," I said. "None that I want to."

"What of your lady in Philadelphia?"

"I think she loves me. I think she would have me prove myself to her before our affair is settled."

"Prove what?"

"I'm not sure, but I think I am closer to the doing of it here than any other place."

"Not here," he said. "Beyond the mountains."

I looked to the west. You could see the Blue Ridge clearly.

"I would go with your army there."

"Then I would have you do it."

He turned his horse.

"One thing," I said.

He halted. I think he was wearying of this exchange.

"Please on your honor do not call me 'Tick' again," I said. "I would not have the name any longer. I will be Tick to no man."

"Very well," he said, and put heels to the flanks of his mount.

We did not shake hands.

———

We crossed the Patowmack at the upriver ford and came upon the main Will's Creek compound on the twentieth of April. In the warmth of spring, all the settlement's dogs were loosed upon the surroundings and they came gallumphing up at first sound of our procession, barking in the manner of fiends and lunatics. Appearing in the trees to the rear of them was just the sight for which I'd had some yearning—a dark-haired beauty in a brown cotton dress, running toward us over the wildflowers.

Once out of the trees, she halted and stood letting the column flow around her until I drew nigh; then she leapt forward and came to my stirrup.

"I am pleased to see you well, Captain Morley."

What a lovely journey's end. "All thanks to you, dear lady," I said, slowing the mare to the most leisurely of walks. She flushed, or so it seemed in the bright sun.

"I was of the thought you'd not be coming to us again—that you'd be at sea or some'eres. But when I heard there'd be so many soldiers, I guessed you'd have to be among them." She paused. She was blushing. "I hoped so."

It was unseemly to remain in the saddle while this girl proceeded on foot—and barefoot at that—in the manner of camp follower. I pulled reins and slipped to the ground.

"I brought you another book," I said, having decided to give her my copy of Franklin's *Poor Richard's Almanack*, knowing he'd not mind, given the fair recipient.

Her look now was serious. I wondered if I should not have instead acquired for her some pretty shawl or kerchief.

"I hope I shall have the chance to read it," she said. "Nothing now is certain."

"What do you mean?"

"There's sorrowful news, but I should not be the one to tell you it."

———

We got the sorrowful news from Captain Trent, the officer who'd been sent to build us the fort that Washington and his force had come to guard and finish. Trent stood not at the Forks, but at the gate of the Will's Creek settlement with other welcomers, all as solemn.

"Major Washington!" he cried, running up, uninformed of George's promotion.

"Sir?" Washington drew up his horse before the man.

"The fort is lost!"

Washington blinked. "Lost? Is it yet even built?"

"Half-built, sir. Then burned. And taken by the French!"

Twenty-three

Trent expanded upon his news for us amidst victuals and refreshment. His report was distressing—our worst fear, save a general uprising of the region's Indians—but it should have been expected. Had not Captains Joncaire and St. Pierre told us precisely what was going to happen?

The fort at the Forks had fallen just three days before our return to Will's Creek, where Trent had been seeking supplies to make up for those that had been promised by Dinwiddie but not materialized. Poor Trent had been busy as well trying to stem the flow of desertions. Gist had also been absent from the Forks, off scouting up along the Monongahela, using his plantation for base.

Left in command at the construction at the Forks, then, was a young and inexperienced Ensign Edward Ward. With just forty men at hand, he'd been proceeding as best he could with work upon the fortifications, which had advanced only to the state of a crude stockade. Young Ward could not count even on his newly appointed lieutenant, the trader Frazier, who was up the Allegheny and on his own commercial business.

Frazier might have been of enormous usefulness in all this, but as Washington discovered to his immense disgust, the trader viewed his title of lieutenant more as honor than duty, and spent his time securing profit for himself and provisions for none of us. The ensign's only ally was the helpful Seneca chief, Half King, who had turned up at the Forks with a few retainers, but no useful force of warriors.

Receiving warning of French canoes on the Ohio from our old servitor Davison, who was roaming the area, Ensign Ward had just sent to Trent for instruction if no reinforcement was available. There then appeared bearing toward him on the river an enormous fleet of canoes and *bateaux*, carrying close to if not more than a thousand men—French marines, *coureurs des bois*, and Indians—the entire party led by a *Capitaine* Claude Pecaudy de Contrecoeur. They landed, marched upon the construction site at the Forks, and gave Ward the choice of decamping or being instantly attacked, as he was trespassing on French property. *Voilà*.

Ward had turned to Half King, who suggested he attempt delay, for he'd had word that Washington's "army" was on the march. (What paltry, miserable succor that would have been.) But Contrecoeur would have none of that, and reissued his ultimatum. The unfortunate ensign had no choice, and so abjectly abandoned the works.

As there was no actual war on, Ward and his men were allowed to keep their weapons and tools, and permitted also to camp nearby while the French destroyed the English works, pulling down the stockade and burning what logs and timber they had no use for. Ward and his party departed the next day, heeding Half King's fears that the Indians in Contrecoeur's force might turn this incident into a war if Contrecoeur himself wasn't willing to do it.

As the forty English marched off, the French had begun laying out the lines of a new, much larger fort of their own making, following the time-tested designs of the great engineer Vauban. Ward said Contrecoeur had told him it was to be named after the Marquis Duquesne, the newly appointed governor of New France.

There was little to do for the present but wait there at Will's Creek for Dinwiddie's promised supplies and reinforcements, with the hope the former would precede the latter. The Colonel took over the Ohio Company storehouse and office as headquarters, which meant that we, his aides and officers, could most usually be found in the adjoining ordinary operated by Mr. Ennis.

George had been provided with Gist's cabin as quarters, but kept little in it, as it had only Anne Gist as resident. I camped nearer the store.

It was not the happy advantage I had hoped, having us there at Ennis's, as the custom of so many officers and sundry others kept the tavern-keeper hopping, and more so his help, including daughter Mercy, who seemed to appear before me only when bearing trays or jugs or platters. She gave me smiles, which made me happier, but unsatisfied. Surely they were the only smiles to be found in the settlement.

Matters were far more worrisome than the Colonel at the outset could have reckoned upon. Trent's frontier volunteers were continuing to desert, claiming their pay was less than agreed upon and that Washington had no legal command over them, as he held a Virginia commission and Will's Creek was in Maryland colony—though I think love of their scalp hair was also a factor in their reluctance. Frazier continued absent, as did Gist. Indian agent George Croghan, deputy to the great William Johnson of New York, had been in charge of acquiring and transporting to us the wagons and additional supplies promised by Dinwiddie, but there continued no sign or word of either.

The governor and Burgesses would have to be persuaded of the precariousness of the situation. Washington sent Ward off to Williamsburg with a small escort, instructing him to describe events and the size and nature of the French force as vividly as possible.

"What I fear are the Indians," George said to me quietly in a moment when no other was present. "I do not think the French want war, not yet. Otherwise, they would have fired on Ward's work party at the Forks. But their success may encourage all the Indians in this country to take up the war wampum and bring hatchets against us. We simply cannot let that happen. It would be the end of everything. We must have a demonstration of some kind to impress them with our might, a countermarch—something to keep the Indian head down. I'll think upon it. You, too."

I must confess my thoughts were then more with Venus than with Mars. Losing all patience, I fetched Mercy that night from the scullery, where she, two sisters, and some other settlement women were hard at labor on our account. She offered no complaint, and walked with me through the darkness to the river, which glimmered faintly with the starlight. Had I put Susannah from my thoughts? No, I could not. But my mind was far more firmly fixed than ever before on the lady at hand.

Mercy's thoughts, understandably, were on French and Indians. "How bad off are we?" she asked.

"The Colonel's worried. He's not been a commander long, and I think this scares him."

"Scared is what we all are. More traders and settlers came in today. After what happened to your young ensign and his fort builders, fear's spreadin' through these mountains like fire."

"Washington understands that, though he's had not much experience in this country."

"He's had experience enough. If not with war."

"What do you mean?"

"Nothing. I misspoke. Pay no attention, Captain."

There was a tree just behind me. I leaned back against it, and Mercy gently came back against me. I put my arms about her waist and soft, flat belly. She made no objection. I found my breath coming more quickly.

"It's a lovely spot to be at night," I said. "Especially this night."

"Night or day, there's beauty enough for any soul along this river. I've been most content here. These mountains are like those in the north of Ireland, except here we have the warmth and sun and all these trees. It's my father who's got the itch to move on. He wants his own grand place, like Mr. Gist's plantation beyond Chestnut Ridge. Grander than that, someday, he says. He's in mind of a castle of wood, kin to the castles of all their lordships back home. But he's too many daughters and not enough sons. Still, he dreams it. And he's gettin' impatient here. We've just been waiting—on you soldiers, to make the Ohio safe for folk as us."

"I'm no soldier," I said, "but I can tell you it's going to take a while."

"When do you leave for the Forks, Captain? That's your purpose, isn't it, to drive them French back where they're from."

"I would have you call me Thomas."

"Thomas." The word came most softly, floating.

"As I would call you Mercy."

"Mercy I am, Thomas. When do you go?"

"The Colonel would like to move out tomorrow, but he isn't certain where best to go first, or quite what to do when we get there. And we need supplies"

"Tomorrow. As soon as that?"

"Could be tonight if some courier comes riding in with more ill report or orders from on high. We'd leave without another biscuit."

The river was becoming faintly more visible now, a shimmering glimmer in the shadows. We could hear the flow of its waters. The spring night now seemed full of sound—insects and frogs, owls, the breeze in the tree-tops, odd splashes in the river made by who knew what. There was a fragrance to the air. I sensed we were sharing the same thoughts.

"I like you well, Thomas Morley."

"And I you, Mercy."

What of Susannah Smithson, you ask? I can only say she was not there with me, and had no such mind to be. For all I knew, I'd be in no other place again. Washington was taking our situation most seriously. We all were.

Life was terribly short—especially here.

My hands slid up her gown and came over her breasts. She put her own hands up over mine and leaned back her head against my chest.

I held her more tightly. Gently, she lifted my hands from her bosom and stepped forward. In a moment, her gown had slipped from her. She turned to me.

"Do not leave me with child," she said softly. "I would not be a mother unmarried."

———

All was bliss to me the following day, but there were other reasons for such a disposition. Reinforcements arrived, new companies led by newly made captains. George Croghan came into camp with a some additional wagons laden with provisions and forage, bringing with him also the legendary Andrew Montour—who was as fascinating to me as I had been to Chief Shingas.

Montour was not so tall as I, but taller than the average, very dark of hair and countenance—looking indeed more Indian than French. He wore a blue coat, as I'd been told—French Navy I think in origin, and in need of further tailoring, for it was at once too short and too loose on his sinewy frame—and badly in need of laundering besides. His face was very much as bright a crimson as advertised. His custom was to make a red dye from some natural element of the earth and mix it in solution with bear grease, the resultant goo then applied thickly enough to avoid the need for frequent renewal. I hadn't the courage to ask him why he so decorated himself. For his part, he took an abiding, and I fear acquisitive, interest in my own blue nautical coat and its superior qualities. If I were to fall to French musket ball or Shawnee tomahawk, I knew this garment would not have long to wait for a new owner.

Mountour also now bore a captain's rank in the militia. Captains, captains everywhere. Better more musket bearers, food, axes, shot and powder.

And Indians, at least those disposed to our English cause. Dinwiddie's hopes for help from the friendly tribes of the south—he'd promised hundreds of Catawbas, Cherokees, and Chickasaws—appeared ill founded. Washington had thought there might at least be some feelings of kinship between Virginia and the Cherokees, as the tribe was adopting numerous of the white man's ways, including the taking and keeping of African slaves, and there was talk of their actually adopting a written Cherokee language.

But no southern warriors came to Will's Creek at all. Instead, we got a reinforced independent Royal company of redcoats from South Carolina under the command of a Captain James MacKay, bringing our strength to something more than three hundred fifty. Whatever joy we took from this was rapidly diminished.

MacKay, who arrived in a coach and four, of all grand things, dragged God knows how through the wilderness, possessed a regular King's commission, and was of no mind to serve as subordinate to a mere militia officer aged only twenty-two years and with the most minimal experience in the command of troops. Thereafter, though Washington continued to issue direct orders to the other company commanders, he was compelled to *consult* with MacKay and negotiate concurrence in his wishes.

He and I were not speaking much privately, but he confessed another irritation. He'd discovered that, as a militia officer, Colonel or no, he was earning something like half MacKay's pay!

All this further poisoned an already contentious atmosphere about the place. Idleness is the worst duty for a sailor or soldier, and our men were liking their situation not at all. Desertions continued, the daily ration of rum was illicitly expanded through an assortment of surreptitious means—in which innkeeper Ennis had a part, no doubt—and quarrels and disobedience became more frequent. Floggings were a regular part of the daily routine.

I remained Washington's loyal subordinate, but my sympathies were much with the men. Their pay was miserly, and not yet forthcoming. The food was not good, and insufficient in quantity. The addition of reinforcements only worsened our problems of transport and supply, yet there was no sign of wagon, cart, or spare animal. Only MacKay's resplendent coach.

He was, to be sure, a *gentleman*, and the Colonel with great deference treated him as such, more so than he did any of his other officers. For all MacKay's grand manner, he was a good soldier—as I'd have occasion to learn in good time. I'd not see his like again until making the acquaintance of General Burgoyne in this American rebellion.

Our men there at Great Meadows had come to fight, but neither Washington nor MacKay could offer them battle. Though the news from the north continued to be worrisome, there was no war.

But there were constant threats of it. Two traders reported parties of French and Indians at large in the countryside near Gist's plantation. Gist himself rode in at last, tight-lipped and grim—beneath that silent facade, full of fury and despair. A force of some half a hundred French under an Ensign LaForce had come up to his house under the guise of hunting for deserters, but looking ready to burn the establishment as they might a prize of war. Had the ever-present Half King not happened on the confrontation and claimed himself to be but part of a great Seneca host friendly to the English, they might have done so.

LaForce had moved on, but there was no good intelligence as to where. Gist had left his sons in defense of the plantation and hurried here in hope of help. Washington quickly ordered Captain Stephen and twenty-five Virginians north to keep watch over Gist's holdings, cherishing the "plantation" as a European commander might some named place on the map. I'd learned enough of the frontier to understand that such habitations were easily made and unmade. One could burn an Indian village and be safe in the knowledge there'd be another in full flower within a week.

Knowing the high regard the investors of the Ohio Company had for the scout, and unhappy with his grousing and lamentation, George ordered Gist to Williamsburg to make a full report and beg the Burgesses and Dinwiddie for our necessities—as well as for information as to the whereabouts of Colonel Fry, who was supposed to be in command of all this mess.

Washington was sending letters to Dinwiddie at such a rate I feared our force would be depleted altogether through conversion to messenger. He showed me one missive still freshly inked, and I was astounded to read in it a demand that the governor grant Washington the favor of being removed from his commission, to serve unpaid in any capacity in lieu of command, or, as he put it. "I would rather prefer the toil of a daily laborer, and dig for a maintenance, provided I were reduced to the necessity, than serve upon such ignoble terms."

What was this? At bottom, 'twas another complaint about his pay. Were the lives of the settlers the Colonel was here defending worth less—in terms of how highly paid their rescuer—than those defended by officers with regular commissions in other of the King's dominions?

I counseled the Colonel against sending this, knowing that if it found the eye of some Royal emissary of His Majesty's, it might be taken as impertinence, but off it went regardless. The dispatch rider had not been gone a day, however, when Washington suddenly called a council of war. He'd just then received a message from Half King, now camped up near Great Meadows, telling him. "Come to me when you are ready."

The longer we dallied here, however, the less ready we would be. The Colonel proposed to march now, cutting a wagon road if he could. He desired to use the Great Meadows site as his base camp. But with the Forks now in French hands, his goal was no longer that place but a nearer point from which he could threaten the Fort Duquesne now abuilding and still shield the settlements at Will's Creek and those up and down the Patowmack.

I had no more interludes with Mercy beyond that surpassing night's idyll by the river. We exchanged looks and touches of hand—and once or twice a kiss. But all were busy at that camp, and there was scant opportunity. Actually, I do not think she would have sought one. She had given of her virtue, but not easily. She seemed now to be waiting, though I knew not exactly for what. Perhaps just to see if we all returned.

That last morning, Mercy and I found a moment to walk a while in the woods, and there decided to exchange keepsakes, though neither of us had much possession to offer the other. She gave me a polished quartz stone from the nearby mountains. A hole had been drilled through it to admit a leather thong so it could be worn, and she placed it around my neck. I had nothing so pretty to give her, but there was something I had held dear that might have utilitarian value as well in this emergency—an ivory-handled sailor's knife my brother Richard had given me when we'd first acquired the *Hannah* and I had become his mate.

We kissed farewell in a quiet glen behind the ordinary. When our troops were mounted or in rank and ready to depart, she came to my stirrup as she had upon my arrival and walked with us a way until we reached the head of the old Nemacolin Indian trail that led over the next mountain. Washington had already ordered out the axe men, and one could hear their blades at work on the wagon road out among the trees.

"I must go back now," she said.

"I look to a safer time when you'll have no such need."

"Thomas, I've a question I've kept silent on until now."

"Yes?"

"The Colonel says you are betrothed, and to a lady. He spoke this not to me, but to my father, who asked him most direct."

"This is a misapprehension. What I told Washington was that this lady's father presumed a troth, or wished it so. Between the lady and me, there is no such decision, and my brother has a great ardor for her."

"He does?"

"Oh, yes."

"And you do not?"

"Mercy, I bear her much affection, but when I come back over these mountains, it will be to come to you, if you would welcome it."

Did I mean all these words? I must have done. I kissed her hand, received a lover's smile and that witch's gleam of eye she sometimes gave; then she patted my leg and turned and darted off, leaping and bounding over the meadow.

————

Road-building in such country is the devil's own work, and the result is nothing so accommodating to travel as you might think. All we did really was to clear the way of trees and brush, as well as of those rocks and boulders too difficult to get a wagon's wheel over. I say "all" we did. It was fearsome labor, digging out those boulders. Our reinforcements had brought more swivel cannons with them, but more than once we had to employ black powder meant for those artillery pieces to clear stubborn stone.

Mostly, these great lumps of rock were pried loose with narrow log levers and hefted by shoulder and hand. More than once I saw Washington himself lend his effort to such need, to set a good example.

But yard by yard, ridge by ridge, like some creeping snake, our long column at last attained its goal. Descending Laurel Ridge, we came to Great Meadows and spread out over its green grass as though upon a bed. I was troubled to find the ground along both of the intersecting creeks still soft. Indeed, as men and beasts trod back and forth over it, the grass in places wore away to mud. But here Washington settled our camp, making a well-organized arrangement of it.

First, though, he drew together a force of some seventy-five men, placed them under the command of Captain Hog and sent them west to take and hold the juncture of the Monongahela and Redstone Creek with orders to apprehend any French who approached or chase them back from whence they'd come, whichever proved the most possible and practicable.

He also sent out scouts along the ridges that overlooked the Great Meadows valley, and dispatched as well hunting parties into the woods nearest us. I was impressed. If only he hadn't kept the remainder of our party in this low-lying, defenseless place.

" 'Tis charming ground for an encounter," he said.

A wagon and then another joined us from the south, but no word came from Dinwiddie and there was none from Gist. At length, Stephen and his mounted group of two dozen came riding in, bringing with them Gist's family, who were now afraid to remain on the plantation, with or without the head of their household.

The Colonel sent these civilians on to safer ground at Will's Creek, with a request to relay to Gist to hurry himself back to us as soon as convenient upon his return from the capital. I thought it folly to have sent the scout to Williamsburg in the first place. Now all we could do was wait. George seemed unwilling to progress much further without the man.

True. The Colonel and I now knew something of this country, and we had Trent, Frazier, Croghan, and Montour. But it was Gist we'd learned to trust about all wilderness lore and matters. Gist in fact might suggest a course of action. The Colonel seemed run out of them.

I took advantage of my own idleness in this place to better familiarize myself with the ordnance and disciplines available to those in the King's army, learning this from Captain MacKay, the first professional soldier I'd yet encountered.

George II's own son, Prince William, the Duke of Cumberland, had been commander-in-chief of all redcoats since 1745, when he'd presided over that butchery of Scottish Highland clans—men, women, boys, and helpless babes—known as the Battle of Culloden. Though many thought him a fat-as-a-pig, sadistic incompetent when in the field as commander, having lost numerous engagements in Flanders, the Prince was credited with having brilliantly reorganized and re-equipped the King's regiments—at least so said MacKay, whom I found a reasonable and likeable fellow.

One of the Duke's recent improvements was to replace the old Long Land Service Musket, an unwieldy weapon with a barrel fully forty-six inches in length, with the more useful and handy Short Land Service Musket, whose barrel was but forty-two inches long, though it was also of .75 caliber and just as deadly.

The older, longer weapon compelled its firer to lean backward while proffering the musket forward, just to maintain balance. A barrel of forty-two inches encouraged a more erect and centered stance, improving the aim. The new weapon also had a steel spring bringing tension to the trigger, enabling one to squeeze it with carefully measured pressure. It was a handier weapon for massed volleys, MacKay said.

"Of what use are volleys in thick woods like these?" I asked.

"Have you ever been witness to one—fired by infantry massed in rank?"

"I've never witnessed volley shot of any kind," I said.

"Well, it's murderous, sir. A thing of awe. Within a hundred yards of it, no one can long stand."

Unless, of course, one was standing behind a tree.

———

The Colonel's impatience and irritation increased almost beyond tolerance. He wrote letter after letter, paced the ground outside his tent, took to horse and cantered about the area, and drank inordinately, at least for him.

I stayed nearer him now, but avoided congress unless addressed. One afternoon he interrupted yet another letter he was writing to investigate someone's report of smoke glimpsed to the east of us up the valley.

I'd been seated on the ground near the open facing of his tent. Shortly after he'd pounded off with Mercer and two other riders to make his reconnaissance, a breeze stirred and caught at the papers on his writing table. His two manservants were elsewhere in the camp, attending to other duties, and when the loosed sheets of paper took flight over the grass, I jumped up to recover them.

Well, yes, I pray forgive my insufferable prying rudeness in this, but there was one letter there, inked in such passion the words leapt off the page, and I read them each. You can guess the recipient, and that it was not His Honour the governor.

"You have drawn me, or rather I have drawn myself, into an honest confession of a simple fact," he'd written. "Misconstrue not my meaning, doubt it not, nor expose it. The world has no business to know the object of my Love, declared in this manner to you . . . ."

Clearly, the letter I had given him back on the road had been Sally's antidote, not her poison.

Was there not some stern "rule of civility" that forbade the writing of such letters to a married lady—to the wife of a friend and benefactor?

I took the papers into his tent, admonishing myself to keep in mind the follies of misplaced speculation. The circumstance brooked other possibilities just as logical, if not more so. He and Sally could be mere friends and speak and write thus to each other in utter naturalness. What I took for passion might be no more than deeply heartfelt amity. Mrs. Fairfax was of a flirtatious bent, and cast her charm about freely upon all, with no carnal intent. Her secret meeting in the woods with George just downriver from Alexandria that spring day a year before might have been no more than her impulsive reach for a means of ending a quarrel—the leaves and mud upon her hem merely what one might expect upon any gown that had been worn upon a riverbank. I'd no knowledge that she'd ever blessed him with more than kisses. In behavior, if not inclination, the relationship of George Washington and Sally Cary Fairfax might well be among the most chaste in the colony.

I suppose there are those who might believe all that, and do.

I did not. I do not.

There was another line in that letter. I glanced o'er it quickly before I returned these pages to the table and placed them securely under weight.

"One thing above all things in this world I wish to know," he'd written.

But he didn't state the question. What could it be? Was he emboldened now to ask for marriage? Was I responsible for that?

I heard hoofbeats, but those of a single horse. Looking to the tent opening, I saw approaching not Washington, but Montour, who'd been off across the mountains to the west and north with Half King. He looked hot, and very excited.

"Tanacharison say the French are now coming for you," Montour said after I told him the Colonel was briefly absent. "He find the tracks of two men along the trail on Chestnut Ridge. The track lead to a rocky hollow, where he thinks a larger group is camped. They may be hiding there to wait to attack our camp. Tanacharison say come now!"

Twenty-four

If Washington had been hesitant and indecisive since arriving at Great Meadows, his resolve returned the instant of hearing Montour's news. The Colonel quickly organized a party of forty men, including the twenty-five led by Captain Stephen, who would serve as his second-in-command on this expedition. I asked to go as well, having tired of hanging about. It was the only thing I'd asked of Washington since our contretemp, and he granted me it—muttering something about the usefulness of my knowledge of the country.

We gathered our weapons quickly and formed up for the march. It was decided to proceed all of us on foot, in the manner of the Indians, as some stealth would be required approaching the French, and nervous mounts were no friends to that. As there were not mounts for all, our pace would have been the walk at all events.

Montour said Half King would be waiting up on Chestnut Ridge, some six miles to the north and west of us. The day was fast advancing toward its end and the sky clouding up. We'd be moving through the dark.

It didn't matter. The moment had come to meet the French. We had to reach them where they were, and not where they might choose to surprise us.

I don't think the Colonel liked it much in the infantry, especially after the disagreeableness of our walk through this country during the winter. But he saw the need and grumbled not—at least not aloud. I followed his example. In time, I got used to the march again. After a while, so did my foot.

Not a third of the way up the ridge, the day abruptly ended of a sudden as a murderous tempest came roiling over the summit, blanking out all trace of light. Its only virtue was the lightning, which at intervals, in hellish fashion, illuminated the way. Otherwise, all became as black as tar, and as wet as if ocean waves entire were dropping from the sky.

I'd secured myself a place in the line of march right behind the Colonel, whether he liked it or no, and stayed within reach of his back throughout the devilish, twisting climb up the ridge and onto the gentler ground that followed after. Others with us were not so skillful at keeping the way. Even in the thudding rain I could hear the cries of those stumbling off the trail into boulder or tree or rock slide. I lost count of the times we halted the column to wait for stragglers to rediscover us. I don't think I said but two words to the Colonel in all those hours, and he spoke to me not at all. His attention was concentrated on Montour, who served as our principal guide. At this he was excellent, having no fault save nimbleness and the fast pace he set.

We reached the meeting place on the ridge just at the first glimmer of gray in the eastern sky. I recognized the spot as the same point of prospect that had filled me with such awe when Gist had urged me up to see its limitless view. Now the clouds made a thick curtain across it.

Half King stepped out from the trees and searched among us in the dark shadows for Washington, whom he approached finally with his hand raised in greeting. I don't know if the chief recognized me, but I nodded to him. He seemed smaller than I had remembered, but that might have been the darkness.

With Montour also engaged in the conversation, Half King told Washington what was afoot. His scouts had found the French camp, in a steeply sided rocky glen only a mile along the ridge to our right. Their party numbered five and thirty, the Indian said, and they had set out no sentries or scouts.

The Colonel was joyful. Thirty-five? He had forty-one English men at arms, counting me, plus now Half King's Indians. We'd earlier heard reports that the chief had as many as sixty of his tribe with him, but he met us here with only thirteen. Still, that made a force of fifty-six, the Colonel included. Unlike poor Ensign Ward's impossible odds, we outnumbered these French by nearly two to one. Ward's humiliation would be avenged, if only in like kind.

I had no notion of battle, mind. There was excitement, and breaths came quick, but it was rather as in preparation for some boy's game of the field—choosing up sides, marking the goals. For all our weaponry, I hadn't a thought of death or bloodshed. I knew these French—or their like. We had dined with them. They were men such as ourselves. Americans, one could call them.

To have made camp without sentries or scouts was a peaceful sign. We had done so ourselves the winter before. These French might well be couriers, bringing a message to us as we had to them. Washington was busy in further interrogation of Half King, so I raised my concern with Captain Stephen.

He clapped my shoulder. "I'dna worry about a peaceful purpose with those lads, Morley. If they meant to be peaceable, they'd be camped along the trail, in the open, not hiding in the bloody rocks."

The rain had ceased, and there was a hint at the horizon of breaks to come in the overcast. Washington ordered us all to check our firearms and load with fresh powder if warranted. When that was done, he ordered those carrying muskets and rifles to screw on bayonets if they had them. As I returned a newly primed flintlock pistol to my belt, the import of this preparation came home to me. Now I was frightened.

I might soon have to kill a man. In a very short time I was going to find myself in a situation where a pull of this trigger might send a ball crashing into the skull or heart or stomach of another living, breathing man—toward whom I bore no real ill will. I thought of our French hosts at the fort, of the charming Joncaire, the courteous if cold St. Pierre. I could not possibly imagine reason enough for wanting to kill or wound these men.

I reminded myself of the scalps I'd carried to Dinwiddie and Franklin, and the report of dead settlers fed upon by hogs. It failed to change my outlook. It was my most earnest hope that the Colonel's mind now held something of the same reluctant thoughts as mine.

Half King and one of his warriors, with Montour just behind, led the way as guides on point. Washington and I came next, with Stephen in our van to relay the Colonel's commands to the column that stretched behind us through the trees.

The leaves were dripping-wet, drenching us anew as we moved through the trees and brush, but the rain was to be thanked for soaking the ground and making of it such a silent path. Up and down the slopes and hillocks we went, winding around clumps of brambles and large boulders, eyes ever forward, sometimes lifted to the eastern sky. If grateful for the morning, we did not yet want it bright.

Much sooner than I expected, Montour, only twenty or thirty feet ahead of Washington, came to a sudden stop, raising his hand. The Colonel turned and gave the same signal to Stephen, who likewise compelled the column's halt. Most of the men sank to one knee, crouching, waiting, though a few stood, lifting their rifles or muskets to the ready, leaning back against tree trunks, eyes darting about warily.

Washington was moving ahead to confer with Montour. I quickly followed, amazed that so bulky a man as George could transport himself so nimbly and quietly. I heard Montour whisper something, but could not ken it. Washington nodded, then motioned to me to signal Stephen and the column forward.

As I obeyed, Washington, at a crouch, crept quietly forward, vanishing from view into some thick bushes just ahead. As I came up to join him, Half King and his tribesmen, moving so silently they might be floating above the ground, emerged from the same thick brush Washington had gone into and came back toward us, leaving our path after they'd passed by and slipping into the woods.

Ignoring a sharp pain to the knee of my bad leg from a rock I'd not noticed, I edged forward, creeping into the thick overgrowth after Washington and finding him lying just beyond it, belly-down at the very edge of a ledge that overlooked the glen. I crawled out beside him. He turned his head toward me, seeming pleased that I was there, then brought his finger to his lips for silence and returned his attention to the scene below. There were bushes here, too, but sparser. Their lower branches, though masking our presence, permitted extensive view.

The west, south, and east sides of the glen were of steep-walled rock a good forty feet high where we lay at our corner, and not much less elsewhere along it. The fourth side of the place, on the north, was open to the trees and a downward slope of the mountain ridge. I guessed Half King and the other Indians were now down that way, or would be soon.

Because of the night's rain, there was a heavy mist hanging in the glen, shrouding somewhat the huddled figures below us. A good number of them were sleeping beneath bark shelters laid on upstanding sticks. I saw two men who were awake, crouched to either side of a small, smoky fire by the rock face opposite us. All the others seemed still to be wrapped in their bedding, lying about the floor of the glen where comfort could be found. Muskets were stacked, nearly all in the dryness beneath the bark shelters. There were indeed no sentries. More confoundingly to me, there were no Indians. Were the French so bold they'd move through these mountains without natives to guide them?

Washington gave me a quick smile, then eased himself back a little on the rock to turn toward Stephen and Montour and get on with the deployment of his force. It was a simple enough maneuver. He bade, with hand signals, the first thirty or so of the men in line to take up positions in cover atop the rock faces to the right of us. When they had passed, he raised his hand again and directed the remaining troops along the ledge to our left.

I held my breath. How such an assemblage of amateur soldiery could complete this task without dropping musket butt to stone or kicking rock over edge amazed me, but they managed it. Each man came to his assigned place as if it were home to him, found sufficient cover, and eased behind it. Had I not known they were there, once they were settled, I'd never have noticed them.

There was sunlight now, and soon the gloom would give way to brightness. Two or three other of the French began to stir, and one rose to amble to the side of the glen and make his morning relief.

If this matter was to be resolved in our favor, the Colonel would have to act with celerity. The course to me seemed obvious: He should have each of our men take precautionary aim, as most had done, then call out to the French with the announcement that they were surrounded and helpless. There'd be no need of firing a single round, except as last resort or to give example. We could take them prisoner, parade them through Williamsburg as the Romans had paraded their captives. If this was inconvenient, we could simply relieve them of their arms, take their parole and send them back to Duquesne as humiliated as Ensign Ward had returned to us.

All Washington had to do was call out, now, with words well chosen.

I looked to him, but his eyes were fixed on the tableau below. I remembered then that he spoke no French. Here I could be useful. I tried to remember the word for "surrender." *Abandonner? Abandonnez! Laissez votre armes!* Something of the sort.

"George," I whispered.

He ignored me.

"George. The French word. It's—"

Washington's huge hand reached out and clamped itself over my mouth. When it finally withdrew, I scarce dared move, let alone speak, for fear next time he'd hurl me over the ledge.

More French were stirring. One had rolled over on his back and seemed to be staring right at us. Now was the time for the Colonel to call out. This was the moment to effect our purpose.

Instead, he was moving, his left knee sliding up, his shoulders lifting, his arms carefully extending. He reached for his pistol; then, with that long device in hand, slowly, resolutely, and irretrievably, began to rise like some great tower, until he was standing at his full, extraordinary height.

That man directly below rolled over, clawing for his musket.

Twenty-five

Captain MacKay had described the massed volley as a thing "awesome." Well, it was all of that. I don't know how many of our men fired in that first instant of Colonel Washington's "battle," but it was most of 'em, and they did so almost in unison—their only command provided by that one poor Frenchman's reach for his weapon. The flash and smoke seemed to come from all directions, the mingled reports resounding as a single ringing blast that echoed back and forth across the stone. The acrid scent of powder gave a sting to the nose.

The fellow who had groped for his firearm with such ill-considered desperation died quickly, hit in three or four places and sent rolling by the force of the bullets. I saw others rise from their shelters and quickly fall. The one making his morning toilet left this life sitting in it. Another, still rolled in his bedding, lifted his head, then dropped it forever, not moving again.

A number did get to their weapons without hindrance from ball and shot, stood where they were, or found cover and fired back. One of our men on the cliff opposite fell forward, crying out, his musket clattering down the rock face ahead of him. Washington leveled his pistol at the general melee, firing it without much aim, the ball cracking against a boulder near a running Frenchman. It was not an occasion to be thought a coward; I jumped to my feet to stand beside George, ignoring a branch severed by a gunshot that came flopping down against my shoulder. I left my flintlock saddle pistol in my belt, though. I could not bring myself to touch it that day. Odd, for I'd fired deck guns without any qualm at menacing pirates in the Caribbean.

Our men were reloading, the Frenchmen below attempting to form a defensive rank. More bullets cut through tree leaves about us. A few determined fellows below had decided on the Colonel as a favored target, yet he stood there tall as ever, without even flinch. It took every ounce of courage I possessed or might borrow to remain there at his side.

He was putting powder and ball into his long-barreled pistol, keeping his eyes to the action. His face was flushed, excited—I daresay rapturous in his delight. Here at last he was made true soldier.

Through the foggy veil of gunsmoke woven into the morning mist, one could see that the French were pulling back, step by step, most holding discipline, some still firing.

Our soldiers loosed another volley, less in unison this time, the shots coming in a roll, sounding in the instant each weapon came ready. More French fell. Finally, all those still standing below turned and ran, some dropping their muskets. Our own men were cheering, or shouting oaths at the departing figures as they crashed on into the brush.

"Reload!" shouted Captain Stephen. "Reload!"

I thought him too wary. The French were done and away from us pell-mell.

But no, amazingly, it wasn't so. I saw figures emerging from the brush again. The French were running back. What lunacy was this? A counter-charge? Against us on these rocky cliffs?

'Twas prudence that had brought them. They came back into the clearing dropping weapons and flinging up their arms. Behind them, I could ken the reason why. I'd heard such savage screams only once before, and those in mockery, on that snowy day when the Indians at the French fort came forth to greet us with whooping forms of intimidation. These cries at the glen were meant in more earnest. Half King and his Senecas had now joined the battle, though it should by then have been over. All the French were standing in a frightened huddle. One was shouting *"Envoyé! Envoyé!"* Another waved a white cloth.

"Cease fire!" came the shout from Washington. "Down to them! Down to them fast!"

Half King and his dozen or so shrieking warriors reached the glen just as the first of our soldiers did. Thus prevented from reaching their helpless quarry standing huddled in our mercy, the Indians settled for the dead and, I fear to say, also for some of the wounded.

I'd clambered down and leapt to the floor of the glen by means of a cleft between two great slabs of rock. Despite my unfortunate foot, I hurried forward without stumble, coming up to Half King just as he knelt over the writhing form of a young French officer. I heard the words, spoken in French, "You are not yet dead, my father." Up went tomahawk. I shouted "No!" or thought I had, but the word was in my mind. I was so stricken by the horror of it, I had not actually uttered it aloud. Down the weapon came, then up and down again, the action repeated several times.

I stood there transfixed, gaping, seeing now what Half King was about. He had chopped the man's skull open and was now bathing his hands in the brains, lifting them to the air and letting the matter drip between his fingers, muttering Indian words throughout. At length satisfied that he'd completed enough of whatever ritual this was, Half King pulled forth his scalping knife and removed a long strip of bloody flesh and dark hair, then stood. Behind him I could see the other chief, Scarroyaddy, bearing a trophy of his own.

We exchanged looks, but not words. Then they began to whoop.

My stomach was clenched tight, but there was nothing in it to disgorge. My fists were clenched tight, too, and I would have hit the Indian, or Washington, or something, if I could, but my arms of a sudden were completely drained of strength. Finally, I sank to my knees and took a very deep draught of air. Then, averting my eyes from the poor French officer's ill-used head, I searched through his clothing and leather pouch. I wished him to have identity.

I found military papers, a map, and a letter. I was reading hurriedly through it when I sensed men standing behind me.

One was Washington, the other, Captain Stephen. I rose.

"He was their commander," I said, amazed I could produce words at all. "Ensign Joseph Coulon de Villiers, *Sieur de Jumonville*. He bears this letter. It's to you—to whoever commands English forces here. It's a summons for you to appear before Captain Contrecoeur at Fort Duquesne and explain your presence on lands in the domain of His Most Christian Majesty."

Washington took the letter from me. "It's in French," he said.

"As your letter was in English."

"My letter?"

"Last year. The letter we brought from Dinwiddie to the French commander in the Ohio."

"Yes."

"George—"

"Colonel."

"Colonel, then. This *Sieur de Jumonville* was on the same manner of mission. His comrade was shouting '*Envoyé!*' Ambassador. This officer was traveling as ambassador. That's what they were trying to tell us."

Washington frowned. He folded the letter and put it within his coat. "I will have Van Braam translate this more fully. Thank you, sir."

"They were an armed party, Morley," said Stephen. "Five and thirty armed men, and lying here in hiding. Look at this camp. They've been here two nights and a full day at least. I judge they were waiting for us to pass. I'd wager they were plotting an ambuscade of our column or baggage train. Or they were spies."

"We were spies," I said. "At Le Boeuf. We counted canoes and *bateaux*. We walked the measure of the fort. Yet they let us pass with heads intact."

"These men were part of the army that threatened our Ensign Ward with immediate attack," Washington said.

"An attack that woulda seen them all slaughtered in a trice," said Stephen.

I sought the Colonel's eyes, but he kept them from me.

"These men reached for their arms, sir," he said.

He turned and walked back to the center of the glen, barking orders.

Had this been murder? I tell you, to this day, I do not know. Had I been a farthing less in doubt, I would have shrieked the word at him for all in America to hear. But I could not.

———

We lost a man dead, so described to you earlier in this passage, and three wounded, all walking. The French casualties were ten killed, one wounded, and twenty-one prisoner, with three others escaping. One, a Canadian militiaman named Monceau, succeeded in reaching the Forks and told the tale to the commandant there, as we would discover not long after. Our Captain Stephen, reverting to surgeon, attended upon the injured. His skill proved enough for the wounded Frenchman, shot through the thigh, to survive the march back to Great Meadows, carried on a litter by his fellows.

We left the French dead where they lay, Washington not wanting to risk the delay consequent to a burying of them. There were more than a thousand French in this country now, by all reports, and we could expect large parties after us. There would be strong desire for vengeance in this.

Half King and his Indians decided to come back with us, taking to the trail forward of our main body, which was well, as we kept our prisoners to the rear, screening us from any pursuers. The stout little Seneca chief, who I think was older even than Gist, moved along in great ease, as effortless as a horse.

Then, of a sudden, he paused, waited for me to draw near and fell in beside me. He took my pistol from my waist, smelled it, then handed it back, emitting a sort of chortle. His hands and arms were still stained and streaked with his victim's gore.

"You did not fight, my brother," he said.

"You surely did, if you call that fighting." I tapped the front of my skull. "Why?"

He looked at me, but gave no expression. I lifted my arm and pretended to tomahawk myself. "Why? *Pourquoi?*"

"To kill him. We kill *beaucoup* Frenchman. *Mais*, we need kill more." He looked back down the trail at our prisoners. "They should die. Too many French in this country."

"It's wrong."

"Wrong? What do you say, my brother?"

"Why did you . . ." I started to ask, but could not finish. I made a hand-washing motion to show my meaning.

"The French, they boil and eat my father," Half King said.

I'd heard this. I presumed the "French" he spoke of were Indians allied with the French, but perhaps not. *Coureurs des bois?* French traders? Boil and eat? This wilderness was indeed a place worthy of Swift.

"I know not the courage of this officer I kill," he said. "He is not a great general. I take his scalp. I take more, but not his heart. He who is at the Forks. Contrecoeur. I take his heart soon as I can."

"I hope not soon."

"Soon. Yes."

"Chief Tanacharison," I said, "if there was to be a war now, would it be fought like this?"

"War is war, Captain Thomas."

———

The wounded began to tire, and the frequency of our rest breaks increased. During one of them, I went to Washington's side as he looked after the state of the injured Frenchman.

"He sleeps. I think he will live till Fort Necessity," the Colonel said.

"Fort Necessity?"

"At Great Meadows. The round hut I've had them building as a store-house there?"

"Yes?"

"Surround it with a stockade and we have a fort. I shall put the men to it directly upon our return."

"You don't want to return to Will's Creek?"

"If we do that now, Tick, we surrender the Ohio. Have we not just won a victory?"

"Victory? George, we have won a bloody slaughter. And we shall pay for it."

"No more such talk, sir. I warn you."

He stepped back to the middle of the track. "Form up! Form up! We move now! Stir yourselves!" He looked down at me. "Your maimed foot, Tick, it holds up?"

"Yes."

"No other wound?"

"No, though I stood by you—after you chose to stand, when you needed not."

"I do not understand you, Captain Morley. Now help get the men moving. We've a long way to go. You'll sleep well tonight."

"Not I."

"No? You've been afoot this long night. And now a battle."

"My dreams will wake me."

"Dreams of what?"

"Our victory. I expect I'll hear the screams."

He was not paying attention. "So brief an encounter. Not fifteen minutes. And everything ours. An amazement."

"George, you could have called out to them. Or fired a warning shot to speak for you. They would have seen their circumstance. No fight would have been necessary."

His eyes were aimed straight ahead. I think he had ceased listening to me. He was composing in his mind.

"I heard bullets whistle," he said aloud. "Believe me, there was something charming in the sound."

I felt quite ill.

Twenty-six

The main body, still gathered on the mushy plain at Great Meadows, cheered our return—with happy shouts aplenty at the sight of so many French prisoners in tow. But the excitement over our encounter soon enough gave way to anxiety. Every man in our regiment knew the strength of the French army near us. It required no great sagacity to realize we'd provoked 'em mightily.

Washington sent our prisoners on to Williamsburg immediately, then put every available man to work on the stockade, or at digging trenches. I wanted to go on to Williamsburg with those poor devils. I wished more than anything to stride aboard some ship and sail unturning across the sea, never to return. My hands felt as sticky and bloody as Half King's had been, though I'd not lifted a weapon. I wished to wash them, and myself, over and over again.

The Colonel would have none of this from me. My presence at Fort Necessity was commanded. As I had not realized, though I should not have been surprised by it, none of the men in his "army" had had any real experience with cannon save myself and the seaman John Shaw, who'd been on a gun crew in the Royal Navy.

All Washington possessed were swivel guns—a naval as well as a field weapon—and these of varying size, the largest no more than three feet in barrel length. Taking the two largest of the nine in our little regiment's possession—each firing one-pound shot—I set them in holes scored and drilled in the top of two wooden posts standing at either end of our oblong fortification. The installation had to wait upon completion of the stockade fence, but I got it done. I assigned Shaw the gun at the south end and myself that at the north and nearest the presumed approach of the French, and recruited a man each to help us with the loading.

You may ask from whence all this military zeal on my part when, amidst that infernal musket fire and tomahawking at the glen, I shrank from bringing even pistol to hand.

However we might sort out our roles in that lamentable event, we were the small party now, hanging on to this last outpost in the Ohio, and sore outnumbered. 'Tis true I felt a powerful shame and guilt for Jumonville, and always would, and do today. But there was a comfort in this martial labor at Fort Necessity. With luck, we might extract some portion of honor from this second act of our adventure and so assuage our shame—fighting fairly, against strong odds.

When not inspecting the progress of the work and the supposed strength of the fortifications, the scouting reports, and the regimental victualing, Washington busied himself with correspondence—official and, I fear, otherwise. He shared some of the purely military letters with me, asking for my literary advice, which I was chary of giving. What he'd writ was full of boastings, but also pleas for supplies, warnings of trouble to be expected along the Virginia frontier, and declarations that he would fight to hold this position until reinforcements arrived. His own words would be more effective without another's artifice and embellishment. They showed his true mind. Dinwiddie and his colonial officialdom could judge accordingly.

So I urged that the letters stand as writ, though I disagreed with some of what he said, especially in one letter. A passage of it sticks in my mind, even now. Washington denounced the French protests and their claims to have been traveling as envoys as "many smooth stories."

"They were confuted in them all," George wrote, "and by circumstances too plain to be denied, almost made ashamed of their assertions."

Nonsense. The French had shown themselves in no way confuted, or ashamed—simply angry and frightened. But this was not occasion to voice such disputatious thoughts. Riling the commander would be of no great assistance to our cause in this emergency—or to our skins. The Colonel would shortly pay a penalty quite dear for what had been done—far more fearsome stuff than my reproach. Still, I felt it keenly.

Hog's company came back to us from forays west to Redstone Creek, of no mind to linger out there longer with so many French and Indian on the move. The Forks of the Ohio were now emphatically French. Gist's plantation was abandoned. There was no other position for which to fight than Great Meadows here, unless it was Will's Creek.

I would guess the Colonel sent a letter to Mrs. Fairfax with every express dispatched to the Virginia Tidewater. Considering what we'd been through, and what was likely to come, I supposed that forgivable, whatever George William Fairfax might think. Yet each letter reproached me the more for my failure to keep my promise to Mistress Sally.

The bloody affair with Jumonville had taken place May 28. By middle June, Gist was back in camp from Williamsburg, and with wagons! They carried uniforms—what a fine time for that—and munitions. Better, one of them carried upon the driver's seat two women, Gist's daughter Anne and the lovely lass who'd been in my mind's eye ever since she'd gone flitting away from us over the meadows on our departure from Will's Creek.

Mercy hopped down from wagon to ground before I could get near her. I saw her searching for me among all the milling soldierly, but her quick glances found me not, allowing me to circle around her wagon and come upon her from the rear.

"The most beautiful lady in all America," I said, slipping my arms around her.

"So, 'tis you," she said, without even a look over her shoulder.

"Who else would make so bold?"

"I'd have none else, though some have tried to change my mind on that since last we met."

I turned her around, gently, but swiftly. "And who be they?"

"Some brutes and louts, the kind we have so regular about the place." She pulled forth from a pocket of her skirt the small knife I'd given her, unsheathing it. "I find they can be discouraged with this pretty gift."

We laughed, though her revelation worried me. Had it really come to her needing that? What barbarism had descended over this land?

We refrained from too much public display of our affection, though her hand remained in mine as we strolled about the camp. I caught myself thinking how glorious a sight she would be if adorned for a promenade along Philadelphia's Broad Street in elegant city finery. Certainly she was Susannah's equal in beauty, with or without silk and satin. In beauty of mind and heart, she was surpassing.

Earlier, with I think good intention, and certainly with careful words, Washington had spoken to me of Mercy's lacks. No fortune, or hope of one, no family lineage, no fine manners, no schooling in the graces, paltry education, no prospect of improving her station, no great fondness for the bath.

"I like her, Tick," he'd said. "You've found a pleasurable companion in these wilds, one that any man would envy. I hope you keep her friendship. But you've a future, Captain Morley. You've made important friends—and have the means to prosper. I've not the slightest doubt you'll do well. Susannah Smithson's the sort of girl for that life. And you do bear her affection. I can see it. Why, you've all but set the wedding date."

"I'll wed in love, sir."

He'd slapped my knee. "And so you shall. I'm simply telling you on which horse I've placed my wager."

That was when we'd still been friends, or counted ourselves so. I'd no idea what he might be saying now of her—nor much care.

I wished for Mercy's company in private, but neither she nor the military circumstance provided opportunity for that. Mostly she was with Anne Gist, helping with camp work and preparations. We were all quite busily employed.

Finally, in the midst of a sultry afternoon, I contrived to draw her away for a while and up the slope of the round hill that overlooked our Fort Necessity.

The hill had trees to the back but only low bushes to the fore and down the forward slope. I do believe I could see every man—and dog and chicken—of our party from that summit, which alarmed me. The Colonel would need a deep trench indeed to avoid hostile fire from this height, yet the one he'd ordered dug was but of two feet. His central storehouse looked small and crude from up on the height. The circular stockade around it was taking shape, but in no way seemed formidable, being only some sixty-odd feet in its diameter.

I drew Mercy into the trees to the rear of the hilltop. There were wood-cutting parties out everywhere, so I was not emboldened to make our reunion a more intimate one. But I kissed her. When we finally drew apart, she reached within my shirt and pulled forth the leather thong, until she'd drawn out the beautiful quartz mountain stone she'd given me.

"So you've not lost it in your famous fight with the French at the glen."

"No."

" 'Twas to bring you luck. And has it?"

"I stand before you unscathed, in body, if not in mind."

"You are bothered in the mind?"

"Vexed and troubled. I can't bear the thought of what's to come, yet must take part. I couldn't leave these men, though at first I wished to." I kissed her hand. "Glad as I am you did, you should not have come to this dangerous place."

"I'm no fine soft lady of the city, Tom. Here on the frontier, a woman goes where she must, and likes it. If I can be a help here, I will be."

"You brought Anne Gist."

"Nay, she brought me—or rather, persuaded her father of the wisdom of bringing the both of us with him. There're other women here. We shall be content."

"What does Anne want of this place? To be with her father?"

"Not him so much. It's the Colonel."

"The Colonel?"

"It's her tale to tell, not mine. Come and let's be back with 'em. I'm not liking these woods so much. Settlers have been coming into Will's Creek telling fearful tales."

———

We found Gist and daughter at the Colonel's tent, where Gist had delivered upsetting but exciting news. On the march, Colonel Joshua Fry's mount had broken rein and thrown our commander, killing him. Washington was now the senior man, and in full charge of all the regiment.

His rank as matters stood was still lieutenant colonel, but a promotion would have to follow soon. A thousand Frenchmen might be on the march, coming to kill us, but George Washington was there a most happy man.

He'd have been happier without the presence of Miss Gist. The handsome Anne was much enhanced to the eye by the high color of her discontent, but her looks to the Colonel were as dark and trouble-filled as those that had been cast his way by Mrs. Fairfax that strange day in the Alexandria public house. What was afoot?

Whatever his relationship with Mrs. Fairfax, George had otherwise been deuced unsuccessful at love, with several eligible young Virginia ladies of the Tidewater and Northern Neck having rebuffed his proffers—for the most part, according to Sally, because of his lack of estate, though one or two might have been afrighted by his inordinate size and strength, and his capacity for dominating whatever scene he might stride onto, however awkwardly,

He afrighted Mistress Anne not at all. She seemed somehow hovering near him always, more a tick than ever I. Once I caught Washington asking Gist if he'd make his daughter relent, but obedience appeared not among her virtues.

Half King's Indians returned from prowls through the forest with ever increasingly worrisome reports of French soldiers and Delaware and Shawnee allies moving over the mountains. One day came news of a large party—perhaps the army Contrecoeur had brought with him—coming straight for us overland.

Washington did not like the advice Half King gave him upon receipt of this report. It was to retreat to Will's Creek or Winchester, and not return unless with a strong army of our own.

There was small chance of that. Gist said that the Burgesses had become irked with the governor over some small fee Dinwiddie was charging and pocketing as concerned property transactions, and they'd balked at voting him more funds, or even authorizing more military expenditure on credit. There was also talk that the His Majesty in England was developing a marked distaste for having so many civilian colonists under arms, organized as the militia—though that had been Franklin's goal and plan from the start.

George scoffed at Half King's every caution. "Our fort's near done and I'll not abandon it. Certainly not without firing a single shot."

The Indian, of a sudden, shouldered his own rifle and loosed a round in the direction of the round hill where Mercy and I had been, rousing all the camp.

"There is your shot," he said. "This is no good place for a fort. No good place to fight. You will all be killed. We will not stay to die with you."

Washington chided Half King roughly for a bit. Then, realizing the possible cost of that, he began pleading in the most deferential manner for him to stay. I did so also. The Seneca chief had led us into that confrontation with Jumonville and so should remain to share the consequences.

He was not persuaded.

"We are brave as you," Half King said. "But we are not so foolish as you. We are your brothers, but you do not learn from us. Fight when you can win. Do not fight simply to die. You will die here if you stay. We will not stay."

He gripped my hand and arm strongly, though Washington would not so engage himself. "We are your brothers," Half King said again. "We wish you well. If you live, we will meet again."

In a very few minutes, he and all his Indians had vanished.

———

Next to go were the women, and not of their own will. Washington commanded them to return to Will's Creek.

As true now in General Howe's Royal army, and even in Washington's ragged band of rebels at Valley Forge, it was custom and long had been to have women accompany soldiery on the march, in camp, and even unto battle. They are there as wives, officers' as well as enlisted men's—I hear reports of General Washington's Martha now in residence at this Valley Forge. They come as washerwomen and sutlers as well; and of course as whores, or at the least, ladies of convenient virtue with nowhere else to turn for support of themselves than with an army. In the usual run of events, they are noncombatants. In Europe, 'twas ever thus. The Maid of Orleans had given much offense in donning armor.

But in the American wilderness, they oft lifted musket when compelled to do so by circumstance. It was said that the woman who could not shoot well was a worthless thing in the wilds. And, as Gist told me, the Indians had small regard for the European notion of chivalry. When making war, they shed blood among both sexes of the enemy. They disliked any white person in their country, whether in skirts or breeches.

Captain MacKay's independent company of regulars had come to us with women among their baggage. The frontiersmen in Trent's group had several wives about also, a number of them Indian squaws. 'Twas in no way unnatural for any of them to stay if they wished, and it seemed they did, especially Anne Gist.

But Colonel Washington was most resolute against it. Gist said he saw no great risk to his daughter, or to any of the women, suggesting rather that they would be most useful should we begin suffering wounded. At that, George became all the more adamant. The females must all go back to the Patowmack, and the soonest possible. We knew the French army was coming. Our Indian scouts had now left us, and though we'd positioned a few outlying pickets, including one on the round hill, their warning would not be much in advance of its subject. The women must be safe.

MacKay agreed with the Colonel's finding, so that was that. The women quickly went, taking two wagons. Anne was flush of face in her unvoiced anger when the time came to depart, and began to weep. Mercy was anxious, partly for me, but also for concerns she'd not shared with me. The other women were as compliant. I think two or three husbands slipped away to join them up the trail in the woods.

My farewell to Mercy was decorous and chaste. There was so much unsaid and undone between us.

"I would see you soon, Mercy Ennis."

"And I you, Thomas."

We kissed again, but it was fleeting.

She drove the lead wagon. There were two mountain ridges to cross and the roughest kind of track to follow, most particular on Laurel Ridge, well-named for that hellish vegetation that grew o'er it. I supposed there wasn't much this lass could not accomplish with her mind put to it. What remarkable waste to have such a flower grow in this wild desolation, instead of in some civilized bower.

The women, led by a small mounted escort we could ill afford to spare, lurched their wagons over the Meadows' mushy creeks, then moved slowly across the valley and into the trees and passed from view.

Gist stood with me, watching.

"Will they be safe?" I asked.

"Safe as here. Safer when they get to Will's Creek. I'll wager they'll be gettin' more male escort from this place before the day is done."

It was midday. The men bent themselves to renewed and suffering effort on our fortifications. It was now the third of July, and a day as hot as boiled, steaming water. Every man save Washington and MacKay was down to shirt, if not bare chest. I busied myself with the two swivel guns, shoring their mounts and wishing we'd had time and situation to position the others.

The sky was gray and the cloud layer was thickening. I thought of Mr. Franklin's long discourse on the lightness of warm air compared to the weight of cold. This hot air hung on us as thick and heavy as a woolen cloak. I poured sweat from simple standing. How could the colder be the heavier?

Not two hours had gone by after the women's departure when the first musket shot of the battle sounded. It was from our own lookout—the man at the top of the hill—and had been fired as signal.

The fellow came pell-mell down the slope. Washington was not waiting for his spoken report. He and his officers were shouting commands for all to turn from labor to arms. A wavering rank was formed in front of the westernmost trench; another faced toward the hill.

More ranks took position, to the right and left. A few men stood about oddly where they figured they'd get clear shots. The order was given to screw on our bayonets. I had my pistol in my belt. I checked its load and priming. Then I pulled my long knife from its sheath, touched the point, and replaced it. Finally, I went to my main weapon—the swivel gun I'd positioned on our right flank on a high post of the stockade fence. It had been loaded with several musket balls. The man I'd taken as my crew stood waiting patiently, firing match in hand. I saw that at the other end of the stockade, seaman John Shaw had mounted his platform with matchstick high. He saluted. I liked the man.

I was struggling to elevate the barrel of my piece higher toward the hilltop when the first French appeared, emerging from the woods to the right of the foot of the hill. They assumed a loose formation and an instant later, fire barked—a small fusillade coming in ragged fashion. At that range, most of their shots went low or otherwise awry, but one thudded into the roof of the storehouse, sending bits of its bark roof and splinters flying.

Our brave Colonel, standing in front of the stockade wall, smartly gave an order to fire in reply. On reflex, or impulse, I set my match and boomed off my shot. The report sounded ferocious, and the balls flew up the hillside with a zing, but chopped a few bushes shy of the top and hit no flesh.

The French went hotfoot back for the trees just as our musketry loosed a volley—those to the right on MacKay's command. Again, no harm that I could see came to a man on either side.

Every man of us reloaded, then stood looking about, most with eyes to the hilltop. There was another patch of forest opposite our left flank and, alas, within musket range of us. From behind its trees, a hundred men or more—most of them Indians, but a few French in white uniform—suddenly ran forth, halted in telling proximity, and fired a fusillade at us before we could thwart them. I saw three of our boys hit and knew there must be more went down, hidden from my view by the curving wall of the fortification.

Washington, furious, ran to that side, bellowing a desire for response. It followed briskly, and I saw some Indians drop. Most of the enemy, shooting as they went, retreated back into the forest and behind cover, from which they commenced a peppering fire. More of our men fell. The Colonel shouted a command to withdraw from ranks and seek the protection of our own works and defenses. MacKay issued the same order to his company, sounding an echo. That gentleman made such a fine target in his bright red coat, I wondered he didn't attract more French rounds.

This swivel gun of mine now had no worthwhile target. I put my crewman in my place after reloading, then shouldered my way through the mob of men who were crowding inside the stockade walls. At length I got to the other swivel piece, which covered the now deadly woods to the left, wondering why it was silent.

Shaw and his man were standing at the gun, but below the top of the wall. It wasn't cowardice that kept them there, not really. I stepped up on their platform and rose head-high over the stockade.

The enemy, still mostly Indian, was keeping up a serious fire, but offering absolutely no targets, shooting from behind trees and brush, only smoke puffs signifying their presence.

"Try firing at the smoke," I said. "If naught else, it'll keep their heads down."

"A waste of powder, Captain, but I'll fling 'em a few hard shot, just for your honor."

He put match to hole and the little cannon made its report. I saw some blur of movement beside a distant tree, but could not tell if this signified death or injury.

With sudden thud and crack, three musket balls in quick succession struck the stockade fence before me and I felt a tearing stab of pain—in, of all surprising places, my face. I fell back, backside striking ground, then clutched at my cheek.

"Shit!" I meant to say, but it came out something else, and the word hurt me as much as the initial wounding.

It wasn't musket ball, but a wooden splinter. It had pierced my cheek, striking a tooth and glancing off against my tongue. Without hesitation, without care to further tearing, I yanked it out. Blood was gushing freely.

Washington had come back into the stockade, and strode quickly over. "My God, Tick. Are you slain?"

" 'Tis a wooden splinter—not lead," I said, the words coming mushed. It was certainly no time to complain of "Tick," though I had sorely tired of hearing it.

He put his hand to my head, tilting it back slightly.

"I'm well," I said, spitting out blood. "Don't neglect your men."

"What can we get for you?" He was seriously concerned, ignoring all else.

For my part, I was angry. I blamed him. Jumonville was his fault; so was this. I wondered if I looked a monster.

"A bandage then, please," I said. "And whiskey." I'd learned the healing powers of that, and wanted it applied quick.

The slave Hercules was at the Colonel's side.

"See to it," Washington said, handing him a key. "The storehouse."

Reclining on the ground, I had no view of the battle outside, but I could hear the gunfire intensify, and then fall off. Shaw's swivel gun whanged out again; then he descended to kneel by me.

"How fare ye, Captain?"

"I'll survive." I looked to see Hercules running forth with a band of cloth and a jug. "With help of that."

Pain's somehow the easier endured with gunfire all about. I filled my mouth so full with whiskey, it squirted out of the wound when I swirled it. Then I swallowed, poured more spirits on the cloth, took two more swallows, then tied the cloth as tight as I could around my jaw and head. I'd not be giving orders to anyone for a bit. The dressing stemmed the blood sufficient. As there'd been no great force to the splinter's blow, I wasn't dizzied and found my feet, taking stance at the parapet again.

We had more men down. Their comrades were bringing them in. The firing on both sides had slackened, though our men's faces had become blackened by the powder of our own part of the exchanges. The gunshots now were delivered by sharpshooters, most of them on the French side.

They had a feast of targets—all four-legged. The stockade was small enough for the human host it might have to hold. Our animals, as a consequence, had been left unpenned to wander about the meadow—horses, cattle, the few pigs, the many dogs.

One by one these poor creatures were struck and fell, the horses screaming, the cows with a grunt or bleat, the pigs with a squeal, and the dogs in every manner of temper. This mischief went on through the afternoon, till all the large beasts were down or dead.

Our men were angered, especially those out along the trenches. One poor dog, caught out in the open, took a round that shattered a foreleg. With tortured limp, it began loping about in crazed circles, yelping. Someone should have put the poor thing from its misery, but the men in the trench along the left flank instead began calling to it to come to safety among them. One, unwisely, lifted his head to better do this, and died for his trouble, quickly but horribly.

The dog continued oblivious to this sacrifice on its behalf. From MacKay's company, a man rose from the earthen bulwark and, at a crouch, on the run, pistol in hand, hurried toward the animal—I think to bring it in, not to dispatch it, as a rifleman could have done that from the safety of the trench.

This brave fellow was an officer, a lieutenant I recognized named Mercier. What reckless and wasted courage, I thought, as he nipped along dodging bullets. The dog was lying on its side when Mercier got to it—too late for both. A round slapped into the lieutenant, and he went sprawling. He got up on one knee and turned to fire his pistol into the woods. It discharged, but he was struck again by our adversary.

Instant volleys roared forth from both our forward positions, causing a flutter of leaves to fall throughout the woods before us. Two men then leapt over our shallow earthworks and went after the lieutenant, pulling his arms around their shoulders and attempting to drag him back. Intrepid lads, they were not touched, but yet another ball found Mercier, exploding a crimson burst from his chest. He sank, a deadweight. They had to pull him in like a log.

And then it commenced to rain. In all the fiendish inclemency we had endured on our winter's expedition to the French forts, never had we encountered a deluge like this. I could not recall many like it at sea The rain on the night's march to Jumonville's glen had been a mere pattering sprinkle compared to this. A wall of water, it seemed, a wall miles thick.

It's in the nature of sudden summer showers to end as quick as begun. Not this. The heavens poured forth a seeming inexhaustible supply of rain. It must have been borrowed from other continents, for not all the clouds above all North America could have sufficed to bear this drench.

Men staggered in it. The sounds of musket and swivel-gun fire seemed pitifully small and lost in the thudding splatter of the rain. We began to worry more about this monstrous wet than the battle—to our peril. As I went to the gate to help bring in some of the wounded, I collected a fresh hurt myself—again from a jagged splinter, this one tearing into the muscle just above my right knee. I cried out and sagged to the ground, this time working the wooden shaft free with great care, tearing open my breeches at that spot the better to see my work.

What shall become of me, I wondered. A maimed foot. A bleeding hole in my cheek. Now a skewered knee. And doubtless hours' or days' more battle to be fought.

I still had my little jug of whiskey. The open storehouse door had drawn more soldiers seeking theirs, not all that many of them wounded. The stockade was crowded with standing, sitting, and supine soldiery, leaving barely a place to step. Its dimensions were suited for perhaps fifty men, and Washington had more than three hundred in his force.

Limping, I returned to my original place. My one-man crew was working the swivel gun himself in my absence.

"Damned powder's wet!" he shouted through the rain.

"Leave off till we need it!" I shouted back as best I could, offering up my jug.

He took a thirsty draught. There were men drinking everywhere.

The downpour continued without slack. I thought of Mercy and the poor women, who should by then have been well up the ridge, though there was no telling in such wet. Wherever they were, I was grateful it was not here.

I heard someone crying out, having no idea whether it was man or beast or from what quarter the mournful sound was coming. It seemed not to matter. It seemed not real. Washington was unreal, or at the least, remarkably multiplied. He seemed to be everywhere. Wherever I looked, there he was. When I looked there again, he was somewhere else—bellowing forth more commands than I knew existed, and to no point I could comprehend.

I don't know how many hours passed in this manner. I think I slept. It was hard to tell the difference between slumber and waking.

What stirred me at last was the feel of water. Not that I was not sodden enough from that ceaseless rain, but now I felt a deeper, colder wetness. I looked down. I was sitting in a small lake. The creek that ran to our rear and the other that coursed along our left flank had each swollen over its banks and spread a flood through the stockade fence. The surge was almost over the top of my legs and gurgling into the storehouse—where the powder was.

With pain, I pulled myself erect, then hobbled stiffly over the sprawling wounded to the storehouse door. Men were sitting there on powder kegs, drinking. They looked at me as they might at some ghostly spirit.

I retreated, finding Washington now at the parapet with Gist, studying the enemy through a spyglass. How he saw a one of them, I know not. Ragged streams of mist were trailing from the low clouds, obscuring hilltop, trees, and all.

"We should retreat!" I said. "Be done with this, before another man dies."

The rag with which I'd bound my face had loosened and fallen about my neck. My words were understood, but he did not reply to them. He only stood staring through his glass.

"It's not numbers but position that will tell," said Washington. "We have a fort, and they do not."

"Those people have no need for one," I said, my words coming each with hurt and spurts of blood. "They can sit up there and wait for us to starve—or drown. The creeks are pouring through your works."

Washington glanced down at the muck at his feet, then returned his gaze to the enemy. "Tend to your wound, Tick. Then back to your gun. We'll need every man."

"I had your word. No more 'Tick' "

This was ignored. The sky was lowering further. No, 'twas the advancing hour. The summer evening was upon us. What were we to do in the night?

A shout came from the forward position facing the hill, where MacKay's company was deployed in their long trench, above their knees in mud. It was a call to cease fire. Two French were coming out of the woods beneath a white flag of truce. There came another shout. "They want a parley!"

Washington shouted out to MacKay: "They're not to come within our lines! Tell them we've no mind to surrender!"

We watched the two Frenchmen, one an officer, trudge across the mucky field and halt just before the trench. MacKay strode up to them. I knew he spoke no French but guessed they had some English, or would not have been sent. After MacKay relayed our sentiments, the two Frenchmen conversed among themselves for a moment. Then the officer hurried back to his people, leaving the private to stand there idly, holding his white flag.

Without much time passing, the officer returned. He and the private conversed again. Then the officer spoke to MacKay.

The latter shook his head, more in confusion than negation, then came over to us.

"As best I understand the gentleman," MacKay said, "their commander, a Captain Coulon de Villiers, desires a conference with some urgency. He says if you send an envoy to him, he will guarantee the man's safety—on his word as a gentleman."

That word was enough for Washington. "Very well," the Colonel said.

"I'll go," I said. "My French is good—as you've seen."

Washington looked down at my injured knee, which I'd bound with the cloth formerly binding my cheek.

"I'll send Captain Van Braam," he said. "And that Swiss man, Ensign Peroney. He speaks French, too."

"George, please. I can be of help here."

"They're officers commissioned in the militia," said the Colonel, "and Van Braam is the equal of this Villiers in rank. We must comply with protocol in an exchange of this seriousness." He paused. "But you may accompany them, if you're able. Give me an account of their strength and position, and your own apprehension of what's been said."

Limping, I started forward.

"Something you might care to know," said MacKay, walking with me to the Frenchmen. "This Villiers is brother to the slain Ensign Jumonville."

———

We made slow progress across the field toward the enemy position—the two French leading the way impatiently. Van Braam splashing along behind them, not wanting to be there. Peroney hanging back with me as I brought up the rear—too slowly, leaning on a musket I had taken as crutch. With the thick overcast, the evening's light was disappearing fast.

A few words in French were shouted to us from the top of the hill. The officer with us responded in kind. A moment later, two French soldiers came running through the gloom from the trees, each carrying a lantern.

I had wondered where the French commander had positioned himself for this battle. I was surprised to find him in a large campaign tent pitched almost exactly upon the spot where Mercy and I had embraced.

The man I took to be Captain Villiers came forth to greet us with considerable charm and grace—as though we were old and well-liked acquaintances, and not murderers of his brother.

"*Bon soir, Messieurs,*" he said, ushering us in with a sweep of his hat. "*Il fait mal temps, oui?*"

I nodded. Van Braam, looking uncomfortable, stepped up to the small folding writing table set at the center of the tent, which leaked. A great drop of gathered water struck me on the nose.

"*Je suis Capitaine Van Braam de Virginie,*" said our spokesman. "*Celui, Ensign Peroney. Et cet homme est Capitaine Morley, un marin. Un chef de bateaux. Il est bon ami à* Colonel Washington."

It was the best French I'd yet heard from Van Braam.

Villiers took note of my bandaged knee and had a rickety stool brought to me. Van Braam and Peroney remained standing. Brandy was poured out, and we each took a drink, to express our amity. I glanced about. They had hung one of the lanterns on the tent pole and there was another on the table, but the illumination was dim, and flickering. The downpour had finally lessened, but it was breezy, and the air still wet.

The French captain picked up a piece of paper from the tabletop. It was covered with writing in a careful hand, but had become blotched and blotted from the rain.

Holding on to this document, Villiers spoke his piece, in too rapid French. I had trouble following it, and Van Braam seemed to ken barely at all. If Peroney understood, he gave no indication, contenting himself to stand there, watching and waiting. He was indeed Swiss, but I think spoke better German and Italian than French.

Villiers led with his most telling argument. He said there were more than a hundred Indians and possibly five times that number, allied to his cause en route to this battleground and expected in the morning, all with the tomahawk up and scenting English on the run. If hostilities were not ended by the time they arrived, Villiers said he could not guarantee our safety.

He had no idea of taking us prisoner, he said. We were being offered terms similar to those given our Ensign Ward. We were to surrender our fort and return to Virginia. We could keep our colors and most of our arms, even one of the swivel guns. All that was required was that we sign this paper, which contained in the text of the surrender conditions the promise that we would not return or make any establishment "at this place nor on this side of the height of land for a year counting from this day."

Van Braam stood stupidly, as though waiting for more. My eyes sought Villiers', which seemed to glitter a little in the wavering lantern light.

" *'Cette côté de la montagne?'* " I asked. *"Est-ce que vous voudriez dire* Laurel Ridge?"

He smiled, gladdened that at least one of us comprehended. *"Oui, et aussi les autres à la Rivière* Patowmack."

"Pas Will's Creek?" I said. *"Nous gagnons* Will's Creek, *n'est-ce pas?"*

"Mais oui, monsieur. Celui la est sur l'autre côté des montagnes."

He wished all us English to pull back to the other side of the mountains, but counted the settlement at Will's Creek as that, and ours to keep. The terms applied only to Washington's poor little regiment. Even if they included every English soldier under arms, so what? Let them keep their damned Ohio. No one in our party save Washington and the Indians really wanted it. Our duty in this parley was to stop the killing.

He stepped forward and handed me the paper with another sweeping gesture, but at the end, placing it in my hands gently. *"Regardez, s'il vous plait."*

As I said, the light was dim. I was rather a bit dizzy from my wounds and exertions after all, and from lack of sleep and sustenance, and too much whiskey. The paper was damp and the ink ran in places. It was a damn hard job, reading the thing. I perceived the words in blurry snatches: *". . . entre les deux princes amis . . . mais seulement avenger l'assassin qui . . . establissement sur ses terres du Domain Du Roy . . ."*

Van Braam stepped to me and pulled the paper from my hands. He had the rank here.

He read it to the bottom and back up to the top, then nodded. "Seems agreeable." He repeated in French, *"Agréable."*

Villiers smiled. I had a fleeting impulse to raise the matter of his brother, but thought better of it.

"L'apportez à votre Colonel Washington," Villiers said. *"Pour signer."*

Van Braam nodded again. *"D'accord."* Peroney smiled. As best I could manage with my cheek so torn and swollen, so did I.

We would live.

———

Washington peered suspiciously at the page, frowning—evidencing great frustration at his lack of this foreign tongue. We were crowded into the storehouse of Fort Necessity—the Colonel, Captain MacKay, Gist, Stephen, Montour, and the three of us who'd been to parley—all those with whom Washington usually took counsel. The wounded remained but the drunk or men who'd taken shelter in there had been run out.

"You've read it well, Van Braam?" Washington asked.

"Twice through, Colonel."

"You, too, Tick?"

"Best I could."

Washington still stared at the paper, holding his huge head in both his hands. "I cannot believe the generosity of these terms," he said.

"He meant 'em," said Van Braam.

"If we don't accept, we die," said Gist. "I'd take seriously his talk of more Indians on the trail. Those he's got here are worrisome enough. Their idea of victory's got more to it than our promise to stay out of this country for a year. They'll want our hair."

The Colonel looked across to MacKay. "You find these terms honorable, sir?" he asked.

"We keep our arms and give parole. 'Tis commonly done on the continent. I know this officer's family. He has another brother of high station, *le Chevalier Villiers*. A French knight. I'd accept this captain's word, and give him ours."

"But the other brother is the now dead Jumonville."

"You said yourself, Colonel. It was a soldierly encounter."

Without hesitation, Washington took quill, dipped it in ink, and signed the paper boldly. The two French emissaries were waiting without.

The Colonel stood, waving the paper in the air to dry the ink, then folding it carefully.

"All right, 'tis done," he said. "I declare this not surrender, but truce. We'll withdraw, regroup, reinforce, and by God, return. But in due time."

He went to the door of the storehouse, gesturing to the French officer, who came up quickly, a look of eager curiosity on his face.

"Tell him it's done," Washington said, handing the man the folded paper. The rain had nearly stopped.

"*Tous est complet,*" I said. "*Nous allons l'accepter. Pour l'amité.*"

"*Bien,*" said the Frenchman. "*Je suis très content. À demain.*"

With Washington staring after him, the officer rejoined his companion and the two of them set off for their lines. If I had then known the true import of what was in that letter, I would have taken out my pistol and shot the man dead before he took another step. Or perhaps myself.

Part Two

Those of us not on sentry duty or tending to the wounded slept where possible in the muck. I was counted among the casualties but treated my wounds myself and simply, again with external and internal applications of whiskey, and so avoided hospital, which was situated within the general misery of the stockade.

The patch of muddy ground where I took my few hours' slumber was outside the palisade and just by Washington's tent. I wished to be at hand if the French came upon us with more business and translation was necessary, as I really now had no faith in Van Braam. Waking in that place at the first touch of dawn, I glanced about groggily and found Washington seated on a camp chair at the entrance to his tent, leaning forward with his elbows on his knees and gazing sadly at the misty, shadowy field—that which he had earlier so boastfully proclaimed "a charming field for an encounter."

He noted my stirring. "Well, Captain," he said leadenly, "would you append your name to this adventure?"

In the faint light, the scene was as gloomy as I decidedly felt. There were two men lying just beyond my feet. By his snores, I judged the one to be asleep. By his wounds, I judged the other surely killed. A dead dog, paw stiffly extended in the air, lay just beyond. In the near distance was the wreckage of a farmer's wagon. The still-lingering smell of gunpowder and a damp, sickly odor clung to the mist, mingling with the woodsmoke from the few campfires. There was no rain. What surprised me was the quiet. There were more than a thousand soldiers here—and Indians.

"I would not deny my part in it," I said, then paused. "And you?"

He hung down his head. "It's all my work. Every man down I put there."

Do not misunderstand. There was no self-pity in his speech. He was only facing fact.

I heard two sentries talking, standing easier now with the increasing light. Somewhere a dog barked. I'd thought them all shot.

"George, may I speak to you as friend?"

"I should be grateful for a friend. I'd not thought to have any this morn."

"I might fault your choice of ground for this fight," I said, "but once in it, I'd call your conduct in the battle resolute, unflagging, an example to all. No officer of regulars could command more steadfastly. You were woeful outnumbered. Three to one, and so many Indians. They're the author of this lamentable result."

He lifted his head. "And more to come."

"But . . ."

"Yes? What?"

"What nags at me still is . . ."

Without much tact or grace, I was trying to broach again the subject of the affair at Jumonville Glen. The Colonel, getting to his feet, cut me short.

"What nags at me," he said, "are all these fine men dead. I shall always see their faces."

He strode forward two paces, looking about, then back at me where I still reclined.

"Let us have coffee from my good Hercules, and then be about our work, Thomas. Your wounds?"

My cheek was slightly swollen; my knee, painfully so. "Still there," I said.

"You must attend to them."

I looked for where I'd left the whiskey. Stephens had risen, and George began walking toward him.

There was drumming in the French camp, and in short order, French troops were lined up before our wretched little fort—arms at the ready but standing at ease. They watched our preparations for departure as might spectators at some public amusement.

This was provocation to resentment, but we soon had reason enough to be glad of all those white coats and fleurs-de-lis. The Indian force that Captain Villiers had used as threat did in fact materialize as promised, arriving not long after sunup. I don't think there were above a hundred of them, but they were of a mind to make battle, or at the least to enjoy the fruits thereof, and would have done so upon our hapless persons had the French not provided restraint. I made them out to be Delaware, none of my acquaintance, nor any so desired. They made murderous noises and looked upon our scalps and possessions with great longing. I think they had expected a great bargain in arriving just after the fight—so much pay for little labor. They felt cheated in their expectation, however unearned or deserved.

Washington called a council, but there was little discussion and no disagreement as to our course of action as he proposed it. We'd pack up all we could carry and remove ourselves from this horrible place with the utmost dispatch.

For a force of just under three hundred, our losses were awful. Thirty dead in the entire regiment, of whom ten, including Lieutenant Mercier, fell in the ranks of MacKay's independent company of South Carolina regulars. Of wounded in all respects of injury, including my own, we had some seventy. More than a third of the Colonel's command was casualty.

He was himself unhurt—miraculously, for all his exposing himself in the fight—unless one counts the wounds to mind and spirit, which in his case were perhaps more grievous than any of our men displayed on body and limb. I'd not seen so stricken a look on any man's face before. His blue-gray eyes seemed dead, his flesh all drawn and dirty and haggard. He had not looked so bad in all our winter's ordeal, not even that night on the island with Gist when we thought we might die.

There was much to do before departure. What powder could not be carried was broken from keg and scattered about the sodden ground so to be no use to the enemy. Anything made of wood that was of use but could not be carried was smashed and broken up to the greatest extent possible, including the stocks of muskets belonging to those so wounded they could not carry them. The edible food was separated from that gone rotten, with the latter a larger amount than the former. The medical chest had to be left behind, its contents divided up and borne by the able-bodied. All our horses had been shot dead, so the axes were put to our wagons, and to MacKay's fine coach as well. I thought this last act might anger the French, who perhaps had eyed the vehicle as a handsome spoil, but Villiers simply looked on coolly, as though we were about nothing of importance. It occurred to me he likely had no great desire for that elegant conveyance, knowing its total worthlessness in that country.

The swivel guns, alas, resisted disabling. We took one, the smallest, but had to leave the rest behind for future French mischief.

Some Dutchmen traveling with the French came among us as we prepared our retreat, finding Van Braam and enjoying conversation with him in their common tongue. Afterward, he told the Colonel he'd learned from them that the French had lost some three hundred people in the clash. Washington seized upon that number for his own report, but I did not believe it, and neither did Gist, MacKay, or Stephen. We British had been the ones exposed in our position. Except for that one sortie from the woods to our left, the French had remained largely behind cover throughout the engagement. There was sharp instruction here, for those who would see it.

Van Braam was given more opportunity to converse with his erstwhile countrymen than perhaps he'd bargained for upon meeting them. Villiers added a condition that had not been contained in the surrender agreement—that which Washington still referred to as "truce." The French captain demanded two hostages be retained by him until the twenty-one men we'd captured at Jumonville Glen and sent on to Williamsburg were returned. This was not negotiable, Villiers said.

We didn't argue. The Colonel picked the two himself. Some have said he chose Van Braam as punishment for the incompetence the Dutchman had too often displayed, but I think not. Washington's other choice was his good friend Captain Bob Stobo. I think he still thought well enough of Van Braam's merits and wanted a French speaker to be one of the hostages all the better to acquire intelligence. Neither man was overjoyed to be given this duty, but both accepted it in soldierly fashion. Villiers seemed a decent man. They should come to no harm—perhaps less than we.

In his official report, Washington wrote that we marched out of our fort with arms borne proudly, drums drumming, heads high, and colors waving. In a French account that I came upon quite a long time later, they said we'd fled in desperation, abandoning considerable numbers of arms and colors. Neither retelling is correct. I think we might have dropped a company standard or two, but the rest survived. No man ran. All walked, in rank and file, save the more badly wounded, who were borne on litters. We walked out as proudly as the occasion permitted—in my own case, limping badly. Someone did start a drum dully rapping, but was discouraged by his fellows and the sound trailed off.

Our dead were left where they were. There was no fit burial in this mire, and we dared not take the time to attend to them at all events, lest more Indians arrive and change the weight of French debate upon the disposition of our living. Perhaps the French would be so civilized as to attend to burial.

We had fifty miles to go to reach Will's Creek, the most of it up and down. Ascending the first ridge in our path, we discovered Indians following us—at a leisurely pace, but relentless. Once upon the summit, they became quite impudently obvious—in the manner of carrion, or sharks at sea, hovering nearer their expected prey. Finally, Washington ordered our rear guard to fire a volley at them. None were hit, but after that, they hung far back.

———

The wound to my cheek was improving appreciably, the swelling gone, the puncture closed and healing. That to my knee was quite the reverse. The flesh there remained red and puffy around the point where the splinter had struck, and blood continued to ooze from it as I walked. I bound it as tightly as I could, but there was small improvement. By the time we were back atop Laurel Ridge, the knee had stiffened. Descending the other side, I found myself in pain that increased in steady measure.

Putting a third of our surviving force to stand watch on picket, we camped in the next valley, all sleeping who were not at arms. The following morning, we got as far as a shallow reach of the Youghiogheny, in its southern headwaters, and fell out again to either side of the trail where it reached the river ford. I did not think I could manage another step, but hobbled over to join Washington's aides and officers who gathered 'round him to discuss some problem.

It was a simple one. We had nine wounded failing so badly they cried out in their hurt almost constantly. Their litters were difficult burdens and slowed the march dangerously. They'd have to be left behind until the main party reached Will's Creek and could send back horses to carry them. It would take days, but there was no choice.

They should not be left alone. I volunteered to stay. My fellow mariner John Shaw remained with me. They left provisions enough to feed all of us for a week, plus several muskets and a pistol each, with ample ball and powder. Our encampment was established in a bush-shrouded hollow not far off the trail on the side of the river nearest Will's Creek. The best that could be done was done.

Before he rode off, Washington came over and sat beside me. "You need not do this, Tick," he said.

"My name is Thomas."

"Tom, then."

"My leg hurts so bad that I count myself one of these poor people," I said. "It's Shaw here who's making the sacrifice. We'll be glad of the horseback ride, when you can send back for us."

"You've no soldier's obligation in this. You're not part of the muster."

" 'Tis fine. I think we've discouraged the Indians well enough. And who can say? Perhaps Half King will turn up, as he so remarkably often does."

Washington stared down at his boots, which were black leather but so covered with mud they seemed fawn-colored.

"I've left two friends with Villiers," he said. "Now you."

" 'Twill have you held in better regard by the men. No favorites."

The soldiers who had dropped to rest were now rising to their feet. There was some grumbling.

"The bullet's whistle has lost its charm," he said.

"I was ne'er its swain," I said.

Washington glanced at my knee. "MacKay and I must ride for the capital. When we can fetch you up to Will's Creek, can you wait there until I return?"

"Will's Creek is where I yearn most to be."

He looked at me. "Miss Mercy." A faint smile.

"Yes, but after that, I would be away from here, from all this wild country. I want no more of it. Not a single bullet more."

"You would marry that girl?"

"I think that I would."

"Then you must content yourself with these mountains, as I think she would not leave them. Not for long."

"You little know her, sir. How can you say that?"

"Her friend Anne Gist has told me this, and believes it strongly."

Anne Gist.

He looked again at my still-oozing knee. "Perhaps your wound shall keep you on the Patowmack."

Another officer had started the men on the track, the first of them sloshing across the ford. Washington looked to them, then back at me.

"Are we still friends?" he asked.

I did not think our paths would cross again. "Yes," I said.

We shook hands.

"You're a damned brave fellow," he said.

"We are all brave—to have come here in the first place."

He was off, his mind turned now to his shambles of a "regiment."

But no, he stopped and looked to me again.

"I hope I have not killed you," he said.

They'd left us whiskey, not so much for the pleasure of Shaw and myself, but for our comrades, the terribly wounded, who most had need of it. As Gist counseled, it would ease their pain and abate their cries and moans, so they'd prove less an attraction to the Indians. We gave the conscious wounded as much as they could take, but that was not much. These men were sorely off.

A young boy shot through the belly died before sundown. Ere the twilight was gone, an old man, his left leg lost to the surgeon's blade, succumbed also.

Shaw suggested we employ some tactic to safely pass the night. We'd take watches and position ourselves some distance from the wounded to avoid surprise—I in deeper brush downstream a way, he in some trees across the trail.

The sky was clear and starry, and the night fell cold. I slept badly in my discomfort, and so was awake and shivering when the first light of morning came upon the eastern horizon. I sought the warmth of the whiskey and had just returned the jug to earth when the first of them leapt upon me, a young brave with a bone tied in his topknot and knife and hatchet in hand.

The saddle pistol I'd taken as companion came to my fingers as though of its own volition. The ball caught the Indian in the brow and blew out the top of his skull. He died looking upward and fell with eyes still open, as though curious as to the whereabouts of the rest of his head.

I rolled over and sat up, wishing to shriek at the pain in my knee but somehow managing silence, staring at the fallen man as I reached for one of two loaded muskets. Now I knew for certain I'd killed a man—for my own life's sake, and in battle. I felt nothing, neither remorse nor exultation. Perhaps it was my fatigue.

As I sat there staring at the brave's dead face, two more abruptly rose up from nowhere. Shaw, more awake and alert than I, dispatched one with a musket shot through the chest that flung the man back nearly as fast as he'd been coming. His companion continued forth, bounding toward me through the air before Shaw could raise another weapon or reload the fired one.

I had a second musket. I couldn't remember if it had been loaded, but its bayonet was thoughtfully screwed into place. The poor chap died upon it, screaming horribly. I cried out myself. The force of his skewered body shoved the musket butt sharp against my swollen knee.

That was the lot of them, unless some undetected survivors had run off at our stout defense. Making certain the dead were dead, we then went to see to our wounded. None had been touched in this brief fracas, but that would not have mattered.

All had died during the night. Every one of them. Their faces made me shiver.

Again, there was no burying. We gathered up what of their personal effects served to identify them and such weaponry as we could carry, then took to the trail with intent to put some distance behind us, much as I could manage dragging my leg. When I faltered, Shaw, who'd assisted ships' doctors in his time, examined my knee and decided it required some surgeon's work.

Whiskey was brought into service once more, poured generously over the injury. I cried out again as Shaw put the sharp point of his sailor's knife to the swelling. I shan't disturb your content with a description of the hurt or the corrupt fluids that came forth. Once drained, however, the now-flattened wound evidenced the point of a piece of jagged wood that had escaped my notice in initial treatment. Shaw drew it out, then reapplied whiskey. Leg rebound, I was hopping along not an hour later.

As we continued our slow progress over the next ridge—that which divides the rivers flowing to the Atlantic from those flowing to the Ohio—we often heard odd bird and animal sounds behind us, especially at night, and surmised they might have a human source. But we had no further contact with Indian pursuers until we were down in the following valley. It came late in an afternoon, after a considerable rain shower.

I don't know why the fellow picked that very instant to loose his arrow. Perhaps he just wasn't very good at this sort of thing. The shaft he shot missed both Shaw and me, hitting a tree high and obliquely and breaking in two. We'd learned enough not to stand about and gape, and threw ourselves into the brush, Shaw firing his musket in the general direction of the bow shot. I lay there waiting.

Another arrow struck, again hitting a tree, just above my head, but sticking. With pistol in hand, I rolled to the right, lifting my head above a scratchy clump of weed with grave caution.

Sweat dripped from my brow into my eyes. Insects buzzed. Somewhere I heard a crow calling. I scarce breathed. My knee was throbbing with the same rapidity of my heart.

Of a sudden, this young Indian brave leapt from a quarter I hadn't expected—tomahawk raised—right for where I'd just been by the tree. Surprised that I was not there, he hesitated a few seconds—to his penalty. Shaw's musket barked and the Indian's chest splattered red. He crumpled. I dropped my head as more arrows flew. Why hadn't they sent braves armed with guns? Or was this a war party in search for precisely such weaponry? We'd hidden the guns we could not carry when we'd left our unfortunate comrades back over the ridge. Strange that this lot hadn't found them.

I heard Shaw reloading his long piece. My musket lay on the ground by the dying Indian, where I'd dropped it. I held my pistol with care. Its round gone and I'd be helpless, but for my bush knife.

Nothing more stirred. I wondered if they were moving about in their quiet way, circling behind us. It commenced to rain again, lightly this time. Sound enough, though, to cover footfalls.

I looked behind me, all around. Nothing but raindrops. Then something rumbling like thunder, only it was too regular and continuous. It grew louder. I heard the sound of hoof against loose stone. A moment later, the trail, as much as I could see of it, was full of a thundering swarm of horses, though I noticed but two riders.

The quantity of the hoofbeats sufficed to flush our game. Three nearly naked male figures leapt up from the brush, amazingly close before me, and ran in darting zigzags away from the swelling equestrian din. A shot was fired, I think by Shaw again, and then another from one of the horsemen. One Indian dropped like stone. Another, wounded, commenced yipping, but vanished like a rabbit into the greenery.

Our rescuers pulled rein—the two of them leading a whole string of horses. I recognized one of them as the helpful Davison.

He dismounted and walked over to check the dead Indians, rolling one over with his foot.

"Wonder you boys ain't dead."

"How is it you've reached us so fast?" I asked.

"Washington sent runners on ahead to Will's Creek," said Davison after a spit. "His main party was walkin' so slow. Currin and me moved out fast as we could, as there was dyin' men to save. Where are they?"

"Their dyin's done," said Shaw.

"Just you two? Now we got all these mounts to spare."

"Them fuckin' Indians gonna get 'em if we don't move out now," said the other man with Davison, the woolly bearded Currin I remembered now from our trip to the French forts.

Shaw helped me into a saddle, then, not liking it, pulled himself aboard a horse. We turned the string and set out on the trail, moving at a resolute trot and walk.

The trail was too narrow to ride abreast. Crossing a meadow farther along the way, however, Davison brought himself to my side.

"Somethin' I forgot," he said. "Letter fer you. From the Ennis girl."

He dug into his shirt and produced a grimy, sweat-stained folding of paper. It had been closed with wax, but there was no signet imprint upon it. I opened it, discovering it was two things.

The outer paper was the frontispiece page of the novel I had given Mercy upon our first meeting. There was the inscription, written in my hand, complete to the "Thomas Morley, Captain." I could not comprehend why she would have torn this from the book, until I looked at what it was wrapped around: another letter, quite familiar, writ in a different hand and language. It was the second "confession" Susannah Smithson had penned of our "most carnal" relations, intended as counterweight to her father's wrath and plotting.

I thought I'd lost it somewhere in this wilderness, but no, I must have left it among my things at Will's Creek.

Where Mercy had come upon it.

Twenty-eight

The news of the defeat at Fort Necessity had spread quickly through the mountains, and frightened settlers were beginning to seek refuge at Will's Creek.

As they'd come in, others had left.

Washington and MacKay had galloped off to the capital at Williamsburg to make personal reports to Dinwiddie and the Burgesses. The Colonel had left Stephen in command at Will's Creek, with Gist assisting, the both given instructions to improve the settlement's defenses until such time as a proper fort could be built. Stephen's task was complicated by a more distressing departure—the continuing desertion of men in the ranks.

None in the Virginia regiment had been paid. A number were of the mind that as the French seizure of all the Ohio had effectively negated the Crown's promise of some share in two hundred thousand acres for each man, they were no longer bound by the contract of enlistment. Others, much like myself, had lost all taste for soldiering.

By ones and twos and large groups, they'd been slipping away. Washington and MacKay might have held them through sheer force of character and leadership. Stephen and Gist could not.

It was no enhancement to matters that Half King, who had reappeared of a sudden at Will's Creek with wife Queen Alequippa, assorted family, and a handful of braves, just as quickly decided to abandon the place for one much safer—a village called Jemmy Arthur on the eastern slope of the Blue Mountains in Pennsylvania. Half King said that the better portion of the Mingo tribe had now gone over to the French and that he and his kin would be offering themselves up to be killed if they remained in the Ohio country.

He was disheartened. To his mind, we would never wrest the Forks or anything else back from the French.

There was for me a worse defection. Just three days before I came into Will's Creek with Davison and the others, a panicked Mr. Ennis and all his family had fled the settlement. They, too, were headed for Pennsylvania, but were making for Carlisle, where Ennis had once worked, or some other settlement well east of the mountains and beyond the reach of tomahawk.

Mercy had gone with her family—apparently without remorse or hesitation. She'd left no note for me, nor word of any kind.

My impulse should have been to gallop off after her at once—and so it was—but neither Gist nor my afflicted leg would permit it. Gist impressed upon me strongly how pursuit would do no good, even were I well.

Mercy's father had come upon Susannah's scarlet letter among the things I'd left behind in his storeroom for safekeeping. Not knowing if it had some import, Ennis had had one of the French-speaking traders read it. Soon all the settlement had known its contents, improving my reputation among the mountain men and soldiers, but utterly destroying it with the one for whom it mattered most.

Gist said that Mercy had before that been reluctant to depart Will's Creek until she'd had felicitous word from or of me. After the revelation of that letter, she'd wished to be gone at once.

"She won't be back, Tick," said Gist. "She told my daughter Anne so."

I knew not what at all to do—what possibly I could do. If reluctant to ape the dreadful conduct of my brother following the demise of his Jamaican love, I fear I did so all the same. Telling people I was attending to the healing of my knee, I kept to bench and jug. I suppose I persuaded myself that if I waited long enough, she might still return—come leaping toward me over the meadow grass, much as I had first looked upon her.

———

One afternoon, reclining on the bench outside what had been Ennis's store, I lifted my blurry eyes to what seemed to me a drink-induced apparition— Half King and two of his braves entering the compound through the main gate, the stout little chief heading directly for me.

I feared the rest of his party had come to some harm, and wobbly stood. Looking at me straight in the eyes, he placed both his hands on my shoulders. His words came out slowly.

"Your woman is gone," he said.

"Yes. For Carlisle. Where is your own family, Tanacharison? Are they well?"

I was imagining every terrible thing.

"My people are well," he said. "They go on to Jemmy Arthur. I and two warriors return here, so that you know what happened."

"What . . . ?"

His hands gripped my shoulders harder. "Ennis is killed. Two daughters killed. By Indians. I think Ottawa. There are now many Ottawa in these mountains. The Ennises sleep murdered by the trail to Raystown."

"Mercy?" I was shaking badly. How unbearable it was to hear a single one of his words. But I urged him to continue, as if her escape might somehow be mentioned as an afterthought.

"She is gone," he repeated.

"Dead?"

"Same thing. She is gone."

Now I gripped him by the upper arms. "Where, Tanacharison? Damn all, where did this happen?"

I was shouting. I commenced to bellow foul oaths. I think I threatened Half King. I know I said unkind things about the Indian race. And George Washington. And Susannah Smithson. And Benjamin Franklin. And, not to be forgotten, my worthless self.

"Thomas! Stop this!"

It was Gist, standing in the store doorway, looking, I think, as stricken as I, but fiercely solemn. Captain Stephen was with him.

"Go with Half King," Stephen said to me. "Take your man Shaw. Take anyone you wish. And horses. Whatever you need. But cease this hysterical display."

———

The bodies were still at the site of the ambush, nearly a day's ride from Will's Creek. Half King and the two young warriors led the way. Shaw had come with me, as had Gist, now tearful. Ennis had been a friend to him, and he loved those girls much as his own.

He had us hang back a bit from the Indians trotting ahead, as though to delay the inevitable. 'Twas no point to that. The horrors there were why we'd come. I moved up to Half King.

Ennis's wagon, axle broken, was lying on its side, the hitch jutting at an odd angle. One dead horse lay in its traces, beginning to bloat. The other had been taken. The wagon's contents, which I believe had included a substantial supply of spirits, had been looted.

There were arrows as well as musket-ball holes in the wood.

"Ottawa," said Half King, pulling an arrow free.

Gist nodded.

"Chief Pontiac?"

"That wouldn't be my hope," said Gist. "But it's my sense. He's out here. He's got more hate for us than any other."

Half King studied me, then moved on.

The Ennises were by trees just beyond, all three of them stripped of their clothing. Faith, two years younger than Mercy, was laid out straight, almost formally, on the ground—blood on her chest from a grievous musket-ball wound and on her brow from where she'd been scalped.

Chastity was tied to a slender, nearby tree, her hands bound behind it. Her body had sagged forward, especially her head, which was half off where her throat had been cut. Why she so harshly treated and the other merely slain?

I turned away to the brush at my side and vomited seemingly everything I had drunk or eaten in days. Then I sat back on my heels, regaining my breath, feeling absolutely dead. But I'd not finished my duty here. Half King was waiting, by yet another tree. One more corpse.

There sat Ennis, naked and nearly bald from his scalping, legs splayed, arms akimbo. His hands had been cut off, as had his genitals. His abdomen had been carved open into a cavity large enough to admit burning coals. They'd burnt out. The opening now buzzed and quivered with flies. There were other mutilations, as there were on Chastity's drooping body.

"These are done—these cuts, these marks—after he and older girl die. Long time after. Other Indians. Maybe not Ottawa."

"Why?"

"To show contempt," said Gist. "To show they're not afraid of us. They are not afraid that we'll do something powerful bad to them for this. They mean to show they think we're done in this country."

"Three, four tribe leave their marks," said Half King. "Mingoes, too. It is not commonly done. But this they do." He peered at the poor girl's ruined flesh as he might some trail sign.

"What of Mercy? She is alive?"

Half King shook his head.

"What do you mean?" I asked, grabbing his arm. "You told me she was 'gone.' Nothing more."

"She's taken, Tick. Good as dead," Gist said.

"But the woman at White Woman's Town. She was taken, and she's lived all these years!"

"She's a rare 'un. And she wasn't taken in a war."

"But . . . what will they do to her? To Mercy?"

"Don't ask, Tick. Put her from your mind. Lest you go mad."

I took the pistol from my belt and ran a few paces into the woods. I was indeed quite mad. Blood-crazed, I was. As I waved the pistol about, it discharged. I knew not where the bullet flew.

Gist's hand caught at that arm. Shaw was there to seize the other.

"We'll bring her family back," Gist said. "We owe her that. We must go do it now. Your pistol shot could be heard far."

Half King left us there, to continue east as he had started before this woeful distraction. I had no blame for him in his haste to be away, but I wished our parting was not so fleeting. I was not to meet with him ever again.

———

We buried the bodies almost immediately upon our bringing them in to Will's Creek, as much with a care to the fears and feelings of those in the camp as to concern for Christian niceties. Amazingly, there turned up two men claiming to be clergy among the refugee settlers at Will's Creek. Each spoke something before the dirt went in.

I took a lock of each sister's hair. I know not why, for I knew none to give them to. Then I went off into the woods, lay down on the ground and cried—for hours into the night.

I awoke, sick as with the plague, at morning, finding the settlement much astir. An express rider had come in, bearing a letter from Washington. It was to Stephen, but a portion of it related to me:

"If Captain Morley has survived and is in camp and reasonable health, I wish him, if he will, as I cannot spare her father from the field, to transport Miss Anne Gist from Will's Creek to a place of safety at Belvoir plantation and into the care of Mr. and Mrs. Fairfax, who have agreed to receive her.

Allow him a wagon and whatever else he need. Extend to him my respects and gratitude.''

It was well he'd written this, for I'd no intention of offering him opportunity ever again to speak such words to my face. Whatever Mercy's fate, its cause lay in Jumonville's Glen.

Twenty-nine

Our journey from the wilderness to the Tidewater had three distinct phases, as measured by the topography and turn of conversation.

Bumping along through the forests of the wild Patowmack Valley north of Winchester, Anne Gist assaulted me with lamentations over Mercy's passing—when none could be as deeply felt as my own. If I hadn't been so steeped in remorse and guilt, I should have liked to strangle her by the time we got over Ashby's Gap.

Once in the Piedmont, she turned her talk to Colonel Washington—her words a constant pester as she questioned me about his disposition toward her and her father, his wealth and holdings, and the general train of his affections as concerned the women of Virginia. I could not speak with any great authority on any of these matters but one, and in that I was painfully discreet. When she persisted in asking about *amours* and dalliances, I finally bellowed at her to still herself.

And so she did, especially as we came upon the northern reaches of Alexandria and into the country of fine manor houses and great plantations. I'm sure she felt—as I initially did—a mixture of awe, envy, and disgust, and the sense of being an interloper. Bold as she was in the rough country of mountains, Mistress Anne was a timid mouse on the wagon seat beside me as we rumbled up the drive to Belvoir.

———

Shaw and I were not received into the house. Sally Fairfax appeared upon the steps—looking as grim and dark as a New England widow when Anne Gist and her belongings were brought inside.

Finally, I called her name and she descended, with slow dignity, to the dusty drive and came upon the wagon's side.

"A good day to you, Captain Morley," she said, her voice as mournful and leaden as Washington's had been the morning after our defeat at Necessity.

"And you, Mrs. Fairfax."

She studied my face sadly, then looked to the river. "Miss Gist informs me you have suffered a grievous loss, Captain."

"Yes."

"I knew nothing of this Miss Ennis. You did not speak of her to me, though we are friends."

"I am sorry, for she was most worthy of being spoken of."

Her eyes caught mine again, a quick glimmer of sharpness in her look. "It is not a good thing to try to keep secrets in those mountains, Captain."

I could not ken her meaning, and then I did. I could think of nothing to say.

"I fear this is not a convenient occasion to invite you to share in the hospitality of our house," she said, "though I will have refreshment brought you. Where now do you go? To join the Colonel at Williamsburg?"

"No. I go home. To Philadelphia, and I know not where thereafter. I don't know when we shall meet again—Sally."

She lifted her chin slightly. Her dark eyes were moist, ail drained of charm and flirtation. "Then the day is doubly sad," she said.

She lifted her hand and, as knee allowed, I bent over and kissed it. Sally had no further word for me, nor I for her.

———

Much as I had been "Tick" or "Leech" for my constant closeness to Richard, in such way did our lives now differ that I entered Philadelphia dreading the prospect of our reunion, postponing it until I had dealt with more amiable business first. For his companionship, and in pitiful small recompense for saving my life, I'd promised Shaw a decent berth on one of our ships, and sent him on to the Delaware waterfront to find Riggins and make arrangements.

Franklin I found not at his home or place of business, but at a coffee-house of his frequent patronage, where he'd gone to seek news of events in the mountains. He was thus enormously glad to see me.

He scribbled down everything I told him, which was all I could recollect, save that interesting part about Miss Gist's transfer to the house of Fairfax and the possible reasons therefor. The town was much awash in battle and Indian news, most of it wrong—so the better part of our time was passed in correcting what he had been preparing to report in his newspaper from the flood of rumor borne with every arriving horseman, coach, wagon, and boat.

The falsehoods were excessive whatever their leaning. In some reports, the French were poised to pour out of the mountains and drive the English from North America. In others, Washington had suffered defeat but slain hundreds of French in the doing.

"If we killed more than two of them, I should be powerful surprised," I said. "On our part, we lost thirty—one tenth our number—dead on the field, and numerous perished thereafter, including some nine left in my care. Settlers have been attacked and slain." I wiped my eyes quickly, not wanting to dwell on this subject. "And Indians died, too. I and a mate killed three or four ourselves. But no 'hundreds'—not on either side."

"You say, 'left in my care.' You stayed behind with wounded?"

"Yes. For naught, as they all died."

He squinted at my face. "You were wounded as well?"

"Yes. My knee also. Wood splinters. All is mending."

He scribbled further. "Captain Morley, I shall see you made hero, too. Perhaps nay so great as Lieutenant Colonel Washington, but ranked with Gist and Stephen, and this Captain MacKay."

"How are there heroes from what happened at Necessity?"

"How? The public clamors for them. Battles are great sport and they need their champions."

"They would not find great sport if they stood there in that meadow that next morning—or if they'd seen the naked remains of an English girl made victim to Ottawa hacking."

He laid a hand on my arm. "All war is a horror, Thomas. But wars are inevitable, as recurring as rain or snow. The trick is to turn them to some good end, as I think may now be in prospect."

"What good end? The prosperity of the Ohio Company?"

"No sir. The good end of unity and the spread of patriotic spirit. Heroes unite us. Danger unites us. King George must now send us money and guns for our defense. I go soon to organize a conference of governors, perhaps including some chiefs of the Iroquois. When this thing has run its course, our King will find America a changed place."

"But there is no war. Just that battle, and now all is lost. The French possess all that country. They are building forts, and will soon have all the Indians with them. 'Tis hopeless, Mr. Franklin."

"No, 'tis hope *full*, Captain. The greater the challenge, the greater the need for unity. Think on all these colonies with their own men armed, sir. The relationship with the Crown will change markedly, yes?"

"I care not. I am not going back to that place, nor staying here."

There was laughter from another, quite crowded table. It occurred to me it was the first I'd heard since we'd joined battle so many weeks before.

"Whither go you, then?" Franklin asked.

"I would go abroad, if the means be found."

"To Afrique?"

"Never. To Europe."

"I would have you rejoin Washington for another adventure."

"Adventure? Sooner Afrique."

"He has good chance of success, don't you think? With sufficient arms and men?"

I sipped the last of my coffee. "As a leader of men, sir, he is magnificent, compelling, irresistible. Many would follow wherever he led though hails of bullets. But as they would follow, he needs someone at his side to tell him where he should go."

"You!"

"No. Gist, or Stephen, or MacKay, if he'll heed them. He has no need for me."

Franklin mused upon this, then changed the subject. "Susannah asks after you. She is in great melancholy."

"That is fair, for so am I."

"She thought you dead, and will cheer this good report. I do think she would marry you, Thomas—but I fear not in the present circumstance."

"How not?"

"She has spoken to me on this. She is miserable in her father's house, and would be away. She would marry to escape it. But for her to marry you with her father's and your brother's blessing, that would require your acquiescence and participation in their trade in slaves. Susannah knows how much that is against your wishes. She would marry you free of them, but not poor. Never poor. And poor is what you'll be without Mr. Smithson and your brother. Do you comprehend?"

"I do."

"I am a wise man, Thomas, but I haven't an answer for you."

———

But I had an answer of my own.

I'd by then begun to think quite earnestly of Italy, of the beautiful artist Rosalba Carriera, and the more glorious possibilities of life of which Italia was such symbol. There was to my knowledge no painter or draughtsman of any great skill in the colonies. It seemed at least plausible there might someday be profitable employment for a young man with schooling at this trade. In the main in America, one earned most at the painting of public signs, of course, but there was or should be also interest in portraits, landscapes, storytelling paintings. I'd done a few sketches—most of the tragic Mercy, some of Susannah, one each of Washington, Half King, and Gist. They were less clumsy than I'd feared. I felt encouraged.

I found my brother as expected at home—sprawled in a chair as he might now be at any hour, decanter at hand—fair drunk, but at least not so far gone he could not understand my proposal, which I presented to him after the most perfunctory greeting and summation of my travels. I told him I was now willing to relent in my claim on Miss Smithson, provided I might procure the wherewithal to commence a new life in Europe and there undertake the study of art. Said wherewithal, I calculated, would amount to a thousand pounds—

I had come upon Richard with this at just the right point in his daily journey to oblivion. He was still rational enough to comprehend the nature of this offer, but not of mind sufficiently keen to ponder its motive and possibilities. The size of the amount suggested came as a shock, almost sobering him, and prompted near-yelping complaint. He had no such sum at hand, he said, especially for the support of a vagabond youth in foreign fleshpots.

I had ready answer. The sum was not for me, but for her, was it not? A measure of her value? Would he want a bride worth less than a thousand pounds? And was Susannah not an acquisition to be amortized over life? Small sum then in that regard, especially as such a marriage would do much to strengthen his partnership with her father.

Could he find Susannah's better or prettier anywhere in the colonies? Nay, not in any town or country village. As for the availability of the monies I required, he had only to turn to his old friend Credit, which was to say, to Mr. Smithson, who surely would be pleased to proffer the sum to gain such a pleasing end.

My brother argued that dowry, not loan, was the custom. Were Smithson to part with a thousand pounds in this, it should be in that form. I countered that Smithson was no customary fellow. He loved coin far more than even daughter. If he could attend to dowry as repayable loan, why, that to him would be serendipity. He'd rejoice at this union as few fathers.

I wished to leave for Europe as soon as absolutely possible, and with all required monies in hand. I gave Richard just two days, and persuaded him of the wisdom of waiting until I had quit the city before he formally asked for Susannah's hand, so she'd find less choice in the matter. He assented, eager to achieve all results, his humor much improved, if not his sobriety.

Richard had little ear for my distressing misadventures, or of the calamities occurred and occurring to the west. His mind was on the awaiting prize—Susannah, naked in his own bed. As I thought upon it, a thousand pounds was cheap for such a treasure. Many a man would measure her in a league with the bride of Troy.

You are thinking what a cad, varlat, and villain I was. Selling off a lady like so much meat by the pound, without a thought to her own mind or feelings or wishes. How differed this from slavery and the auction block? And to one's own brother. Not mere villain, I, but Shakespearean villain!

I could not agree more. He who'd carry forth such a scheme would be scoundrel indeed. 'Twould be despicable, most particularly so in consideration of the fact that I still had much affection for this lady.

But I was no scoundrel, except from Richard's and Smithson's view. Rather, I was a plotter of no little cleverness, and with a sharp eye to just result. Recall how brother Richard "borrowed" the ill-gotten inheritance of our stepmother? It was just such a trick as that I had in mind—with full intention of repayment, of course. He'd see his thousand pounds back, however long it took.

But he'd not have Susannah. Neither would her father.

Richard took the full two days I'd asked. I've no notion of what haggling he might have had with Mr. Smithson, or of how much of my barter details he related. He didn't live up quite to his end of it. I received but nine hundred fifty pounds. Old Smithson again, true to his habit of taking a little off the top.

No matter. It certainly sufficed. With that much in hand, waiting only until I knew my brother and Smithson were at business—Richard was truly cogent only in that period from midmorning to midday dinner—I flew to Susannah, with whom I'd corresponded—in French so neither her father nor Richard would guess the way of the wind.

Susannah had agreed to my scheme almost at once. Rather than poverty with me or wealth with my brother, she'd chance the stakes in that place where she had come to womanhood: the England of such wealth, station, and marriage prospects as to make any in the colonies seem shabby.

When I came to her door that morning, she was ready, taking with her only such traveling clothes as the two of us could carry, and leaving behind for once her personal maid.

We made our dash successfully. Good Riggins and the still-friendly crew of the *Hannah* took us upriver to Trenton. As we set upon debarking there, he held me back.

"I was not in mind of telling ye this, Tick," he said, "for y've got enough sadness on you. But you should know it. Richard is after selling the *Hannah*. He wants all his ships in the slavery work. I'm to be master of one. I'd rather be master of a slops jar, but sooth, it's my only chance at master. And with fears of war about, there aren't so many ships going forth as before. I'd not be sure of a mate's cabin any other where."

"I am sorry for thee and for me and for the *Hannah*," I said. "But there is now absolutely nothing I can do to alter matters. You might inform Mr. Benjamin Franklin of the impending sale of our sloop. Perhaps he'll know of a worthy buyer who'll treat her with affection. As for your becoming captain of a slaver, I can only leave that to your conscience."

"So I'll be guided," he said. "As you'll see."

———

From that place, we coached across Jersey. A barge brought us over the Hudson to New York, where we had a choice of no fewer than three merchantmen leaving for London within the fortnight.

We chose the ship of soonest departure, though it was far from the most capacious and accommodating—or the most seaworthy. Even in summer, one good storm a week could be counted upon in the North Atlantic. We were more than five weeks crossing, and in the most violent waters.

I feared Susannah would die. Our cabin was more box or stall than chamber, and she kept to its rude board bed throughout the weather's torment, sick as a starved cat. She retched every day till dry, and I was hard put keeping liquids in her. Her face drained of all its rosy blush and turned the color of an old sheet. Her exquisite blue eyes grew rheumy and blood-flecked. Her flesh came to hang from bone. I held her tightly, as though I could press my own good seaman's health upon her, for hour after hour.

This is how I came to know how deeply I cherished and admired this lady, and would always, always be her friend. I was, however—alas—reminded of how Mercy had cared for me, and this did make me doubly sad.

While Susannah slept, assuring myself that she might survive the next few hours, I took myself to the deck, became friends with the chief mate and acquainted myself with the captain. He knew of our now several Morley ships, though was not personally acquainted with Richard, Ambrose Butler, or Smithson. A Boston man, he was no friend to the slave trade and berated me for the use of our ships in it, but I was able to wean him from this hostility with persuasive protestation of my innocence in that practice—and my hatred of it. As master of the *Hannah*, I'd traded only in such salubrious products as wheat, rice, whiskey, rum, indigo, and tobacco. So convinced, he took a liking to me, and had me to his quarterdeck and table, when Susannah's condition permitted.

He and I fell one night to discussing a most intriguing notion, and I was sorry for the lack of Franklin's presence. The subject was ice. In a cool, dark place, such as the hold of a ship below the waterline, covered with sufficient cloth to ward off the warmer air, the captain thought ice might be prevented from melting for days and weeks—possibly for a month or more. Taken to the tropics or some like warm clime, could not ice be sold like farmer's produce brought to market?

To what end, I countered—a momentary cooling-off of brow and body? What of drink, he suggested, and the cooling potion that ice fragments might make of, say, a good punch? An interesting idea, but who would pay for such novelty? In Charleston or Barbados, a cup thus cooled would swiftly warm again. What price for that? The captain shrugged. He had a lively mind, and turned to another subject. Still, I would have liked Franklin's thoughts on the matter. I've since passed the notion on to my kin and heirs, at least those of a seafaring bent. Perhaps one of them shall make a successful enterprise of it. The Good Lord knows the times my thirst would have been all the more whetted by the expectation of refreshment as cold as wet.

Poor Susannah, whose masquerade on board was as my wife. I ministered as best I could manage to her every need. I bathed her, head and foot. I emptied her slops and washed her clothing. For the rest of her life, no matter whom she married, I doubted there'd ever be man so intimately involved with her. I fought to keep her in sustenance. I held her in constant embrace. Still, she faltered and declined. One night, with the ship's roll so bad I feared our spars were dragging in the whitecaps, I was certain each hour was her last. I told her I loved her, with perhaps more meaning than was justified, but I don't think she comprehended a word.

Somehow, in the calmer morning, she rallied. With clearing skies and a friendly sun about, I had her brought up on deck and kept her in comfort there. When we reached Portsmouth four days later, she was thin as bones, but walked off the ship herself.

On land, like a transplanted flower, she prospered, took food and drink with the relish of our hearty crew, each day her returning beauty surpassing itself. After almost a week on the coast, we took the coach for London—she well enough to devote frequent portions of the journey to practicing a coquette's hand ballet with her fan—and found quarters where she could restore herself complete and renew acquaintance with her old schoolmates, some now of lofty station indeed. As she completed her correspondence, I planned. Whither to go?

A stop in Paris, certain. The French now intrigued me much. I'd advanced in their language. I knew of the beauty produced by their culture. I wished to see Notre Dame and the Tuileries. But then where? The Venice of Rosalba Carriera? Florence? Rome? What of Portugal? The fame of that country's cultural richness had spread even to the American colonies. I was Protestant, and Catholicism lay heavily on that land, but so did it upon Italy. Perhaps I should travel beyond—to Greece, Byzantium, and the Turkish Empire, or . . .

Or all of it, till my money was fled. Then I could work passage back.

I had small wish to remain in England. My status as a colonial colored me as bumpkin wheresoever I went—though such was not the case with my worldly Susannah. Once they'd discovered her among them, her old school friends drew her to their bosom, and to their residences as guest. One school chum, now a marchioness, invited Susannah into her household indefinitely, promising to protect her from fatherly reach. It was ideal. I was convinced Susannah would find herself a marchioness—if not a duchess—by the time I'd ended my travels and artistic schooling.

She took to this lofty life as bird to a tree, but I wanted none of it: the foppish waste and extravagance, the endless tittering gossip and vacuous calumny, the grotesque decadence, and constant painful groping for amusement.

I went three, four, perhaps five times with Susannah to balls and dinners, nearly all an agony of prattle, and painful more for my awkward ineptitude at the dance—both minuet and gavotte as strange and terrifying to me as I'd once found the wilderness. The best I could do was that clumsy, clomping Virginia country dance that had been the extent of my repertoire at Sally Fairfax's entertainments. This did for the gavotte—though not without producing giggles—but was no meet substitute for the courtly minuet. Susannah, alas, abandoned me. She had entered her glory. A magnificent powdered wig now crowned her much lovelier golden tresses, and her blushing countenance was powdered and painted to a hue more ghostly white than that presented me on the sickliest portion of our voyage. Upon this, incredibly, was a painted facsimile of the blush, and hideous black "beauty patches" were stuck here and there, looking dead insects.

Yet, it was the fashion. I could scarcely tell one great lady from another, and certainly not their age—as might have been the aim.

Susannah's mastery of the fan was complete. I could myself not help but be once more smitten by her gifted employ of it. With flutter of lash and curl of smile, she imbued the flimsy device with magical powers beyond all science. She had a trail of men by the end of every evening.

In such fashionable company, for all my reading and high adventure, I remained her simple rustic, a dolt bereft of wig or powdered hair or rouge. But I remained her friend and she mine.

Not that my London stay with her was totally without pleasure. I took her to a recital of the music of the most talented Mr. George Frideric Handel, hearing his oratorios "Samson" and "Solomon," and twice to Covent

Garden, there to see David Garrick and Margaret Woffington in John Van-brugh's *The Provoked Wife*, from which Susannah took much delight, and also Garrick's own *The Lying Valet*. I thought how much Washington would have enjoyed both evenings, yet never had foot of his put once on English soil.

For all this intellectual stimulation, for all the joy I took in Susannah's blooming restoration, I wished away from this damp and jaded place as much I had from Great Meadows after the "Battle of Fort Necessity." Her friends here, like all their kind, were shallow, useless, pointless snobs. I despised their life.

Also, I had reason to fear for my own. Susannah might well be under the marchioness's protection, but not I. Foul-tempered Smithson had been robbed not only of a marriageable daughter—a crime in his colony as it was in mine—but of a thousand pounds sterling. In his mind, I'm sure the ar-tifice of my brother's "borrowing" made no difference. 'Twas his money, and I'd run off with it. A man of his means could buy well-placed friends in London as well as Philadelphia. I was as much the subject of his as Richard's wrath.

So off I went by sail to Calais. I settled fully five hundred pounds on Susannah—it was all hers, yes? by the fairest measure—and thought the remainder sufficient to all my needs. She tried to press upon me more, so well-situated now was she, but I wouldn't accept it. The dear lass was also generous with her flesh.

This I did accept, on my last night in London. We were still friends who bore each other much affection. This to her mind made firm the bond, and it would be our last opportunity. I could not strongly differ.

She by then, I think, had no notion of marriage to the likes of me under any circumstance. She spoke to me of love after our last night's *couche*, but not in the sense of romance or marriage. I was part of her heart, and always would be, she said, no matter what manner of man she took as husband.

I could see she was looking forward with some relish to a play at that game, a principal sport of the aristocracy in Britain, as it was throughout Europe.

For my part, with refreshing honesty, I could pledge the same sort of love. As for marriage, I thought myself as good as married—for all my life—to a woman who could never abandon me, for she was dead.

Susannah wished to augment my baggage with the gift of a sword—an old and dented weapon belonging to one of her reacquainted friends, yet still a handsome, burnished piece. I declined.

"You cannot look a gentleman without a sword," she said.

I told her I'd no wish to look a gentleman, as it would only draw atten-tion to the possibility of the treasure I'd be carrying about, though I'd taken the precaution of sewing the heavy coins into clothes, hat, portmanteau lining, and other safe places. I had a small pistol with me, and my excellent knife from the frontier, a weapon of awesome size and malevolent aspect, given me by the good Gist from his stores. This should see me through the streets of Paris and the alleys of Rome, as it had through Fort Necessity.

I'll ne'er forget our last embrace, nor she, I think. We'd saved each other. It counted much.

———

Life is so relentlessly curious. Scant months after leaving an American frontier made a hell for all English by the French *coureur* and Indian ally, I found myself in Paris, capital of the Most Christian Louis, and there as resident.

Yes, there I was, hurrying along through the swirling mob at the Valois arcade of the Palais Royal to my favorite wineshop, glancing up at the brooding facade of the Richelieu Palace as though it were a landmark familiar to me since infancy, and exchanging oaths, salutations, and imprecations with all and sundry encountered in that bustling public way, my French tongue managed almost as nimbly as a native's.

Oh, the mud, the filth, the smells, the squalor, the din of that place! The most crowded quarter of Philadelphia was but a slumbering village to this. The supposed grandeur of the governor's palace at Williamsburg or the plantation houses along the James could in no way compare to the magnificence of these Parisian palaces and public buildings. And the gardens! The Tuileries! All America, even England, seemed wild and scrubby compared to these intricately verdant enterprises of this French king and the monarchs enthroned before him—most especially Louis IV. I wondered there was coin left in all the kingdom that hadn't gone to pay for it.

Yet one walked mucky, foul streets through poverty so desperate its human sufferers seemed wormy things. I'd ne'er seen so many rheumy, meatless children—and all so scarce alive. The Most Christian Louis had no coin for these flowers. In London, I'd found much of life there as bitter as the depictions in those brilliant prints of Master Hogarth. But the grotesques of Hogarth's "Gin Lane" were pale copy to the garish maelstrom of Paris.

Yet I did love this French city. True, I'd been bound for Italy. But, once in Paris, I advanced not a step farther south than Ville de Juifs and the Porte d'Italie.

For all the musket balls and arrowheads boring into flesh back in the American forests, here there was no war. I arrived anticipating scorn and abuse—the treatment a Frenchman might now expect in Philadelphia or Alexandria. But, initially at least, I found all was amity here between the English and French. I and my sketchbook were as readily accepted as though I were some student up from Provence.

If there was hostility and tension in the air, it was between the French classes. Dinwiddie himself and the shabbiest Virginia country farmer or dockside navvy seemed close kin indeed when one pondered the chasm that separated the poorest and noblest French castes. In America, a George Washington owed an innkeeper like Ennis the respect of a "Sir" and "Mister," and to a barefoot maid Mercy or Anne Gist every gentleman's courtesy, no matter that he signed himself "gentleman." For all the corrupt influence at his disposal, Smithson had been subject to the same law as I, and had been bested by it.

In Paris, any *comte* or *duc* or mere *sieur* could run down a Mercy with his carriage and think no more of it had she been a dog.

I took a room in the Latin Quarter—in a shabby house facing a narrow street but on a topmost floor, providing a plenitude of light. I found an artist-engraver willing to add another to his few pupils. He taught me much about line, less about color. For that, I made café friendships and won invitations to the studios and workrooms of more accomplished painters—including François Boucher, at whose establishment I met the celebrated Jean-Honoré Fragonard, an immeasurably accomplished painter precisely the same age as young Washington and already the winner of the Prix de Rome.

We talked of Rome. Fragonard derived his style from Giovanni Tiepolo, yet he shared my fondness for Rosalba, and indulged me with some conversation. His paintings followed religious and allegorical themes, excelling most in the rhapsodic flair of the background landscape and the captivating charm of his subjects' faces.

He wished, he told me, to secure the patronage of someone of liberal, even licentious leanings—perhaps a generous noblewoman. He wanted to break free of religious themes and embrace those romantic. He asked me numerous questions about England, though I could provide but paltry answers. Well-placed in marriage, Susannah might well prove just the noble lady Fragonard sought, but not yet.

The young genius had little interest in my art or thoughts upon it. I intrigued him only because I was an American and had been in the forests and mountains that now laid such claim to French excitement and imagination. He wanted to talk about Indians. He had never seen one. I provided him such a sight, with a quick but facile sketch of Half King—a vivid reproduction of memory. Fragonard was delighted to have it, but made no judgment on my talent, or lack of it.

Still, it was an encouraging encounter. My work improved in output and accomplishment. I won my master's praise—finally—and a few small commissions, most of them assisting him or other artists. I invested money enough to obtain oil paint for a serious work. Serious? Deuced somber. Fragonard's paintings, even the most dourly theological in purport, seemed to float with an inner esprit and lightheartedness. This canvas of mine was heavily moored in melancholy. It was a portrait. Of Mercy.

My initial hope was to recreate her on canvas as I had first seen her, the forest nymph coursing over the fence. But I couldn't get it right. After several failed attempts, I left the woods as they were but painted over her, restoring her image in much nearer perspective as a standing figure in the center of the canvas. I cannot say I brought her back to life, which was my artist's goal. Her wild beauty was there, though. I managed a representation of her dark and flowing hair real enough to want to touch. But she was a ghost in this picture. Her dark eyes held not the sparkling light of love and daring, as I so well remembered. They were accusing, staring, grim, apocalyptic. I had created an object with which to haunt myself.

And deservedly so.

Nay, I did not decide to destroy it. In a sense, I had transferred a portion of my guilt and regret from my spirit to the canvas. I felt freer. And I felt the lift that comes with completion and accomplishment. I had painted a painting, as no man I knew in America could say—not the sage Franklin, not the heroic Washington, not the rich Smithson. And it was good enough, I thought, to hang in the governor's palace, where the public might see it. So few were such places in the world, even here in Paris. Art was for the pleasure of the upper classes. Fragonard knew his world quite right.

And the world of Italy. He'd discussed it not so much in terms of art as in terms of history, in the same context as we talked of Indians. He referred to the American natives as "savages," for their cruel customs, but did we not extol the Romans as icons of civilization and grace, and were they not as barbaric? Could what the Ottawa had done to the Ennis family be disparaged, and not the bloody amusements of Nero, Caligula, and the Colosseum?

Walking the streets behind the Louvre Palace one chill evening, my thoughts of Italy fell upon Lorenzo di Medici—he exalted as "the Magnificent"—as great a friend to art as Italy had produced. But was not his daughter Catherine, as Catholic Queen of France, the same who loosed the assassins upon the Huguenot Protestants who'd come to Paris for the wedding of their Henry of Navarre to Catherine's daughter Margaret?

Starting that night of St. Bartholomew, had not this Catherine urged the assassins forth through these very streets until some fifty thousand Protestants, women and children among them, lay piled and stripped and bleeding upon this very earth I walked?

Except for tattoos and length of hair and sex, how did haughty Catherine differ from the bloody-minded Chief Pontiac? Lover of music that she was, as her daughter was lover of literature, how was she not savage?

Europeans had been in North America a century and a half. If all who had fallen to arrow, tomahawk, war club, and scalping knife were heaped in a pile, as were the Protestants that royal wedding night, would not they make mere knoll to the French mountain?

I would kill Chief Pontiac if I could, and any of his Ottawa warriors. I would be gladdened to see them die as Mercy's sisters perished, or poor Jumonville. But I would not call Pontiac savage. Not more than these.

I sought warmth and diversion from these morbid contemplations and turned toward my favorite wineshop. The hearth was aglow with its blaze, gladdening me. The bluster of winter had fallen upon Paris with some force.

Someone at my table before me had brought along a French newspaper and left it there. I seldom took note of newspapers. My small time at ease I devoted to book reading. Something about the page attracted me, however, and I pulled it into precise view.

The words near jumped at me. *"George Washington, l'assassin de Jumonville . . ."*

The phrase struck me as though a great stone. I had last looked upon those words the previous summer, had I not?—by flickering lantern light in the rain-soaked tent of Captain Villiers. "George Washington, assassin of Jumonville." Wounded, groggy, a little drunk, and pummeled by the battle we'd just been through, I'd paid little attention to them, given them no great weight. In my mind, I don't think I'd bothered to translate them from the French that night, but just assumed their meaning. Young Jumonville had died. Washington commanded the force that killed him. The work had been at the hands of Half King. There had been a fight. *N'importe.*

But here reprinted was the full text of the document Van Braam and I had brought back from Villiers' camp—the surrender terms we'd all urged George to sign because they were so generous and our misery so great.

It was a confession! Here was another word, *"Je."* I. "I, George Washington . . . the assassin of Jumonville."

"L'assassin." The murderer.

My head snapped back. I blinked, then looked over the rest of the newspaper page. The reprinted confession was part of a long polemic against the English. It contained accounts of the fighting at Jumonville Glen, including one from the French Captain Contrecoeur, who was quoting the escaped Monceau, the Canadian soldier who had fled the glen in time to keep his life and freedom.

"In the morning, at seven o'clock," Captain Contrecoeur had written of Jumonville's party, "they found they were surrounded by English on one side and Indians on the other. They received two volleys from the English, and not from the Indians. Through an interpreter, Monsieur de Jumonville told them to stop, as he had to speak to them. They stopped. Monsieur de Jumonville had the summons read to them, my summons for them to retire, of which I have the honor to send you a copy. While it was being read, the said Monceau saw all our Frenchmen coming up behind M. de Jumonville, so that they formed a platoon in the midst of the English and Indians. Meanwhile, Monceau slipped to one side and went off through the woods."

What? There'd been no such reading, no platoon formation. There'd been no time for it. This had been an ambush, without complication, the death-dealing volley fired the instant that hapless French soldier groped for his musket.

Another account in the paper was that of an Officer Drouillon, who'd been sent back to Williamsburg as prisoner and now, apparently, exchanged as a free man. His retelling was even more fanciful.

"Mr. Washington might have taken Notice w'n he attack Us at about

7 or 8 o'Clock in the Morning, y't neither we nor our own Men took to our arms; he might have heard our Interpreter, who desir'd him to come to our Cabbin, y't we might confer together, instead of taking that Opp'ty to fire upon Us."

There'd been no "cabbin"—only a few birch-bark lean-to's.

There was an exchange of letters reprinted here also between Contrecoeur and Duquesne, governor of New France. And they chilled my blood the most.

"I think, sir, that you will be surprised at the shameful way the English are acting; this is something which has never been known, even among the most uncivilized nations, striking at ambassadors by assassination."

Duquesne had replied: "I did not expect such a sudden change, sir, as the one you report in your letter, nor that the English could have pushed their cruelty so far as to assassinate an officer bearing orders from me. Yes, this murder is unique and can be avenged only by shedding blood. If the English do not hasten to send me the murderers as a proof of their disavowal, a step which they ought to take at the very scene where the assassination was committed, then lay a heavy hand on everything that can be found belonging to that nation."

In Europe, I had found no sign of war. The two nations remained at peace—as though blithely ignorant of all events in the wilderness of America. Hence my happy abode here in the French capital. But this newspaper page quivered with a raging call for war. This was a beating of the drum— and it was damned loud.

What could one say? I knew these accounts to be false—outright lies or hysterical fancies. Yet belying this judgment were the words signed by my friend: "I, George Washington, assassin. . . ." That was fact.

And signed because of me.

Hand trembling, I left coin enough to cover cost of my drink, then repaired to my drawing master, who was well acquainted with those in the printing trade. He said similar treatments of the events in America had appeared in Paris journals. There was an official *"Précis de faits"* from the King's government as well, circulated throughout the literate population and including line-drawing illustrations of the handsome Jumonville in life and the murderous deed itself: a fiendish Washington, very nearly bearing horns, firing a pistol ball into the head of an innocent, helpless French officer.

My teacher, curious at my shock, asked if I were acquainted with this murderous monster George Washington. A coward, feeling trapped in the midst of millions upon millions of French, I replied only that I had met him. I explained my agitation as arising from the bloody nature of the incident described and my fears that it would bring harm to the good relations of our two realms.

He was a good man, this teacher, and clasped my hand to show our own good relations still intact.

"This will mean only more fighting out in those faraway woods, where there is always fighting. Here in Paris, it is small matter. *Rien.*"

My mind's eye filled with the image of Mercy's sister, tied naked and bloodied to her tree. Small matter. In the faraway woods.

Even then I knew better. A king's *"Précis de Faits"* of such inflammatory execution was intended to pound the war drum all over the world. France and England had rival colonies not only in North America, but in the West Indies and the Asian land mass that was India. And here in Europe, war between the two nations was always only an express messenger's hard ride away.

Of a sudden, I felt terribly vulnerable and afraid. Worse, I felt a guilt more overpowering even than that I'd so long suffered because of Mercy.

"This murder is unique and can be avenged only by shedding blood," Governor Duquesne had written to his officer. "Lay a hand on everything."

This was my fault! I could not and cannot even now blame poor Van Braam. He was dolt, and not so wonderful a swordsman, either, but he was not the man who pushed that paper upon Washington and urged him put his name upon it. I did that in the name of peace, but now it proved I'd laid match to powder. If finger was to be pointed for the sorrows of all those settlers, for Mercy, her father, and her sisters, it was to me.

I stood condemned by the worst possible accuser: myself.

There was less of my money left than I'd hoped to husband, but enough to meet my transport needs and extended expenses. I had no guess of what all must be done to expatiate my sin, but knew it included going before Dinwiddie in person and absolving Washington from responsibility—if not for the deed, certainly for the word. If there was to be war, the fault would be mine.

Also certainly was I obliged to return to Will's Creek, there to stay until the danger had concluded. I could not remain taking the pleasure of Paris cafés and ateliers. I could not repair to the comforts of Susannah's bosom and circumstance. Not then. Every arrow loosed, from Laurel Ridge to Will's Mountain, by right should have naught but me as mark.

There were no English, or even Dutch, ships at Calais bound for an American port just then, and I dared not take a French one, lest war indeed begin and I become seized contraband. With my small possessions and now treasured oil painting, rolled as canvas, I crossed the channel on a packet.

———

Susannah thought me altogether crazed to be returning to North America for the passionate reason I gave, but she had thought me lunatic, as well as lover, from our first meeting.

There was no more thought of "lover." Susannah had now acquired a beau—a young British army major of high family—and wished no jeopardy to her prospects. Well enough. I was full of martyrdom, or at least contrition. The juices of sexual passion had quite dried.

The English newspapers were full of American matters and more alarming than the French, whose reports the British press repeated, but with comment, none of it kind. The general apprehension expressed was that the French were lying about Jumonville's "murder" to justify their incursions upon England's domains. An article recounting the "Battle of Fort Necessity," an amazing compilation of falsehoods and erroneous surmises near a year after the fact, stated without equivocation that Washington had been tricked into surrendering the fort. In another broadsheet, the "Affair at Jumonville Glen" was related as an ambush of British troops staged by the French and their savage Indian allies. Walpole had uttered his remark about the backwoods militia officer setting fire to the world. The King, with the blessings of Parliament, was appropriating funds and sending troops to suppress a French invasion of the middle colonies. War seemed inescapable, and soon.

In London's "society," as faithfully and daily reported to me by Susannah while I waited my embarkation, there was whispered talk. Washington was said to have committed a murder of a Frenchman and so provoked this clash—a "rumor" spread without knowledge of original source. The Frenchman, in one version of this nasty chunter, had been cuckolded by the Colonel, who had left his wife with child! There was also chatter of colonial sedition against the Crown, and plots by Quakers and Pennsylvania Catholics seeking to prevent a British military response.

My own name was occasionally mentioned in this bandying. Some said I was one of Washington's fellow assassins. Others that I had fled his wrath in cowardice or fear of reprisal for having informed upon him. The fact that I had been in the wilderness and involved in the momentous events now reported attached a certain notorious celebrity to me, as word of my renewed presence in England—as guest of Susannah and her hostess—gained currency.

"My scornful commentary against you in Philadelphia is withdrawn," Susannah said. "You are famous now as friend of the bloodthirsty Washington. If you stayed, you would be more famous yet. I wonder the King himself has not asked an interview of you."

"I've no taste for fame or kings," I said, perhaps too proudly. "My only wish now is for America."

"A lady in England might take offense that that is your only wish, sir."

"A lady in England should not doubt my affection."

"A lady will take a kiss as proof."

As asked, this was given, and no doubts remained. I then wished her most well with her major.

For all her circumspection, Susannah made a point of taking her farewell of me in that most public verdure known as Pall Mall, with a still better-remembered kiss, and gave me something of herself—a lock of her golden hair, ribboned together and placed in a small, emptied snuffbox.

I have it still. Those of Mercy's sisters are kept in another.

Thirty

I arrived at Yorktown in early April 1755. Like some pilgrim in haircloth, I was bound for the highest authority obtainable in Virginia, before whom to declare that the surrender at Fort Necessity and consequent confession were all a doing of my humble self.

Whether there had indeed been assassination to confess to was another matter, but not one for my public pronouncement. I doubted I could spare Washington guilt for that, but I'd do my damndest to spare him the presumption of it—especially of any placed on him that belonged with me.

Then, as now, I was unsure of the truest nature of my feelings toward the Colonel. At times I loved him as I did my brother, even more so, for the better brother he—and God as witness, the better man. At other moments I could find myself near to fury at the man, for his vanity, his barely concealed snobbery, and titanic ambition—for his so cavalierly thrusting himself into great events and making such a shambles of them, then blithely turning to the next as though what went before had been merely practice.

Whether I was to be his friend, his enemy, or someone simply quit of him, I had come to undo my wrongs to him, just as I intended to go into those mountains and perform the same for my sweet Mercy. That was why I was in that part of North America that bloody summer—not politics, not soldierly or sailorly ambition, not monetary gain, nor any other reason. I was there as penitent.

Hiring a horse at the Yorktown port and pounding hard for Williamsburg, I made firm in my mind precisely what I'd say to His Excellency, Fat Bob Dinwiddie, whatever embarrassment to myself. But events had moved on ahead of me. I pulled rein in the gravel court of the governor's palace, discovering no one to greet me save two sleepy sentries and a clerk—the latter a replacement for my laconically unhelpful friend from earlier visits, who had died just the month before of the bloody flux. Franklin had an interesting scientific theory as to the source of that ubiquitous ailment, but this is not the appropriate place for that.

Frustrated, hot, and much fatigued from my journey, I went to the nearby public house where I'd once made reunion with Washington, and found it as full of news as grog, at least what was news to me, most of it bad.

Franklin had had his conference in Albany, New York, the preceding summer, and it was one of no little moment. He'd assembled chiefs of the Iroquois' Six Nations, who still counted among their members the western Mingo Senecas now so bent on tomahawking us—as well as commissioners from nearly all the colonies. In accord that the frontier must be defended, and by the colonies themselves, they'd taken up Franklin's radical proposal for a near-autonomous colonial federation, with President-General and other seditious notions, and sent this and other requests and recommendations off to London and the Board of Trade, which administered the affairs of the King's American dominions.

About the time I had first arrived in Paris, flirting with whores in the public markets and drinking in *vin ordinaire* and *la vie des arts* as the air itself, the British Board of Trade had begun consideration of these brave proposals, found them preposterous, impudent, frightening, and too abrim with "the Democratick," and summarily rejected them. I had known none of this, caring more then for the opinions of Boucher and Fragonard than for those of the Lords in London.

Though all agreed the French must be driven from the Forks, there was no concord on strategy or route, and there was no provender to feed or munitions to arm such a conquering force. An ardent supplication asking muskets and powder for new militias had been made to England, but without satisfactory reply.

Worse for my cause, Dinwiddie had been so disgusted by the performance of the "Virginia Regiment," both before, during, and after the Fort Necessity debacle, that he'd virtually disbanded it, breaking it into separate companies with no officer higher in rank than captain.

Our Colonel become a mere captain? I could scarce contemplate this eventuality, and neither, you may be certain, could Washington. According to my thirsty newsbearers in that public house, he'd angrily resigned his commission and removed himself to Mount Vernon, which his remarrying sister-in-law had left to his proprietorship. He'd ceased all communication with Dinwiddie.

This was quite old news—months and months old, some of it—but as I'd heard none of it, it was all the same to me as express. Of more recent report, I was informed that the colony had received just now two entire regiments of the British Army. These troops had thus far invaded and conquered only Alexandria, though their mission was to restore all matters in the colonies to the King's liking—this, mind, at the colonials' expense. Talk of all manner of outrageous new taxes to pay for the soldiery was the *sujet du jour*.

Washington and Dinwiddie were now in Alexandria, having hastened to that Patowmack town for some important sort of meeting on military matters with the newly arrived army. "Meeting" or court-martial? Was George in the dock?

My horse was less impatient than I, and at Fredericksburg I was compelled to acquire a fresh one. Fleetly now, I coursed along the rolling road north through the sweet greenery and wildflower blaze of the Virginia spring. Falmouth, Stafford, Dumfries, Colchester—I galloped and trotted on, passing quickly through them, taking my rest in the saddle or at roadside. Even Belvoir and Mount Vernon I hurried past, clattering exhausted finally onto the streets of an Alexandria I found not only crowded beyond all memory, but full of red-coated soldiers

They were fresh from duty in Ireland, and many of them Irish—their rough, yet musical speech reminding me much of the Ennises'. Several of the sentries stationed about the town treated me unkindly, even though I announced wherever possible that I sought audience with Dinwiddie and it was a matter of some import—what were Washington's words?—to the Crown! Half these louts I encountered had no ken whatsoever as to who Fat Bob was.

One sergeant knew of the governor, however, and passed the intelligence that Dinwiddie was at that hour conferring with a General Braddock of His Majesty's forces and other worthies at the Carlyle house, which I knew to be one of the finest residences of the town. The wife of merchant Carlyle was a Fairfax, sister to Sally's husband George William. I'd met both Mr. and Mrs. Carlyle, and once talked at some length with madam. I assumed I'd be welcome.

I knew not this Braddock, but it seemed to me I'd advance more swiftly among these lobsterbacks by calling forth his name rather than Dinwiddie's, and so I did. No further impediment did I encounter.

The Carlyle house sits on a bluff overlooking the shore of the river, its gardens descending to the bank. On the street side, one enters through a gate and goes along a gravel walk that leads through what is more grassy court than garden. Soldiers were at the gate and also standing about the court, as were many prominent gentleman of the town and colony. A most consequential trouble had drawn them. I feared more and more for Washington.

I had with me about my person and saddle all my paltry few belongings, but these included my oil painting of Mercy, removed from frame and rolled tight and wrapped in cloth, and carried in a leather dispatch case of long proportion with a wide shoulder strap—a gift of Susannah's in London. I was tired and angry, full of impatience, and came riding up to that house on the fly, stirrups asplay. As I did not discover till later, the soldiers at the gate mistook me for an express rider bearing a message for the great ones within. I thought only that I'd at last encountered some courtesy.

The same presumption of messenger was made by all. Doors flew open, corridors cleared. A final portal remained closed to me with a redcoated grenadier before it. I said only, "General Braddock?" He swept aside and I pushed in, swinging open both of the double doors before me.

I'd expected to find only Dinwiddie and this general, perhaps taking refreshment. I meant to spill forth my confession all at once, before anyone could stay me. Instead, I found I had burst into a high council of the colonies' most powerful men, all in the midst of grave discourse.

There was a large table at the center of the room and about it sat seemingly every important man in the English Americas, save Franklin and Sir William Johnson, the great Indian agent, though I later learned Johnson was simply elsewhere in the town at that moment.

Dinwiddie and Braddock were dominating all, looking twin monarchs in their respective civil and military finery. The general, late of the Cold-stream Guards, was even older and plumper than Fat Bob, and much meaner of countenance, with great black, bushy eyebrows and a glutton's greasy lips and chins. Others about the table included Governors Sharpe of Maryland and Shirley of Massachusetts, DeLancey of New York and Morris of Pennsylvania, Dobbs of North Carolina, the twenty-nine-year-old commodore and son of the Earl of Albermarle, Augustus Keppel, and more ruffled and red-coated deputies, aides-de-camp and gentry than I'd seen gathered in a single room before.

And all eyes on wretched me!

Washington stood in a corner, nearer Braddock than Dinwiddie, remaining utterly still but staring at me with so much indignation, alarm, and anger you'd have thought me Chief Pontiac wielding a war club. Yet I had come to offer him succor. Here he was, obviously in the dock, brought to the bar of these powers. I would save him.

"Sirs! General Braddock! Excellencies," I stammered, looking from one to another. "Before you proceed further, you must know this. It was I who failed in the translation of those surrender terms! Not Colonel Washington!. The mistake was mine. I—"

"Who is this boy?" said Braddock, a most haughty fellow, turning to Dinwiddie.

The governor sighed and cast down his eyes. "A young sea captain, General. Late a scout in the Ohio. He's been twice out with Washington against the French in their country. Er, our country."

Braddock's color was rising. He would not look at me further, as if it were a grievous imposition. Instead, he brushed me away with a disdainful gesture of hand. "Gawd, what a place," said he.

I stood gape-mouthed as Washington, more quickly than I'd ever seen him move, stepped forth from his corner and came 'round the table, taking my arm hard and propelling me about toward the open doors to the corridor.

"But George—"

"Be quiet!"

I obeyed. Who would not? He kept hold of my arm as the doors slammed closed behind us. I tried to resume my protest but he continued on with me in tow. We took another turning, went through another door, and down stone steps to the front garden. The river beyond was full of ships and boats.

"What in hell were you doing?"

"Setting things aright. That confession—"

"I will not hear of that again! Do you understand?"

"Damn thee, sir, do you realize I've come all the way from France just to—"

"France? You've been to France?" He stared at me as if I'd said "moon."

"Yes. To Paris. To study art. I came back because—George, the newspapers there. They're full of vile calumny. They call you assassin, murderer!

There are pamphlets and broadsides, too—published on order of the French king. They're screaming for war and your head. George, they would justify every killing on the frontier now in your name! The English papers have taken up the cry, and vow a fight. And the gossip, sir, in London—"

"Thomas—"

"I came back to assure their lordships here that it was not your doing, that you meant not to sign a confession, that—"

"Damn all, Tick, shut up!"

I did so. A soldier was looking at us. I took notice that Washington was not in the blue and buff and red facings of a militia officer, that he wore no silver gorget of rank. They'd said he'd resigned.

Resigned? Or been dismissed?

"My situation is unclear, but I am at no hazard—unless by your ill-considered office."

"What?"

"Is your horse spent?" he asked.

"No. I managed a good one this leg of the journey."

"Good. Go get upon him and ride for Belvoir. I'll join you late this evening, perhaps in time for supper. Tell Mrs. Fairfax that I may be bringing an important guest."

"But George—"

"Go. I'll explain all. The King has set things right."

———

Neither Fairfax was at the house when I arrived, George William being somewhere back in Alexandria—odd that I'd not seen him, though he might well have been in that room of the Carlyle house, for all the time I'd had to seek acquaintances—and the lady of the plantation having absented herself for a late afternoon walk.

Rather than wait, I set out on foot to find her. Belvoir boasts some two thousand acres—or did before the Fairfaxes' recent abandonment of it for England—and I feared I might have to trudge every one of them, but I spied her from the river bluff upon which the main house sits. The land there is a neck where Dogue Creek reaches the Patowmack—not far downriver by vessel from Mount Vernon—and it was along the sandy shore of the latter I spied her walking. I made a fearful, sliding descent of the bluff to join her, attaining a measure of surprise and adding to my rearmost portions a substantial covering of dirt and leaves.

How happy was I always when this lady smiled, though she did so thinly, almost sadly.

"Thomas. You drop upon me as though from Heaven."

We embraced warmly, more than compensation for my rude welcome in Alexandria.

"We thought you dead," she said, though I think without full seriousness. "No letter. No word whatsoever."

"Not dead, but I thought I was in Heaven—well, rather Heaven and Hell combined."

"Combined? What place is this?"

"Paris, madame. I was in Paris."

"Thomas Morley! You've been to Paris!"

She touched me as though by this I'd attained a magical state. I wasn't certain she'd ever been out of Virginia, for all her being a Cary and now a Fairfax. At all events, she could not have traveled farther than Charleston or Philadelphia—and I knew she'd not been to England, though her husband kept promising that. Friend I'd been, but now I held her esteem and wonder.

"Is it as they say?" she asked.

"Paris? It is everything they say, and ten times more," I said.

"And London? Did you visit London?"

I told her everything as we resumed the sandy promenade, speaking as I might to my own sister, among these revelations the curious manner of Susannah's and my departure from Philadelphia, and the duplicity engaged in to secure the finance for our travels. When I spoke more of the squalor of Paris than the glitter, she turned me quickly back to news and doings of the English capital, and pried from my memory seemingly every sight and sound I'd witnessed. She loved my telling of the theatre, and took vicarious pleasure at Susannah's social progress. Small wonder these plantation ladies made such empresses of themselves in their own domains. They had so little else to make of their lives.

We reached the point at the confluence of the Pohick and Patowmack and walked to the end of a sprit of land bent downriver by the current. Standing there, it seemed only water all around us, as though we'd walked out onto the river. The sun was lowering behind us and there were great birds swooping low upon the water, for the fish were running. I saw eagles with snowy heads.

I pressed her for news. Was Mistress Anne Gist still present? Was she in communication with her father, and was he still in the mountains? Had his news borne any word of Mercy Ennis's fate?

Sally looked at me with such sweet melancholy. Anne remained in Tidewater, she said, but passed much of her time now helping out at the nearby residence of Colonel William Fairfax, Sally's father-in-law, as quarters at Belvoir were too confining to have the girl in permanent residence—whatever that might mean.

Yes, letters came regularly to Anne from her father, Christopher. They said nothing of Mercy. The atrocities continued in the mountains and the settlers were continuing their retreat from the frontier, but Will's Creek remained unharmed and unattacked and still in the hands of the English. It was being transformed into a fortress—at least, fort—a last redoubt that might yet be saved, now that the British army was here.

"George would be on the march against the French this very hour, but it's all now in the hands of governors and the general," she said.

"Does he stand in trouble with them? The confession he signed . . ."

"He was faulted—by some—for the loss at the Meadows, wherever that is, but there's been no reproach for any confession. I should think now all is forgiven, certainly by his friends, and he is not without them in Virginia. George is master of Mount Vernon now, and a good neighbor to all."

"You were a good neighbor to accept Miss Gist."

"Please, Thomas. I would not speak of this. Were she to stay at Mount Vernon . . . there would be talk, you can be sure. That is why she is here."

"Talk of what?"

Sally cast her eyes down and took my hand. Tears came welling forth. "Thomas, speak of this to no one."

"You may always count on me for that."

She spoke nearly in a whisper. "Miss Gist has not been with child."

"What?"

"Miss Gist has borne no child."

"Of course she has not. She is unmarried."

The look I got declared me naif—or the most damned fool.

"When she came, I had been made to understand that she was with child. Did you not know this? You brought her here."

"I knew only it was the Colonel's wish. He was not there to explain."

A long silence followed. Her eyes fell closed, and her lip trembled, but she said no more on the matter, except then to ask, "How long do you reckon that these troubles with the French and Indians will endure?"

I shrugged. "That's a matter for that general in Alexandria to decide. For the French part, I think they have already all they seek in this. The Indian? He would live here, on this river, without us. This Northern Neck. It belonged to them. Pocahontas was kidnapped somewhere along these Patowmack River bluffs, did you know?"

"Hers was a sad yet lovely story, but that was so long ago. The tales we hear now. These natives would strip us to our skin, flay meat from our bones and eat us. What they did to your friends the Ennises . . . I'm sorry, I should not speak of it. I fear for the Colonel, and for you, Thomas, if you go back there. I fear for us all."

The tide was rising, the river nearing our feet. Her tears had not abated. She was looking distraught and miserable, and her husband and Washington would be joining us soon.

"Sally," I said, "I gave him your letter."

"My letter?"

"Last year, before we marched for Great Meadows. You wrote one, then changed your mind and wrote a second letter to displace the first, which you wished me burn.

"Yes. Now I remember. Too well." She choked slightly and commenced to cough.

"Sally, I must confess something." I was so full of confession at that time.

"Pray spare me."

"Nay, you must know. I mixed those letters up and could not then tell the one from the other. So I gave him one picked at random. A vexing habit, my clinging to things I should discard. It's cost me dear. I destroyed the one remaining, but I know not which it was. I am sorry."

"Thomas. You gave him the wrong one."

" 'Tis so? In no respect did it change his abundant affection for you. I contented myself I'd done no great harm."

Sally turned away, her face coloring. "When you marry, Thomas, choose well."

The river was lapping at our shoes now.

"I would have married Mercy Ennis."

"Did you love her?"

"I still do."

"Then you chose well. Come, we tarry overlong." She took my hand and we leapt back to safer shore.

"I have a present for you," I said.

———

I had brought a gift to Susannah in London—a lace-and-silken fan of expensive manufacture, and the latest Paris fashion. But thoughtless I, nothing for this good friend of Virginia. My painting of Mercy would be hers, if she'd have it.

Despite my care in packing, the canvas was a little damaged, cracked and bent at the lower right-hand corner and scraped a bit where I'd painted a grove of trees in the background. Sally reacted to it with I think favorable astonishment. She'd not seen much art in Virginia, damaged or no.

"This is wonderfully pretty, Tick. Most attractive to the eye. But I fear the cost too dear."

We stood in the great entrance hall of her house, a chamber full of light, with the door open this nice spring day.

"Not at all, my lady. I am the artist."

" 'Tis true? You did this? You?"

I nodded, grinning foolishly.

"It's quite majestic. And very much our countryside. Who is this somber maiden who stares at us?"

"It's her, Sally. Mercy Ennis. At least as best I can recreate her."

"Oh Thomas, you must keep it then."

"No, please. It's the only oil painting I did while I was in France—that I've ever done, or finished, at any rate. All the rest were drawings and pastels. I mean for you to have it, if you've a place for such poor work in your house."

"I shall cherish it." She kissed my cheek. "No matter what," she added a little sadly, and began to roll the painting up once more.

I was guest to supper, and Washington did bring another, Captain Robert Orme, a ranking aide to General Braddock and the bewigged epitome of all that was finest in His Majesty's forces—and all that I despised. A handsome fellow, to be sure—though long of chin and exceedingly pale of skin—of such good family I think my Susannah might even have left her major for him, as that fellow was only brother to a minor baronet. This Orme was perfect in every detail of uniform—replete to highly polished black dragoon's knee boots and silly small tricornered hat covered in gold braid—thoroughly powdered besides, and even the tiniest perfumed. His brows seemed permanently arched, his eyelids perpetually in droop, his lips in immovable curl. He treated all present as social equals, even myself, but I think this was mere courtesy extended to the Fairfax house. For all the rest of America, excepting his good friend Governor Robert Hunter Morris of Pennsylvania, whose name found frequent mention, Orme was all contempt and disdain, especially as concerned the colonial military.

He had attended that afternoon a drill of the Virginia troops, more new recruits than old ones.

"They performed their evolutions and firings as well as could be expected," he said. "But their languid, spiritless, and unsoldier-like appearance, considered with the lowness and ignorance of most of their officers, gives little hopes of their future good behavior."

The last words were taken with two pinches of snuff, and thus more sniffed than spoken.

George William Fairfax, though his father was addressed as "Colonel" through hereditary right, had small understanding of military details and took Orme's commentary as inarguable, or at least not worthwhile disputing. Washington, though he'd seen his own "languid and spiritless" acquit themselves resolutely enough at Fort Necessity, made no comment.

I was less politic. "There are good men in Virginia's service, sir. Captain Stephen, our scout Christopher Gist, many, many more. I've seen them fight. They might be poor soldiery upon the drilling field and parade, but they know those woods and mountains, and they know their foe—which out there will be the Indian."

"The Indian?"

"Yes sir. The French alone could not withstand you. It is because they've won the Indians to their side that they possess the Ohio."

A flash of Orme's eye told me he was no friend, and never would be. He looked to George William Fairfax, his lips curling all the way into a smile. "There's your problem, sir. Your military counsel comes from sea captains, and young'uns at that."

Young'uns? Washington was not quite three years older than I, and Orme not yet thirty. I was twenty that year. More than man.

Fairfax smiled back, politely, as Orme returned his gaze to me. "Your Indians, sir, are a wild, unruly rabble. Aborigines. Upon the King's regular and disciplined troops, it is impossible they should make any impression. 'Tis General Braddock's view as well, and his good friend the Duke of Cumberland, heir to the throne and the architect of our designs in this campaign."

"Mr. Gist can take you to a hundred burnt and bloodied cabins where the Indians have made a most profound impression," I said. "Until you've put a stop to that, you'll have no victory."

Now Orme just laughed.

Poor Sally, her charm had dimmed. She was weary, and found no amusement in the talk of war. At her husband's suggestion, she retired after the supper's sweets. A somber figure, head bowed, back straight, candle held in two hands, as though appropriate to some mournful rite, she slowly ascended the stairs.

Port was brought, and sherry. Orme set about instructing me.

Braddock would have us all in Montreal by June, if boastful words were substitute for victory. After a healthy sip of the fortified wine, Orme leaned back and set forth the grand plan as authored by Cumberland, gesturing broadly with a sweep of arm and hand, as though the foe would be routed as easily.

The French were to be hit in four places at once. Braddock would strike from here, take Fort Duquesne, then sweep north to the Lake Erie forts and thence east again to Niagara. There he'd meet a force under Governor Shirley of Massachusetts, which would attack from that province and New York. In the meantime, Sir William Johnson, with colonial irregulars and his Iroquois allies of the Six Nations, would move north and seize Crown Point on Lake Champlain, while a fleet from New England would land an armed force in Acadia.

Braddock's army was more than meet for the task, Orme flatly boasted. He had the 44th Regiment, under Sir Peter Halkett, and the 48th Regiment of Colonel Thomas Dunbar's, both just arrived from Ireland and numbering in total some 1,350 men. Most were seasoned veterans, though both regiments had been brought up to strength with some "recruiting" among convicts.

Added to this would be about half a thousand colonials—Captain MacKay's Independent Company from South Carolina, another from New York, three Virginia companies, at least one from Maryland, and a group of rangers from North Carolina. All these did not include scouts, pioneers, artillerists, sutlers, wagoneers and others, plus a unique unit of some forty or fifty seamen from Commodore Keppel's Royal Navy flotilla anchored by the town. Experienced with ropes, blocks, and tackles, these sailors would haul and wrestle with the artillery—twelve-pounders, six-pounders, how-itzers, and field mortars. With such guns in play, Fort Duquesne would likely be reduced in a day.

"Twelve-pounders?" I asked. "Over Laurel Ridge?"

"I raised that point with His Excellency," said Washington, turning to Orme. "The tracks over some of those mountains are no more than a horse wide in some places—if that—as you know. But General Braddock has a plan to deal with such obstructions. He will build a road as he goes."

"Then you'll get there next year," I said.

I fear I was too impertinent in my tone. Captain Orme's smile now more exactly resembled a snarl.

"Hannibal crossed the Alps, young sir. You are acquainted with this general and this feat? Your Appalachians are but hillocks compared to the Alps."

"The Second Punic War," I said. He'd picked the wrong bumpkin for that impress. "But he lost fifteen thousand men in his passage, of forty thousand at the outset. He had to recruit among the Gallic and Celtic tribes to reinforce, the equivalent of our American Indians. But the Indians are already recruited—by the French."

My knowledge impressed him. I caught myself in mid gloat. It had been luck he'd hit upon a history I'd read. There were a multitude I hadn't.

"No Indians have ever taken field against such a force as we'll have, Thomas," said Washington. "The Spanish conquered Montezuma with fewer men than will march with Braddock."

"Does our young ship's captain here intend to join our expedition?" asked Orme. "Our seamen will appreciate another hand on the ropes."

This was smack across the face with gauntlet. "I am not a part of His Majesty's Royal Navy, sir. I go to Will's Creek, but on personal business."

"Surely no 'gentleman' has private concerns in such a place," said Orme.

"Then I am no gentleman."

He became very matter-of-fact. "What is your business there?"

"If at all possible, I am going to find and kill Chief Pontiac."

A dead silence fell. Sally's husband toyed with a small table knife. He had never much liked me, I think, and at that moment was doubtless pondering how soon I might be going elsewhere.

"Captain Morley's intended was kidnapped and feared murdered by Indians," said Washington, with some delicacy. "They are believed to have been Ottawa, led by this fierce Pontiac. They are western Indians who have come to fight with the French against us."

"Then they shall all soon be dead," said Orme, passing fingers to lips in response to an incipient yawn. "This Chief Pontiac among them."

"I would have a care, sir, not to put yourself near them until they are dead," I said, proceeding to describe the state of the bodies of Mr. Ennis and his two daughters when I came upon them.

An even stonier silence followed.

I rose and bowed to George William. "My apologies, sir. I think I will retire."

The door to the Fairfaxes' bedroom was ajar. As I passed it, I heard Sally coughing. I paused.

Not coughing, crying.

———

In the morning, on my way to the necessary, I encountered Washington returning from it.

"I leave today," I said. He stopped.

"But Thomas, why not wait and come with us?"

I nodded toward the house behind me. "I fear I have worn out my welcome already."

"You are always welcome at Belvoir."

"Not always."

"Captain Orme? Think nothing of that. All our Virginia officers respond to him as you. He's a good man, though, I think. Certainly an excellent officer. I expect you are merely unused to the ways of English gentlemen."

"Too used to them, George. And I would not go anywhere beside the likes of that one. You said *we* march. I thought you had resigned your commission."

"It resigned me. I commenced my service to this colony as adjutant major. Can you imagine me mere captain? Subservient to MacKay? Now that I have gained so much of the general's confidence?"

"It's in a good cause."

"All the more reason I be permitted to serve at the highest possible rank. I've applied again for a Royal commission in the regular army, nothing lower than major. General Braddock says there are no such vacant commissions available and that I would likely not wish to pay what one costs these days, even for lieutenant. But a way might yet be found. Dinwiddie remains obdurate, so displeased is he with the Virginia regiment. I am vexed. Still, I would go with Braddock to the Forks, if a way be found. He takes some getting used to, our general, but I like him. And I think he favors me. Every day he asks my advice."

"There is no unhappiness over your 'confession'?"

He grimaced. "There was, there was. But I have persuaded all that it amounts to French distortions of the truth."

"With war the result."

"Yes! The army's here. With armies, war. And I will be part of it."

He seemed to fidget, looking over the meadow to the river bluff, then back to me. "The combat here shall be quickly concluded, I think. You've seen the troops, Tick. Did you see the guns?"

"Those twelve-pounders will be a hell of a haul over Laurel Ridge—

and Chestnut. What Braddock needs more than cannon are Indians. Have you any?"

" 'Tis hoped. Dinwiddie has promises from his fellow governors in the Carolinas of Cherokees and Catawbas who will fight for King George. Christopher Gist has gone down that way recruiting. We're to meet him at Will's Creek, which is now Fort Cumberland."

I wondered at the whereabouts of Gist's daughter. At Will's Creek, she'd not strayed far from Washington, yet here there'd still been no sign of her.

"What of Half King?" I continued. "Cannot he find braves to join us?"

"I've a sadness to relate, Tom, for I know you were fond of him. Half King is dead. Last fall, at Paxton in Pennsylvania. Lord Fairfax was much devastated by the news."

Paxton was east of Carlisle, in the Piedmont of the Blue Mountains. Safe. A refuge.

"Killed?" I asked.

"No. He came there sickly, and in a few days died. He'd been very melancholy, I'm told."

"His fortunes did not prosper much as a British ally."

"They would were he with us now."

"We should do something for him, for his memory."

"What he would like is for us to kill many French and Indians. Those who were his enemies."

"George, I fear this campaign will not succeed."

"You err. This is the mightiest force ever set foot in North America. If only I could find my part in it." He was fidgeting.

"You do really wish to march with Braddock?"

"Yes! But not as captain. Not as nobody."

I thought a moment. "I think I know how you can do it."

He put a hand to his belly. "How?"

"As civilian."

"Civilian? I told you, sir, I will not be nobody. A civilian on a military campaign? I might as well be wagoneer, or pioneer with axe. All would outrank me."

"No sir. None would outrank you. You would be as I was when I accompanied you last year. You say you enjoy the general's favor. Your status would derive from that."

"He does favor me! I've served him every day since his arrival. Beyond favor, I daresay he depends upon my advice. There're few else about who know the country there, unless he hires Gist. But what of you? Will you join this army? I would have you with me again, as I would Gist. Let me sign you to the rolls as civilian scout."

"No rolls, no musters. I've no wish to serve under orders. I go back only to settle scores on behalf of those I've wronged."

He looked extremely uncomfortable.

"Including you, and my failing part in that confession," I said. "And for my part in the murder of Ensign Jumonville."

Washington appeared not to have truly listened to a word of it. He had turned and was heading up the path to the necessary again.

"But you've just gone," I called after him.

"I know," he said, hurrying faster. "I fear I am afflicted."

Thirty-one

The best part of war is the going to it, is it not? The gay colors and martial airs and blood-stirring drums, everything festive and celebratory, glory in promise if not in hand—and all of it mere days or weeks in advance of the smoke and confusion, mangled limbs and screams, stench and sickness, fatigue and terror, vermin and filth that are the truer nature of the military enterprise.

The town of Alexandria gave a jolly good show for the departure of the first of Braddock's regiments, Major Sir Peter Halkett's 44th Foot, which, with banners flying and drums tapping, marched for Winchester on April 10. The next day, Colonel Thomas Dunbar's 48th Foot creaked out of town in the midst of similar jubilation, taking with them General Braddock himself in his glorious carriage and plumage, all the colonial troops, the vast baggage train and principal artillery, and the assorted and sundry camp followers, including, as with the 44th, a sizable number of women.

This half of the army followed Halkett's tracks only to where the road drew opposite the mouth of Rock Creek at the place it empties into the Patowmack, just by a long, wooded island and three small, rocky islets, where I'd once come close to grounding the *Hannah*. Finding shoal water there shallow enough to provide easy fording, the 48th crossed the river and marched north through the hilly country of Maryland, taking a farmer's road to Frederick Town, where Braddock hoped to acquire more provender and transport and make rendezvous with colonial officials from Philadelphia, there to further discuss Pennsylvania's role in the war effort, such as the Quakers would allow. After that, he intended to strike westward through the Maryland mountains and come upon Will's Creek from that side—clearing that portion of country of any presence of the enemy while Halkett came on similarly disposed from the south.

Conspicuous by their absence in either division of troops on the march were Colonel, now Mister, Washington, and your correspondent.

The "affliction" besetting George that morning at Belvoir had not relented, but increased in its miseries. They were in fact now raging, and he was compelled to repair to Mount Vernon and confine himself there—never far from necessary or chamber pot.

I'd had the flux only mildly in my time. Franklin, as I was about to relate earlier, thought the malady was acquired through the drinking of water, that people poisoned their vitals drinking water tainted with the piss and other bodily toxins they regularly dispensed about their habitations. At all events, Washington was suffering it prodigiously, though he gave no complaint save one of thirst, and impatience with the duration of the thing.

There was a high casualty rate to this damnable plague, but I did not think Washington's life in terrible danger—never so near perishing as Susannah was on our voyage to England. But George was in a monstrous bad way in all other respects. He had sister Betty, sister-in-law Anne Washington, and hordes of servants to attend him, but their presence I think only increased his misery. He could not bear to have women see him in so foul and weak a situation. The thought of Sally attending upon him while so wretchedly indisposed struck him with great horror—though I think, some days, she did.

I had dispensed with "Tick," yet I found myself powerless to abandon George. I took quarters there at Mount Vernon and served him, sometimes welcome, sometimes not. From all reports, both halves of Braddock's army were moving with painful slowness, for all the clear and open road before them, and it would seem an easy matter to o'ertake either—should Washington recover in timely fashion.

He did not particularly, but tiring of his frustrating circumstance, of a sudden decided to join the general no matter what. You know, I have seen the man retain his coolness of mind under fire with bullets zinging through his clothing. I've seen him endure the worst imaginable ordeals, including that of our frozen night upon that Allegheny River island. But never have I witnessed such display of raw courage, fortitude, and resolve on the Colonel's part—or any man's—as when George grimly rose from his Mount Vernon chaise longue and set out to take his place with the army.

He could barely sit a horse, but did so, braving discomfort unto pain and risking more embarrassment than a man of his inherent dignity should be made to bear.

I think he wished terribly to have been part of that grand pageant of departure down Alexandria's high street, with drums and fifes and Mistress Sally's farewell kisses. Instead, we rolled out of Mount Vernon's stable yard at daybreak while all ladies were sleeping. If there was to be embarrassment, he'd not have them witness to it.

They were spared. I was not always.

———

Have I told you that Braddock was a voluptuary? This you might surmise of a man so physical in his tastes. He was sixty, but age seemed to diminish none of his appetites. He'd been at Gilbraltar before his American posting, and from all I'd heard from my fellow mariners about the pleasures to be had in that part of the Mediterranean, I'd say he'd never hungered for very long.

America was another matter. The ladies of Alexandria and the Northern Neck were flirtatious enough, but gads, not brazen. Unless he wished to indulge himself with females from the lower social stations—which for the common soldier in the wilderness meant Indian women—the general would find himself a bull in an empty pasture. But, veteran campaigner that he was, he'd come prepared for the road. Disembarking with the baggage from Braddock's ship had been a tall, red-haired, and handsome woman, I think Irish, and little seen thereafter—except about his quarters, and again briefly at Winchester, and one day at Will's Creek.

Over the years I've heard tales of the general having gone into battle with "his mistress," but this is not true. Of Braddock it must be said he did not favor women near or about the field of combat. He kept their numbers in our train as small as possible, and was good officer enough not to flaunt a bad example before ill-disciplined troops.

This red-haired lady was little apparent when we arrived in Frederick. In fact, we found the general fallen into the company of a Philadelphia colonial official by none other name than Benjamin Franklin! I came upon them dining together at the principal public house of the town, engaged in ribald discourse and, as I would learn later, preparing for less vicarious pleasures at a private house of Franklin's incomparable familiarity that evening. Whether the handsome Irish lady joined them is a matter for unseemly surmise.

Franklin, upon seeing me, was most anxious to renew our friendship, and even more so to embark on one with Washington in person—though shocked he was, joining our party outside, to find our brave Colonel barely able to dismount.

If feebly, Washington stood. Franklin examined him as he might some new scientific wonderment, then stuck out his hand and shook the Colonel's firmly—perhaps too firmly, as I saw George's eyelids sag in queasiness.

"You are the very giant I perceived from all accounts of your adventures, good sir," said Franklin as we sought the shade of a tree. "I am sorry to find you unwell, but once you are restored, I am sure there will be no Frenchman or Indian who can long resist you."

Puzzled by such gushing rhetoric, Washington muttered some vague reply, then shuffled to a near stump and sagged his huge body onto it. Franklin, still chattering, followed—to my amazement, seating himself in cross-legged Indian fashion on the ground. I knelt, on my good knee—the other still a discomfort.

"Captain Morley joined us at our refreshment," Franklin continued, "as I'm sorry you could not, Colonel. We addressed the subject of your wish to serve the general as aide-de-camp without military rank. The general asked my opinion, wondering as to the suitability of an arrangement so lacking in orthodoxy."

Franklin slapped Washington's knee. I was so glad it was not mine.

"Well, sir," he continued, "I replied with all candor that the single most very important thing the general could do to assure the success of his campaign would be to have George Washington attend him on it. No man in the colonies, save Sir William Johnson I said, has his skill with Indians or knowledge of the country or handiness with the French. No man better understands the greatness of the need to sweep the French lily from the Ohio country—from all this continent. 'He would be sharp spur to your army,' I told him. 'And eyes that will see what you know not is there.' In sum, indispensable."

Washington revived a little, color returning to his face, his eyes more widely open. "And his reply, sir?" he asked.

"He is pleased to invite you! Glad he is to have you for military reasons, but also to have another *gentleman* among his official family. He asked, if convenient, for you to call upon him in his quarters this afternoon."

"At what hour?"

"I would suggest this very moment. As I have discovered dining with him every day since he arrived in Frederick, he is fond of a bit of spirit with his coffee after the midday dinner, and I suspect he is at that now. Tarry and I fear you'll find him napping, and in no way disposed to waking. Or visitors. Except for his personal circle."

"It was thus when he was in Alexandria."

"Another thing, dear Colonel. You must be to great excess sanguinary in your remarks on this endeavor, for that is the general's mind. His words to me were this. 'I am to proceed to Niagara and having taken that, to Frontenac, if the season will allow time; and I suppose it will, for Duquesne can hardly detain me above three or four days, and then I can see nothing that will obstruct my march to Niagara.' "

"Except the lying-about here in Frederick," I said.

"Be still, Thomas," Franklin chided.

Once again Washington reached inside himself for strength and managed to rise, offering words of thanks and farewell, then slowly moving off toward the house Franklin indicated.

With Washington gone, Franklin had news—and questions—for me.

"Where have you put the beautiful Miss Smithson? There's a price in gold in Philadelphia for that knowledge—and your head! The forgiveness once granted you is well withdrawn."

Frederick lay just south of the Great Wagon Road that led quite directly to Philadelphia—connecting it thus with Winchester and the Shenandoah Valley. If Franklin could come to us with so little inconvenience, so could others. Here I should not linger long.

"She is in England," I said. "And happy. I think she'll be soon married, and to advantage. An officer of good family."

"But not to you?"

"Our friendship no longer leads in that direction. I found my love beyond the mountains. A lady who now is dead."

"Pray accept my sorrows and condolences."

"I thank you."

"I've small good news for you. Smithson and Butler have absented themselves from Philadelphia to tend to other business. You should be safe from them for the time the army is here. Your brother Richard remains in the city, but stricken by what he views as the theft of Susannah, and disconsolate at what he deems your criminality, he is insensibly drunk all the day. He is so drunk that I wonder if he drinks through the night in his sleep to awake in such stupor."

I cast my eyes down. "I would help him if I could, but he will do nothing that corks the jug. I mourn for him."

"Indeed you must, Thomas. Smithson and the vile Ambrose Butler have absented themselves to better indulge their greed. They are both gone to Africa, and thence to the Caribbees, on one of their ships—that mastered by your good man Riggins."

"Riggins? I'd hoped he'd take no command of a slaver."

"These are hard times for sailors. Your Richard sold your sloop, the *Hannah*."

"I feared he might."

Franklin winked. "Fret not. The purchaser was a friend, and the sale one of my own arrangement. She'll be waiting for you, if you do not tarry long in making your fortune."

"I've no interest in fortune."

"Right you are. War first, then fortune. But to continue, Butler and Smithson have taken ship to Africa and Hispaniola to set about what I would deem most treasonable. If there is war—and look about you, there it is—all trade with the French will be forbidden. Yet those two rascals go to the French Louis's colonies in the West Indies to assure themselves a continuing supply of Negroes from Afrique—Negroes sold now at a premium price. They are war profiteers, sir—as bad as spies. I commend your brother his drunkenness insofar as it keeps him from this odious mischief."

"To hell with them," I said. "They matter not to me. When this quarrel is settled—when I've done my duty here—I'm leaving. I don't know where, or care. Perhaps to Europe. Someday to Italy."

Franklin's countenance grew serious. " 'Someday' indeed. You'd best content yourself with these environs, Thomas, for I fear this affair with the French before us is a quarrel that will be a long time in coming settled."

He took me back to the public house and stood me to rum punch. His conversation then, alas, turned to wagons, which as Washington's associate, I compelled myself to listen to as necessary to duty, though I'd pale interest.

Franklin said Braddock had come to Frederick not only for provision, but for wagons and whatever else necessary to sustain the army in the field. His requirement was for a hundred or more vehicles at the minimum, but days of scrounging the Maryland countryside had produced only twenty-five, and those acquired through corrupt intermediaries who'd delivered shabby cartage for premium prices.

Incredibly, Franklin promised Braddock no fewer than one hundred fifty wagons, to be procured by honest shilling, with Franklin and his son William acting as Crown agent. There'd be driver and four horses to a wagon, plus fifteen hundred saddle or pack animals. The price for the former would be fifteen shillings a day, and two shillings a day for the latter, unless the horse came without saddle, which would reduce the rate to eighteen pence the day. All wagoneers and drovers would be exempt from soldiers' duties.

I fear I could not share the man's excitement in this.

———

That night, a message came to Washington by military messenger.

> Sir, the general, having been informed that you expressed some desire to make the campaign, but that you declined it upon the disagreeableness that you thought might arise from the regulation of command, has ordered me to acquaint you that he will be very glad of your company in his family, by which all inconveniences of that kind will be obviated.
> I shall think myself very happy to form an acquaintance with a person so universally esteemed, and shall use every opportunity of assuring you how much I am, Sir,
> Your most obedient servant,
> Robert Orme,
> Aide-de-Camp."

So, George was to be an aide to the general, without the bother of rank.

"I would have you serve me as I serve Braddock," Washington said. "You remain civilian, but duty-bound to me. I see no better way for you to travel with the army, and I'd not have you go up there alone."

I agreed, but only to the Forks of the Ohio. From that place, I'd return. I presumed that by then, I'd have my duty done.

———

I began to wonder about Braddock's generalship. He had split his force from his other regiment and gone all the way north to Frederick, thinking there was a direct road from there continuing west on the Maryland side of the Potowmack to Will's Creek. But there proved to be no such track—exist as it might in the great minds of the military planners in London. Braddock was compelled to follow the Great Wagon Road back across the Patowmack by means of William's Ferry, and thence onto the road to Winchester in the ruts laid by Halkett.

Washington rallied—promotion and advancement were always restoratives for him—took food as well as drink, and kept his saddle with minimal interruptions. With Braddock trailing such a long and slow baggage train, we had little fear of falling behind.

Halkett's 44th Foot had passed on through Winchester by the time we arrived, but elements of his soldiery and train were still in the town.

It was a rowdy place at the best of times, possessing some sixty crudely built structures, a great many of them taverns. Though it would later become a fixture of his life, Washington still called the town a "vile hole."

The farmers from the outlying country and the town tradesmen were decent enough folk, but the trappers, hunters, wagoneers, laborers, layabouts, thieves, vagabonds, and Indian traders were numerous and a constant plague—all of that compounded by the army's presence. Gambling, drinking, whoring, fighting, and murdering were so prevalent here in what they called "The Wild West" that the small log courthouse at the center of the place was more in business than the taverns, if that can be imagined.

The worst of it was the Indian women, who came to the town to exchange the use of their bodies for whiskey, rum, or money. They could be found aquiver in the weeds and bushes almost any time of day. It was well that Winchester was then so thickly surrounded by woods, but some of these ladies were in such haste to complete their commerce they plumped themselves down in the open wherever their partner might have them. I saw one couple so disported, with the Indian "maid" hanging forward over a hitching post, and this upon a morning.

Everywhere the punishment whip was in play. I saw one poor wagon driver, a man about my own age named Daniel Morgan, take four or five hundred lashes on his bare back from a drummer's whip, this for knocking down some British sergeant or officer. When through, his back was as red as a soldier's coat, the skin laced and tattered, yet he kept his bold and cocky grin, and with the help of a companion, retook his driver's seat and returned to the road.

"They lost count and skipped a stroke," the man told me later. "I took four hundred ninety-nine hard on my back, but they skipped the last one. I owe it to the King, but he'll not have it, the fooking bastard."

Morgan was a hired civilian, paid to transport flour, salt, and other necessities to the new Fort Cumberland at Will's Creek and return to Winchester for more, but despite his flogging, he remained with the army when it finally launched itself over the mountains. I made friends of a sort with him, and his companion, another young rustic named Daniel Boone, hoping that in their travels or sport with the Indian ladies, they might have picked up some word of Mercy and her fate, but they had none.

Washington said that had Morgan's insolence occurred in his command, he'd have likely had the fellow hanged or shot for striking an officer, but I think my friend George was merely in a foul mood. I could not deny him it, given his physical distress.

———

Braddock and the 48th had left Winchester on May 7 and spent a little more than two days on the dusty trail leading through the hills along the Patowmack. When we forded a stream called Cherry Run, Gist told me of a great cliff not far from there called Devil's Nose, and a dream he'd had of hurling an Indian enemy from it. I should have liked a diversion to see the oddity but there wasn't time. We were in Will's Creek on May 10.

The settlement had grown some in the passing year, with the population swollen with refugees, but the whole of it was now dwarfed by the great fort that had been built on the Maryland side of the Patowmack, just across the creek from the main settlement, facing the Ohio Company store and what had been Mr. Ennis's ordinary.

This fort was rather badly built, to be sure, thrown up in great haste the previous fall and improved in places over the winter, but for all that, tremendously strong, with four great blockhouses in the corners and substantial artillery. There were *abattoirs* and trenches established on two sides, with the Patowmack and Will's Creek protecting the fort from the southern and eastern approaches. It was no wonder to me now that no French claim had been pressed upon this place. If only Mercy and her father had been more sure of that, and less fretful to depart.

But then, I was most to blame for her impulse to flee.

On that same May 10 of our arrival, official orders were posted proclaiming. "Mr. Washington is appointed aide-de-camp to His Excellency General Braddock." That paper, and the entry made in the headquarters' orderly book, was as good as colonelcy to friend George. In most respects, in Braddock's name, it empowered him to give commands, yet required him to take none, save from the general.

His duties those first few days were confined to attending upon the general and keeping up said orderly book, but he minded not, given the vicissitudes of his lingering condition. He forbore uniform and gorget, of course, but adopted a blue suit of clothing of similar hue to that worn with red facings by the Virginia militia, and added to it, in military fashion, a sash. This had a dual purpose; it supported a sword and scabbard slung from the waist, and in case of wound or other injury, it provided the wherewithal for sling or litter.

I retained my nautical fashion of blue coat and white breeches—both pair I'd brought with me now well-stained by travel—but disdained sash or sword. I did acquire some good black boots, though not so fancy as Orme's. As mounted scout—we had horses aplenty for such purpose—I wanted no saber banging about, but otherwise amply armed myself with a saddle pistol, a smaller flintlock pistol for my belt, and the same long deer-slaying knife Gist'd given me.

Braddock had brought huge sums of money with him from England, and while much of that was retained in Williamsburg to be sent later to where he directed, he had some fifty thousand pounds' sterling under guard in his baggage. Yet he felt this insufficient, and on May 15, dispatched the under-utilized Washington all the way back to Hampton, Virginia, where the expedition's paymaster had stationed himself, to fetch an additional four thousand pounds to be distributed to the men, and return with it in time for the army's departure at the end of the month.

A challenge, this, for any fit rider, but Herculean for a man so undone by the flux and lack of nourishment. I urged George to beg off for reasons of health, but he was adamant he should go.

He bade me stay behind and not accompany him. "If your Chief Pontiac should present himself, and you not there for the killing of him, you'd not forgive yourself—or me," he said.

As Washington departed, Gist arrived, his mind hard on finance. He'd signed on again as guide and scout for His Majesty's forces, but was still in mid haggle over the price to be paid for his services, for accounts outstanding from his last service, for the loss of his plantation in the King's employ, for pack animals and supplies he'd brought in, and sundry other sums he believed owing.

Gist came highly recommended by both Dinwiddie and Washington, so the general was of no mind to ignore him, but he for certain found Gist's demands and protestations pesky and disagreeable, and so foisted him onto the high and mighty Orme, with instructions to settle these affairs and get on with plotting the course for the Forks. I was attendant upon one of Orme's conversations with the mountain man and must declare it hilarious. Gist was relentless, ignoring all disdain and insult, persevering until he walked away with a sack full of money.

Braddock forbade any address of me by the maritime honor of "Captain" lest it confuse the enlisted men. It would not do for some ill-chosen word of mine to send troops off where they shouldn't go. I accepted the "Mister" gladly. When I wished to repair to the ordinary with Gist for whiskey, a "Mister" needed no one's permission.

We sat at table there one afternoon, by the light and airy breeze of the open door. The whiskey was not so good as that of the late Mr. Ennis, but did for the day.

Gist gave me a steady gaze into my troubled eyes.

"Still no word of her, Tick. No sign. No rumors. Nothin'. I've been down the Blue Ridge almost to Carolina and back, and over to the high waters of the Youghiogheny. Nothin'. Countin' her, there's been now some one dozen settlers took by the French Indians, I mean beyond those they've killed and left. Only five of those captives been recovered. One woman, cut up bad, and four men—all burned, and I'd say from the look of them, tortured first. God, Tick, it tells you. I wish 'twere otherwise, but you've got to give her up."

"Not yet." I drank.

"When you were at Belvoir, did you see my daughter?"

"I did. Briefly. As I was leaving."

"And is she well?"

"She is well."

"And happy?"

"Not happy, but well."

"Why not happy?"

Gist looked older. His beard and hair were longer than I'd seen, but it wasn't that.

"I think she does not favor the people there. I think she would be here."

He thought upon this, pursing his lips in and out, then finally lifting his cup.

"I think she would rather be with Mr. Washington," I said finally, "than with his friends."

"Well, she is safe." Gist paused. "I brought a few Indians in to fight with us. You remember Chief Monakatooka, the Oneida who partnered up with Half King your first time out?"

"I do indeed. He is called also Scarroyaddy."

"Got him and seven braves. George Croghan's taken charge of them. He commands rangers here and will direct the Indians on point."

"Eight Indians, to screen this army?"

"Got American scouts, some British light horse in the van. And Groghan's got some Mohawks comin' in. Some fifty braves, plus their women." He looked at me. "What's your work in this?"

"I'm here to serve Washington and kill Chief Pontiac." Youthful bravado. I regretted the way that sounded soon as I heard it.

Gist smiled, but in kindly fashion. "You got people talkin' about that. Let's hope Pontiac don't get word of it, lest he come alookin' to kill you. He's like that. Big on vows and proclamations. But how's the general puttin' you to use?"

"I assist Washington, who serves officially as Braddock's aide-de-camp with Orme and all those 'gentlemen.' I suspect I'll be in some fashion courier. I mean to be forward when there's fighting, where they'll be Indians."

"Then you'll be up with me, and welcome for the scoutin'." He finished his cup and leaned his elbow on the rude table. "Though you'll need less bright a coat. You know about Half King?"

"Yes."

"I heard he was ailing, and that it might be his time, and so I rode for Paxton. He dead when I got there, but I was in time to see his spirit off in ceremony. I talked to Alequippa. Got drunk with her. She said Half King left words for you, a kind of prophesying."

"Prophecy?"

"He said to tell you all your questions about Mercy will be answered, but the answers will not make you happy."

I thought upon this. How could they? "I should expect not."

Gist rose. I could never get quite used to how long it took for him and Washington to become fully erect once they commenced rising.

"This is goin' to be a hellish war, Tick, what Colonel Washington brung upon us. They oughta name it for him, like Queen Anne's War. But this won't be like those little ones before. We're goin' to decide who owns this country with this one, and 'twill take a good deal of killin' before we have everyone agreein' on it."

"That's why I'm here." More youthful bravado.

"That's why we're all here. Only some's for the killin' and some's for the dyin'."

———

If Winchester had been a "vile hole," Fort Cumberland was becoming one viler. The mixture of so much soldiery, refugees, camp followers, Indian women, and frontier rogues and rascals—plus rum for the apparent taking—all confined in one place, proved too much for even King's army discipline. The fights and other mischief were maintained at a pace exceeding Winchester's, and the fornication was close on to biblical. The men, in uniform and not, were forever pouring rum and whiskey down one end of the squaws and intruding themselves on the other, with loud abandon and prodigious in the public view of it.

The consequent flogging went on apace, as though just another amusement at this ribald country fair, with no effect upon the profligacy of sin. At length, Croghan's Mohawk braves, tired of seeing their women so misused, protested to Braddock. He treated them contemptuously, but ordered a curtailment in the liquor ration.

Yet still the depravity continued—at great cost. The Mohawk braves became pronounced sullen and angry, and went to Braddock again to protest. They were received this time instead by Croghan and Orme—and what a painful audience was that.

The general did ultimately respond, with yet more costly effect. He banned the Indian women from the fort, settlement, and surrounding camp—driving them hence as pariahs. In fact, he ordered a sharp reduction in the number of women of all races to be allowed upon the march.

Before the problem with the squaws, the orders had stipulated "six women of the line" to be assigned to the traveling hospital, six women per company allowed to each regiment and the independent companies, four women to each of the Virginia and Maryland companies, two women to the seamen's detachment (hah), and two women to the troop of light horse.

After the Indian *amours*, Braddock decreed. "No more than two women per company will be allowed to march from this camp. A list of names of them that are allowed to stay with the troops to be given into the Major of Brigade, and any woman that is found in camp whose name is not in that list will for the first time be severely punished, and for the second, suffer death."

Women would suffer death, aright, but not by noose or firing squad. For all its severity, this order was greeted with much winkery. I know for fact that when we were compelled to divide our army again, something between thirty and fifty women marched with the first contingent.

I recall a letter that came to hand before we left Fort Cumberland, ill-writ and from a woman named Martha May, who'd been sent to gaol in Carlisle for speaking ill too freely and loudly of a colonel.

> *I have been a wife 22 years and have traveled with my hus-*
> *band every place and country the army has marcht too and have*
> *workt very hard since I was in the army. I hope yr Honor will*
> *be so good as to pardon me this onct that I may go with my*
> *poor husband one more time to carry him and my good officers*
> *water in ye hottest battle as I have done before.*

I brought this note to Orme, the nearest staff officer in authority. To my surprise, he read it through, smiled, and scribbled, "Petition of Martha May to carry water to soldiers in the heart of battle approved."

He'd done her no kind office, but that he could not know.

Braddock was not so arrogant or unwise as to grant himself exemption. The handsome red-haired lady, glimpsed once by me at Cumberland, at some distance, identifiable by her fine dress and hat, was not noticed again.

The Mohawks were all soon gone, taking to the woods after their ladies, and the few Oneidas and loyal Mingoes who made up Scarroyaddy's little band were all that was left of our native allies. Their interest lay more in settling score with old Indian enemies in the French camp than with any loyalty to King George II or his representative, General Braddock.

"He is a bad man," Scarroyaddy told me, relating to me also that Braddock had been overheard declaring to Orme and others that for all their alliance in the British cause, "No savage should inherit the land."

"He looks upon us as dogs," Scarroyaddy continued. "He never hears anything of what is said to him by us. When Gist tries to speak for us, the general listens to Croghan instead."

Washington, Gist, Croghan, Franklin—we all pressed upon Braddock the keen need for Indian scouts in this enterprise, and I believe he understood it. But he could not bring himself to treat civilly with the aborigine, and paid for this disdain.

No Catawba or any other southern Indian from the Carolinas ever did join our ranks. I later learned Governor Dobbs of North Carolina had withheld them, though some were ready to come north and fight. He had some private quarrel with Dinwiddie and this was his means of waging it.

Good Franklin arrived with nearly all the wagons promised, and heaps of victuals besides. These vehicles were not all in the best working order—indeed, a few collapsed ascending the first ridge—but he'd done his best, spent all the eight hundred pounds given him by Braddock for the procurement, plus two hundred pounds of his own wealth. Whatever our cause in these forests, here was the man who believed in it most.

He brought me a letter, boldly addressed to me but more discreetly writ entirely in French within, and from Susannah.

She bade me well, said she missed my company, hoped I should prosper in my purposes upon the frontier and that I should not perish from them, and then added that she was shortly to be married—by summer's end—

having become officially trothed to her major. As she noted in postscript, now she would be free of her father's despotism in perpetuity.

She signed it, *"Avec tendresse."*

————

Washington came galloping up on May 28—four hundred miles ridden back and forth and all in less than two weeks! He was much the thinner for his late illness and exertions, and came out of the saddle weakly, but withal, the slenderness improved his looks.

I wondered if, in that brief time, he stopped at Belvoir, but gave the curiosity no voice. He said nothing to Gist about his daughter.

We'd have to move soon. The army was damaging itself through quarrel and drink. You invite sickness when you crowd soldiers into one place like that for long. Yet our general wished to wait—for more provender and equipment, and most particularly for better animals. He had money enough to buy the strongest, fleetest horses in the land, were the locals willing to sell him any, but this was seldom the case.

June came, and on the evening of the sixth, Washington, Franklin, Gist, and I gathered to ourselves by a campfire, disdaining shelter to sleep in the open, for it looked to be a handsome night.

Washington was brooding, and seemed glad to be with good friends and away for once from the general's "family."

Franklin had through this visit, as on the last, been on friendly terms with Braddock, but now he spoke words of small amity.

"I would warn you good men to press your knowledge and advice upon the general whenever warrantable, and with full ardor. Allowed his own mind, I fear he'll seek trouble and find it."

I was shocked at the harsh judgment coming from someone so practiced at the "useful grease" of flattery. Gist nodded slowly, smoking his pipe. Washington sat still, gazing at Franklin, waiting to hear more.

"Young Shirley has written a letter," Franklin said.

He referred to a young man about my own age, son of the governor of Massachusetts and serving in this venture as Braddock's official secretary on the march. There were few in that army more intimately involved with the general.

"It went out two weeks ago," said Franklin, "writ to Governor Morris of my colony, good friend of Washington's good friend Captain Orme. Young Shirley's words bordered on mutinous. 'We have a General most judiciously chosen for being disqualified for the Service he is employed in, in almost every respect,' he wrote. 'He may be brave for ought I know, and he is honest in pecuniary Matters. But it's a joke to suppose that Secondary Officers can make Amends for the Defects of the First.' "

Franklin leaned nearer.

"Sirs," he said, "you are all of you secondary officers in your way, and

I strongly commend you to make no joke in amending the defects of this general! Our cause is too great."

More nods from Gist. An owl called. I thought of Mercy, she with me in the embrace of the woods on a night as starry as this. In my pocket, still crinkly with freshness despite its travels, was Susannah's letter.

I had as well that curl of her golden hair. And the polished mountain stone of Mercy's. If an Indian, I'd have been well-totemed.

Washington had a strong, clear baritone voice, but when he was vexed, it sounded grumbly.

"The general is no friend to these colonies," George said. "We're all the same as Ireland or Gilbraltar to him. He will represent us in a light we little deserve, for instead of blaming the individuals as he ought, he charges all his disappointments to a public supineness. He looks upon the country as void of both honor and honesty. We have frequent disputes on this, which are maintained with warmth upon both sides, but especially on his. He is incapable of arguing without warmth, or giving up any point he asserts, let it be ever so incompatible with reason."

I should here point out that on that day, George had argued with His Excellency over plans that, once Fort Duquesne and the Forks were attained, called for the building of a road east to the sea through Pennsylvania. Braddock would not expand the one already cut through Virginia. That colony's prosperity was not the general's concern, though it consumed Washington.

I said nothing on this subject then and won't belabor it now. But I will note that years later, long after all consequent to Braddock's march passed into mist and legend, I found reference to the general in a letter from Washington.

"True, true, he was unfortunate," George wrote. "But his character was too severely treated. He was one of the honestest and best men of any British officer with whom I have been acquainted. Even in the manner of fighting, he was not more to blame than others. Of all that were consulted, only one person objected to it."

That lone objector, of course, was aide-de-camp George Washington.

Thirty-two

On June 7, Braddock finally ordered his army forth into the mountains. The next fort ahead of us belonged to the French.

This departure from Fort Cumberland was not so festive as that from Alexandria, but the sheer size of the combined force set in motion gave the event the aspect of tableau. Soon enough, tableau macabre.

I rode mostly with Washington and the general's "family," though increasingly with Gist and Scarroyaddy up well in advance of the army. Once I fell back among the Royal Navy fellows, who were hauling artillery back behind the 48th and just ahead of the wagons and livestock.

Though Braddock had frowned upon it, Washington took to calling me "Captain" so the men would not mistake me as his servant, or of a rank not equivalent to officer. I was sometimes messenger, but mostly scout—pursuing not so much The Enemy as His Excellency the general's curiosities and vexations, as in "Someone ride to apprise me of what all that shouting is back there," or "Will someone ride to the van and inform Mr. Croghan to slow the pace of himself and his Indians." Several times I was sent to range to either side of the column in search of sources of fresh water, as many of the streams and runs that of normal cut across this way had vanished in the summer dry.

It was scary out there alone on the flank. I was glad I had traded my nautical blue for a drab brown coat.

Painful slow was our progress, even on the flats. Scouts and Indians would proceed, followed by the vanguard and flankers, who'd hold position while the pioneers—some six hundred strong and counting two hundred skilled axemen—would whack away at trees and brush, lever aside boulders, and smooth the way by plucking rocks or covering stony runs with shoveled dirt. They needed twelve-feet width on the road they made, for the largest of the wagons to pass, and it was hard won, every inch. Black powder had to be used to dislodge some of the more stubborn rock.

By June 11, we'd not gone much more than a dozen miles. Can you believe that? Mercy could have managed that in a morning on her fleet little feet. Washington, Gist, and I had done it in a day in the freezing depths of winter. The column was by then stretched to more than four miles long, and two nights the rear guard camped where the vanguard had broken camp the previous morning. At this rate, we'd greet the French as old men by the time we got to Fort Duquesne's gates. Even Orme conceded the difference between the simplicity of maps and the reality of mountain ridges.

Braddock, visibly concerned, ordered two six-pounder cannon and four mortars sent back to Fort Cumberland, and had wagon cargoes lightened, with the excess dispersed upon the packhorses as well as officers' spare mounts, who liked it not. We were carrying 140,000 musket flints, 54,000 nails, 10,000 sandbags, 1,000 hand grenades, 2,980 swords, and 600 shovels, among sundry items more.

On June 18, the main part of the army passed through a dark, forbidding wood that the locals, such as any remained, called "the Shades of Death," and at its end came upon an open valley I remembered well as "Little Meadows." There our pompous little quartermaster, Lieutenant Colonel Sir John St. Clair, had established a forward camp, including a small but highly serviceable fort erected in extremely quick time by a Major Chapman. Would that Fort Necessity had been so well-considered and constructed.

To this forward base, the only thrown up in advance on this campaign, we had come but twenty miles.

Barely repressing his fury at the slow progress, Braddock called a council of war. I was not, to be sure, invited to it, nor was Gist—only the general's "family" and senior officers—but Washington was, and I was sent to summon him to it. I found him in his tent, suffering a most awful relapse of the flux, and a high fever besides. Once again the sheer power of his will lifted him to his feet and propelled him staggering forth to the general's tent. I accompanied him, helping him keep his feet, then lingered just outside should he have need of me.

Thus I was privy to the discourse. Washington, sounding perfectly cogent and not at all someone hard put to maintain wakefulness, described the way ahead for the benefit of those officers present who knew nothing of it, which was all of them. It was, he observed, rougher country than what we'd crossed thus far, most especially the Laurel and Chestnut ridges. He urged Braddock to transform the larger part of his force into a flying column, leaving some of the artillery and nearly all the baggage with the remaining troops.

Traveling lightly, the larger group would move as swiftly as possible to the Forks, there to take position and hold the French within their fort until the rear guard came up with the rest of the artillery and the wherewithal for a siege. The long summer dry, which was approaching the proportions of a drought, had drastically lowered the levels of all the streams and rivers, rendering the Allegheny, Youghiogheny, French Creek, and other watery French supply routes impassable. Washington said he was therefore certain Fort Duquesne had not been reinforced and would not be by the time Braddock's army reached it.

This was sound counsel. It truly was. One cannot always take into account every possible mischance.

St. Clair, as timid as he was pompous, argued contemptuously that no professional officer would deliberately weaken his assault force when approaching combat, especially in a country so wild and little known and offering so many opportunities for ambush.

But Orme and Lieutenant Colonel Thomas Gage—the same who is

now a general, and whom I've had as guest to my Philadelphia table in the present rebellion—agreed with Washington, and so did Braddock.

Halkett's 44th would serve as the major component of this flying column, augmented by two independent companies, the Virginia militiamen, some pioneers and Navy men, thirteen pieces of artillery, including twelve-pounders, and thirty wagons—in all, some thirteen hundred fighting men, well equipped but poorly victualed. The other detachment, commanded by Colonel Dunbar and including the 48th Regiment, would follow along as fast and best it could.

In this manner did we proceed after that, but our progress was not much improved. Washington seethed.

"Instead of pushing on with vigor, without regarding a little rough road," he complained, "they're halting to level every molehill and erect bridges over every damned brook!"

If our pace seemed improved, it was only because Dunbar's rear guard was now moving even more slowly than we. If we were to stop, I wondered, would they commence moving backward?

More trouble. Washington's flux now smote him with great vengeance. He simply could not sit a horse anymore, as an army surgeon admonished him. George was so sick he could not muster even indignation when a covered wagon was brought up to transport him. Though I wasn't much experienced at it, my offer to serve as driver was accepted.

On June 25, we began to take note of French Indians. Trailing the column, lurking to either flank, they waited for stragglers, deserters, hunters, foragers, drovers—anyone straying from the main body. The first attack was upon a party of three officers' servants and a wagoneer who'd gone into the woods after stray horses. All four fell to ambush, the servants killed and scalped on the spot, the driver suffering a fatal wound from which he died after rejoining us. All eyes and ears kept sharp after that, but still the hovering Indians continued to pluck victims each day.

One of the surgeons, a Doctor Murdock, prescribed a substance for George called "Doctor James' Powders," a restorative for many ailments. Washington found it worked for his, at least in that it restored his spirits and reduced the frequency of his complaint. Still, he could not take to saddle. Our wagon and team were slow, the former in ill repair and the latter ill-guided by this correspondent, and we fell behind the lead column, ending up eventually in Dunbar's detachment. Striking a large rock and smashing down into a gully not long after, our wagon had its right front wheel shattered and the rest of its structure badly damaged.

Captain Stephen came up with a hundred mounted men leading a train of packhorses bearing flour for Braddock's advance column ahead and invited George to join him, but it couldn't be managed. Soon a line of wagons approached and we commandeered passage for George in the most comfortable of them. I took to a saddle horse and rode alongside.

We caught up with Braddock on July 8. He had made camp two miles off the Monongahela River at a place I knew to be about ten miles short of Frazier's cabin and but twelve from Fort Duquesne. We were as good as at our goal, if the French and Indians would permit.

There were some four hours of daylight left, but Braddock was feeling cautious this near the foe and wished to creep forward in hushed, careful, tentative movements. He posted reinforced pickets to reduce the menace of Indian attacks upon our periphery and ordered nearly all the scouts—not that we had many—forward into the forest in search of any French on the march toward us, or sign of ambush. The rest he commanded to take their ease, as the army would rise at 2:00 A.M. for the next morning's march.

Washington thereupon decided he'd not go an inch farther in any wagon, but would get himself into a saddle and stay there if he could. His best preparation, he thought, would be prolonged slumber, and he set to it on a bedroll in the open, without wish for a tent.

If not as sick as George, I felt as weary. I took a bit of food and whiskey, lighted a pipe, and was well-disposed to sleep myself. But no sooner had I dropped head to earth when I felt my shoulder being shaken and looked up into the grinning face of Christopher Gist.

"Scarroyaddy and me are going up to the Forks to reconnoiter the French. If you want to kill Ottawas, maybe you'd want to be there with us instead of here."

I looked to Washington, who was snoring. I hadn't come out here to dispense Doctor James' Powders. I struggled to my feet.

―――――

Gist usually rode horseback on the march and Scarroyaddy did sometimes, but on a prowl like this, we went afoot. A mounted man moving through thick forest might as well be an army, for all the stealth he'd achieve. Riding horseback at night through trees and brambles was no joy at all in any event, and the noise made would beckon a foe as much as would a clanging gong.

So we walked. I had exchanged my boots for moccasins, and felt every stone and twig sharply until remembering to lighten my step in Indian fashion and cease the white man's tromp.

Our pickets were nervous about us as we came through them on our way out, though they could mark us well in the light of afternoon and we gave the proper password. Gist said that in the morning, on our return, 'twould be better the army came upon us than we upon them. There were six of us out on this jaunt. Scarroyaddy and three of his warriors leading, in single file, with Gist and myself bringing up the rear, staying close together.

We spoke softly, and Gist kept a constant eye on the brave ahead of us. Four, five, six, a dozen times we stopped stone-still at his signal. I never heard anything worrisome enough to provoke such alarm, though I'm sure Scarroyaddy did. Wild animals broke cover numerous times when we surprised them—even I was moving with extraordinary quiet and gentleness—but we never saw a man.

That is, until we'd got across Turtle Creek and came in view of Frazier's cabin. It looked intact, the several small outbuildings as well, just as I remembered. The little structure seemed as inviting in the now-fading summer's daylight as it had that frozen morning we'd walked across the ice to reach it. I felt oddly sentimental, and had an impulse to visit it.

There was neither smoke nor flicker from cook fire. No sound save that of birds. Trader Frazier had moved back somewhere near Fort Cumberland. I thought I might have a look around, and advanced that way perhaps three paces.

The Indian brave ahead of Gist gave him a quick growl. Gist sent me a woodland sound for alarm we'd used on our previous marches. I halted, took note of his disapproving countenance, and retraced my steps, embarrassed. As I was preparing to resume the correct path, I glanced back at the cabin and will swear to you today, I saw a shadow by one corner move.

Thereafter, I was Tick to Gist's back, listened to everything, and said nothing. Some distance on, filing through a ravine and ascending the rise at its narrows, Gist and I saw a sitting figure at the top, his back to us, his musket leaned against a tree beside him, the strong scent of tobacco coming from his pipe. I would not have guessed him Indian, but in Indian fashion, he wore no shirt.

Our own Indians had seen him well in advance of us. As we stood there, motionless and uncertain, two of our braves leapt at the fellow from either side—one going high and the other low. In a trice they had him prone, his throat cut, and his scalp become Indian treasure. I'd not eaten, and was grateful.

Gist and I crept up and were chilled indeed to discover the victim a Frenchman—probably an officer. He had three grouse beside him; he'd been out on a shoot. It was a sign at least that they'd not expected us English quite so near.

Scarroyaddy and his braves had sufficient reward now for their trouble—taking the Frenchman's weapons, money and valuables, and game. They bid us return to Braddock's camp with them, but Gist declined, wanting to get as close as he could to the French fort.

After a quick look around, the Indians slipped back into the ravine and commenced their return. Now it was just Gist and me, within a mile and a half of the Forks and the enemy fort—and how many French and native allies? Some of the more panicky reports made to us by inbound settlers had put the French strength at two or three thousand, counting Indians, but that seemed doubtful. As Washington observed, the rivers were low, and it was a long walk from Montreal. Still, we had to see.

All we managed to glimpse was, remarkably, behind us and to the east, a column of smoke rising white in the twilight from a small valley. Gist pressed on regardless, heading toward the Monongahela riverbank to creep up along the lows and come at the fort from a direction we'd not be expected.

There was a large tree rising over the bank. Gist moved to the right of it and I swung 'round to the left. Immediate to my dropping to the lower ground, this enormous Indian with a painted face and great bone through his hair rose of a sudden before me.

Thirty-three

The Indian and I stared at each other for an eternity of immobility and silence—he desperate to know if I was French; I to know if he was Ottawa, and neither of us certain.

The night was nigh, but we were near the open space of the Monongahela, and the twilight's glow served to limn us both. He was much painted, and possibly a chief, because—odd as it seems to judge so much in an instant—he struck me as very proud.

His eyes went to my belt and its weapons, as mine did his. I had a pistol, but it would have been difficult to advance and cock that weapon—and the report would have brought all hell down upon us. Instead, I shifted my hand to my long bush knife. The Indian carried a musket, but we stood too close for him to bring it to bear without my taking hold of the barrel and thrusting it aside.

In his belt—and he was otherwise completely naked—he also carried tomahawk and scalping knife. His left hand was moving toward the latter thing, his right still holding the musket. In this numb, timeless vacuum, my mind pondered possibilities. My bush knife was longer than his scalping blade. If I pulled forth my weapon now, I could gain advantage. He might block me with his musket, but if I darted to the side, swiveling as I lunged with my knife, I could get him.

I did not want to kill him. Not then. I wished him to speak to me of the fate of Mercy Ennis. It was likely he knew nothing at all of her abduction—or murder—or anything about her. But I meant to know, no matter how I learned it.

The timelessness snapped. Gist suddenly loomed up behind the Indian like some shade rising from a grave. In a swift movement, he hit the man athwart the head with his rifle. I heard a crack, saw the head knocked to the side, and watched the Indian sag and crumple to his knees, and then fall headfirst to the soft earth.

Gist grabbed my arm.

"Is he dead?" I asked as he dragged me on.

"Don't know. Haste, Tick! Run!"

Ran we did, commencing a sort of lope that moved us over ground without too great a crashing of brush.

"Do you think you killed him?" I repeated between breaths.

"Maybe. Why didn't you? Had your knife out."

"Chris, he might have told us about Mercy."

"You don't want to know about Mercy. Keep up, Tick!"

He was pulling ahead. Gist was more than twice my age but a better man for this country. I kept hitting toe or knee against things he avoided nimbly.

"Was he Ottawa?"

"Might of been, with that hair ornament. Too dark to tell."

"Could he have been Pontiac?"

"Don't think so."

"Why not?"

"You'd be dead."

———

We were in time pursued. Gist heard them before I. There were not many, but they persevered. When it became apparent we could not outdistance them with the night descending, Gist urged me to run on by myself, straight along the trail, such as I could see it, and fast as I could manage, not to stop till he called my name. Meantime, he'd attempt to throw them off the track.

He told me afterward what he did. As I crashed on, he flung himself into some brush beside a thick tree. Two braves—that is all there were—came swiftly up. Gist sent one sprawling by swinging his rifle against the man's shins. The other brave whirled about, a tomahawk leaving his hand and whizzing just by Gist's hair, but before he could bring up another weapon, Gist's rifle butt went into his gut, and down he went, too. This quick action bought us some five or six minutes, and both of us escaped into the night.

Reunited at Turtle Creek, we slid down a long, steep bank into the water, waded upstream a way to throw off trackers, then ascended the opposite shore, another high incline. The steepness of these banks disturbed me. The creek here was not far from Fort Duquesne, and an ambush at this point could easily be waiting when the army came up. Beyond this watercourse, traversing heavily wooded and rugged ground, was a deep defile Gist called "the Narrows." Braddock's troops would have to pass through that as well to advance directly on the fort.

That place offered even more appetizing opportunity for waylaying. As we on our patrol had now certainly alarmed the foe, we could expect Indians, and even French regulars, at any time and any place.

Walking softly, we kept on in darkness in search of a safe place to rest for the remainder of the night, but blundered into Braddock's pickets instead. More than one musket was discharged at us. It was Croghan who heard and recognized Gist when the latter commenced a calling out, and so saved our lives. The noise made in all this was most regrettable, but better that than Gist and me slain.

———

It was still the thick of night when the army got up to prepare for the march. The troops seemed in surprisingly good spirits—a contrast to the sour demeanor they had more usually displayed in these mountains.

At the morning council of war, Gist warned them of possible ambush in the defiles we had encountered. The army the previous day had come through an extremely dangerous-looking long valley, emerging without noting a single Indian, and so were now disposed to incaution. There was a hopeful notion afoot that the French were in such awe of the British numbers that they were falling back, likely to abandon their Fort Duquesne and the Forks without shot or dispute. Gist tried to dispel this optimism.

"The Narrows're not fit for an army this size," he said. "And once you get through there, you got Turtle Creek. The water's low but the banks are high and steep, and damned impossible for wagons. Reducing the grade could take hours and we could get caught there should the French be out of their fort. Scarroyaddy and us come across some Indians and a French officer outside the palisades. The Frenchman's dead but those Indians, except for one of them, got away breathing."

Washington, looking terribly thin but still ready for the saddle, concurred in Gist's warning. He'd remembered this country better than I—in fact, had made numerous entries and maps concerning it in his several notebooks. He apologized for not informing the general of these dangers himself, pleading his illness.

"Damn all, then," said Braddock. "What's to be done?"

"Go 'round another way."

"Where?"

Washington looked to Gist. So, with only the slightest of condescending smiles, did Orme.

But Gist did have a solution. The Monongahela was also low in this near drought. Instead of pushing forth through the Narrows and attempting the creek's steep banks, he urged Braddock to turn the army back across the river, progress along the opposite bank in relative safety, then recross to the fort side once past the mouth of Turtle Creek and its dangers.

The general, surprising me, saw the sense in it. Only St. Clair demurred, suggesting the army wait here until Dunbar could come up, and only then march on the fort in the safety of increased numbers.

He was ignored. Avoiding such delay was why the flying column had been formed. It was time for it to fly in earnest. I had much the same feeling, a mix of fear and exhilaration, as when I'd been at sea and a storm approached. Live or die, I had no choice but to be in it. Live or die, here I was with George and Gist and Braddock. We should all sail forth now together, and all questions to be decided would be.

With the hour just past three in the morning, Braddock ordered Gage's advance guard forward to follow the detour suggested by Gist, and once back on the Fort Duquesne side of the Monongahela, to seize a bridgehead. This he would hold until the main body had come up and crossed.

Gage's troops moved out noisily, with some grumbling that I attributed to nervousness. We all felt it. In some of us, it was manifest as eagerness.

Gist was going on ahead again with the point, this time on horseback. He asked if I wanted to accompany him. Where else to be? I looked to Washington.

"Serve us there, Tom," he said. "If the enemy's found, ride back with all dispatch and tell us where they be. You know the ground."

Orme, of all people, sent an orderly to fetch me my horse. While waiting—Washington had turned to assisting Braddock in a study of some map—I checked my pistols, refreshed my ammunition and water, and walked a few paces into the trees.

I'll admit it, I was seeking some sense of Mercy's spirit. I was there in her cause and wished her blessing, her forgiveness, some sign of a spiritual awareness of what I was about.

I felt a thrill, what the French call *frisson*, as I groped my way into that gloom. I stood there a moment, then succumbed to an involuntary shudder, as though I had felt a touch. I took it for her blessing. In silence, I told her that I loved her.

Once mounted, Gist, Croghan, and I placed ourselves at the very tip of the renewed advance, with only Scarroyaddy and his warriors trotting on foot before us.

The Monongahela bottom had its slippery rocks and was three hundred yards wide, but the water scarcely came to a man's knees. We made the first crossing easily and moved upstream along the opposite shore without incident. Scarroyaddy pointed out the mouth of Turtle Creek as we went by it, continuing on to the next ford, where we stopped and looked and waited. Not a sound from the French. Not a sign.

We dismounted. Leaving the three of us white men to cover them, the Indians fanned out and hurried into the river at a crouch, muskets held at the ready. They vanished into the brush on the farther shore, then reappeared as silhouettes much higher up, among the trees.

Scarroyaddy waved us forth. Gist and Croghan went first. I followed with the horses, splashing too loudly. Behind me I saw a troop of light horse come down to the shore, shiny helmets glinting in the increasing glow of sunlight.

No bullet sang, but reaching the opposite bank, I made a terrible discovery. Gist had noted it, too, and was staring at me.

The weeds and brush at the water's edge were high and the trees thick enough to obscure a disturbing fact. The ground just beyond sloped up steeply and high, worse than the banks of Turtle Creek. This natural bulwark would have to be torn down and graded with picks and shovels before artillery or wagons could get up it. We might otherwise be leading the army into a predicament far worse than anything that had yet threatened it.

"Ride back and tell 'em," Croghan said. "We need troops up here. And all the pioneers."

I splashed back over the river and moved my horse with some speed through Gage's advancing body, urging that officer to get his men over the Monongahela quick, but not stopping to explain.

Braddock accepted my unhappy news with equanimity, ordering a sizable work party of pioneers up from the rear to attend to the grading problem. Whatever worries this new obstacle presented were balanced by the good news that we'd got our scouts across without a shot being fired and that Gage would soon be in position to hold the ground. All might yet go well.

I rode with Washington a while along the river shore as the column pressed on. He still seemed unwell but was quite quick of mind now, and much concentrated on the situation.

"A charming field for an encounter?" I asked, hoping to make clear my jest.

" 'Twill be the more charming once we're past it," he said.

"You are happier with our general?"

Washington glanced at me. "He is the only general we have."

We pulled to the side of the trail to let a file of axe men pass. The rising sun showed the path clearly.

Again I carried the totems of Mercy's polished crystal and Susannah's golden hair. I glanced at Washington's clothing. Tucked into his boot, puffed out just below his knee, was a pale blue cloth—a Lady's handkerchief, or modesty cloth.

"Are you thinking of her?" I asked..

"Of whom, sir?" he said, his voice low and somewhat stern.

"Your Sally."

He turned to face me square. I could see those large eyes clearly now, and they were not upon me happily. "We all have our duty, Thomas," he said. "See to yours."

With that, he turned his horse and moved back to his general.

———

Gage's men were nearly all across and into their position by the time I got back. I splashed past the last of them and spurred my excited horse up the steep, sandy bank. Gist and Croghan were standing well into the woods beyond.

"We'll be here too long a time, digging down that damned riverbank," Gist said. "Must be twelve feet high."

Croghan produced a small jug of whiskey, drank a deep draught and passed it round. "From here on, it'll be easy. These are sparse woods."

"I don't count it easy," said Gist. He took a pull of the liquor. "Not till we're past it."

Through all this, not a shot, a sound, or any glimpse of foe. Where were they? We were but a few miles now from our goal. As memory served, the ground hereafter was not so hilly and the trees spread much farther apart, almost like a park—just as Croghan said.

Gage, apparently at Braddock's urging, ordered all scouts forward to the remains of Frazier's cabin, with his advance party following. The habitation, as I'd not noticed in passing it the late evening before, had been burned on this side of it—all gone to charred timbers and dead coal and ash. No wonder it was uninhabited.

The sun was now bright crimson in the morning haze. The birds called. Insects buzzed everywhere. The laboring men at the riverbank raised a hum of their own with their muttering and grunting.

A bit of biscuit was served, and water. Those with liquor added that. By noon, the bluff was leveled and by two in the afternoon, the entire army was across. This day looked to make up for all the follies, miseries, and sundry misadventures thus far suffered.

Washington came up now with word for the scouts and Indians to move still farther out, screening both Gage's vanguard and St. Clair's working party, which would labor to make the trail into a more passable road as they went. George, who'd pulled his horse alongside mine, bade me stay with him.

"You seem in better humor now," I said.

"Crossing that river restored me. All our army moving through that water like a tide themselves. I tell you, Thomas, it was the most thrilling sight my eyes have known."

"The British Army can look a splendor," I said. "They're good at that."

"The general has pronounced his plan," Washington said. "It seems sound and prudent."

It was simple. We'd all march on until about three o'clock, then make camp, for it would be twelve hours since our starting. We'd be but three or so miles from the fort, and it would be a simple stroll the next morning to commence our siege, with cannon drawn up. The French would learn of our presence before then, of course, if they had not already, but no matter. We were too large a force to be attacked whilst entrenched in encampment, especially with artillery deployed.

"I'll keep hold my doubts till the last round's fired," said George. "But the worst we've got behind us. That long valley. The Narrows. Now Turtle Creek and the Monongahela. The rest's an easy walk, though I wish we had more Indians."

I leaned forward in my saddle, looking to watch the main units coming along. "At all events, I shall not sleep well tonight," I said.

"You're not much a man for killing, are you, Tom? Despite all your vows of vengeance."

"I must say I'm not."

"In truth, nor am I. There's a certain glory to battle, but it's not in the blood."

"When first we came this way," I said, "all this ground seemed ours. Now I feel an invader . . . in a foreign land."

"Not foreign yet."

He clicked his tongue and with a gentle flick of rein against his horse's flank, bolted forth and was away. There was no horseman so good in all this army.

I watched the army pass, as might a small boy watch a parade. Not counting those few regulars up far ahead with Gist and Croghan at the point, the advance party of Gage's numbered some three hundred men, both mounted and foot. Their column stretched some two hundred yards as it went by me.

Following Gage's mixed force were the elite grenadiers of the 44th Foot, and behind them, an independent company from New York led by Captain Robert Cholmley, beside whom rode Captain Horatio Gates—Horace Walpole's godson, and though then twenty-seven, an army officer since becoming a teenage lieutenant.

Next came the forward working party, led by St. Clair, axe men employed to either side but having no great labor to make on this stretch with so much space between the trees. There were engineers in this group as well, whose efforts would be needed most when we reached the fort and commenced to lay siege.

In line next was a string of wagons bearing, among much else, ammunition and tools, and guarded at their rear by a squadron of Virginia light horse, commanded by George's friend Captain Robert Stewart, who'd been with us in the defeat at Fort Necessity and been wounded.

Then came more pioneers, and the sailors from Commodore Keppel's fleet, who'd earned their meager pay hauling cannon over mountains and building endless bridges but were at leisure here, the major artillery pieces trundling easily along just to their rear with little need of their muscle.

Following behind them was a mixed contingent of the resplendent general's guard—the main body—some five hundred troops, both mounted and foot, moving along either side of the line of wagons. Riding in their midst, aides Orme and Washington to either side, was Braddock, attended also by a small mob of attendants and servants. To either side of this column, prodded along by a few drovers, were two herds of cattle, screened on their outer sides by Braddock's flank guards.

At the rear of this main body and wagon train came along the odd lots of sutlers, traders, and women—whose numbers this day (Braddock's earlier order being no longer well regarded) came I'd say close to fifty, including two quite older women and perhaps three or four young girls.

Though commander of the 48th Foot that made up the better part of the main body, Sir Peter Halkett was on this afternoon back with the army's rear guard, a force near two hundred strong and all Americans, most of them Virginians. Captain Adam Stephen was here, leading a company of rangers that would have been better put up at the front, ahead of the less knowledgeable Gage. Here also were Captain Robert Stobo; Captain Peyroney, the Swiss-born officer who as ensign had accompanied me for the surrender parley at Fort Necessity, and numerous others of my Williamsburg, Fredericksburg, and Alexandria acquaintances—all veterans of this country, unlike the Irish regulars, yet kept back in the rearmost file.

Despite Washington's strong endorsement of these men, Braddock continued to think the colonials less than soldiers, and would have them only in the rear.

I felt sorry for them, and swung back there to ride with Stephen a while—he glad of my company. I turned in the saddle just once to look back at the river, now completely clear of soldiery. I felt an odd chill, realizing fully how cut off we were. Colonel Dunbar was many miles to the rear. No other British troops were to be found this side of Fort Cumberland, and that lay now more than a hundred miles behind us. We were great in number, but we were alone.

I had a brandy flask and shared it with Stephen, then realized I had tarried too long away from my place at the front of the column and bade him farewell. Giving spur to my horse, I swung out into the parklike woods to canter my way forward along the column's right flank.

The army looked such a bright red river in the green. You couldn't miss a man of them—at least not in the regulars. Spying Braddock's party, I waved my hat to Washington, who responded with a lift of hand.

On and on, coursing through clumps of brush and over fallen logs, I rode past the sailors and guns, the cows and wagons, grenadiers and pioneers, all the way back up to Lieutenant Colonel Gage. The trail the army was following here led up a slight if long incline, beyond which I could not clearly make out the rude road's continuation. But the grade was easy. I suddenly felt quite giddy, a peculiar, thrilling happiness. We were but a short march from all we desired to do. Why stop at all this day? Why not just press on?

I gave a slightly crazed little yell. I was near one of the forward-flanking parties. There were twenty-five of these little groups all along the line of march—each a sergeant and ten privates. A few of the fellows in this one gave me an odd look.

Slowing to an easy trot, I passed a larger knot of men—twenty infantry led by a lieutenant—then the most forward-flanking party, and then a small body of light horse. Gist and Croghan were just ahead.

Something caught my eye forward and to the right, but it took a moment before I realized the significance of what I saw.

This was a small but commanding hill off to our side, its outline clearly perceived in the relative sparseness of the trees. It seemed harmless enough. No one was visible upon it.

But such a height would be a gift to an enemy attacking from that flank. That hill was as much a hazard to us as the Narrows and the banks of Turtle Creek, which we had so carefully avoided. Why hadn't Braddock moved to secure that mound until the column had passed? Was it haste, or great confidence in our situation? I thought of galloping back to him—or at least to Washington—and making gift of the intelligence that to this side lay what seemed to me, student of the Punic Wars that I was, a threat of no little potential.

But every man in the forward half of the army could see that hill and its barrenness of troops. Surely Braddock could, too.

I rode on. Perhaps Gist or Croghan knew something of the situation—or at least could advise as to what might be the best course of action here.

Spurring my horse forward once more, twisting it in and out among the trees, I passed the small body of Gage's light cavalry. A moment later, rounding a clump of brush, I came in view of the scouts and noticed Gist suddenly rise in his saddle, craning forward.

An instant later came a quickly rolling crash of musket fire. I heard a singing bullet fly over my head. It was quite high, but the sensation was not pleasant. I saw smoke among the trees ahead, and heard someone shout *"Tirez! Tirez!"*

"Shoot! Shoot!"

Those were not our men.

Thirty-four

As my horse pounded forward up the slight incline to the scene of combat, I looked quickly back to see how alone I was, relieved to note Gage's small troop of light horse coming up fast. Behind it were three or four score of infantry in tall hats running at the double. To the right of the column, in flanking position, more red uniforms. To my side on the left, a few more soldiers—the whole of us now lunging along toward the smoke hanging in the air ahead, the troops pressed toward it by officers.

The heat of the day had become that enveloping, almost palpable presence I'd come to hate on this march as I had the cold on our first trek over the mountains. I wondered how these running men in their heavy equipage could long endure, how they could even see with all the sweat that must be running into their eyes. The nearing prospect of battle wouldn't dry them much. It did not me. I envied the pioneers engaged in felling trees and leveling banks. They had stripped to shirts and skin.

More musket fire from the enemy ahead, a louder staccato of reports than before, adding to the pall of smoke—which I now could smell. Trotting my beast, I saw Gist drawn up tall behind a tree on the left, reloading his long rifle, no horse of his own in view. Two puffs of smoke exploded from brush just across the trail from him, but I realized it must be coming from our own Indians. Yes, there was Scarroyaddy, leaping up and yelling for having hit someone in the French party, then quickly gone from view, seeking other cover wherein to reload.

The musketry before us seemed more sporadically triggered than volleyed, marking it, I thought, as Indian. There seemed a hell of a lot of it directed toward me, with whizzings and thunks all about and one ball ticking my hat and knocking it yards behind me. In the saddle, sitting so high, I was a splendid target. How they could have missed, I know not, but suspect it was both the range and my mount's erratic progress, for it was quite crazed with the noise and jerking about.

Wishing to live a bit longer, I pulled it up and leapt quickly to the ground. Holding my horse's reins in trailing hand, I hurried crouching toward Gist and his protective tree, my mount somewhat calmer without me on its back—at least until a musket ball hit my saddle cantle, just where I would have been, causing the mount to buck. I pulled the reins hard and kept going.

The British redcoats coming up behind me now converged into a small mob, rushing toward the smoke, their officers driving them with imprecations. As they came up, I saw two or three of them drop—one quite near and grotesquely dead, lying faceup with nose smashed and gushing blood. The light-horse cavalrymen mingled there were taking bullets, too. But just behind them, a massed, better-disciplined group of infantry was approaching at the double and presenting a slightly broader front—though the way immediately ahead of us was narrow, the trail running through brush and gully.

My task then should have been to hurry back and make a report. With the enemy encountered and engaged, however unexpected, this was time to bring up the main body in preparation for useful deployment. But all I'd "scouted" were noise and smoke and French voices. I needed some knowledge.

Gist, when I got to him, was not firing, but waiting for a fair target, his eyes flicking back and forth. I don't know where Croghan was. I didn't encounter him again for several hours. Taking my reins in my left hand now, I pulled the pistol from my belt, checked the prime, and leveled at the enemy, but all I could see before me were smoke and vague silhouettes.

"How many?" I asked Gist.

"More'n we want."

I heard more Indian yelling from the French side. It grew louder, and then there were the bobbing heads of warriors on the run advancing—hundreds of them!

There came also shouts from our side. The light-horse troop, poor devils, were now all down or fled, but the massed infantry came crashing by Gist and me, abruptly halted, and presented their muskets with the front rank abruptly dropping to their knees—a sweating officer bellowing what sounded like parade-ground drill commands all the while.

Gist and I moved ahead ourselves—a bit out of this fight—to the column's left flank, into a patch of brambles that tore at our clothes and faces and hands but which we ignored. It was odd ground here. As I say, the trees were so high and broad in the branch there was great space between them, as in a park, but here and there brush and brambles grew in bunches and patches, providing ample cover for those combatants who got themselves down on the ground. The French Indians had been seeking the lip of this small ridge, and were now coming over it. My pistol still seemed rather useless but Gist raised his rifle, sitting back on his heel slightly to better balance its long barrel.

The Indians came nearer still, trying to spread out into the trees, in warrior custom. But they were not given the time to do so. The British infantry fired a volley that bowled over the mostly naked men with great violence, at least those the most advanced. Then, obedient to procedure, the first rank of British fell back to reload and the next line of troops presented to take the other's place. The look in the eyes of those turning rearward was deuced fearful, but discipline was holding.

Another volley. More French Indians down. This infantry officer of ours was a cool fellow. Suddenly he was a dead one, his hat, wig, and part of his head sailing backward as three separate projectiles. The remainder of him tottered, then fell stiffly sideways.

The British infantry, unsettled by this loss of its competent leader, now fell back a few paces en masse, to a point just behind us. More French

Indians came up, firing from cover where they found it. I could see some of their faces clearly, though not enough to recognize tribes. The warriors were wearing highly individual war paint beyond my ability to discern tribal difference.

Two of the brutes flung themselves behind a rotting log just ahead of us, and I could see dark topknots and gleaming pates. Still I couldn't bring myself to shoot. It wasn't that I shrank from joining the ranks of killers here. I'd killed, had I not? I was afraid to discharge my weapon and be caught helpless in the act of reloading. My other pistol was in my saddle.

Another, more ragged volley from our side. Several Indians fell, but many of our soldiers were dropping, too. Now the Indians suddenly began running back. I've read ludicrous accounts about Indians attacking forts and such in mobs and being mowed down like hay, but that's codswallop. The Indian does not charge pell-mell when he would expect defeat and his own passing. Confronted with that possibility he turns back and seeks an easier way. The Indian fights in a manner to survive his victories—if by deceit, ambush, and murder, all the better. So much less the risk, so much better assured the triumph.

What happened here was that, made to march with the French soldiers like troops and expecting to catch us at some more distant place—likely Turtle Creek or the Narrows—the enemy Indians had been caught by surprise in the collision of the two unsuspecting columns. This wasn't an ambush on their part, or anyone's. It was a colossal accident.

The enemy, at least, was trying to retrieve the situation. I could hear someone shouting to the Indians in French, calling to them to pull back and regroup. Then I saw the fellow, standing at the center of the trail. He was European, another of their handsome young men. I'd later learn his name was Captain Daniel-Hyacinthe-Marie-Lienard de Beaujeu—a pretty name to go with face. Beaujeu translates to "beautiful gambit," or "pretty play," as in gaming or cards. He wore leggings and boots, but his chest was bare in Indian fashion, except for his gorget of rank. He was altogether quite magnificent, seeming a heroic character out of antiquity, if not mythology.

He was an impossibly brave young officer, standing there so incautiously in the open and so close before us, a sword in one hand and a pistol in the other, but he was also a smart one. Though ordering his Indians to turn away from the front of our column, it was not to retreat. Rather, he was urging them to go roundabout and advance again out along both our flanks. I could see several warriors moving now in this manner through the trees to my left. In a minute or two, they'd be behind me, and more were following their path.

Gist's rifle discharged. The ball struck this remarkable Frenchman squarely in the chest and sent him flying backward, feet going into the air.

There were French Indians all over the field now. They'd been following this officer's instruction to fan out to the sides with much diligence. The man's magic with them must have been powerful, because his death brought them to a halt. As they stood, wavering, a flail of British bullets cut some more of them down.

I thought that now—if we seized this moment—a British rush with bayonets could yet turn these Indians away from us and back upon whatever main French force there was up the trail, breaking it or stalling it until our main body could come to the fore. We had stumbled upon our enemy without the slightest notion of their presence, surprising them as much as ourselves, but we could have our victory nevertheless, and soon—if only our men would move.

A charge down the trail and then oblique movements to either flank, spreading ourselves into a line across the woods, creating a wide front and sweeping all before it, bringing up our cannon to emphasize our point. Those French Indians who had been running along the sides of our column would be cut off, and would quickly perish. We'd have the day.

Where was Braddock? Washington? Halkett? Orme? Where was any to order the charge?

But we had no officer there capable of effecting this, nor men, I think, who could manage it. I shouted at the soldiery near, till my words came hoarsely, but to no purpose other than to vex them. One frightened fellow turned and fired a shot at me! It missed, but what did this portend?

The French Indians were all running now, but in sadness I saw it was indeed no retreat. Another one of these shirtless *monsieurs* had come up and was doing just as the slain Beaujeu had done—sending those Indians back around the sides of our column, trapping more and more of us the farther back along the army they progressed.

This man was another captain, name of Jean Daniel Dumas, as I'd learn having a drink with him in Paris some years after. He told me the worst casualties the French suffered that afternoon were in this initial collision of forces. After that, things began to go their way quickly.

Though this Dumas stayed much farther back from us then Beaujeu had been, Gist was marksman enough to have dropped him with a careful shot, but our able scout was not now interested in that. He pulled me down close, so he could be heard above the din of shouts and shooting.

"We stay here and we're dead, Tick. The Indians're getting to all sides of us."

"What do we do?"

"I'm going back to our militia. See if we can organize a way to fight ourselves out of this. These damned regulars're too scared. It's bad, Tick. Worse'n it looks."

"I'll go with you!"

"Nay, Tick. Go—"

An Indian came rushing up with musket in left hand and tomahawk rising in right. Gist shot away much of his stomach with his rifle in a one-handed firing, then rose in a crouch backing away, drawing me with him, ignoring his victim's hideous and loud lamentation. That brave must have hurt horribly, for normally the Indian is unwilling to make evident his pain and weakness in so unmanly a manner.

"You go to Washington, and get to him quick," Gist said to me as we backed along. "Tell him what's happening and that Braddock must see to the flanks. This army's got to get off the road and into those woods."

"You come with me," I said, gripping my frightened horse's reins tightly. "Ride postillion."

"No," said Gist. "I'll get shot up there, and slow you. Go! Keep your head down! Ride fast!"

As he spoke, more of our infantry came up. These men hadn't fired a shot, but their faces showed strain and apprehension. They'd never been in such country. They'd never fought Indians.

I swung into the saddle, pistol still in hand, head kept close to my mount's. Gist darted across the trail just ahead of me and into the brush and trees opposite, moving toward the rear. More gunfire sounded.

This newest infantry section to come up halted abruptly. A sergeant, standing next to a frightened young lieutenant, barked out more orders, and of a sudden I saw the flash of bayonets going to rifle barrels. Then they began marching off the trail, into the woods to the side—toward that unoccupied hill I'd marked as a threat to us. A sharp fellow, that sergeant or lieutenant, whichever was issuing commands.

But not ten paces in that direction, a barked order from somewhere in the column stayed them again. They about-faced and marched back to the trail, where they collided, mingling with another section of infantry moving up the path from behind them. More shouted orders came, sounding contradictory.

An Indian to my right had broken cover and was running to a new and closer position. I could not be so truant in this fight. Friends were dying. I fired my pistol and he went down—I don't know whether from wound or prudence. I stuck this weapon, now with barrel hot, into my belt and yanked forth the bigger saddle pistol, shoving my heels into my horse's flank.

The mount needed no such strong suggestion, charging forth in a mad gallop in the direction of peace and sanity. As I moved away from the fighting, red-coated soldiers along the trail leapt out of the way. I could see the incipient panic in their eyes. One snatched at my reins.

"What's happened?" he shouted. "Where're you going?"

I should have told him. Instead, I pushed him away with my foot and urged my horse on. Just ahead, men were unlimbering two artillery pieces, six-pounders that had earlier in the day been at the head of the column. I recalled Orme asking Gates during the last river crossing if he would continue with the guns at the point, as they'd kept getting in the way when obstacles were encountered.

"No, sir, I think not, for I doubt we shall have much occasion for them," Gage had said, "and they are troublesome to get forward before the roads are cut."

I saw Gage now, sitting mounted in portrait-painter's equestrian tableau with two aides. I came at him with hooves thundering.

"Morley!" he said with raised hand. "What ho?"

"Sir, the enemy's well upon us!"

"To the front? An ambuscade?"

"No, sir, but they are on your flanks now!"

He looked completely in a dither. I never did hear either of those six-pounders report. I maneuvered my horse around one of them and then darted to the trail again, taking a quick look back. There were redcoated men following me now, running fast, and not in military maneuver. One had dropped his musket. Looking ahead again, I saw a bare-chested mob mixed with soldiery and several grandly garbed officers in a knot at their rear. It was St. Clair's working party. Picks, shovels, and crowbars where muskets were needed. Many heads turned toward me as I galloped around them and by. I wondered if I looked as apprehensive as they, if they took my wild rearward ride to be flight.

Was it? In truth, I was scared to death. At Necessity, I'd been groggy, wounded, half-dead, and fairly drunk. Here, I heard every gunshot, shout, and scream. Every bullet seemed headed toward me.

There was an enormous report of volley fire, coming from the point. I turned my horse about, staggering to a stop, and looked over the heads of the working party to where Gage and his infantry had been. Most were still there, but he'd got a rank or two of them off the road and into the woods on the right. They'd loosed a volley and were preparing another. Volleys still? At Indians now hiding behind hillocks and trees?

No. I could see these redcoats' target. A huddling group of their own soldiery. I was enraged. They were firing at our own flanking parties, whom the Indian marauders were driving in on the column—and the firing was telling.

A bullet-severed branch came down on my head with a rush, a sharpness there cutting my brow. The damned Indians moving along the flanks had arrived this far down the line. If they reached the river behind our rear guard, we'd be cut off from that escape route and surrounded. How many of those Indians could there be?

Heels to horse again. Ahead now was a seeming endless train of soldiers and wagons, the troops coming on, their twin files sliding ahead of the more slowly moving line of wagons like boot coming off foot. As I drew near, they showed no intent of stepping aside for me, so I turned and sallied out beyond the trail, cantering again through the woods. A few Indian rounds came whining close, but none struck me or my mount. I was worried more about my horse stumbling and tumbling. At such a speed, the trees here would kill a man as good as a musket. At last I swung in again when I spied

Braddock and his officers. Some damned redcoat near the group had his musket up at my approach, but I just kicked it from his hands, as wrathfully as I could manage. Why weren't these men out in the woods, fighting?

Braddock, his fatness bulging and bouncing, was at a rough trot—Orme and Washington, as always, riding to either side. They pulled rein at my headlong approach. I almost crashed into the general. My horse reared and whirled about once before I could claim control of it and speak. There was no shooting as yet this far rear, but the noise forward was still dreadful, and coming nearer.

"The French, sir!" I shouted. "And Indians!"

I fought for calm. Of course it was the French—and Indians. Who else? Some Quaker farmers? Orme spoke. "How many?"

"Three, four hundred I could see. I think many more coming. Mostly Indians."

"I trust Gage is on them with great vivacity," said Orme.

Vivacity? Not even tenacity.

"There's much confusion." I extended my arm and waved it about from one side to another. "The Indians are now to either side of the column, sir. There and there and there! General, it is a peril!"

Braddock commenced a long stream of profanity, then said: "We must move up the main body at the double quick! Grenadiers! I want some of Halkett's grenadiers!" He turned to a young officer behind him.

"Lieutenant! My respects to Lieutenant Colonel Gordon. I want his full party to detach from the line and move up to reinforce the vanguard. And with all dispatch."

"You would detach him from the baggage train, sir?" said Orme.

"Baggage be damned!" said Braddock. "I fear we need save the day!"

The young lieutenant behind him took note and bolted his mount in the direction commanded.

Washington leaned toward the general from his saddle, speaking his first words of this exchange. "And the Americans, sir?"

"Yes! Them too! The Virginians. Move them forward. But leave sufficient rear guard."

Well now, an honor. The Virginia militia invited into action before the Maryland men. With an enormous if, alas, unsavory smile, Washington now leaned from his saddle the other way, toward me. "To the Virginians, Tom! Fetch 'em up! Stephen and Polson; Peroney if you find him!"

Thwit, thwit—two bullets racing by. The damned Indians now this far. I looked behind me, out to all the left of us, but could see nothing of them. *Swack!* A stout tree was hit. More firings, and then an awful neighing scream! I whirled my horse around.

Braddock was hit! No, 'twas his horse struck in the neck, going down and taking the general with him. He was a nimble fat man, though, popping out of the saddle and rolling away onto the ground before the dying mount could collapse heaving upon him.

Washington leapt from his own steed and was at the general's service in a trice, offering his arm. In the same moment, he looked back to me and reprovingly shouted: "Get the Virginians!"

What a ride through lunacy and hell was that which followed. The wagon train, which had been traveling between the two files of the main body, seemed in its rearward sections to have many masters, and they in little agreement as to conduct and course of march. Some were trying to move ahead, some trying to pull off the trail to admit more soldiery, and others, damn them—the majority, I fear—were trying to turn 'round however possible and head swiftly back to a land where no Indian hollered nor bullet flew.

All the meanwhile, Braddock's young lieutenant having posthaste delivered his message, the grenadiers were crowded about the path in commencement of orderly movement. Unfortunately, Lieutenant Colonel Gordon couldn't simply tell them to run ahead to the front. These proud and practiced troops had to be maneuvered, parade fashion, into a proper procession for the march, and it was nigh impossible to do in that mad swarming. Two officers were standing idly by, as though waiting for carriage horses to be hitched, conversing as one proffered what looked to be a snuffbox. I felt the urge to kick that, too, but kept on.

In the midst of all this bumbling and stumbling, the wagons backing and wagoneers cursing, the horses pawing and protesting and churning up dust, were all manner of other beasts; two pigs coming from I know not where and chased down the crowded trail by a young girl; a pack of dogs snarling for first lick at the open bowels of a shot horse; cattle braying and bumping, some with tongues lolling from the steamy heat.

Slapping my own miserable mount ever on with reins on rump, I pressed forth, dodging around more artillery—big twelve-pounders stuck there with nothing to shoot, the cannoneers standing as though for inspection. Behind them, the Navy men, little armed, lying or sitting about the ground, heads turned toward the chaos up the way but such nonchalance in their looks as if it was no concern of theirs.

Another mass of mixed humanity crowded the trail just beyond, sutlers and traders, the "scum of the earth." Also many of the women. I saw one lady, age indeterminate for her face and hair were streaked with dust and dirt and sweat, tottering along toward the battle with two water buckets that, for all I knew, she'd been toting since crossing the river. One had nearly all the water splashed out of it and the other had a hole through the side from which the water was pouring in a stream.

When had I last drunk water? This was all going into the earth, and judging by her daft expression, she had no ken of it. I reined my horse. The Virginians could wait these few brief seconds.

"Madam!" I cried, kicking my feet from the stirrups and sliding to the ground. She kept on tottering. No one was paying her any mind. Catching up, I put a hand on her shoulder and she turned 'round, this dazed, uncomprehending look still there, a half grin on her face. I guessed her age at twenty at the least, as she was missing many teeth.

"Madam, some water, please." She just stood there. I leaned over, cupping my hands into the still-laden bucket, bringing the cool liquid to my lips.

The water brought thirst for more. Down I went with cupped hands again, then slowly, carefully brought them back. Just as I was fully erect again, a musket ball came from nowhere, passed through one side of the woman's head and out the other. For an instant, but one whose memory I still bear, she remained standing, that foolish expression utterly unchanged, then fell as rags to the ground, the buckets dropped. I went to my knee and lifted her head, but she was of course gone. I pulled her to the side of the trail. Two ragged-looking men went for the bucket with the hole for the water still in it.

More firing. The Indians were now some two thirds of the way down our column. I returned to my saddle, my horse protesting, and thumped doggedly on along through another group of women. A man stood in my path just beyond, drinking from a keg I guessed contained rum. I kept my horse steady on and let it knock the man from our way. More stragglers. Some wagons whose drivers had decided on early retreat. A smart-looking group of red-coated regulars, Captain MacKay's company, trying to keep the teamsters going forward, but also skirmishing with Indians now. I saluted, pounding on.

Then at last there were our colonial militiamen. Not standing in the road like mindless men, they'd pulled off into the brush and were sitting and crouching in clumps beneath the trees both right and left. Some called out to me.

My mount was running at its fastest now, but freely. I'd moved my hands to the pommel, letting the reins hang loose. All to the sides was a blur. The trail was clear. Ahead I could see a bright, shimmering line of blue—the river!

It beckoned so. I do believe that for some seconds—it seemed minutes—my mind flirted with the notion of escape. I do not know to this day what prompted my lapse—the death of that unfortunate woman, a moment's neglect of the restraints on my fears? But I at last managed some small courage. Her name sounded. I pronounced it myself.

Mercy.

My horse's head turned sideways to the left, then twisted up to the right as I sharply drew back reins. It slowed, skittering, bucked once, rose up on its hind legs, then came down, circling round. Its flanks, all its ribs, were soaked and lathered, its eyes bulging.

I looked 'round. I was entirely alone. I'd gone all the way past the end of the column and now was some yards to the shy of it. All that was near me was a limping, scrawny dog, river-bound.

I headed back, turning off the trail into the woods, toward where I'd find remembered faces.

"It's Morley, Washington's man!" shouted someone, a happy-sounding sighting.

"Don't you know how to stop a horse, Morley?"

"Where's the fight? What's happening?"

"Where's Washington?"

I looked about the faces of those gathering 'round me. "Where's Captain Stephen?" I asked.

"He took his company up the left there, after some Indians."

"We ain't seen a goddamn thing back here, but we been hearin' plenty."

"You there, sir," said a voice behind me. "Who do you seek?"

I turned my horse to see a tallish man wearing spectacles, a blue militia officer's coat and drab brown trousers. He carried no sword but had a pistol in a crimson sash.

"I'm Thomas Morley—with Washington. He sent me back to fetch the Virginia companies."

"That's us. I'm Captain William Polson." I remembered. A storekeeper and bookseller of Hampton. I'd visited his establishment.

"We need haste, sir," I said. "The van of the column has plowed into a lot of French. Braddock's called the main body up, and you Virginia companies are needed, too. Got Indians on both flanks. They're killing us."

He had no horse. I descended from mine again and pulled it protesting forward.

"I'll show you," I said.

———

Returning to the melee ahead was much the same as intruding one's hand upon a fire after having it once burnt. But my courage had fully returned, what there was of it. At all events, both cowards and brave men were dying equally here. The Virginians I'd found were anxious to get in the fight, feeling marooned and useless standing idled at the very rear.

There were three companies of them now, for Stephen joined our rapid march, and Stobo with him. MacKay's independents did not, turning to meet another need that had arisen. I could hear his men making sharp reports of musket to a new threat off to the right and rear. The damned French Indians had now gotten along the entire column and were attacking the back of us! MacKay was all that could save us from being cut off from the Monongahela.

I saw dead now here and there along the entire way. Among them was a young woman, shot in the back, not far from our heroine, the water carrier. Men in civilian clothes lay sprawled and bloodied, including the one I'd seen drinking from a keg. And now, soldiery—white breeches and leggings and those crimson coats—looking broken toys.

Some of our Virginia men dropped, but the whole of us kept going—past wagons, past guns, into throngs of soldiers seeking order, but causing confusion.

Braddock had his grenadiers and much else of the main body quite farther along now, and he had gone with them. Pushing our way through these complaining redcoats, we got to a point where I could see the general's party—and damned exposed it was.

I began to run. Where I found strength for this, I could not say. My thirst was terrible again, my clothes so soaked with sweat I felt aswim. The whining bullets were a constancy now. There was inspiration enough for my zeal.

Braddock was on a different horse, his wig gone, his face flushed deep red with heat and perplexity. Washington was afoot, his own horse down and dead. Orme was still on his original mount, peering through a spyglass, at what I could not say, as all we had of the enemy in perception were his bullets.

"Forward, you men, you Americans!" cried Braddock. "Bolster the front."

Polson, just behind me, shouted some obedience and led his company onward with a wave of the arm. I turned to Washington. A ball had torn the shoulder off his coat. Another, most miraculous, had pierced two holes in his shirt, neatly side by side, perhaps passing through a fold as he'd leaned forward in the saddle.

He hadn't noticed this. Looking down at these apertures, he commenced to laugh, not a little repressed hysteria bubbling free in that.

"You're not hurt?" I asked.

"No, Tom, but you?" He touched my forehead and his fingers came away with sticky blood.

"A tree branch," I said, remembering. "I'm well."

Washington clapped me on the shoulder.

"I fear a dire shambles." he said, turning away from his general. "You stay with the Virginians. The right flank needs them most. The firing's hottest there. Gordon's gone up but . . ." He shrugged. "I don't know."

I pulled my mount forward and set its reins in George's hand. "Take it," I said. "No room for a horse where I go."

Another clap on the shoulder. Stephen and his men were coming by. The captain called out a greeting. An older, portly man nearby him of a sudden sank to his knees and peered at his rounded stomach, from which blood and gore were oozing. Stephen went to help him but by then, the fellow was dead—I think from the shock of assessing his injury.

We ran. The bullets were coming from both sides. At lengths along the line, the British soldiers were forming back to back in several ranks, firing volleys that seemed to go high in the air.

Ascending an incline now, we came upon the most grotesque sight of this combat, a carnage monumental in its grandeur. Gordon's grenadiers had run up as commanded, colliding in horrifying impact with Gage's advance guard, hurrying back in full retreat.

It was awful. The men appeared leaderless. I could see two officers down and one definitely dead. Soldiery was milling about frantically, shouting and cursing, some crying. Muskets were being discharged every which way. And men were falling, some to Indian fire from the left, but most from a devastatingly constant and direct fire coming from that hill to the right, the one I'd passed and seen the menace of on my first advance to the front.

Polson had seen it, too. He moved his men out into the woods. Taking to the cover of the trees, they progressed piecemeal forward, leapfrogging, one man covering while the other advanced.

The French-and-Indian firing from the hill was still heavy, but not so effective against Polson's tactic. The enemy instead poured most of its lead over the heads of the Virginians and into the writhing mob of redcoats on the trail behind. If we could take that hilltop, we'd have a strong point on which to anchor our line and make some martial sense out of this chaos. At the least, we'd have the Indians on this side of the column flanked and on lower ground—and cut off from their fellows. We could establish a front, instead of receiving fire from all directions.

Polson, small merchant and bookseller, could see this. Gordon and Gage could not, or would not—or had lost complete control of their men. Somewhere in that melee was St. Clair, but he'd in no way I could see made his presence known and felt.

Stephen was beside me, pointing down a line of trees.

"We've just got the Indians out of there, and killed some," he said. "All in great quickness. You get at 'em like this and they'll run. I'll keep my men moving this way 'round to the side of the hill and enfilade their position. Probably some French up there, too. Tell Polson to keep pressing the front like he is and we'll have 'em squeezed."

Not a clap but a thump on my shoulder from him and he was gone, running low in zigs and zags from tree to tree, rejoining the main portion of his company.

Someone's musket had fallen. I picked it up and checked its load, then set off for Polson, crouching and running, coming up to three men and passing on before I finally found him. He'd been taking Stephen's instruction without hearing it. His men were spread out through the woods, advancing well. If there were French on that hill, behind shelter and waiting, we'd have a hard time of it. But the Indians would scatter once they'd lost their cover. We might yet have the day. At least that hill.

Then there was a horror of musketry crashing all about. I say horror in speaking not of only of its violence, but of its direction. It was coming from our own line, from the column on the trail, from the bloody British Army. And it was not aimless. Here a Virginian behind a tree went down, gasping. There another. Another and another, all shot through the back.

Some of them, alarmed to see what was at work, desperately sought the outward side of their trees, but there the enemy saw them, and down they went. Some started running back toward the road, but were hit in both chest and back. Polson shouted to the redcoats to stop their damned shooting, their damned murder. A brief faltering of the musket fire let me hear the reply.

"We got orders! Fire on the men in the trees!"

God Almighty, I swear I would have signed a subscription to the most seditious of Franklin's pronouncements right then and there. I'd mind enough to go over to the French, who—whatever else might be said of their cause—at least fought sanely, and damned well.

The shooting resumed its intensity. More Virginians fell—blood spurting from their backs! I rolled over, lifting my musket with some strain and aiming at the lout who'd told us about his "orders." A hand shoved my barrel to the ground. It was Polson.

"Don't do it!" he said. "I'd shoot him myself, but if we start doing that, they'll kill every man of us and claim reason!"

Shaking his head in fury, frustration, and incredible sorrow, Polson began calling his men back, telling them to crawl back to the road, keeping flat.

We could have taken that hill, damn all! We could have walked up and pushed the French and Indians from it in accord with Stephen's plan. I shall always know that we could have done it.

But that grand chance was gone. I crawled along, my face much in the dirt, musket balls flinging bits of it into my eyes, the shooting still coming from all directions. I tried to think of Mercy, but all that came to my mind was that water woman and her mad grin, and the bullet's visitation. What "war" was this when women so perished? What "honor" and "glory" in such as this? I never wanted to hear those words again, not spoken by men in King's uniforms.

The nearer I got to the column, though, the less willing they seemed to shoot me. The regulars weren't firing out of malice or mischief, but in insane panic. All around them, men were falling from wound or death, yet no Indian could be seen. So they shot at anyone they could see, any poor soul not wearing the King's red uniform. Many fired high. At what, flying Indians? At God? What wretches, these. But when I got near their feet, they spared me.

Reaching the trail, I stood up, warily, but found myself ignored now. Two other men of Polson's company came straggling in, one missing the lower part of an arm. Gist slipped out from behind a tree, hurried a few paces and joined us on the trail, looking deadly grim.

"Where's Captain Polson?" I asked.

He pointed behind him. Twenty or thirty yards distant, the man lay dead. All about the woods we'd crawled through were men's bodies, some still moving, most not. Polson's company had ceased to exist, nearly all victim to British ball.

These craven redcoats were tightly packed now, striking each other with their weapons as they turned to reload. They were crammed back to back, side to side, wedged together all along the trail sometimes five ranks thick, sometimes ten. Where were their officers?

Most of these gentlemen were strewn about the trail side, some of them I think struck by British rounds, too, and with unfriendly purpose.

One "officer" decidedly was not dead. Washington, galloping up now on yet another horse, pulled rein with coattails flying, stopping at the point where Stephen's company had gone into the woods. Dismounting, he waded into the British line with sword in hand, pulling soldiers this way and that and bellowing to cease fire. Why any of them didn't bayonet or shoot him, I don't know. He was not in uniform, bore no rank, and as best I could recollect, had never issued a command to these men before. He'd been seen throughout the march as part of the general's "family," but that was small money in this quarrel. These men had ignored and defied commanders they'd had for years, and as I note, had shot a few.

Yet bold George, towering over them like a wrathful god, lashing them as much with those icy blue-gray eyes as with the fury of his voice, had them cowering before him—most of them anyway.

He saw us—Gist and me—and shoved his way close. "Where is Stephen? Where is Polson's company?"

"Stephen's with his men in the woods. Polson . . ." My eyes went tearful. I waved helplessly at the woods behind us. "Through the back, George. British rounds."

Washington raged. I think he would have run his sword through all the redcoats at hand had not one of them just then taken a shot in the groin and fallen over screaming. After that came more shouting, from back in the woods. Men were running toward us, darting from tree to tree. It was Stephen's company. Unsupported by a frontal assault, his flanking maneuver had failed. Captain Peroney had also taken his Virginia company out into the woods—in support of Stephen—but caught too much of the British fire from the rear that had murdered Polson's men. Now he was coming back as well.

As I knew would happen, one or two of the fear-crazed bastards in ranks before us loosed fire on these Virginians now. George snatched away my pistol and blasted it toward one of the fool soldiers, just missing his head. In two strides he was at the file and striking the idiots with the flat of his sword, bellowing, "Cease fire! Those are our men!"

And so it passed. Wherever Washington was in this mad melee, he commanded. Stephen got his men in with only a few new casualties, but barely able to restrain himself from murdering the British.

"You dogs!" He shouted at the regulars. "You infamous dogs!"

Stobo's Virginia detachment had gone up the column to support the vanguard and been caught in the chaos of Gage's collision with Gordon.

Stobo and his survivors were now pulling back, hurrying toward us in a mob. The crammed British ranks to either side of Washington kept to their discipline now and held their fire. At his order, a platoon even moved forward off the trail, spread out to make a space between each man and knelt, presenting arms toward the enemy—the whole of it greatly reducing their risk.

But if George thought he'd set an example here for all the army to follow, he was as deluded as some of these fool King's regulars. Elsewhere up and down the line, madness and cowardice reigned intertwined. And all the while, our numbers steadily decreased. The French could not possibly be suffering in like fashion. I wondered how any of them could be hurt.

The Indians were little exposed. One would appear of a sudden beside a tree, fire his round in a second or two, then vanish before a reply could be made.

Gist, impossibly calm, was playing marksmanship games, waiting with rifle aimed at a chest-high point on a likely enemy tree. When, as often occurred, an Indian appeared, off went Gist's round and gone was the warrior—usually for good. If all the army were doing this, we could have strolled to the fort come supper time with naught to stay us. But Gist had few emulators. I took a dead man's musket again and tried Gist's trick, but picked unproductive trees, or became impatient and moved my aiming point just as the original grew head and shoulders to the other side of a tree trunk. Sometimes I simply missed. Muskets were not rifles.

A runner came up. General Braddock's respects. Could Washington return? Captain Orme was wounded, St. Clair was down, and so was Halkett. The two six-pounders at the point had been taken by the enemy and might soon be used against us.

George was trying to get litter-bearers assembled to take the wounded back to the river, but had met with little success, as few of the uninjured soldiers were willing to put down their weapons to attend to the less fortunate. At all events, there seemed little headway for stretchers to make on this crowded trail to the rear.

Before Washington could fully respond to the messenger, we heard a loud burst of noise at the head of the column and strained to see its source, wondering if it was one of these lost cannon, fulfilling the messenger's prophecy. Just then another runner came up. Now the wagon train and baggage behind was under severe attack. Could the Virginia companies be spared to help again at the rear?

Not only spared, but eager, at least to be away from this anarchic place. With Stephen leading, they moved out, pushing redcoats aside and dodging gunfire as they ran.

As he headed back for the general, Washington continued to pull the line together in some discipline as best he could. I saw Lieutenant Colonel Burton farther along the column, managing the same orderly accomplishment. But elsewhere—up and down the trail and all around—it was awful. The regulars were now packed twenty or thirty deep, fighting each other for a chance to get to the center, there the safest, or so they thought. Other ranks were standing in form but had recommenced these mindless volleys into the air. They'd leave the field having killed as many birds as men—if leave they could.

Another runner with Captain Orme's respects and serious news. The general was down with a wound and Mister Washington's presence was desired immediately.

All else was now forgotten. "Tick!" said Washington. "Attend me!"

He moved in great strides. I followed as best I could, but fell behind.

Braddock down. Halkett, too, and St. Clair. Burton was next in line of command, but he was forward with Gage and all but trapped. Who could lead? Orme? He was wounded, though well enough to be sending messages.

The man who should command was there ahead of me. To think they had made him a civilian aide because no sufficient military rank could be found for him.

But now arrived another messenger. And where was Orme finding these? I was at George's side before the fellow spoke. It struck me the dispatch he bore was that Braddock had died.

No! Good God, it was to inform us of an advance! And one ordered by the wounded Braddock! As a last gasp of our bleeding army, instructions now had been sent to Burton, doubtless with Orme's respects, requesting of the lieutenant colonel to please detach a body of one hundred fifty men and, with two artillery pieces, advance upon the hill to the right and clear it of the enemy, so that this French enfilading fire might be suppressed?

Had Braddock been shot in the head? A wound that left him capable of issuing orders but possessed of no brain to think them first? The hill was gone to the French for good. Victory was gone. Any man was lucky who'd leave here with his life.

Poor general. When we got to him, we found he'd suffered a minor wound, but also additionally a grievous one—all with the same bullet. It had gone through his arm and then into the side of his chest. He lay on the ground, his head supported by Orme's arm and knee.

"Mister Washington?" Braddock's voice was surprisingly strong and clear. I'd have thought him wheezing and gasping, coughing blood—though there was sufficient of that staining his white shirt and lace.

"General." George said, kneeling. "Rest yourself."

I caught myself thinking of a painting here: "The Death of Braddock." To adhere to popular taste, it would need more officers in the background.

And, of course, Indians. Here, there was only the young lieutenant employed as messenger for a background figure, himself unscathed through all this bloodshed. For all the relentless shooting, we saw not a single Indian about us.

No, untrue. We were treated to the sudden and incredible sight of four, five, a dozen Indians leaping up all around us, as though transformed through some magic into humans from tree, log, and bush. They must have observed the general go down—perhaps one of them had shot him—and now had come for their prize: his hair. I might have laughed—and perhaps in mad, demonic fashion, did so. Without wig, old Braddock had scant any stubble to grab hold of.

But the Indians came gleeful toward him nonetheless, whooping and yelping. We had soldiers and wagons all about here, but the soldiers were preoccupied with their own essential interests. To resist these attackers, there was only us: myself, Gist, Stephen, Washington, the wounded Orme, the stricken general, the useless young lieutenant.

Not so useless. He pulled a pistol and slew one of the Indians—himself dying in the act as a war club smashed his skull. Washington near cut off the head of another attacker with his sword. He had discharged my pistol and I'd failed to reload it in the heat of things. Seeing a large, nearly naked man almost upon me, I went frantically for my long bush knife, stumbling as I did so and nearly toppling forward.

This clumsiness saved my life. His tomahawk came down, not slicing into my head but in more glancing fashion, striking muscle and bone at the rear of my shoulder. It hurt insanely, but I managed to get my knife from its scabbard and into the man's stomach, just below the breastbone. I'd meant to stab him higher, but he'd been in mid bound when I struck at him. We crashed to the ground together, I rolling on top of him, then off and onto my back. He clutched his belly, blood streaming through his fingers. He made no cry of hurt or anger, however.

Struggling, the Indian then somehow got to his knees and wielded his weapon for one more blow at me. His arm was so corded with powerful muscles, I think he could have killed me yet even if he'd had all the blood drained from him.

But his chance was gone. In went my knife again, blade aimed higher. His head went back, and then his body fell backward at the knees, his lower legs caught beneath him.

Now I got to my knees. I could manage rising no further. Pulling free my knife and keeping its blade before me, I crept over the dead man and looked at him carefully, holding my left arm tight to my side.

Pernicious fate. It was him, he from the scouting night I so well remembered, the same marking of war paint, the same thick neck, He had a scabbed-over, ragged-edged cut across the side of his head—the same put there by Gist's rifle butt.

There was something else. I grabbed the small, sheathed knife that hung by a leather thong around his neck and yanked. The thong did not break. Shifting myself, I pulled it free off his head.

I knew what I'd see and there it was: the scrimshaw portrait of the

Hannah on the ivory handle, the chink in the hilt from when I'd dropped it once while high in mast shrouds upon a capstan, the same maker's name inscribed in the blade.

This was my small sailor's knife—given in intended troth to Mercy and now returned to me in this horrible manner. One way or another, this newly dead brave had gotten it from her. What else had he done? I should not have wanted even to begin to imagine.

I stared at the little knife, more decorative tool than weapon, running my fingers over it as though I might pick up some sensation of her touch. Then slowly I took full note of my situation. The sound of battle, absent these past moments in my intense concentration on life and death, returned with a great roar. Stephen was at my shoulder, pulling the cloth of my coat and shirt apart to examine the wound.

"By God, Morley. He almost had your arm."

The pain came on with everything else. My friend the fighting doctor produced as though from nowhere a flask of whiskey and poured some into the cut before handing me the rest. Washington was beside me, too. He took the linen stock from his neck and handed it to Stephen for a bandage, which Stephen quickly and tightly wound about my shoulder.

"It's a deep and nasty cut he made on ye," said Stephen, good doctor that he was. "But it's bled clean. Your chance is good."

I felt dizzy. I looked about me. There were four fresh Indian bodies here, three within reach of me. The others who'd tried for Braddock had fled, but doubtless not far.

Everyone stood. I did the same, but not easily.

"This battle's lost," said Gist. "They know it. They want Braddock's hair and they'll keep coming till they get it. His heart, too, if they can manage."

Orme looked horror-stricken. Washington glanced about and shouted to two soldiers running by. "You there. Halt!"

He seemed to have encountered the only two obedient members of Halkett's shredded regiment. They did as bidden, while Washington pulled the sash gently from the general's still-heaving chest. As I have said, the sash does double duty in battle. If one is wounded, it can be made into sling, or placed under the arms and back for a kind of litter.

"We have to get the general to the rear," he said to the infantrymen.

They must have wondered where that was. I stared at my dead Indian, villain of my life. His eyes were turned upward, but otherwise he seemed all a calm. What could he have told me of Mercy?

"Is he Ottawa?" I asked Gist.

"Yes."

"I think he's the same Indian who almost killed me when we were scouting—the one you clubbed with your rifle."

"He's been clubbed," Gist said. "Probably slowed him some today. Probably why you're breathing."

"But the same one?"

"Maybe."

"Not Pontiac."

"Surely not Pontiac."

I held up the sailor's knife. "This was Mercy's. I gave it to her."

"I remember. You want his scalp?"

I turned away. "No."

"Well, I do. He may be a famous warrior, or even chief. If Scarroyaddy lives through this, I'll ask him."

All this talk while bullets still flew. It seemed to me we'd used up all the bullets in the world, but still they came and went. The noise was unabated—it was hellish loud, but we'd become used to it. Another Indian appeared just off the trail and started a run toward us, but someone's round felled him. We were getting used to that, too.

Washington, Orme, and the others were moving off, heading toward the river, half carrying, half dragging, the heavy Braddock. A few wagons were squeaking and crunching by, having got themselves loose from the confusion up the trail. They were vexing Washington sorely, for they would not stop to take aboard his general. After the one rolled by, so would another. The wagoneers' faces matched that of their struggling horses, impassive, yet barely sane.

George yelled and cursed the drivers as only he can, waved his sword about. But, high in their seats, they paid him no mind. They were bound elsewhere, no matter what.

Finally, he pulled pistol, standing squarely in the path of the next wagon like a highwayman.

"You! Stop!"

"Needn't aim your piece at us, Colonel Washington. You after a ride the hell outa here?"

It was that young Dan Morgan, he of the flayed back who'd taken his lashes so blithely, complaining afterward that he'd been cheated his full number. Were he in the militia, and the circumstance less desperate, he might have paid dear for his impertinence, yet he was helpful. The only one.

"I need no ride," said Washington tersely. "It's for this brave officer."

The mirthful look on Morgan's face when he saw his passenger's identity was indescribable. Here was a woodsy with wit enough to savor irony. Here was the author of his fleshly torment, now in such a state himself.

"All right. We'll accept the burden, though this wagon's small," Morgan said. "Lift him up."

It was a struggle, but they managed. I tried helping, but the rigors of the day, and the bleeding, too, proved more than I could stand up to and down I went, head swimming.

When I awoke again, I was also passenger in Morgan's wagon. A regular army surgeon had been found and placed aboard as well, the three of us jammed together and the previous cargo dumped. Braddock eyed me balefully, but had no strength for words. His hand rose, then limply fell. His eyelids drooped, but it was to sleep he went, not death. Not yet.

I raised myself up, the pain encouraging my wakefulness. We'd hardly gone a hundred feet. I could see Washington and Orme, standing together, looking forward up the incline. I don't know what they might have been saying, or planning, or hoping—but all of it was for naught. Straining some, I could see through the bullet-torn trees that Burton's advance toward the little hill we'd attempted earlier had stalled and faltered.

Then all was undone for good. The column, such as it remained one, was struck by the most fatal occurrence of all. The ammunition, fired so wastefully into the air or comrade's back, was running out. Stunned by this fact, the soldiers seemed struck as hard a blow when the swift word came of Braddock's falling. To their crazed minds, there was none to take the general's place, and no hope. Here and there, and then all at once, they turned toward the river and commenced to run.

From where I sat in the bumping, creaking wagon, it seemed a charge. With a din of panicked shouts and caterwauling, they came back toward us down the trail like a red river in flood, throwing down muskets, throwing off packs and haversacks and all encumbrances.

Washington and Orme—the latter now growing in my esteem, the former elevated to godlike stature—tried to stem this onrushing tide, but to no effect. The fleeing redcoats just kept hurtling by.

Worse, their victory all but complete, the Indians and French—I could ill tell them different, what with so many French stripped to waist—rose from their cover and expended their ammunition willy-nilly, pouring in fire upon the British soldiery without any worry for their own defense. Assessing the futility of what was now mere officer's empty gesture, Washington and Orme rejoined us. Without causing Morgan to stop, they flung themselves up either side of the wagon.

"Whip your horses!" Washington cried. "All speed or we perish, and the general with us!"

Whip Morgan did, but no animal there needed great encouragement. There were four horses in this team and they were sound and steady beasts. We careened along, thumping and bumping over roots and stumps and gullies, yet we did not o'erturn, Washington and Orme hung on and did not fall, I did not give unmanly voice to my jarring pain, and poor old Braddock still did not die.

Screams, shouts, cries, curses, Indian whoops, and animal bellows; the most awful, horror-struck faces; wagons capsizing, cannon, too; continuing gunfire, flames in the brush, the stench of smoke and gunpowder and sweat and ruptured bellies; shrieks then, I think from women. God, I'm sorry, but I followed my brave general's good example and closed my eyes.

I opened them when of a sudden I felt the wagon rush and thump down an incline, heel over like a ship in sudden gust, then slam back down and slide with a great splash into water. We were at the river.

Bolt upright, I looked back on the trail that was to have taken us so easily to Fort Duquesne. I'd thought that having been so continuously overtaken by the fleeing soldiers, our wagon would have ended up last, but the way behind us was still clogged with vehicles, animals, and men—the latter in uniform and not.

Washington and Orme had jumped off. George had raised both hands cupped to mouth and was shouting. "Find the Virginians! Have them form a rear guard at the farther shore!"

Someone shouted in obedient reply. Morgan's wagon was stirring a great wake. So were the other wagons. One went over, onto a man, pinning him. He drowned in water not up to a knee.

We were almost to the far shore. I leaned forward and touched the general's leg, peering into his face.

"No," said the surgeon, whose shirt and breeches were one great stain of blood from his day's labors, and who looked the tiredest man who ever labored at anything. "Let him sleep."

The wagon struck against a rock, then swayed and bumped and was out of water and onto the shallow bank of the opposite shore. I looked upstream and down and saw men there, still armed, most in blue coats, some in buff and brown, holding the position. The Virginians. Again, they had followed orders before hearing them.

"Hold, driver!" I shouted.

He glanced back at me, then pulled reins. "What for, you?"

"I would dismount."

"Shit, you're a fool."

The wagon never stopped, but slowed enough for me to clamber over the side, drag foot, and drop, landing on arse but evading the rolling wheel. I don't think I did myself further injury, but I brought upon myself another dose of pain I needed not, and from which I spent several minutes recovering.

Staggering to my feet, I trudged off the road into the high weeds of a hillock that heightened the bank. Passing among the men, I found an exhausted Gist, lying in the grass and cradling his long rifle, which he'd not dropped once—his eyes fixed on the macabre parade still crossing the river. In the distance, as yet unseen, you could hear the Indians coming.

"Should've formed the rear guard on that side," Gist said, spitting. "Won't do much good over here, unless the Injuns start across. But they won't. On their side is where they'll have their fun and plunder."

I had no weapon left but the little sailor's knife I'd given Mercy, now stuck tight in my belt, and my bush blade. It occurred to me that I wanted no more weapon. I wished not to carry rifle, musket, or pistol ever again. I wished to be in Philadelphia, sipping milk punch with Franklin in his chamber of eccentricities. I wished for my Paris wineshop.

Gist was looking at me, showing a weird smile. "You're 'bout the only man on our side got what he wanted today," he said.

"This?"

"You killed the right Indian."

"I no longer wish to have what I wanted," I said. "I would have it all taken back."

"There's words in the scriptures about that."

I found tears in my eyes, and wiped them away.

The trail continued full of walking men. I turned to look toward the tree line to the rear of Gist and me, where I noticed three British officers, reasonably intact, gazing at the river and talking. I could scarce believe it. One of them was Gage, not so long before, our man at the point!

The last of our soldiery was into the river now, along with the last of the wagons. Gist hunched down to present his long rifle, squinting down the barrel at the opposite bank. All along our shore the Virginia militiamen were doing the same. Washington and Orme were on our side of the water now, Orme continuing on toward Gage, Washington looking back at the killing field.

There was more to come—the worst. Those straggling soldiers and vagabonds weren't the conclusion of our people. As I should have realized must occur, the poor women were the last to reach the river. They came on, exhausted and stumbling but running as best they might, skirts lifted or dragging, plunging into the water, which slowed them awfully.

And behind them came the Indians—gleeful, riotous fiends and ghouls on Walpurgis Night—trotting in a great dusty cloud, yelling in merry triumph and appetite for prospective slaughter.

I did see two Frenchmen step before them and try to stay their progress, but these *monsieurs* were brushed aside, their intended gallantry for naught.

The Indians were out of all but long-rifle range from our position, and they took their bloody time about their awful business. Cut and hacked and sliced and stabbed, screaming all the while, our dear ladies fell one by one into the streaming flow as we watched appalled at our helplessness. The sunlight was gleaming on the water, but I'd swear the color turned to red.

There was no keeping any Englishman here now. We hurried to the trail and set in haste upon it, our limbs numb but somehow moving, propelled along by the strength of our will to be away.

Washington and Gist came near me, Stephen, too. How we loved each other then.

"They fought like soldiers and died like men," Washington said to me, as to the entire world.

"Who?"

"Our Americans."

"Yes. They did."

"You are well, Tick?"

"Not of mind."

He put his hand to my shoulder. "If you take to a war again, be careful of your cause," he said. "They're all like this, I fear."

I'm not sure I shall ever be able to explain why, but those words uttered at that particular time of a sudden enraged me. This bloody-minded man was giving advice to me to take care in the choice of war or cause? Better one take care in the choice of comrade. Better one not stand at the side of a *friend* upon the edge of a rocky glen as he commits *murder!* What had Washington said in the aftermath of Fort Necessity? " 'It is all my work—every man down.' "

Whatever exaggeration had been employed in the French polemic against him, it was all bitter truth to me now. It was all his work—every man down, every woman hacked and screaming before our eyes. If all war was like this, then war be damned. Then Washington be damned.

There he'd been, the great heroic figure of the battle, dashing hither and yon through the fray, smiting the cowards, rallying the men, saving his general, commanding the retreat—and all with horses dying beneath him and bullets tearing unminded through his clothing. Yet he was the architect of the stage on which he strode. How he must have yearned for this "war." No wonder Franklin had sought him above all others for his *agent provocateur*. " 'Major Washington, Hero for Our Times.' " Major Washington, *"Assassin!"*

"Assassin!" I shouted, nearly in his face.

"What?"

"You are a goddamned murderer! It's all true what they wrote. This is your work! This is your desire! You are murderer, a bloody murderer—and any man who follows you deserves to be called the same! Murderer! Murderer!"

I was bellowing. In quick reply, I felt a blow to the back of my neck and I went down to my knees.

It was Stephen who had done this. He and Gist dragged and lifted me to my feet. The pain in both my neck and stricken shoulder was as the worst agony of Hell itself. Holding my arm tight, Stephen leaned to my ear.

"Stop this, damn you! Would you now stir men to mutiny? Aren't we already a bloody wreck?"

Gist had my other arm. "Keep your peace, boy. Every man here has trouble enough!"

Washington strode up the trail a way, then whirled about, hand defiantly on hip—still the heroic figure.

I spoke no more.

Thirty-five

The only good thing that can be said of that retreat from the Monongahela was that none of the enemy came after to try to kill us.

Gist, as so usual, had been correct in his judgment. We had left so many corpses and so much liquor, loot, and weaponry behind as to occupy our Indian enemy for days, and not a one of them showed up in pursuit. Instead, we were goaded on by the demons of our fears and imaginings.

Wounded carried in litters died and were discarded at roadside. Walking wounded died and dropped where they last stepped. Many simply sat or lay down and hoped to die, and when that failed, got up and stumbled on.

Many of the horses who'd got loose in the fighting had rejoined the column and came ganging up amongst us—providing mounts for the surviving officers and a fair number of others. As someone rated the equivalent of officer and garishly wounded—bandages were wound around my upper arm, shoulder, chest, and back where the tomahawk had cut me—I was offered a horse and I took it.

Poor Braddock, more Orme's and Washington's dependent now than grand commander of an army, had lost his ride when Morgan's wagon slipped a wheel. Washington tried to waylay soldiers to make a litter for the dying general, but all refused the entreaty, even when accompanied by threat. Wagon drivers rumbled by with no regard, either. Finally, the sad old man was put back upon a horse and tied onto the saddle with a jury rig of sash, rope, and bandage—swaying ludicrously in this seat as the horse resumed the way.

I spoke no further word to Washington. As companion to Braddock, he was held back to the general's hobbling pace at all events.

At last we reached a small advance camp that Colonel Dunbar, perpetually far to the rear, had ordered men up to erect. We tarried there not long, but I noted that the respite seemed to revive Braddock a little. His conversation improved from mutters and babbles to cogent instruction on improving our lot.

But not long after we took to the road again, he faltered and sagged to the side at the angle of a gangplank. Someone reached to loosen his bonds for a better securing, and down the general went, never to rise again.

It was 13 July, a day as hot, dusty, and sweaty as those preceding. Braddock had given up trying to issue commands, and for some time he'd not spoken much. Washington was again at the general's side and helped lower him to the ground. At Washington's order, the entire column stopped while Braddock was put resting against a tree.

"Who would have thought it?" were the words I heard from him, and I heard no other. Then he died.

We all knew how much the Indians desired his hair. If there were any skulking at the rear of this column, we guessed they were there in hopes of that prize. Speaking to that concern, Washington had the general put into the ground right there in the roadway, then covered deeply. After that, he bade all the men, horses, and remaining wagons and artillery caissons to pass over the site, so it wouldn't be noticed—except where he marked it on his map. I noted it was a scant two miles from Jumonville Glen.

———

Washington was looking gaunt and weary, and beginning to sway himself in the saddle. I kept back from him, leaving him to Gist's care if he needed it, and fell alongside a mounted soldier who'd caught up with us after having been left behind back at the Monongahela by the shift of battle.

His name was Duncan Cameron and he was a private in Halkett's regiment. Caught out in the woods where he'd gone to escape the desperate, huddled mob on the trail, he'd taken refuge in a big hollow tree, watched the forward aspects of the battle, and the horrid aftermath as well, until he could himself withdraw across the river.

He had a tale to tell, which he later officially drew up and Franklin printed, so this comes to you as he told it.

"I'd not been there long before these ravenous hellhounds came yelping and screaming like so many devils and they fell to work," he told us as he described his refuge in the tree. "About a foot above the entrance into the tree I was in, there was good foothold for me to stand on, upon which I stood, and against my face there was a small knothole facing the field of battle, by means of which I had a fair prospect of their cruelty. What panic was I in when I saw one of those savages look directly at the knothole. As I apprehended, he gave a scream and came directly up to the tree. But what inducement he had for doing it, I cannot tell, for he went off again without showing any signs of his discovering me. The whole army of the enemy fell to plundering. Though I must do the French commandant this justice, that as soon as possible he could, he put a stop to the Indians scalping those that were not yet quite dead and ordered those wounded to be taken care of. Among the plunder, they found near two hogsheads of rum, and the Indians, as likewise the French soldiers, fell to drinking, and soon got themselves pretty drunk and went off at night to the French fort.

"They did not leave so much as a guard on the field of battle, neither did they pursue you farther than the river, so that if you people had halted but half a mile from the field of battle, you might have returned at night and destroyed most of the baggage. At night, when the coast was clear, I got me out of my hiding place. I found a horse loose upon the road and rode it coming up to you here."

Scarroyaddy, I think the bravest man with the British Army that long, bloody day, caught up to us also, having made a complete reconnaissance of the battlefield.

He'd come off it with many scalps taken in what he held to as honorable combat. The Oneida chief had then lingered in the woods to scout the ground in the aftermath, following at careful distance the triumphant Indians from their bloody revels in the field to the fort.

The chief confirmed Cameron's report on the attempts of the French officers to curb the cruelties, no matter how traditionally practiced, but the restraint was not totally effective. Scarroyaddy told of five British soldiers taken prisoner, stripped naked, and marched to Duquesne where, in full sight of the French, if beyond their ability to intervene, the men were burned alive, their blackened bodies left there where they'd crackled.

En route back to us, Scarroyaddy had crossed the battlefield again by a different route, finding most things of value vanished and the pillaged bodies left there in careless heaps. Except along one stretch of road, where a strange sight greeted him. There he took note of eight women—five full grown and three girls—all of them stripped naked and laid out neatly in a careful row, on their backs. They'd been scalped, but otherwise bore only the marks of their death wounds.

When we rejoined Colonel Dunbar, our nominal commander, we discovered he'd never got even to within fifty miles of the Forks. His force still numbered more than five hundred fighting men and several mighty artillery pieces, all of which together, according to Scarroyaddy, would be sufficient to subdue Fort Duquesne, as now there were only French in it, with all those Indians drunk and fat and laden with booty, heading back to their villages. But cautious Dunbar would have no talk of that. Resolutely now, moving more quickly than our advance guard ever did upon the fort, Dunbar kept us all making for Will's Creek and Fort Cumberland, there to consider our best strategy.

Gist related the strange story of Sir Peter Halkett's slaying. Gist had been in the forest when Sir Peter, the 44th Regiment's commander, had appeared on horseback, attempting to maneuver a body of grenadiers into an attack upon some of the Indians hiding in cover. One Indian—a Shawnee—was sitting exposed on the ground against a tree, having been shot horribly through the knee, that limb effectively destroyed, though the fellow had seemed calm enough.

Our force, including Gist and the preoccupied Halkett, left the warrior to his misery, but as Colonel Halkett moved along, the Indian raised his musket from the ground to take wavering aim at the grand officer. Gist, who'd not taken the time to reload his rifle whilst crossing this ground, hurriedly commenced to do so, but could not complete the task in time. The Indian's weapon discharged truly, striking Halkett a mortal wound. His rifle finally loaded and primed, Gist walked up to the Indian and blew out his brains.

"I never saw a one-legged Indian, so for all I know, I did him a favor," Gist said. "Still, I regret the whole proceeding. Halkett's boy died, too. James Halkett, Lieutenant. He ran up and threw himself across his father to protect him against what other Indians were about—and there were some. They shot the boy for his trouble. Died quick. Before I could reload from the shot I took to kill the one-legged Shawnee."

Gist had brought two of his own sons with him on this campaign and they'd both survived, neither maimed nor serious wounded.

I've noted differing counts of our casualties. The first list I saw had 456 men killed and 421 wounded, including among the latter St. Clair and Burton. The final grisly sum I saw reported, reprinted in Mister Franklin's excellent newspaper, had 63 officers and 914 men killed or wounded of 1,459 under arms and taken into battle. The French losses, according to their official records, were put at 16 whites and 27 Indians. The Virginia companies had been so brutalized you couldn't make one such unit from the four, counting the Virginia rangers.

Someone on the French side became the richer for the trouble. The fifty thousand pounds in coin of the realm that Braddock had carried into the Ohio was left back there somewhere on the Monongahela and it never came back to us.

Our lost cannon got carried up to New York and were used to fire upon British troops in battles for the forts at Lake Champlain.

Still, we came into Fort Cumberland with a not insubstantial force— Dunbar's more than five hundred men and our some four hundred, counting irregulars and the less severely wounded. The place could be well enough defended.

But Colonel Dunbar was no man for any such fight. This "brave" officer—I still cannot believe it—decided as we staggered at last into Fort Cumberland, safe on the shores of the Patowmack and but a few days advanced into August, that what the army needed now was to withdraw to *winter quarters!* And in Philadelphia!

He had all the British regulars save independent companies like MacKay's marching for that place within a fortnight.

I will confess it. I went with them. My wound now hurt more than any other thing I'd suffered in the King's service and I feared it had gone septic. Even good doctor Gist had no remedy for the pain other than friend whiskey, and it was not of abundant help.

My soul hurt. As Gist had noted, my own mission on this campaign had met with its own unique success. It was clear to me beyond all doubt now that poor Mercy had perished, and I had, had I not, taken my vengeance. In dreams and waking, I can still see that scarred warrior's face as it looked the second time my blade went in.

Success I may have had, but it satisfied nothing. All that would assuage me now was oblivion, however acquired.

So, while we remained there in Cumberland, I drank, I think straight on through two days. Then, somehow arising from it—my wound not much better, but my mind clearing—I commenced to arrange my departure. My only desire now was to be gone. I'd need the King's horse I'd taken in the retreat. I'd not add stealing to my sins here. I went to Washington to ask permission.

I found him sprawled and looking near lifeless on a crude bench outside Gist's cabin. He had numerous papers and correspondence about him, as always, but had put them aside for a rest. His more usually flushed face was close to gray and his eyes gone pale and rheumy. His flux had returned and there was pain in his belly. His voice was weak. I quite truly wondered if I should see him again. Some of the bravest and strongest men in the American colonies had perished in this. Men were still dying—every day.

"So, it's Thomas Morley," he said, peering closer as though to confirm what he'd thought he'd seen.

"I'm leaving," I said. "I'm going on—to Philadelphia."

"You're on no regimental muster. You're free to go as you will. I've no further need of your service."

He closed his eyes, grimacing. He was bad off.

I could not depart and leave it all like this. I was unsure of how much I'd truly felt those venomous words I'd hurled at him upon the trail in retreat, how much I still believed them. I didn't want to withdraw them complete, but I didn't want to leave them there hanging in the air about us, as eternal echoes, declaring the end to our friendship. I think I wanted still to be his friend, but without denying the guilt I still felt he rightly bore.

I would work that out later. Then, I kept talking. "If you please, George," I said more warmly, "I shall need a horse, and would take the King's, for there're few others, and none else good for the hard ride."

"Then do so," he said weakly. "There'll be no better accounting of horseflesh than there has been of human."

I stepped closer. "Where will you go?"

His eyes sparked a tiny bit keener. "Where go? I will go back."

"To Belvoir, and Mount Vernon?"

He took a deep breath of air, then let it out slowly. "You do not comprehend me."

"To Williamsburg?"

He rose forward in his seat, his thin hand reaching to grasp my arm, those blue-gray eyes now burning bright with the urgency of his meaning.

"Damn all, Tick!" he said. "I will go back to the Forks!"

With that, he lay back and turned his head away, facing the far woods and the ridge of Will's Mountain rising behind them. I fixed the sight of him like that in my memory, then walked a few paces away.

That was not the memory I wanted. I turned again. "George," I said. "I wish you well."

His hand came up and made a slight wave, then fell.

———

I traveled with a detached unit of Dunbar's light horse. They were slow-moving, not sure of the country, but though I knew it well, I had trouble keeping up with them. By the time we entered Harrisburg on the banks of the Susquehanna, my fatigue was so great I barely held to my saddle.

We were out of the mountains and Indian country now, just a few days' march from Philadelphia over easy terrain, so I was about to let them ride on without me at all events. But I soon had the happiest reason for tarrying there in Harrisburg. Mister Franklin was there! He'd come west from our city in search of Braddock or news.

Most of what he'd already heard had been in the nature of wild reports that had spread before the retreating survivors of the army like a grass fire before the wind. Lingering to acquire a more accurate accounting for his newspaper, not to speak of his Philadelphia politics, he'd accosted the commander of the light-horse troop who'd been my escort—none of whom of course had seen any of the fighting—then sighted me, giving forth a joyful greeting indeed.

After thanking the cavalry officer for my safe deliverance from the wilds, I bade him farewell and then went with Franklin to a public house, where he with glad generosity supplied all my wants and needs. In return, struggling to stay alert and coherent, I told him all I knew, which he found incredible, but scribbled down nonetheless.

Franklin listened to every word, to every count of casualty, to all the British order of march and disorder of retreat, with the most rapt attention. But he expressed no great sadness or anger or any other emotional thing. He digested my news with his intellect, posing a poking question here and there as I told my tale, but interjecting nothing of his own until the very end.

"This is disaster," he said, slumping back in his chair. "Catastrophe! The mightiest armed force ever put on this continent, destroyed in an afternoon—by a few hundred savages."

He shook his head, lifting a tankard of ale to his lips.

"There's instruction in it," I said. "There has been for me. I shall never go back into that country again. For all the rest of my days, I wish never to be more than a short day's ride from the sea."

"Then you return to Philadelphia." He wiped his mouth gingerly with his hand.

"Aye, for now. Price on my head or no."

My news seemed of a sudden to have aged him, or perhaps it was the light, which came oddly from the window.

"I am grievous remiss," he said, eyeing me somberly, "and I feel the guilt of it. Thomas, I fear I have a casualty to report myself. Your brother Richard—he is dead."

I felt no shock or surprise at this. I'd expected it. Not so soon, perhaps, but inevitably.

I loved Richard, don't you know, despite all his ruinous ways and wretched behavior toward me and Susannah. I would have done anything in my power to have seen him restored to health and happiness and sound mind, had that end been possible. I wished him as many years as man has a right to expect on this earth. But what that required had lain solely within his own power to effect, and he had not sufficient will to the task. I daresay he had none at all.

And so he had died, there in his grand Philadelphia house. According to Franklin, the attending physician said it was a fever of the liver that had swollen that organ and poisoned the blood. Richard was bled copiously to rid his body of this evil humour, but to no avail. He perished in mournful lamentation at his pain and fate, never comprehending how much his terrible weakness was to blame for both.

I found this solace in it. Richard's spiritual suffering, which I'd never understood, was ended. If there was a place of posthumous union in an afterlife, he was now with his Jamaican ladylove, as he could not be on earth. I hoped she would forgive him for his ambitions toward Susannah—as I had not.

Also, I was free now to think of him as he had been, my strong and resolute hero, forging a new life and great success for the both of us in this new America, respected by all he encountered. I could put aside my memories of him as besotted fool, disgracing himself at every opportunity.

That image could die with him. I'd keep the earlier one as I might a chosen heirloom, discarding the rest.

"He did not disown you," Franklin said. "I'm afraid I must tell you that he would have done, that it was his intent—so furious was he at your having run off with both fortune and fair lady, in bad bargain. But in his state, as with so many things, he just never got 'round to it. So you are his heir, his only heir."

I shook my head. What mattered that now?

"What you are heir to mostly is debt," Franklin said, much the businessman now. "A most considerable debt. But, with the astonishing way all prices now rise in this war fever, you should have ample left, after selling assets, to establish yourself. The *Hannah* still awaits you—for a fair price." He smiled and winked. "I know, for it is I who now own her."

I found myself smiling, but then a frown came quick over his countenance.

"In Philadelphia, sir, I fear your name is on a warrant, and price still upon your head. The charge is kidnapping, Thomas. The noose for that. It's beyond even my influence to stop."

I took a deep breath. The meal and drink and rest and Franklin's good company had much restored me, though my shoulder ached as though that Ottawa's tomahawk was still in it.

"I'll brave the resolution of all that before any authority," I said. "Susannah is now or will shortly be married to a King's officer, brother of a baronet. There's small kidnapping in that. The letter that came through your good offices bore the news and I have it still.''

"Well, then,'' he said, lifting his cup. His resumed the merriment I remembered the better.

"There is something I must know,'' I said, "and you are perhaps the best man to tell me.''

"Anything.''

I leaned forward. "What is to come of it? The carnage in the forest—what gain was there in it? What reason? There are hundreds dead, Mr. Franklin. If they should now gather 'round us as ghosts, what would you tell them? What would you say? What is the worth of it?''

He glanced around the crowded room. There was some soldiery about—not quite sober.

Franklin gave a quick sigh, then said: "For these redcoats, there's no more worth in their dyin' here than there would be in Flanders or India or on the China Sea. Death's their wage, and they draw it quite regular.

"But for us, the inhabitants of these colonies, there is a worth in it. You've just now told me how well the Americans in that battle did fight, and how well Washington and the others led them, and how they might have actually carried that sorry day if not shot down through the backs by their miscreant fellows—these same who carried on as though their military superior.

"You said there was instruction in it—and there is. If we can raise more armies of our own good Americans, and put them with such leaders as the estimable Washington—and for all you bear grievance against him, Thomas, he is our very best man. He is. If we can take upon ourselves our own defense, begging from King George only the weapons that are the means to it, if we can stand up and seize from this tragedy the opportunity to make all this country our own, then we will have gained a profound worth from it. Every Virginian and Marylander and South Carolinian who fell in those trees died for something.''

"A pretty speech.'' I fear I said that rudely.

Franklin now became most serious indeed. "What's been set afire here, Tom, will become the awfulest war that mankind has seen since the horrors of antiquity. It's my guess that our Sovereign and France's will grapple with each other hideously and everywhere, each seeking the possession of the other.

" 'Twill take the longest time to burn out, and devour soldiers' lives relentless. I wonder that King George will find redcoat enough to defend half the places he'll need to. If that be the case, there may be few he can spare for here. All the better then for America, if we amass guns and powder enough. We can drive the Frenchman out on our own as good as convict soldiery—with men like Washington, men like you. We can do it.''

Another sigh. He drank more ale, and yet seemed sadder.

"But if our Majesty puts great high price on these colonies, and sends his soldiers here before any other place, then it's sad for us, and sad for those Americans who were up there dying. The British Army will stay. The French in time may go, but those Indians will not. They cannot. And as they won't, the redcoats won't. They'll abide with us as master to slave, and every promise raised by this new abundant country will be dashed. Have you ever been to Ireland, Tom—or to Scotland?"

I shook my head. "England only, and France. The West Indies."

"The King has his armies in both sorrowful places—for their 'protection,' but, sooth, to keep them down. In Scotland, after the rebellion they call the forty-five—that slaughter at Culloden—it's a vanquished, perishing land, sir. The populace is taxed to pay the wages of their oppressor, possessing only the right to send some earl or duke's son to Parliament, there to second the Crown's wish. In Ireland it is the same, only the life much worse.

"If the King sends such armies over here now, Tom, that'll be us. That'll be all your brave Americans died for in the Ohio Country, and I'll curse every word I spoke that helped to send them there."

We both stared at the tabletop.

"When do you go back?" I asked.

"Today. You've given me all I need."

"I must tarry here. I should like to visit my friend Chief Half King's grave. The place where he died—is it far from here?"

"Not at all. Any man in this town can show you the way."

"And Carlisle?"

"Near as well, just up a stream from here called the Conodoguidet River."

"The lady Mercy Ennis. Her family was once settled there. Perhaps there's some kin remaining. If I can find anyone, I shall do what I can for them."

"Sad duties you've given yourself, Thomas. But I wish you well on them."

———

I found Half King's grave, though not his spirit—at least none that would communicate with me. I knew little of the Seneca religion but thought I could do no harm were I to leave him something. I still had the long bush knife with which I had slain my foe—who was Half King's enemy as well. I dug a hole to the side of the chief's burial place and buried it, too—within reach of him.

Entering Carlisle, I stopped one or two men I found on the main way and asked if they knew of a family Ennis, or any of that name, but met with no help. There was an ordinary by the grassy place that was the village common, and I went in there, finding no other patrons. There was considerable noise coming from what I took to be the kitchen, but no innkeeper or serving wench in view.

I sagged to a bench, dropping my belongings, then put face in hand. I was so beaten down with fatigue I didn't think there sleep enough left in all my life to restore me from it.

The serving wench at last came up behind me, yet stood there, dumbly, moving no further, saying nothing. My head was low and she may have thought me in some stupor. I turned a little, catching sight of her bare foot—slightly grimy to be sure, but the prettiest foot I'd ever seen.

My weariness had bred apparition.

"Thomas." Just the one word uttered, as her gentle hand came to my shoulder.

I fear I cried out with the hurt of it. When I looked again, the pain had prodigiously clarified my mind, yet there she still was. No apparition.

"Mercy?" I said. "Are you alive?"

Thirty-Six

As it happened, Washington was unable to make a triumphant return to the Forks until years later, and then in circumstances he'd not envisioned nor much desired. But neither did he abandon the frontier to resume the planter's life at Mount Vernon—so close to tempting Belvoir.

On the contrary. If he is to be blamed for what in these colonies came to be called the French and Indian War, Washington acquitted himself most admirably in it—and not in another bloody, glory-seeking plunge into the hostile wilderness.

He instead accepted the incalculably difficult, heartbreaking, ill-rewarded, yet militarily vital, responsibilities of commander-in-chief of a new Virginia regiment raised to defend the Appalachian frontier against further French and Indian incursion.

Assuming at age twenty-four the militia rank of full colonel, he served as lord protector of a frontier region greater in size than many a kingdom in Europe, stretching hundreds of miles from Forts Cumberland and Maidstone on the Patowmack down to Fort Trial and Captain Harris Fort, where the Blue Ridge crosses into North Carolina.

Headquartering himself in Winchester, where he built a stout Fort Loudon—named after yet another glorious commander of His Majesty's forces he sought to please—George established in all a chain of twenty-seven forts or fortified outposts throughout the mountains, keeping the Shenandoah or Great Valley of Virginia in English hands and providing sanctuary for the settlers who were treated now most horribly to unceasing Indian attack.

He manned these all with only a few hundred men, most of poor quality and facing an enemy more than three thousand strong—with sickness and desertion taking as great a toll as Frenchman, Canadian, and Indian. Money was often short, and provender, materials, equipment, and ammunition constantly so. Lawlessness was rampant among both civilian and military populations, and hangings and floggings constant. Intrigues and corruption, both military and political, haunted Washington's enterprise like mischievous spirits.

Compounding all the evils that beset him, Washington was further vexed by a Captain Jonathan Dagworthy. Made commander at Fort Cumberland, anchor to Washington's chain that it was, this officer refused George's authority on the ground that Cumberland was on Maryland soil. After weeks and months of dickering and maneuvering, George was at length compelled to ride all the way to Boston—in the depths of the winter of 1755–1756—and take audience with General Shirley himself to get all that set right.

But for that digression, the Colonel stuck to his mountains, dashing from place to place as enemy attack and other emergency required, coping with sickness, hunger, and mutiny besides. The Indian foe raised bloody hell, getting deep into the Shenandoah on some raids, but for all its ferocity, this enemy was never able to conquer or occupy.

The worst part of it for George were those pathetic, miserable settlers who came streaming into his redoubts in such frustrating numbers. I think he learned more the true cost of war from them than from the battle deaths and maimings he'd witnessed in combat. These unfortunates tore at his soul—as they would any caring man. I received a letter from Washington in the winter following Braddock's defeat. It still moves me in the reading:

> These sorely afflicted people. Their distresses—not an hour, nay, scarcely a minute, passes that does not produce some fresh alarm or melancholy account. If it is so here, Thomas, think upon all that country where there is no palisade, and no army.
>
> I have a generous soul, sensible of wrongs and swelling for redress. But what can I do! If bleeding—dying!—would glut these savages' insatiate revenge, I would be a willing offering to savage fury. I'd die by inches to save a people. I see their situation. I know their danger. Like many here, I participate in their sufferings. The supplicating tears of these women, the moving petitions from the men, they move me into such a deadly sorrow I declare I could offer myself a willing sacrifice to the butchering enemy—provided that would contribute to the people's ease. But it would not. Naught does. Nothing. It is a hell we abide in here, with new torments every day."

To my mind, he was more the hero there in Winchester than ever on his three earlier and more illustrious adventures. When the Continental Congress chose him to lead its ragged armies against the British Crown in the present rebellion, I think the choice of him was prompted more by this later experience against the French and Indian than any of the early.

This is not to say he was entirely resolute throughout his frontier ordeal. I think he resigned, or offered to, on several occasions, so deep was his frustration. He wrote his superiors despairingly of the quality of his militia forces and the general feebleness of his forts. He rode to Williamsburg to openly beg for better. He could not fathom why a Royal commission in the regular army was denied him—still dense to the lineage, cash, and conniving this required—and gathered resentments in himself over this sleight that I think have helped carry him into the field against His Majesty's forces in this rebellion today.

He was frequently ill, on the frontier and on his leaves to Alexandria and home—his old friend the bloody flux again, striking so violently once in 1757 that he came close to resigning his command for real. Through all this, Dinwiddie was harried by the same ailment. Their correspondence must have been painful to read.

But in all this, Washington grew. Except for his deficiencies in education, I never knew a more complete man.

Though I kept to my vow to pass my future life always within reach of the sea—and as far as possible from the Indian lands—I was sufficiently moved by that tormented letter of Washington's on the sufferings of the settlers to make at least some small further contribution to the British cause, and so outfitted a brig as privateer and went voyaging with Riggins down to Hispaniola, Martinique, and Guadeloupe on two expeditions during the height of the conflict.

The first of these forays netted me nothing but expense, plus three men lost to tropic sickness, but we did best a French naval vessel in a small skirmish in the Leewards the second time out, and I took home from that encounter two French merchantmen as prizes—having sunk their escort. The sale of those ships added handsomely to my estate and my crew's and won me a small moment of fame in Philadelphia, but it was a paltry exploit compared to the burden the Colonel bore quietly and without glory out in those mountains, day in and day out through all weathers and all seasons.

You may wonder how, impoverished as I was, I came into ship enough to go careering about the Caribbean after French booty. Well, death was a busy fellow in that turbulent time. Soldiers and innocents were not his only victims.

While all of us with Braddock were so violently engaged on the Monongahela, good citizens Butler and Smithson were completing a voyage from Africa to Port-au-Prince on the island of Sainte Dominique, that which the Spanish called Hispaniola until they lost it to France. They had a cargo full of black gold and were bound for the principal slave market on that island—which is to say, they were preparing to gather immense profit trading in human cargo with the French enemy!

My good Riggins was indeed caught in the misfortune of serving as captain of the vessel, and was having a worrisome time of it, for this particular cargo was most discontented with its lot and the long Atlantic crossing, and was behaving disagreeably, despite heavy servings of the lash ordered by Butler.

When the ship had reached Sainte Dominique and was lying at anchor, just off the bar at night in wait of the morning's high tide to take it into the harbor, the inmates of the forward cargo hold somehow found the means to slip the pins in their chains in the darkness and break out onto the deck. Within minutes, they'd subdued the crew, killing the worst of their tormentors, and had thrown Smithson and Butler overboard. They'd then ordered the surviving crew members to bring the ship close in to shore—actually running it aground. Thereupon they'd released the captives of the other holds, swam and waded onto the beach, and vanished into the jungle, the entire lot.

Smithson drowned before he could be rescued. Butler almost did, but was plucked from near doom by sailors, who'd been ordered into a small boat by Riggins to effect a rescue—though not until the escapees had found their freedom.

Curious that so dependable a ship's master should be so careless and negligent with chain pins and hatch covers. Curious that the captives had so readily spared him.

Riggins wasted so much time getting Butler aboard and searching for Smithson's body that no recapture of any kind was accomplished of the fugitives—a loss in capital of great magnitude.

Butler sought to dismiss Riggins and have him tried on trumped-up charges in the admiralty court—the French location of the crime conveniently omitted. But, as heir to Richard's shares in the business, I had equal voice in the partnership and was able to thwart him in this, as I was in his wish to continue the slave trade. I had big weapons to wield in these disputes. Smithson had left an heir well known to me, had he not? Susannah's vote, if by proxy, was always with mine. I also could bring to bear the threat of reporting Butler to Crown authorities for trading with the King's enemy in time of war. The gallows for that, if a court be pressed.

The quarrel with the French was finally and formally declared a war—known across the Atlantic as the Seven Years' War and fought all over the bloody world, just as Franklin had predicted.

In North America, Europe, the Caribbean, the Mediterranean, the Indian Ocean, and remote places of the far Pacific, men bled and died by the thousands in the rivalry of two kings.

I was surprised when the combat in Europe drew in Prussia on the British side, and Austria, Sweden, and some of the small German principalities on France's—struggling over issues and grievances an infinity removed from Jumonville Glen. It was equally astonishing to hear of French and British troops fighting on the great sultry Indian subcontinent over some crowded filthy city called Calcutta, and in the Philippine Islands, where as you may or may not recall, we British captured the capital at Manila; fat difference it made to Scottish herdsman or Virginia planter.

I don't know that there was ever before so all-embracing and far-flung a war. Neither Caesar nor Alexander ranged so far. I doubt that mankind will ever fight one so expansively again. The expense in lives, treasure, and geography was just crushing.

This war we came very close to losing in America, as you must know. Governor Shirley, serving as general and interim commander-in-chief of His Majesty's forces in the colonies, tried but failed to take Niagara—where he was to have joined forces with Braddock in the effort. Though this formidable-sounding Sir William Johnson of New York ran the French and their Indians off Lake George, he could not budge them from Lake Champlain.

France's Marquis de Montcalm, great friend to the horrible Chief Pontiac, captured Fort Oswego on Lake Ontario and then Fort William Henry on Lake George, where so many English were massacred after surrendering themselves and their arms.

Actually, for a time, it went quite badly everywhere. Some English worthy I'd never heard of named Clive lost Calcutta to the French. Frederick the Great of Prussia, no less, suffered a bitter defeat at the hands of French and Austrians, and that Royal military genius the Duke of Cumberland, for whom our rude little fort on the upper Patowmack was named, had to surrender an army to the French, though not himself, King's son that he was.

Happily, we got ourselves a better leader in 1758, when William Pitt was made secretary of state and prime minister. He sent to North America some decent generals, Robert Moncton and James Wolfe among them, and to sea some first-rate admirals, notably Charles Saunders.

You know the rest—all sunshine after a storm. Canada's Louisbourg was recaptured by assault from the sea, and Fort Frontenac taken on the St. Lawrence River. Fort Ticonderoga and Crown Point fell to us on Lake Champlain, and Sir William and his screaming Iroquois finally did manage the seizure of Niagara, cutting the French from the Great Lakes for good.

Most glorious of all, Quebec was won on the Plains of Abraham, though, alas, with both the great Montcalm and our good Wolfe among the killed of that battle.

And, yes, Fort Duquesne at long last fell to us. Two able officers, Colonel Henry Bouquet, a Swiss mercenary, and General John Forbes led an army made up largely of Americans west from Philadelphia, cutting a new road through the mountains. Though an advance party was shot up badly, much as ours had been with Braddock, Forbes was no Dunbar and pressed on, compelling the French to blow the magazine at their fort and burn it, fleeing downriver into the western woods. A new British fort rose on that spot, named after the great and resolute Pitt.

By 1760, all Canada and the Ohio belonged to the British Crown, but that same year, George III ascended to the throne, dismissed Pitt as too ambitious and set in motion all the machinery of peacemaking—which, given the nature of diplomacy, took three more years to achieve its goal.

But no sooner was the ink dry on the 1763 Treaty of Paris than that devil Pontiac unleashed an Indian uprising against British rule. The attacks spread from Lake Superior well into Pennsylvania and New York, with garrisons massacred right and left and sieges laid upon Fort Detroit and Fort Pitt, though unsuccessfully.

Those bastions held out. But when bad weather set in, and a smallpox plague spread through some of the Indian populations from tainted blankets sent as gifts, the rebellion collapsed. Pontiac was subsequently murdered— not, I daresay, by me or any other white, but at the hand of another Indian.

The toll in slaughtered settlers in that uprising and the long war preceding was just ghastly. Never in modern times of my acquaintance, nor in what I know of antiquity, was warfare so mercilessly turned on a civilian population.

And what was the grand reward for all this suffering? What profit to the colonies who'd waged this war and won?

The French were driven from the Ohio, true, but no British colonists were allowed in their place! All English settlement west of the Appalachians was forbidden by Royal decree!

This was intended as a calm upon the Indians, who had enough to suffer from British garrisons maintained indefinitely in forts throughout the frontier regions. The forbidding eventuality held out by Franklin came to pass.

As with the British regulars stationed in Scotland and Ireland as military establishments keeping order, those put in place on the western frontier of America were supported by means of a tax levied on the colonists. But unlike the King's good subjects in Ireland and Scotland, we Americans had no representation in the British Parliament whatsoever.

Mister Franklin found a neat slogan in that—"Taxation without Representation!"—one he and other newspaper publishers put to good use rousing the rabble in the current revolt. But here I get quite ahead of myself.

After the Forks were reclaimed—and the frontier war as good as won—Washington turned from military matters to more personal concerns. He got himself elected to the House of Burgesses from the Winchester district, largely with the help of Sally's husband, George William Fairfax, and her brother-in-law, the rich John Carlyle of Alexandria, both of whom went out into the Shenandoah and campaigned energetically for George among their many tenant farmers.

He also got himself married.

I do not know for certain when he persuaded himself to abandon all hope of ever marrying the true love of his life. But I think it became obvious to him that when the war was done, he would need perforce to embark on a domestic situation of his own and proceed with his life without his Sally.

His heart not interfering, he chose well. A tiny thing, in reverse proportion both to George's immensity and that of her own considerable fortune, Martha Custis was a chatty, plumply pretty charmer of a widow just two years his senior whom he'd met at a supper party. In addition to all her lands and slaves and monies, she had two children. Washington was as fond of humanity at its early stages of life as he was of the theatre and horses.

The wedding was held in the bride's imposing house on the Pamunkey River, though they afterward settled at Mount Vernon. It was a cold winter's day, January 6, 1759, chosen for a time when the Colonel was back from the frontier. My wife and I were guests, as of course were George William Fairfax and Sally.

It was a difficult time for Sally. She embraced me with great affection, far more of that than she allowed herself with George. I think I stood as his surrogate for her that day. She let me see her tears, knowing I could guess their reason.

We saw the Washingtons infrequently after that—only once again in Virginia, and most often then in Philadelphia, where he came for the increasingly rancorous politics—the same dangerous "Democratick" of Franklin's ardent instigation that I was loathe to associate myself with. I had become a man of great substance in my adopted city and quite content with the state of things. Though I perceived moral right and logic in the side taken by Washington and Franklin, none of it seemed to me worth another plague of bloodshed across the land.

It is said that in measuring the strength of the present American rebellion, its support comes from no more than a quarter or a third of the population, the commonest quarter of that the Scots–Irish folk of Piedmont and the frontier. Another one quarter to one third is judged fiercely opposed to the revolt and happily Tory, while the remaining one half to one third Americans find credit and fault on both sides and wish mostly for the quarreling and fighting to stop.

I would certainly place myself in the latter group, while my wife is among those intransigently Tory. She admired Washington from their first meeting and has never tired of flirting with Franklin, absent though now he must be from our hearth and table as a "wanted man." But their politics drive her sometimes to rage.

Sally, for all her devout belief in the nobility of the names Cary and Fairfax, I rather think is truly Whig, if not Damned Rebel. Martha is simply besotted with George and would share his politics if he came to believe that monkeys should rule all mankind. But with Sally there was an intellectual union with George on the philosophies of governance, limited as her woman's education was on such matters.

To put it in different fashion, I think Sally Fairfax, like George, was truly *American*.

What a wife she would have made for him. Cruel irony it was that they first met after she'd become married to his best friend and benefactor. Cruel fate it was that in 1773, George William Fairfax, perplexed by all the turmoil in the colonies, and needing to attend to some family affairs in the ancestral homeland, elected to take his wife to England for an extended visit, which, in the event, has proved a likely permanent one, with this new war ablaze on sea and land.

Do you know that Washington still tries to write to her? And on occasion, his letters get through! My wife fears he'll have both Fairfaxes charged with treason if he does not relent.

You may wonder how a wife of mine might come by all these Royal and Tory notions as a mere country girl born in English-hating Ireland. The truth, which is both sad and happy, is that I did not marry Mercy Ennis—

though I wanted to and tried, and had her live with me as wife nearly a year from the time I discovered her at Carlisle.

She never told me all her story, or I think even most of it. I sought some hints in her once lively and telling eyes, but found there a strange implacability. I perhaps should not describe it strange, for I've seen it before in Indian encounters—when talking with Half King and Scarroyaddy, or Alequippa.

Mercy would often sit like that, impenetrable, perfectly still, sometimes at a window, often not. I gave her a locket for the twists of hair I'd taken from her murdered sisters, and she'd clutch that oft for hours. Her eyes revealed nothing, though occasionally I might discern the slightest touch of sadness, or sometimes a small spark of affection or gratitude. Otherwise, they were dark stones. Her face was hard as well. I don't mean to say her beauty had lessened. She was sunburned and a little weathered, to be sure, but if anything, her loveliness had gained a mystery, and so increased. She spoke very seldom, usually only when addressed, and her tones were those of a grown woman. All girlish delight was gone, and she had no laughter. Just, every so often, one might notice a slight, sad smile.

The Indian warrior I'd killed who'd been in possession of the sailor's knife had not in Indian fashion become her husband, but neither was their relationship simply one of captive and captor. He had indeed been an Ottawa, and I know little of that tribe's customs, but in some formal way, he'd made Mercy his betrothed—his property, either to be taken as wife or discarded as he chose, but until then, not to be molested. Mercy said this had afforded her great protection during her ordeal. Other women taken on the frontier were not so fortunate.

He treated her in accordance with his custom, but was not harsh. If grateful, she bore him no affection, for he'd slain her father and he'd calmly watched as others slew her sisters. He taught her—as did women of his tribe—many new things about the natural world of the wilderness, toward which she'd had an inclination in any event.

These lessons were to serve her well in her deliverance. It was Braddock's advance and the coming of full-scale war in the Ohio that provided her moment of opportunity, drawing from the Ottawa camp all the warriors to Fort Duquesne to hear Dumas and Beaujeu exhort them to battle against the British.

To effect her escape, Mercy had clubbed, she thought to death, an old Indian man and stabbed quite certainly mortally an Indian woman. She'd swum the broad Ohio at night, naked, holding her clothes in a bundle before her. Then, reaching land, she'd gone north and east, finding the bank of the Allegheny and following it upstream, where she crossed the Continental Divide and descended to the Juniata River, striking south from that stream out of the higher mountains and walking down to Carlisle, where she'd found friends and that position as innkeeper's serving maid—as I'd come upon her. She'd gone all that distance barefoot, and living off the land, armed with nothing more than knife. I doubt I could have managed it myself.

Did I still love her? Gads, a thousand times more. I wanted nothing more than to care for her, as I had nursed the ragingly ill Susannah across the Atlantic, and to do so all our days. I wished to make her wife right there and then, but when she demurred—aye, fell into obdurate silence—I relented, giving her the time I thought she needed.

I brought her with me home to Philadelphia. With reason now to relish my inheritance, I installed her in the grand *Maison Morley*, bought her fine clothes, and packed her off to a nearby academy of Mister Franklin's recommendation for "finishing."

Save that of marriage, she assented to all my wishes dutifully, but mostly sadly. She never spoke of love, but informed me that she still bore me some affection. She withheld her body from me—in truth, I had no wish to press myself on her again before marriage—but allowed me kisses and often touched my hand.

The academy, I discovered, she quite hated, and after a few weeks, I let her abandon that. She disliked as well the social entertainments of the place, quickly sensing the snobbery that too often came her way. She entirely despised, I think, living in the city. She took to sitting for long periods in utter quiet in darkened rooms of the house, and to going for long walks just at dawn. With increasing frequency, I'd find her in the hills and meadows along the Schuylkill, walking or sitting, melancholia her companion.

Some weeks later, on an early morning as I still lay abed, Mercy returned from one of her walks and told me that she was leaving. I was devastated, and generally behaved like a man gone mad. Her response was this same quiet repose, waiting until my anguish had drained away so that I could comprehend the intractability of her wishes. I later found she'd received a letter from Anne Gist, who was still a guest of the Fairfaxes, and hating it.

When the moment of departure came, I bestowed all the money I had in the house upon her, which discontented her but which she did not reject. She set off down the high street on foot, but I had a servant fetch two horses, mount her on one and escort her to her destination, which was down the Great Wagon Road to Winchester, where she was to make rendezvous with Christopher Gist. He'd been made Indian agent for Virginia and the Carolinas and was setting up a headquarters for himself somewhere down in the Shenandoah Valley.

In time, I heard from Gist that Mercy had married some mountain man and gone into that country where the peaks and ridges seem perpetually on fire, and that she was said to have borne him a child.

I did not hear from her for something more than three years, and then in July of 1759, about the fourth anniversary of Braddock's defeat, a crudely worked but lengthy letter in her hand arrived, bearing sad news.

Gist had gone down into the Carolinas bent on recruiting more Catawbas and Tuscaroras to the fighting with the French. He'd met with small
success but acquired from the Indians the damned smallpox and died of it
quite quickly, age just fifty-four.

Here was a man who'd done more to open our frontier than any other,
but ever did that fame elude him. He's quite forgotten now, as blundering
Braddock is remembered everywhere and forever, his name on every place.

As I say, I've never gone into those mountains again, but I once jour-
neyed near them, going to visit Lord Fairfax on business.

Did you know that all through the French and Indian War, and thus far
through this revolutionary one, His Lordship and his Shenandoah properties have remained utterly unmolested by one and all? So respected was
and is he that neither Frenchman, Canadian, nor Indian—and now, neither
redcoat nor continental—has so much as fired a musket ball in his direction.

Before my night's supper at his Greenway Court there in the Shenandoah, I took a long, lonely walk across the meadows, looking toward that
one mountain to the south—Massanutten?—that so resembles a ship
turned to the wind, and I found myself thinking of Mercy with an ache.

I called out her name, without feeling the slightest foolish, and do you
know, there was a stirring in the trees from a sudden rising breeze in response.

I suppose I must be content with that.

Yes, to be sure, I married Susannah Smithson.

Death was a great provider in her case as well. She returned to America
heiress to her father's fortune and wed to her major, who was now baronet
with the passing of his brother. Her husband's regiment had been dispatched to America to do battle with the same French Indian foe as had I—
only in the New York colony.

Alas, he was among the poor defenders of Fort William Henry under
Colonel Munro, and died of tomahawking when his defeated and retreating
column—traveling virtually without arms on their own parole with French
laissez-passe—were set upon by angry Indians in lawless ambush.

So there, in 1757, was I yet unmarried, and Lady Susannah—the title
clung to almost viciously ever since, despite her marriage to commoner
me—a widow. And still the most beautiful woman in Philadelphia, if not
all the colonies, and as worldly and educated a one as any gentleman of
intellect could desire.

This was more than a year since Mercy had left me for the wilds—and
desire Susannah I did, both mind and body. We married quickly and in jolly
celebration. Our combined fortunes, with hers so prodigious to begin with,
made us people of great substance. And by dint of inheritance, we were
both full partners with Butler in my brother's mercantile seafaring.

We not only kept that damned Butler from entangling the firm again
in slave shipping, we gave him one of the ships outright in return for his

quitting us complete. He invested in cotton plantations in the south, continuing his life as northern aristocrat supported by the labor of Gullah slaves. I have been diligent in making sure that all Philadelphia society is aware of that.

Sharp-tongued as she can be, and no matter how painfully conservative her politics, I have delighted in every minute of my life with this golden-haired lady. I love Susannah as I loved her in the full freshness of her pretty youth and as I did as she lay retching and gasping in my arms aboard ship to England. Yet I still love Mercy, as I still love—and I do—Sally Fairfax.

Do you understand this? You must, if you wish to understand General Washington, for I am as fair convinced as I am of anything that not one drop of his passion for Sally has fled his veins in all these years, yet he delights in every minute he is with his Martha.

Thirty-seven

You may remark how curious for a man to denounce another as "villain," before his very fellows, and then continue for years thereafter a correspondence and friendship—and attend upon the "villain's" wedding.

My essential explanation—or if you will, defense—is that both are true things, villain and friend, and also that it is in the way of mankind that the one cannot be had without the other.

Whose friend is perfect? I know no man more good-hearted, civic-minded, brilliant in intellect and better a friend than Franklin, yet is he not also philanderer, adulterer, seducer of young virgins, political intriguer, and now, traitor to his Sovereign? But as I would have the one part of him, I must take the other.

My wife is one of the most esteemed women in all the colonies, and were she instead despised, I would still cherish her with the great ardor I always have. But with her essential good heart and keen mind and beauty come extravagance, a waspish tongue, and vanity.

Sally Fairfax is as dear a lady as I know, but who could deny her provincial airs and, if I may make so bold, unseemly indiscretion? Christopher Gist? As towering a conqueror of the western wilds as ever there strode upon a mountain, yet petty knave with penny and expense accountings. Half King had a noble nature, and deep wisdom. He was endlessly brave and a jolly companion on the travel. But with little bother, he'd happily wash his hands in brains.

George Washington is not perfect. Who would have him so? He is human, a man like all the rest of us. As he was friend that night we came within an inch of freezing to death on that icy Allegheny island, so was he friend when he made that grievous error at Jumonville Glen.

And looming over all of this, of course, is my still lingering doubt.

If the matter at Jumonville Glen was a case open and shut, a terrible sin confessed to and forgiven, the burden of it might now be more easily borne.

But, as I said at the commencement of this, all these years I have not known the truth of it. On nights when the past has troubled my sleep, it's not only for the remembered screams and horrible images that I've fretted in my sheets. There is that doubt. In rising so provocatively that bloody, long-ago morning, did he merely err, or did he commit crime?

British justice found no crime by Washington then, but certainly it does now in this continuing insurrection.

It had been my hope and expectation that this rebellion would subside as all others before it on the soil of North America—that these rebels might give it up and go back to their homes at last, admitting the error of their enterprise and letting King's law rule where it must and tranquillity come again over the land.

It was thus a shock to me the other night, with General Howe and entourage at table, to hear of no such leniency in the mind of the Crown's representative. Very matter-of-factly, without malice or animus, he observed how the fate of Washington and his rebellious comrades could in no way be left a kind one.

The rebel leaders, noted Howe, would all be taken back to England for trial—Washington, Franklin, every one of them. One or two or more would have to be hanged as example, Howe said. The King would have no choice. All the rest would be imprisoned for years and years, and their properties confiscated in partial payment for the cost the Crown has had to bear in suppressing this revolt.

I had envisioned this insurrection ending with formal ceremony—a surrender of sword and granting of amnesty and parole. Not gallows and leg irons. Howe's words have distressed me greatly. I think they did also my wife.

For weeks now, I've heard considerable about the sufferings of George and his men in their frozen hell at Valley Forge, and I've had recurring impulses to help them. I've not given into these promptings for fear that keeping his ragged little army intact would only prolong the struggle and thus the bloodshed. If severe enough, a rough winter like this one at hand might strike some sense into George and his followers, so they'd all go home and we'd have peace again.

Now, says Howe, it's likely to be death instead. Who's more leader of the Damned Rebels than "Mister" Washington? I mentioned hanging. It could be the axe or worse. Vile and many are the medieval punishments still on the English capital list.

There came to hand recently this long pamphlet, "The American Crisis," by a man of my small acquaintance, one Thomas Paine, a fellow perhaps best described as a street rowdy in the printing trade.

There are a few lines in his pamphlet: "Tyranny, like hell, is not easily conquered; yet we have this consolation with us, that the harder the conflict, the more glorious the triumph. What we obtain too cheap, we esteem too lightly. 'Tis dearness only that gives everything its value."

And also: "We are not moved by the gloomy smile of a worthless king, but by the ardent glow of generous patriotism. We fight not to enslave, but to set a country free, and to make room upon the earth for honest men to live in. In such a cause we are sure we are right; and we leave to you the despairing reflection of being the tool of a miserable tyrant."

Susannah all but shrieked when she encountered the words "a worthless king," but I must confess, such boldness thrilled me.

For when this foolish monarch did put aside the worthy Pitt back in '60, did I not remark much the same?

———

I am by no means as compulsively busy as Mister Franklin, but my days are much taken up with commerce and my evenings given over to attending upon my wife's social affairs and the concerns of my children, so it has been in the very dead of night that I've most often repaired to my study and writing desk to labor upon this recounting.

Consequently, I oft go to sleep thinking hard upon it and the events it relates, and often wake in the morning at the conclusion of sometimes dreadful dreams of remarkable clarity about those old times.

In one such recent phantasm, I saw myself trying desperately to kill again the Ottawa brave I'd dispatched while with Braddock at the Monongahela. In another, I have been pursued through impossible woods by an Indian who gets nearer and nearer, and at the end, as I scream—aloud, I fear, vexing my wife sorely—he is discovered to be Half King.

Two nights ago, I found myself, having completed the preceding chapter of this work, becoming similarly vexed by dream as I lay in bed by my wife's warm side.

There was the remembered image of a winter wilderness and George, Gist, and myself sitting huddled around a fire so close our feet were nearly in it, drinking melted snow and thinking ourselves fortunate.

But then I turned to George and asked him calmly, as friend to friend, was he a murderer? His face, as in dream imagined, took on this high color and dark, stern look, and he seemed on the point of explosive rage. I feared he was going to kill me.

Then I waked.

I rose and crept, freezing in nightshirt, downstairs to the kitchen, where I found a fire still glowing and the comfort of strong cider. After stirring the fire's embers to flame, I sat hunched over my cup, letting my mind take me where it would, and it took me to the hills to the west of the city, and what few memories I had of the place called Valley Forge.

There he was, my friend George Washington, camped only a wagon's drive or horseback ride from me.

The kitchen fire went low and my cider cold. I should have returned to bed. It was still hours before the dawn.

No. I knew precisely what I must do.

I fetched three of my strongest and most trustworthy men from their nearby quarters, had them hitch up three wagons, and set out for the countryside to the west. Not directly, mind, though Valley Forge is but eighteen miles to the northwest on the other side of the Schuylkill. Both the exigencies of this war and the nature of my scheme necessitated a detour.

I have this farm, don't you know, out in the country near the village of Darby and on the Darby River. We use it as a refuge in the summer from the city's heat and foul odors, and also as a provider of fresh fruits and vegetables for our table and winter feed for our stables. There are numerous orchards on the place, and when the season for apples is past, we store the usual abundance of them in the form of cider, barrels and barrels of it.

We ordinarily end up selling the most of it, for my wife and our lofty guests prefer wine and I'm really the only one who favors it. But we haven't yet this year parted with much more than a hogshead and the storehouse was full..

It occurred to me then how to put such a plenitude of this tasty, fortified juice to better use. There were freezing men in those hills who could use its warmth badly.

Now, I carry at all times a pass signed by General Howe himself. So taken is he with my wife's entertainments—and her own flirtatious self—that he'd happily sign me a pass to the King's wife's bedchamber if I asked. I am, besides, a familiar figure in this town, and often a sentry will let me progress with no examination.

The two who guarded the Schuylkill River bridge were not of such easy mind, and the ranking one of the two looked my pass over twice, both sides. Three empty wagons on the road without escort at this hour were warrant enough for suspicion, I suppose.

"Where're ye bound?" he asked, still holding the paper in his woolly gloves. He had woolly scarf about his neck as well, but no greatcoat over his red uniform tunic.

"To my farm in Darby," I said, as cheerily as I could muster. "I fetch fodder for my horses and provisions for our table—and some for General Howe's as well."

With that, he handed back the pass but still did not let us on our way. "There's rebels to the west," he said. "A whole army of them."

"At Valley Forge. But I'm not going that way. I'm to my farm at Darby. At all events, those poor wretches haven't shoes and not many clothes. They'll not be stirring from their hovels on so cold a night unless it's because the likes of you lads are coming for 'em."

This sentry seemed to have small wish to be coming for 'em. "Are you armed, sir?"

"No." In truth, I wasn't, though my men had pistols beneath their wagon seats.

"Well, you have a care then, sir. And travel brisk."

He stepped aside and gave a slight salute, afterward returning to the small fire he and his comrade had lit by the side of the road. We creaked out onto the bridge and across the frozen river, making a seemly haste once we got to the other side.

It was six miles to my farm, where resides a manager with wife and family. With all hands pressed, we loaded each wagon with as many barrels as they'd take, then looked about for more solid sustenance and odds and ends that might help, including clothing. With wagons heaped to the very limit our teams of horses could drag up a slippery hill, we set forth now on northerly roads, traveling in increasing light, though, alas, no increasing warmth.

The first of the Continental Army's sentinels was much more forward advanced than I'd expected, taking me by surprise, and he signaled his wish for our halt by discharging his musket in our general direction, the ball whistling by uncomfortably close. He was an older fellow, grizzled and rough-looking, indeed resembling much the men who'd been with us at the Monongahela and Fort Necessity two decades ago. He made us dismount and searched our persons, not greatly pleased to find a pass signed by the British commander.

"You're spies and you'll be dead ones, soon," he said, backing up to level his musket at us.

A useless gesture, this. As he'd forgotten, he'd just discharged the piece.

"No spy would be so fool as to wander about carrying such a pass," I said. "We come to see General Washington."

A sergeant came running up from down the road and drew what I'm sure was a loaded pistol on me. The sentry showed him my pass and repeated my stated business.

"The General? You would see the General, bearing this?" He found this outrageous funny, as I supposed it was. "What have you in those wagons?"

"Cider for your troops and other necessities."

"And these are gifts?" He waved the pass about. "From General Howe?"

"They are gifts from me, so let me by, if you please. Just get word to General Washington that Captain Thomas Morley is here to see him. Tick Morley. Tell him that."

'Twas the first I'd used the "Tick" since the French and Indian War.

"Captain? And in no uniform? That makes you spy sure enough."

"I'm a sea captain. Now, please. A message to General Washington. I tell you, he'll be glad to see me."

"I don't know if he'll be glad, but he'll be seeing you, for you are under arrest."

———

More soldiers came to attend us. We remounted the wagons, and in something of a mob and with great difficulty on the icy track, we ascended the hill. Eyes were fixed far more intently on the wagon loads than on me and the drivers, and I began to fear that my good deed would be ruined by sack and pillage before I could impress General Washington with it, but there was good discipline here.

I was in fact amazed at that, given the ravaging cold and dreadful condition of these men. A good half of the sentries and others in posts of duty had rags wound 'round their feet for shoes, and their blue uniform coats were in tatters. Wound rags did for gloves as well. I could not comprehend that this was the fighting force keeping the British lion at bay.

"We are the army besieging Lord Howe's troops in Philadelphia," one of them put it—a young, scrawny lieutenant with missing teeth and cheeks burnt crimson by the wind.

This officer took charge of our party, and on a horse so frail and unhappy it looked as though it'd just as soon be roasted for dinner to get itself warm, led the procession to a small house set between thick groves of trees. There were two sentries at its door, much better uniformed, who jumped to attention at the lieutenant's approach and did so again a moment later when he came out again, this time followed by a tall figure with a blue greatcoat about his shoulders.

The booming voice echoed over the snow-crusted yard: "Tick? Is it you?"

He came a few paces out onto the snow, looking a giant, and waited. I leapt down from my wagon seat, not so nimbly as in years past, and hurried to him as fast I could manage. Halting, I slipped a little on the frozen surface. We stared at each other, and all there stared at us. His large blue-gray eyes, so fittingly arctic in this place and weather, seemed just as clear and keen as always, and his face was ruddy, as though from good health, and not just cold wind. But he seemed so old! It had been less than two years since our last encounter—though a lifetime in military and political measure. He is forty-five, forty-six next February, and I forty-two. I guessed he looked ten years my senior. Perhaps an end to this war would restore him, as the end of the last one had me.

I heard a dog barking, and men's voices behind me. The tension broke. George took a step and threw arms around my shoulders, and I his.

"It is good to see a friend," he said. "These days, they are few in number."

He took me inside. Martha, thickly wrapped in shawl, bonnet, and quilted dressing gown over her clothing, was in the hall and greeted me as warmly as had her husband. Then she turned to scold a serving girl into bringing us hot refreshment.

George stooped through a doorway to the side and led me into his office. There was a small fire on the hearth, but the windowpanes appeared to have ice upon both sides. Three men were seated at a table almost completely covered with maps and correspondence, and another stood at a near wall, looking at a map pinned there. A fifth, appearing as much a pile of rags as that first sentry, was seated on the floor by the fireside, scribbling something on a folded-over piece of paper.

Washington introduced them, and I received bows or handshakes 'round, except from the scribbler. The man at the map was General Nathanael Greene, "soon to be our commissary-general, should we ever acquire some commissary for him to general," said Washington with some laughter.

Of the three at the table, two were quite young—Colonel John Laurens, an aide-de-camp whose father Henry was president of the Continental Congress, and a Frenchman, the Marquis de Lafayette, who was so exuberant at meeting an old friend of his hero I thought he was going to kiss me.

The other man at table was a Count Casimir Pulaski of what had once been the kingdom of Poland until swallowed up by Russia, Prussia, and the Austrians. He spoke almost no English, but I succeeded with a few words in French. I was curious at his presence in that army, as Washington introduced him as his cavalry commander. As I was sure George spoke no Polish, I wondered how they communicated, but it likely didn't matter. Doubtless they'd eaten nearly all the cavalry horses.

The man by the fireside I knew. In fact, he seemed to be wearing the same ill-fitting, greasy clothes he'd had on at our first encounter four years before, when he turned up at my offices fresh off a ship from England and bearing a letter of ardent recommendation from Franklin, then temporarily residing in London. As Franklin requested, I'd given the fellow some money and inquired after some employment for him, which proved to be in assisting the editor of the *Pennsylvania Magazine*. He was this selfsame Thomas Paine—the last name quite fitting as concerned his loutish manners—and he was a genius, if otherwise a most disagreeable man. In all my readings, I'd never quite thrilled to words as I did in consuming that "Crisis" pamphlet, which I'm told is now in great circulation.

"Captain Morley," he said, getting to his feet, "have you come at last to join our cause?"

"I've joined no cause, either for or against you."

Paine was about to launch into I'm sure a well-practiced polemic about the evils of neutrality and other political sins of omission, but Washington stayed him with an upraised hand.

"He comes as friend," George said. "Old friend. That's all that matters."

"I come with presents," I said. "Three wagons full."

"Presents?"

"Hard cider mostly, for your men. Some smoked meat and flour. Some clothes, and tanned hide that might make shoes."

Washington went to the window, peering at the wagons through the thickness of ice. "I'd no thought of what those wagons were," he said. "There's not enough for all, but what's there will be sorely appreciated."

He turned to Laurens. "See to as equitable a distribution as possible. Start with the hospital."

The young man saluted and headed for the door, but I bade him wait. "There's a parcel under the seat of the first wagon," I said. "It should come in here."

Laurens went out and sent it back with the frail lieutenant. I opened carefully the bound sack, removing seven bottles of fine French brandy— all I had at my Darby place.

You'd have thought I'd brought angels, or chests of gold. They all were a long time in thanking me.

The maid fetched mugs of some steaming dark brew that was introduced as coffee, but tasted something else. Washington had five of the brandy bottles sent to safekeeping for a grander occasion, but one he uncorked and set on the table with instruction that it be shared with the rest of the staff. The other he stuck under his arm. Taking a steaming mug with his other hand and placing another hot cup in mine, he started out the door.

"I want to bring a taste of this fine brandy to my good General Knox, and I want you to meet him as well. Even here in the midst of our starvation, he is so fatted in the arse he can barely sit a horse, or trim a boat, but he's among the very best I have."

It was now well into the morning and the sun had made its warmth a little better known. The wind had dropped as well. Washington started us through the trees and up a slope.

"His quarters are in a house farther along the creek," he said, "but he spends much of his time with his artillery brigade up the hill, where he has a hut he keeps as hot as an oven."

A squad of infantry fell into line behind George at some distance astern, in custom. These he ignored, but when the Marquis de Lafayette of a sudden appeared, bounding over the snow toward us like some frolicking puppy, George waved him back.

"Later, *monsieur*," he said. "I will join you later." We advanced a few paces and, more quietly, he spoke again. "The Marquis' effusiveness is hard to bear, but I am told by Franklin there is a chance we'll have the French on our side in earnest—perhaps with a fleet—so I do nothing that might ruffle feathers. He's able enough, in truth, though I don't think he would have lasted a day with us upon Laurel Ridge."

"How odd that we have traded our old friend for our old foe," I said.

George laughed. "I think of that quite often. That incompetent Gage was our friend. Now he's our foe. I'm damned grateful."

We tramped on through the snow, he sipping his coffee without pausing, I spilling mine but not greatly caring. I could have done with more time inside the warm house, but perhaps we'd soon be entering another shelter.

Alas not. Washington was taking me not only up an arduous grade, but passing among collections of huts set in holes dug in the ground, showing me them as he might major sights on his plantation. The board walls of some were well and tightly built, admitting no wind or cold, but trapping in the stench and smoke with which the unfortunates inside constantly abided. Others had spaces between the slats and board, and so their inhabitants breathed better, but were colder.

Some of the men were outside, and I was shocked to see their condition. More than a few were moving about the snow on the flesh of bare feet. Others wore clothes so torn and ragged, their bodies seemed naked, yet festooned. At least one fellow, taking a hurried pee, was altogether exposed.

Across a swale was a ragged line of tents. The occupants must have seen us, for there came from them protesting, moaning chants: "No meat. No meat. No meat."

I was shocked by this marked degree of want, because for all the redcoat occupation and recurring battles, the colonies were in plenty—most especially Pennsylvania. I knew for fact there was beef enough in this and the next county alone to feed the whole of Washington's army for weeks, much as these herds had been nimbly kept from Howe's in Philadelphia. There were shoes to be had out here, clothes of every kind, and whiskey. The British were not making war or laying siege upon the colonies entire—not with so many neutral or disposed toward them. Their fight was with Washington's army and the seditious and peripatetic Congress. The King's soldiers occupied a few cities and towns, and shelled a few others, but with only a few exceptions, such as that murderous bastard Banastre Tarleton, who waged war like a Hun, His Majesty's forces left the American population and its riches in larger part unmolested.

As Washington explained, the fault for the miseries at Valley Forge lay mostly with the Congress. The system of procurement was no good, and ridden with corruption. The Continental money was neither respected nor accepted. Attempts at compensated confiscation and other rough forms of forage were frustrated by farmers and the like, who hid their goods and provisions, either out of greed or for fear they'd be accused of supporting Britain's enemy and otherwise committing treason.

"I am myself intrigued against, you know, as incompetent," Washington said as we moved on. "There are parties in the Congress who would have that damned poltroon Charles Lee command, or that Irish-born General Conway. They resist my good Greene for commissary and would have Mifflin or some other. If only they could come here and see these poor soldiers of mine. It is not incompetence that has brought us failure in the field. Would that it were, for then I'd gladly step down to assure the better fortune of our rebellion. The cause of failure is nakedness and scurvy and the flux and fever. Are they fools and madmen, our Congress? Can they be so deluded as to fail to comprehend that men cannot fight or walk in winter snow in bare feet? Or with bare ribs and backsides exposed to the wind? And nothing in their bellies? I don't know how many soldiers I have left. There is no fixed count. The rolls keep declining. They die in such numbers you'd think it was from battle. But these are excellent fellows. They may moan and prattle about the lack of meat, they may look like death itself, but by God, they stay. Those who are left with me when comes the spring will be the essence of one hell of an army. If only they could be shod and fed and fitted. This damned Congress."

"I was never its admirer," I said, "the Congress."

We crossed an open space on the upper slope of the hill, then paused. Looking down and around, I could see that Washington's encampment was a considerable establishment in size, if pathetic in condition.

"You know me well, Tom, and so you know I am not uncommonly modest. But it is with great conviction I tell you no other than I can hold this together. These men won't freeze here for Charles Lee or Conway or any other. And believe me, all the troubles I had in the old days with Dinwiddie and the Burgesses over supplies and money and a sufficiency of men, all the desperation of those years trying to hold the frontier, all those horrors piled together make for a mild day compared to this."

"I am appalled," I said.

He smiled, exposing some of the gold wiring supporting his painful-looking false teeth. We were nearing a new group of huts, marked by a wavering row of emplaced cannon. He halted again, drawing me close.

"I know you're neutral in this, Tom, but I must know further. What does Howe plan? I have intelligence enough to know he's at your table frequently."

His question seemed a most serious broach of the "Rules of Civility." To answer it would be to commit treason, or at least espionage. I wondered if it was a test. If I answered wrongly, would he not let me go? Whither friendship now?

"I speak one word and I am traitor," I said.

"There's naught here to hear it but me, and I am already traitor."

I decided to answer—and truthfully. I feared he might just keep me standing here all day if I did not. Besides, I wanted to.

"General Howe does not share with us his troop strength or schedule of transport arrivals and grand strategies drawn upon maps," I said. "But I feel safe in saying he will not stir from our city until you move from this place. He boasts of having you 'pinned.' And he enjoys our city much. Except for the Quakers, it is much more like London than New York, which Howe detests."

"Then I've picked our Valley Forge well. I wanted to be near him, but only just, so I'd have plenty of warning should he come after our army, yet give him as little as possible of it myself, should I decide to move quickly for a strike elsewhere. I'd do that tomorrow if only we could get resupplied. If I ever am, come spring, we'll have an army good enough to fight the whole long year."

We were atop the hill. All about us was a panorama of barren winter, misery, and defeat.

"I think we shall win this war, Tom. We are independent, you know. All the colonies. It is a fact. All it requires now is for a foreign power or two to make recognition of that."

"The French."

"Aye. I think they will. This Lafayette is well placed in their aristocracy, and he thinks so."

"They would aid you, 'assassin of Jumonville'?"

"Their foe is Britain. Come. You must meet Knox."

He led me on through knots of sitting and standing artillerymen to a small building that was more cabin than house. Indeed, it proved to have but one room—and one most commodiously filled by the bulk of a huge officer whose splendid uniform must have been made from two. Not so tall as George, rather more my height, he had a pleasant face and intelligent eyes, though far too many chins. He rose, bidding two aides he had with him to seek the chill outside.

They were doubtless glad of it. The fire in his place was enormous and roaring, and very quickly I was hot.

"Knox," said George in the informality of bonhomie, "this is Tom Morley, a Philadelphia friend. He was with me at Great Meadows and Braddock's Field." He set the brandy bottle down on Knox's crude table. "He brings us presents, some cheer to chase the chill."

"This is a bloody amazement," said Knox. "You are not from Philadelphia, sir. You are from paradise, bearing ambrosia."

He smiled, his brows shooting up. Pouring some of his own excuse for coffee into a cup, he set it down with ours, then filled the remainder of all three mugs with brandy. I started to reach for mine, but he bade me not. Turning quickly about—I feared for the crockery on his small sideboard—he took up a blackened iron poker, shoved it deep into his fire, and waited a moment.

"Now!" he said, retrieving the poker and plunging it into each cup quickly, making a steaming hiss each time. Then he set poker to wall and himself onto a bench and lifted his mug. "There's a fine toddy!"

We sipped happily. I tell you, I've stayed skittish with spirits since my brother Richard's death and my woodland despond after Braddock's defeat, but never in all my life has any drink tasted quite so wonderful as this.

"How did you pass through British lines?" asked Knox, his curiosity, I think, bearing the slightest barb of suspicion.

I explained my pass and our ruse with the mission of gathering horse fodder from the farm.

"On your return then, you must bring back fine presents for General Howe and the sentries who greet you," said Knox.

"I will," I said, "for I intend to come here again."

"But do not give them presents so fine as this!"

He splashed more brandy into his cup without benefit of the heated poker, drank, then rose and drank again, draining it all and giving forth a happy sigh at the end.

"Now I could fight their whole army," he said. "At least until supper." He patted his broad belly. "I am off to examine some new defense we are digging here on Mount Joy—yes, that is its name. We must be better prepared and fortified. And then I'm to the field where von Steuben is making fine European soldiery of our poor farmers."

"Baron von Steuben," said Washington in response to my querying expression. "He is a Prussian general come to help us, and doing a damn fine job of it. We'll have the worthy makings of a grand parade come spring."

"I think he is no baron," said Knox, pulling on his greatcoat. "Nor is he Prussian, nor a general. For all I know, he was a sergeant. But it matters not with the men. He's making the best of them I've seen."

"We've become an army of many nations," Washington said. "You met our Pulaski. He has his flaws. Slept through one battle in a barn, claiming no one came to wake him, though the cannon fire would have waked the dead. You know, I once saw him ride galloping at a pistol placed on the ground. He snatched it up without a falter in the horse's stride, threw the damn thing into the air, caught it with horse still on the run, and loosed the ball at a target, hitting it square. If cavalry were deployed in units of one man, he'd be the best in the world."

"We'll be down to one-man cavalry soon enough," said Knox, "unless our mounts're replenished."

He thanked me again for the brandy and started for the outside. Washington bade him leave the door open, for the excess heat, and for appreciation of the hilltop view.

"This place reminds me somewhat of that lean-to hunting shack where we harbored a night on our way back from Le Boeuf," Washington said, lifting his booted feet to the tabletop after Knox had gone.

"A little," I said, looking to the distant snowy hills visible through the doorway. "But then we had no brandy, or roaring fire."

"We had our youth to warm us. So long gone now."

"It's a grand view from here," I said.

"Not quite 'the land as the sea.' "

"No."

"It's what we fought the French for. Now we fight King George for it."

"Is that why you're here? Why you've writ your name so large on the list of traitors?"

He smiled again. "I could give you a hundred reasons, Thomas. Their barring us from the Ohio country is a big one. And we all have grievances. I gave the King as much as he might expect or want from any soldier, but got nothing for it. No rank, no recognition, no regular commission. Not an acre. But that's a petty quarrel. The thing of it is, we've become a country of our own now—no longer colonies. Virginia, Maryland, each a country—maybe one great country, without need or want of foreign landlords.

"When I was young and my father alive, he had a small forge there on the road north from Fredericksburg. The need for ironwork was great, and there was iron enough in the mountains to feed the forge. But the Crown forbade him to produce more than a few paltry things, lest he compete with the ironworks in England. And so we suffered. We were not rich folk, Thomas.

"Now there're thousands, millions of complaints of that nature—and taxes, and the support of troops occupying lands we're not allowed to live in, and myriad other miseries afflicted. The wonder's not in why I'm here, but why more aren't—though I'd scarce be able to feed 'em."

We sipped. Looking through the open door, it occurred to me for the first time in many years that I rather would like to stand upon that high prospect of Laurel Ridge and look upon "the land as the sea" again. This view looked in that direction.

"Your beautiful wife," George said of a sudden. "She is well?"

"Aye. She is concerned for you."

"I am told she is General Howe's favorite American. Goodness knows, she's one of mine."

"She admires you, General, and fears for your life and safety. But she does not wish you well in your cause. I daresay whoever wins this war will find a friend in our family."

I wondered here if he suspected me of sympathy with her Tory side of things—of coming here in guise of friend, but in truth to spy out all the weaknesses of this crude redoubt and suffering army, in advance, perhaps, of British attack.

But no, he was content to continue in friendship. He had quite something else in mind.

"As yours is a household deemed loyal to the Crown," he said, "you have easy access to the mails. Your Susannah still corresponds with her friends in England?"

"Oh, yes. With astonishing frequency."

He hesitated, studying me. "Do you think it might be convenient for you to get a letter to England for me?"

I thought upon this. Convenient, no. Dangerous, yes.

"I could," I said, then hesitated. "I presume the recipient is a Mrs. George William Fairfax?"

His ruddy face colored even more. "Yes. Of course it is. Damn all, Thomas, you know it. Do you object?"

"No."

"You'll do it?"

"Leave off your signature, which could damn us all, and I will see she gets it as part of one from me—and that she gets it quite directly, delivered unto her own hand. Susannah has friends who can tend to that."

George rose, with some happy excitement, and went to Knox's small writing table, there finding paper and taking quill to hand.

" 'Twill not take long," he said. "I've had it writ in my mind for weeks. It's been eight or more months since I last heard from her, and that the only letter I've received since they sailed for England. Pray refresh the cups again with that good cognac."

I rose to do so, then set his by him. His quill was scratching away with great vigor.

"At all events," I said, "you've all her old letters to console you."

He stopped, looking up, but not at me. "No, alas, I do not. Martha's burned them. Every one."

I had gone to the open doorway, for the heat was fearful. "What?"

"More than two hundred of them, all gone to ash on her order—when I was away campaigning. 'Twas the only thing she's ever done against my wish—though I never gave voice to it. Who'd have thought I'd need to?"

"Could you not have kept them hidden secret?"

"Thought I had. Sooth, I don't think she was bothered overmuch by Sally's letters, for they have always been cautious, and couched in propriety. Every one. 'Twas the others, those from Anne Gist."

"I knew not of those."

"They were many, too many I'd have thought for a girl ungifted in language."

"You two were . . ."

"She had just claims, shall we say, and say no more. My bargain with our friend her father was to provide for her safety at some place far from the fighting. She stayed with the Fairfaxes some years."

"And what of her since?"

"I do not know. At war's end, she went off into the Shenandoah, and then I think to the far end of the valley." He paused. "There where your Mercy went."

I took a step closer to the cold out-of-doors. The wind was refreshing against my face.

"I am almost done," George said, behind me.

I turned to see him take a swallow of his drink, now half brandy.

"Would that I had my Hercules here to tend to the coffee. You recall my servant Hercules? He who learned the French way with cooking?"

"I remember him well. He has not died?"

"No. Escaped. The man has wife and children waiting him at Mount Vernon, but he's fled, and for good. I think perhaps now he's in Philadelphia. You might see him, for he's uncommonly well-dressed. Almost a dandy. We informed his family, through the overseer, and do you know how they replied? They are separated forever, yet his daughter, asked if she were sad, said, 'Oh sir, I am very glad, because he is free now.' "

He had chin in hand, and was staring out the door.

"I have Negroes here among my soldiers," he said. "Free men. They have fought and soldiered well, very well. I could almost not believe it." He raised his head. "I've thought many times on what you said to me on this subject years ago. I think that when I die, I shall leave no slave to any man but themselves. Do you comprehend me? I think I shall have them free."

"Why not now?"

He shrugged. "Without the institution, there could be no Mount Vernon. Not as it survives."

I heard shouting—commands—and the tromp of marching feet ringing through the cold air.

"I tarry overlong," he said. "There. I'm done."

Folding the letter, he took a bar of sealing wax and put to its end the tip of a burning wood from the fire. A large crimson drop of wax fell to the folded paper. He was about to press his seal upon it when I bade him not.

"They'll mark you by it," I said.

"Yes, of course." He brought the letter to me, gratitude softening his eyes.

He put the remnants of the brandy in a drawer. Our cups were still fairly full, so we stood the two of us together by the doorway to finish them.

"I asked her to come back," George said. "When this war is over. That's what I wrote. I fear she may not, as they are on the wrong side of it, but I would make her welcome—the both of them."

"What if her side wins?"

"Then I shall be dead, and 'twill matter not."

He grinned, showing more gold springs in his mouth, and clapped me on the shoulder. "I would have a reply to this. I would hope for one quite like another I once received, in one respect at least."

"What's that?"

"It came to my eye while we were on the road to Fort Necessity. It was the only time in all our lives she ever wrote that she loved me."

I started a bit. "What? You never told me of this."

"You delivered it yourself, Tom, from her very hand. Came riding up to our column, fresh from Belvoir, and dug it out of your pocket."

I remembered. Dug out one of two. The other later burned. The contents of neither truly known. "Thomas," she had said, "you have given him the wrong one."

"I'd thought that letter full of chiding," I said. "An admonition to cease your flow of correspondence, for you were vexing her husband. That was what she told me."

"There was some of that, Tom. Too much of that. She asked me to cease writing. Worse, she asked me, for the good of us both, to remove myself to another part of Virginia, if not to another colony. If not to England. It was written with some passion. She said she asked this of me in the name of love—that she would declare it, she did love me, yes, and that if she hadn't husband live, she'd marry me. But as she loved me, she would have us both happy, and so apart, far apart, forever. As the object of her love, I must obey."

There came into his eyes that farseeing look again, but it was no great wilderness vista he held there.

"But you did not go away," I said. "Except to war."

"How could I, Tom? She said she loved me!"

We stood there for the longest time, as though the mind of each of us was filling with the other's thoughts. But then of a sudden, I think we both wished to be away from this hut.

I drained my cup, as did he. Throwing on his coat again, he started back for the door, but I stayed him.

"George," I said quietly, "I am your friend, and I will do what I can for you, Tory politics no matter."

"Then I chose well when first I spied you and your little sloop that day in Alexandria."

"But as your friend, I must ask you something, and seek an honest answer."

He leaned back against the doorway, facing me. We were standing very close. His uniform was well-brushed, the brass buttons highly burnished.

"Yes?" he said, with some wariness.

"When we were at Jumonville Glen, gathered in hiding all around that cliff top . . ."

Washington put his hand to my chest, as though to brake me. "Tick," he said, "we've crossed this ground before."

"Nay. We've walked upon it, but never crossed to the other side. Not in all these years."

He sighed. "Very well. Let's be done with it."

"We were all of us crouched down in hiding, none of us visible to the French below. A call of our purpose might have sufficed to keep those Frenchmen at ease, to stay their reach for arms, to impress upon them the strength of our numbers and position, and their hopelessness."

"Perhaps. Yet any shout as that might only have panicked them more."

"A white flag of truce waved then, any sign that we were not there to kill them."

"Perhaps. And perhaps is all I'll give you."

"But when you stood up as you did, appearing with such suddeness, and armed—you must grant it was a shocking sight. That one Frenchman who reached for his musket. He did so, George, in fear of his life."

"I expect so."

"But the one thing led to the other. You stood, he reached, our soldiers fired, Frenchmen died, and the war was on. Within a year, it had spread all 'round the world."

"There's truth in that. I've oft thought upon it in all that's followed. Curious how a thing like that could bring on so much. But war was in the air, Tom. 'Twas warlike French who drove our Captain Trent's party from the Forks. The Indians had their blood up. Any small thing could have blown that powder."

"Yes, but you provided the match."

Our eyes were fixed upon each other. It was growing late, and we each had other concerns to turn to—he far more than I.

"What I would know, George—when you got to your feet and stood above that bush, pistol in hand—was that what you had in mind? Did you seek the deaths below as a step to war and glory? Did Ensign Jumonville die because you wished it? To serve the end of your provocation? Your ambition?"

The focus of his eyes altered not a whit. He scarcely blinked. "No," he said. "I wished none of those men dead. I wished only their submission, as the French wished of us at the Forks."

"But why then? Why did you stand?"

A slight smile came to his lips. "Why, Tick, you brought the reason yourself, kept safe in your pocket all the way from Belvoir."

"I?"

"That letter. She said she loved me. Those written words were with me every step on our march into the forest, up every mountain. You cannot know the constant thrill they gave me every time I thought upon them. She loved me. Married, yes, but she was mine. And I her champion.

"Yet there I was, at the moment of battle, but crouching behind a bush—not her hero, but furtive, like some low, predatory animal. If she could have seen me skulking so, what craven thing would she think me? At this, my first soldierly encounter, hidden in the weeds like a snake. No! It was as though her eyes were on me. I would take to the fight to come in manly fashion. I would stand, and let them kill me if they could. But I tell you, Tick, rising in that place, looking down upon them as the battle commenced, I felt immortal."

"It was for her?"

"You know the lady," George said. "I need say to you no more."

Helen of Troy. Sally of Jumonville Glen.

I could hear again the sound of tramping, cadenced feet, and more rhythmic shouting. The wind blew colder now against my cheek.

"And now you're here," I said, "leading an army of scarecrows in this place of want and suffering."

"I've told you the why of that, Thomas. But I'll confide I have a fire here to warm me and keep me that's denied your friend General Howe."

I glanced behind me, but he was indicating his heart.

"If I lose this thing, I shall perish," he said. "I accept that. It's the way of our cause. But should we prevail, Tick, and thus end this war . . ." His expression gentled. "Why, then she can come back."

I took a deep breath. "George, as your friend, I must say that I do not think she will."

"There is hope, sir," he said. "There is always hope. I shall always have that."

And with those words, leaving the brandy bottle behind for his friend, he strode out the door, walking across the snow as straight as a tree.

Select Bibliography

Alberts, Robert C. *A Charming Field for an Encounter*, Washington, D.C.: National Park Service, 1975.

Chartrand, René. *The French Soldier in Colonial America*. Alexandria Bay, N. Y.: Museum Restoration Service.

Clark, Harrison. *All Cloudless Glory: The Life of George Washington from Youth to Yorktown*. Washington, D.C.: Regnery, 1995.

Colonial Williamsburg Foundation. *The Williamsburg Art of Cookery, or, Accomplished Gentlewoman's Companion*. Williamsburg, Va.

Cunliffe, Marcus. *George Washington: Man and Monument*. New York: Mentor Books, 1982.

Darling, Anthony D. *Red Coat and Brown Bess*. Alexandria Bay, N. Y.: Museum Restoration Service, 1991.

Earle, Alice Morse. *Home Life in Colonial Days*. Stockbridge, Mass.: Berkshire Traveller Press, 1992.

Eckert, Allan W. *The Conquerors*. New York: Bantam Books, 1980.

Eckert, Allan W. *Wilderness Empire*. New York: Bantam Books, 1971.

Fay, Bernard. *George Washington: Republican Aristocrat*. New York: Houghton Mifflin Co., 1931. (cq).

Felder, Paula. *George Washington's Relations and Relationships in Fredericksburg, Virginia*. Fredericksburg: Historic Publications of Fredericksburg, 1981.

Ferling, John. *The First of Men: A Life of George Washington*. Knoxville: University of Tennessee Press, 1988.

Fitzpatrick, John C. *The Last Will and Testament of George Washington*. Mount Vernon, Va.: Mount Vernon Ladies' Association, 1982.

Flexner, James Thomas. *Washington: The Indispensable Man*. Boston: Back Bay Books, 1974.

Franklin, B. *The Old Mistress Apologue*. Philadelphia: The Philip H. & A. S. W. Rosenbach Foundation, 1956.

Franklin, Benjamin. *The Autobiography of Benjamin Franklin*. New York: Collier Books, 1962.

Franklin, Benjamin. *Benjamin Franklin*. New York: The Library of America, 1987.

Freeman, Douglas Southall. *Washington*. New York: Collier Books, 1992.

Freidel, Frank, and Lonnelle Aikman. *George Washington: Man and Monument*. Washington, D.C.: Washington National Monument Association, 1988.

Freidel, Frank. *The Presidents of the United States*. Washington, D.C.: White House Historical Association, 1975.

Grant, George. *Highland Military Discipline of 1757*. Alexandria, N. Y.: Museum Restoration Service, 1988.

Grimm, Jacob. *Archaeological Investigation of Fort Ligonier*. Pittsburgh, Pa.: Carnegie Museum, 1970.

Hambleton, Elizabeth, and Marian Van Landingham. *Alexandria: A Composite History*. Alexandria, Va.: The Alexandria Bicentennial Commission, 1975.

Harrington, J. C. *New Light on Washington's Fort Necessity*. Washington, D.C.: Eastern National Park and Monument Association.

Higginbotham, Don. *Daniel Morgan: Revolutionary Rifleman*. Chapel Hill: University of North Carolina Press.

Hugon, Anne. *The Exploration of Africa*. New York: Harry N. Abrams, 1993.

Hurtz, Howard. *An Encyclopedic Dictionary of American History*. New York: Washington Square Press, 1974.

Janney, Asa Moore and Werner L. Janney. *John Jay Janney's Virginia*. McLean, Va.: EPM Publications, 1978.

Josephy, Alvin M., Jr. *Five Hundred Nations: An Illustrated History of North American Indians*. New York: Alfred A. Knopf, 1996.

Kent, Donald H., *Contrecoeur's Copy of George Washington's Journal for 1754*. Washington, D.C.: Eastern National Park and Monument Association, 1989.

Kent, Donald H. *The French Invasion of Western Pennsylvania*. Harrisburg, Pa.: Pennsylvania Historical and Museum Commission.

Klapthor, Margaret Brown and Howard Alexander Morrison. *G. Washington: A Figure Upon the Stage*. Washington, D.C.: Smithsonian Institution Press, 1982.

Kopperman, Paul E. *Braddock at the Monongahela*. Pittsburgh: University of Pittsburgh Press, 1977.

Langdon, William Chauncy. *Everyday Things in American Life*. New York: Scribners, 1969.

Leish, Kenneth. *American Heritage Pictorial History of the Presidents of the United States*. New York: American Heritage, 1968.

Lewis, Thomas A. *For King and Country: The Maturing of George Washington*. New York: HarperCollins, 1993.

MacDonald, William. *George Washington: A Brief Biography*. Mount Vernon, Va.: The Mount Vernon Ladies' Association, 1987.

Macoll, John. *Alexandria: A Towne in Transition*. Alexandria, Va.: Alexandria Historical Society, 1977.

Miller, Helen Hill. *Colonel Parke of Virginia*. Chapel Hill, N.C.: Algonquin Books, 1989.

Mish, Mary Vernon. *General Adam Stephen*. Martinsburg, W. Va.: The General Adam Stephen Memorial Association, 1975.

Mitchell, Patricia. *The Good Land: Native American and Early Colonial Food*. Chatham, Va.: Patricia Mitchell Foodways Publications, 1992.

Morgan, Edmund S. *Virginians at Home: Family Life in the 18th Century*. Williamsburg, Va.: The Colonial Williamsburg Foundation.

Morgan, Ted. *Wilderness at Dawn*. New York: Simon and Schuster, 1993.

Morison, Samuel Eliot. *The Oxford History of the American People*. New York: Mentor Books, 1972.

Netherton, Ross. *Braddock's Campaign and the Potomac Route to the West*. Winchester, Falls Church, Va.: Higher Education Publications, 1989.

O'Meara, Walter. *Guns at the Forks*. Pittsburgh: University of Pittsburgh Press, 1990.

Paine, Thomas. *The Crisis*. New York: Penguin, 1996.

Powell, Allan. *Christopher Gist: Frontier Scout*. Shippensburg, Pa.: Burd Street Press, 1992.

Powell, Allan. *Fort Cumberland*. Hagerstown, Md.: McClain Printing Co., 1989.

Powell, Allan. *Fort Frederick: Potomac Outpost*. Hagerstown, Md.: McClain Printing Co., 1988.

Powell, Allan. *Fort Loudon: Winchester's Defense in the French and Indian War*. Hagerstown, Md.: McClain Printing Co., 1990.

Quarles, Garland R. *George Washington and Winchester, Virginia, 1748–1758*. Winchester, Va.: Winchester–Frederick County Historical Society Papers, 1974.

Scott, Anne Firor, and Suzanne Lebsock. *Virginia Women: The First Two Hundred Years*. Williamsburg, Va.: The Colonial Williamsburg Foundation, 1988.

Sweig, Donald. *Fairfax County Virginia in 1760: An Interpretive Historical Map*. Fairfax, Va.: Fairfax County Government, 1987.

Trudel, Marcel. *The Jumonville Affair*. Harrisburg, Pa.: The Pennsylvania Historical Association, 1954.

Ward, Harry M. *Major General Adam Stephen and the Cause of American Liberty*. Charlottesville, Va.: University Press of Virginia, 1989.

Washington, George. *George Washington's Rules of Civility & Decent Behaviour In Company and Conversation*. Mount Vernon, Va.: The Mount Vernon Ladies' Association, 1989.

Washington, George. *The Journal of Major George Washington*. Williamsburg, Va.: The Colonial Williamsburg Foundation, 1982.

Watkins, Julie. *A Guide to Civilian Clothing during the American Revolutionary War*. Urbana, Ill.: Folump Enterprises, 1993.

Wick, Wendy C. *George Washington: An American Icon*. Washington, D.C.: The Smithsonian Institution, 1982.

Williams, Neville. *A History of the Cayman Islands*. Grand Cayman Island: The Government of the Cayman Islands, 1992.

Wright, Esmond. *Franklin of Philadelphia*. Cambridge, Mass.: Belknap Press, 1986.

About the Author

Michael Kilian has written fifteen books, including the historical novel *Dance on a Sinking Ship*, about the courtship of the Duke and Duchess of Windsor, and *The Last Virginia Gentleman*. Kilian is a Washington columnist and correspondent for the *Chicago Tribune*, writer of the Dick Tracy comic strip, host of CLTV cable television's "DC Journal," Washington correspondent for WGN's Roy Leonard Show, and news commentator for CBC Canada. He has written extensively on the French and Indian War, the Civil War, and other aspects of American history. He, his wife, Pamela, and their sons Eric and Colin, reside in McLean, Virginia, and Berkeley County, West Virginia.